the voice at the back door

ELIZABETH
SPENCER

the voice
at the
back door

With an Introduction
by the Author

Time Reading Program Special Edition
Time-Life Books Inc., Alexandria, Virginia

TIME®
LIFE
BOOKS

Time-Life Books Inc.
is a wholly owned subsidiary of
TIME INCORPORATED

TIME Reading Program: *Editor*, Max Gissen

Library of Congress CIP data following page 367.

For information about any Time-Life book, please write:
Reader Information, Time-Life Books,
541 North Fairbanks Court, Chicago, Illinois 60611

to David and Justine Clay

Elizabeth Spencer

**editors'
preface** With every year Mississippi has become more of a clear-cut symbol, a kind of pole from which to measure the racial attitudes and the social progress of other Southern states. The rest of the United States has been almost as ready to explain itself by contrast with Mississippi as by contrast with Russia. Mississippi has appeared to glory in this symbolic contrariness.

Yet it can be exaggerated. "Mississippi," we need to be reminded, continues to stand for individual men, women and children in all their infinite variety. Their collective character represents 20th Century America far more than it does the special attributes we (including Mississippians) now attach to the symbol.

It is Elizabeth Spencer's achievement that she has written a moving and lucid novel that takes its strength from the tension between the two meanings of "Mississippi." She does not for a moment shut her eyes to race, violence and injustice; her people and her story turn largely around these themes. But they are people and it is a story. Mississippi-born and now self-exiled, she does not use the novel to reject or excuse the society which shaped, among so many less civilized products, Elizabeth Spencer.

In the opening pages of *The Voice at the Back Door*, the reader begins to sense a supra-Mississippian concern with the universal theme of loneliness. Sheriff Travis Brevard, the most respected man in Winfield County, stricken with a heart attack, drives fast to the town square of Lacey because he wants to die in Duncan Harper's grocery store. He refuses to die at home because his wife, Miss Ada, would put him on a pink bedspread and wring her helpless hands. He refuses to die at the home of his Negro mistress because she might be embarrassed by his corpse.

The storekeeper, Duncan Harper, is lonelier than Sheriff Brevard. He had been a great football hero, though without ever committing himself to the game. Now, without really committing himself to politics or to the mores of Winfield County, he runs for election as its sheriff to succeed Brevard. But this proves tougher than anything he had faced at Ole Miss. The campaign is fought in a miasma of duplicity stemming from Harper's desire, which he hides from the voters, to give Winfield County's Negroes fairer treatment under the law.

Against this background the whites and Negroes whose lives touch Duncan Harper's play their lonely hands. No two players, white or black, are really in communication with each other. Segregation is a condition not only of blacks among whites but of whites among whites and of blacks among blacks. Duncan Harper is cut off from his wife, Tinker, by the scar of an old love. Tinker's old adorer, Jimmy Tallant, has become a roadhouse Machiavelli, more honest after his fashion than Duncan's friend Kerney Woolbright, a desolate young moral ruin from the Yale Law School. Beckwith Dozer, a Negro, feels a responsibility which his wife never fathoms. They are all in a ring where no hearts touch. Yet each is struggling to achieve identity through communion.

Mississippi, the symbol, stands for hate and lawlessness. Yet Mississippi, the actual society, is deeply involved with love and the law. "Race relations" in the North is a matter of cold statistics. In Mississippi "race relations" conspicuously includes the personal recognition and confrontation of individual Negroes and individual whites. This fact is the ineradicable and tragic kernel of truth contained in the old Southern lie that Negroes were "better off" in the South. The recognition of another's personality is not love, but it is a prerequisite of love.

As for the law, in what other region of the United States does a consciousness of law and politics run as deep as in the South? Northern and Western communities do not carry in their folk-memories for 30 years the guilt of lawless acts, as Winfield County carried the memory of a slaughter of Negroes in its courthouse in 1919. Urbanized and depersonalized, the great Northern and Western conurbations are not stirred to their depths by elections for county office. The "speaking" at Lacey a few days before the election is like a town meeting gone mad, but it *is* like a town meeting. Even in its cruelty the Southern mob is not faceless. Even in its determination to pervert the law it is deeply aware of the law.

Anybody who hopes to understand the South must learn that the Southern habit of legalism is not 100 per cent hypocrisy. A few decades ago the economic interpretation of history denied the validity of the moral antislavery motive in the North of 1860; the Union was simply industrial capitalism on the march. The same interpretation denied the validity of the Confederacy's concern for the Constitutional rights of states; the Rebels were fighting only to hold on to their human property. It ought to be clear by now that both of these economic interpretations were superficial, yet the misunderstanding persists. The case for the Negro is basically a moral, not an economic, case. Southern resistance to the Negro advance turns largely around theories of law which are no less strongly held because they are misapplied. Economic motivations do not seem to play a large part in Elizabeth Spencer's Winfield County—and that is one reason her novel rings true.

In a most interesting introduction written for this special edition, the author explains that she wrote *The Voice at the Back Door* while living in Italy. "I missed Negroes," she says —a statement that would be quite implausible from a white writer reared outside the South. "The story really started in a moment of love," with her account of how old Senator John, just after the Civil War, found a Negro boy who would accept education. This led to the crime of 1919 which shadows the novel's action some 30 years later.

Returning to Mississippi in 1955 with her unpublished manuscript, Miss Spencer was amazed to find how much of the book was no longer "true." Within a few years, lines had become more sharply drawn. Attitudes had frozen. As a symbol, Mississippi had become clarified. Yet she wisely decided not to bring the book up to date. Beneath the new crust of misunderstanding that followed the Supreme Court's school-desegregation decision, the more human (but not more edifying) Mississippi of her story still pulsed.

Elizabeth Spencer, born in 1921, grew up in Carrollton,

Mississippi, which has a population of about 500. Before *The Voice at the Back Door*, she published *Fire in the Morning* and *This Crooked Way*. Her most successful book was her fourth, *The Light in the Piazza*, a delicate story of an American mother in Florence with her beautiful, mentally retarded daughter. The mother must decide whether to let the girl marry a Florentine who is not aware of her handicap. *The Light in the Piazza* won the $10,000 McGraw-Hill Fiction Award of 1960 and was made into a movie. The literary craftsmanship of *The Light in the Piazza* is superb, but *The Voice at the Back Door* may be a more solid and remarkable achievement. More than originality of plot was needed to extract a glowing novel from the overburden of cliché that lies upon Mississippi race relations.

—THE EDITORS

introduction   Summer politics is one of the things I remember most about growing up in Mississippi, up in the hills.
It was a hot subject, and the weather being what it was,
nothing about it was apt to cool off, right straight on through.
I've never got very close to politics elsewhere, or very well
acquainted with the subject except for what I see in the
papers and magazines and on the TV, but having later worked
on a paper for a while I know that what gets into print is
sometimes quite a bit different from what actually goes on.
I think any paper in the world, though, would choose to
devote itself to society and homemaking columns, high-school
notes and reflections on the Scriptures, rather than try to
report anything resembling county politics in Mississippi,
up in the hills.

   Perhaps it was really no different from anywhere else, only

on a smaller scale, with homemade equipment—I wouldn't know. Would it ever come out in the papers, for instance, what happened to the Beat Two ballot box, which was delayed 24 hours in getting to the courthouse? Some people swore that the pickup truck which was bringing it in from way out in the country had overturned and the box fell off in a gully and no one could find it. It was not found until long after all the other votes were counted, and some people who thought they had offices turned out to be nothing but ex-candidates. Such occurrences always went unsolved for all practical purposes, yet anyone could see that they had been decisive. But what could anybody do about it?

We all took passionate sides in politics, especially if a member of our family or a family friend was running; and we took sides too in the governor's and senatorial races which might be going on at the same time. Presidential races were nothing like these. We voted for President not in the summer but long after the weather got cool; the Democratic primaries were all that mattered in Mississippi, since it had all been settled long ago that only Democrats lived there. This fact had something almost sanctifying about it, for when an uncle of mine went North to take a job and married the boss's daughter and in due course became a Republican, this was mentioned to me in whispers; it was said that we were terribly ashamed of it but could not help it. "Don't mention it to him," they said when he came to visit, not wishing to hurt his feelings.

During Presidential elections it was already November and misting cold with all the leaves fallen and the cotton wagons lining up at the gin, which would be running all night long, and we had a sense, while waiting for the returns to come in over the radio, of being out of things. The country did not go the way we did because the country was not like us, and we had lost the war way back then and had somehow got lost ourselves, or forgotten or misplaced in some way. We had no power; we were important to no one but ourselves. There wasn't ever enough money and nobody understood us but us.

There was that large, implacable, unapproachable thing called the United States. We were part of it only in an extremely tenuous way. We speculated darkly on Big Money Politics and the Middle West and Tammany Hall, but these things were all very distant and strange. My mother related that she went through a terrible crisis of conscience when she voted for Al Smith. She was really shaken and said nothing would induce her to vote for a Roman Catholic again. It was not right for women to vote anyway, but she would never do this again. She was terribly afraid she had offended the God of her fathers in the course of remaining loyal to the Democratic Party.

But none of this was at all the same as those summer home-grown races which went pounding into the home stretch as the temperature mounted and the summer dust grew thicker and blue vituperation bit through the night air at the "speakings" and the grass was parched and your feet couldn't stand the sidewalk any more.

I remember holding my breath and praying for Mike Conner to win something or other while we were driving all the way over to Greenwood to hear the returns come in, and then later we went and sat at the courthouse, and saw them write the tallies on the blackboard. My brother had his first big fight, which got him bloody, because he yelled out "Hurrah for Bilbo!" in a mocking way, and another boy sprang up out of nowhere and knocked him down.

A lot of the talk in this book is only the sort of thing I used to hear around the county courthouse. Our town, Carrollton, is the county seat, and while the town of Lacey in the book is bigger and different in a good many ways from Carrollton, it is in a lot of ways similar, no use denying. Most of what I heard, I heard when I was a child tagging along behind my father or uncle or somebody who was going here and there on business. There must have been a lot of times when nobody thought I was listening (children can sort of melt into the landscape while men talk business); perhaps I didn't think I was listening either.

I had lived all my life in the South until I got a fellowship which took me to Italy in 1953, and it was there I wrote the book. I had planned to write it long before but for one reason or another—a job to hold, poor health—had not been able to. It was very exciting to write about the South from the distance of Italy, for the outlines of things stood out very clearly in my mind. Of course I couldn't speak Italian at first (back then there were those who said I didn't even speak English, but this is not true), and in the foreign cities all the home voices kept coming back as I wrote. I could hear them talking among all those other voices; even to visualize my characters walking or turning their heads was entirely different from what I saw around me.

I missed Negroes. If you have always lived where half the population is black (at least half, for I knew far more Negroes than white people until I got sent to school), then when you leave that, you feel the world is lacking something, and then you know you are wishing to see black skins around. Somehow one never imagined that there would come a time when they wouldn't be there. To write in this book about as many Negroes as I thought I could convincingly imagine was a way of being with them. I liked writing those parts.

Then there had been the crime, the old crime, the one nobody ever really talked about, though the bullet holes were still there in the courthouse wall. The thing was known, but I never got the straight of it. People wouldn't say or couldn't say, or grew very vague. So finally I made it up. Perhaps it is not a good thing to do that. I don't know. I hoped that if a monstrous thing were seen in human terms, its monstrous nature might receive a wound; but perhaps it is not wise to be kind to monsters. The earth is nowhere innocent of some terrible thing. But the fact that it happened in the courthouse, the center of a Southern town, the symbol of justice; and the fact that county politics centered there too—these two things gave me my tale. For if ever a Negro would feel some fatal attraction to knowing, to somehow being a part of courthouse affairs, that Negro, given everything else that had happened to him overseas during World War II, would be Beck Dozer.

But the story really started in a moment of love. I saw that as I went along, burrowing further and further back into local history, back to the Civil War, which is a Southerner's A.D. It started, in other words, when the old man, Senator John, looked across the fresh homemade plaster cast on his broken hip and the morning glitter of the fire, and saw and loved the little Negro boy who stood in the threshold—wide-eyed, frightened, but bursting with the nameless, ineffable hope which had brought him there. For this hope could not have been only the hope for "something better," as some people say, or for the "light of knowledge," as others say. All hope is somehow concerned with love. But was this scene real—was it true?

Was it ever real or true that Aunt Mattie spent a lifetime of devotion to the white people of an entire town and never regretted it, this being the source of her many recollections through all her blind lingering days—the source of her joy? She retained the power to bless and gave her blessing to Duncan's wife Tinker, in whose hands the book rests. But was all of this condemned to have no consequence?

I did not ask myself these questions while writing away in

Italy, but I certainly did when I came back to Mississippi. It was 1955, after the Supreme Court had made its decision ending segregation in the schools, and immediately after the Emmett Till murder, which took place only a few miles from my family home, over in the Delta. During these days there, I realized to my horror that in my absence from the state a precipitate moment had come and gone, and that the local scene which in my manuscript I had hopefully allowed to contain the action—with its many ramifications in love and blessing—had already as good as vanished. Anyone now who believed he might quietly use a local political office to improve the lot of Negroes in the average Mississippi town would not only have to be naive politically—as well as genuine, honest and encouraged by a friend like Kerney Woolbright—he would also have to be a lunatic. I felt then that I might as well have spent my time in Italy chronicling history long past, gone forever, and I saw the painful irony of what I had done: that even while I wrote it down, the tenuous but vivid thread of hope that I thought to be there had been dissolving utterly. Had it only appeared to me to be real?

I remained in Mississippi only a few weeks after that return; then I went to New York.

One goes North on a train, traditionally, and one somehow knows when the trip is definitive and final, when it is true that no return visit will ever erase its meaning. This is a traditional American journey—I do not think it has been written about very much as "going West" has been, or "going East." Perhaps there are ways of understanding why. Yet thousands of people, of every shade of color, of every degree of intelligence and talent, have made this journey and are still making it, and all for the same reason: they don't belong down there any more.

How had this estrangement happened? Whose fault was it? Who knows? Perhaps it was mine. It had nothing whatsoever to do with my manuscript. As far as I recall, no one had even mentioned the manuscript; it had not even been opened since I arrived. I felt that the answers to my particular questions were quite likely in that Beat Two ballot box that got lost in the gully with all those votes locked inside.

All night on that long journey I hung between sleep and wakefulness, troubled by the fleeing away of the beloved landscape in the dark, dumbly haunted by 30 years of memories, and generations of faces, voices, tales. Going North, there is a discriminatory tariff on the heart.

When I at last began revising my manuscript for publication I had to emerge from the shadows of doubts which that visit had placed upon it. It was up to the story itself to instruct me how. For, I reasoned, I had been nothing but a Mississippian when I wrote it, and I had had no motive but to place things there in their truest and clearest light. And if the existence of Duncan Harper now seemed to me impossible, then perhaps in a society gone deliberately blind, a person who has the honesty to see at all will always seem to be impossible. This very impossibility, in fact, may only be a part of the loneliness of seeing. And in this case, inasmuch as Mississippians were still human, there would, of course, still be those lonely, seeing, impossible people.

So just about all that revision meant was the toilsome application of literary craft to an already completed vision.

I had decided to stick to my story.

—Elizabeth Spencer

part one

a
speeding
car

1. On a winter afternoon, unseasonably warm, a car was racing over country roads toward town. Dust, gushing from the back wheels, ran together behind in a dense whirl. On the headlands, the sun cast its thin glare above the sagebrush; it shot through the little trees, the pin oaks and the new reedy pines, and its touch pained the eye.

A large rock of gravel leaped from the wheels and whanged a mailbox. A terrapin, off on a hundred years' journey, missed death by half an inch. The car stitched a shallow curve and plunged downward, shivering: the descent was steep as a broom handle. But though the back wheels swayed, the car held the safe track, the ridges between the ruts, no broader than the edge of a nickel.

The hill emptied into a red road, quiet with sand and clay. Red clay gullies towered around, or fell away from the roadsides. No growth was on them, and some were deep enough to throw the church in. This was where the old-timers said the world was held together. Through this scarlet silence the car darted small and flat; then it ripped over a wooden bridge and was instantly swallowed in the trees of a Negro settlement.

Dogs leaped silent out of nowhere at the flying wheels and raced in pack for a way, yelping. They were mongrel hound and feist, the kind called "nigger dogs." Before the road curved, the oldest dog sat down to scratch his flea, and a young Negro woman, barefoot, stepped out on the front porch, set her hands on her hips, and stared, her eyes, like the road, growing emptier every minute.

One thing about the car: it knew the road. A country car,

after a few months of driving have loosened every joint and axle and worn the shock absorbers tender and given every part a special cry of its own, pushes very fine the barrier that divides it from horses and mules. The road it knows, it navigates: dodges the washouts, straddles the ruts, nicks the bumps on the easy corner, and strikes, just at the point of balance, the loose plank in the bridge.

Five miles ahead along the road the car was traveling, an iron overhead bridge spans a brown creek with an Indian name, Pettico-cow, and a scant mile beyond that, three Negro men were quitting their work at the tie plant, shaking the sawdust out of their shoes, gathering up the lunch buckets and the work jackets. The sun had lowered into the dust line and reddened, staining the dense horizon. The three Negro men moved toward the road. The one who walked off to the side was singing to himself.

> "Quitting time done got sooner
> Most ever-ry day.
> Got to lay off two-three more niggers
> 'Fo the end of the week."

The other two Negroes exchanged a glance. Their mouths were thick and hung slightly open.

"You going to lay somebody *off*, Mister Beck?" the younger one asked.

The one who had sung moved on steadily. "Lay somebody off? I ain't said a word about laying anybody off."

"You wasn't saying it, but you sho was singing it."

"Oh, singing. That's different. You think everything a man sings he got to go and *do?*"

"I ain't studying do nor singing neither. But if somebody going to lay me off work I wants to know hit."

The third Negro was older than the first. He knew by now

that another Negro is the hardest kind of boss to have. "Brer Beck ain't said nothing about firing you, boy. Brer Beck just talking to hisself. Ain't that right, Brer Beck?"

The singer ignored his question. "You niggers ain't got good sense. Did, you'd be in line for some other kind of job."

"They pays good," said the young Negro.

"They pay all right, but you ain't getting noplace. Everything you do, you do because somebody else tells you to. Me, I tell you."

"Yeah, and you got somebody else telling you."

"In a general way I have. But it's me that cuts the big orders down to the little folks. That's you. You don't do nothing but grunt and sweat. And how much money do you get? Not half as much as me."

"That's right, Brer Beck," the older Negro said, softly and with sweetness, but the younger one said, "I could quit this job tonight if I wanted to, and leave you shorthanded."

"Go on and quit then," the foreman answered. "There's plenty more just like you where you came from."

"I ain't going to quit," the young Negro said, "because it ain't but Wednesday. I thinks more of my three days pay than I does of you. Fact, I thinks more of a nickel than I does of you."

"Y'all hush," said the old Negro. "Hit's too hot to qua'l."

"Hush," said the foreman in another tone, and stopped still, listening.

From back up the road they all heard the iron bridge over Pettico-cow shake out a sound like a small foundry. From the deep points of the curves they could hear the gravel tear.

"Traveling," the older Negro said.

They had reached the edge of the road, and for the first time the three of them drew together.

When the car passed, the weeds along the road shook

violently and the three Negroes were momentarily blotted out in the whirl of dust. They climbed up to the road.

"It was the sheriff," said the youngest.

"Sho was," said the oldest.

"The High Sheriff," said the foreman.

"How come him driving that fast?" asked the youngest.

"I seen his two great big old hands, laying up side by side on the steering wheel," said the oldest.

"I seen his red hair," said the youngest; "it was all slid down to his ears."

"I saw his license plates," the foreman said.

When they reached the crossroads, the young Negro turned to the foreman. "You reckon anything done happened?" he asked.

"You know as much as me, boy," the foreman said, and left them there, taking his own road for home, moving perhaps a little faster than usual.

By that time the dusty car had gained the highway, entering it at the point near a large roadhouse painted green, bare as a barn with no trees near, set on a sweep of gravel. Inside, leaning at the window, was a man with a grizzled head cropped close and a strong wad of shoulders beneath a khaki shirt. He turned and called to another.

"You hear that car?"

"Somebody in a hurry."

"It was Travis Brevard, coming in from off the Beat Two road. Heading for town."

"Travis, huh?"

"I never saw him go that fast before. You best run into town after while, Jimmy."

"It's none of our business, Bud. Whatever it is."

"Just the same, I think you best run into town."

"Look, Bud. I'm always telling you. The best way to stay out of anything is not to get curious."

"It never hurts to know."

"It never hurts not to know. Haven't you ever heard that what you don't know don't hurt you? I thought everybody—"

"God damn it, Jimmy. Do you go into town or do I have to go myself?"

"Go yourself? Then I'd only have to go anyway, to get you safe back home. Okay, okay. I'm practically there."

He had never dreamed of not going, from the time he heard the car wheels scream onto the pavement.

But Travis Brevard, the sheriff, having reached Lacey, did nothing but slow to a tame fifteen miles an hour and circle the courthouse square. In pavement and telephone wires, bare trees, and an overcast of dust, the town, beautiful to anyone in the green seasons, now seemed shrunken and drab. But Travis Brevard took his time around the square and looked at everything closely. He was dying and he knew it; it had seemed very important to him to reach Lacey alive.

He chose to stop on the square before a small store front— one glass window and a door. Lettering on the old brick façade above read: HARPER & BRO. GRO.

He alighted from the car, a man strikingly tall, and rested one large copper-haired hand for a moment, perhaps to steady himself, against the warm hood of the car.

Then he advanced on the store.

the sheriff's advice

2. The Negro delivery boy saw him first. The boy, whose name was W.B., was sitting in the far corner of the store, cross-legged on a sack of chicken feed. Duncan Harper, the proprietor, was behind the counter filling the delivery basket with items from the shelves. He first knew that something out of the ordinary was happening when he caught the white flash from the boy's eyes, and saw the rest of him grow rigid as an idol. The storekeeper turned toward the door.

The sheriff had sagged against the door frame, but nevertheless he filled the opening. At his size and the suggestion that his weight was about to land somewhere, the store seemed to withdraw and shrink; to the grocer his property had never looked so small. Drunk, was all he thought.

"Come on in, Travis," he said. "Drag up a chair." But he noticed the reel in the sheriff's step and how riskily he lowered himself to sit down. His face was the color of a red-hot stove. Below the long thin strands of copper hair, the flesh blazed. The hair was wringing wet.

"Duncan," he said hoarsely, "I'm hot as a fox. Cut out that damn gas and give me a cold Coke."

"Sure," said the grocer, thinking that if it were whisky he would surely have smelled it by now. He pried the cap from the bottle and offered it doubtfully. "Travis, you don't look good. Let me just ring and see if Doc's in his office."

"No, you're not," said the sheriff, and poured the Coca-cola down in one tilt of the bottle. He let out a long sigh and the deep red color faded visibly. "Give me another one," he demanded.

This second bottle he sipped from. "No, Duncan, no doctor. I'll have it my way. I'm to the point, you understand, where anything I do will be wrong, so I might as well do what I want to. I knew the next one of these attacks would be the last. I only wanted to live to get home to Lacey. Would you pick a Beat Two gully for the last sight your eyes looked on? But I made it back and made my choice."

"You ought to be in bed," said the young grocer. "I'll take you home and call Doc—"

The other lifted a large hand. "I had my choice, like I said, and I said I would not go home to Miss Ada. She would spread me out on a pink bedspread and stick a thermometer in my mouth and get so scared she would forget her own name. I tell you for a fact, Duncan, I been married to Miss Ada for thirty-odd year, but I couldn't ever age her. She's nothing but a little girl and, God forgive me, but I'd rather die in a gully than on her bedspread." His breath came with difficulty, filling with a noise like a cold wind the long bellows-case of his lungs. "Then," he went on, "there was Ida Belle. Her house is a place where I could go out quiet as a match. She's been my nigger woman for fifteen years and everybody knows it, but it would likely embarrass her to have my corpse on her hands. You can't tell what they're liable to do to a nigger. She might have to leave town."

"Travis, all this talk of dying—"

"Don't butt in on me. Maybe I should have gone to the office just now, but I didn't. Maybe I've just got the big head, thinking I'm going to die, but I don't think so." He settled back, relaxing his long limbs. His breath came more easily. "Duncan, remember when you used to play football?"

"I remember."

"I used to go all the way up to the university on weekends to see you play. I went over to Baton Rouge too and down to New Orleans more than once. We would all go see you play. Then we would come home and read about it in the paper. They called you the fastest running back of the year. They named you 'Happy' Harper."

The groceryman winced. "The newspapers made that up," he said. "Nobody ever called me that. I didn't care for it, but they did it anyway."

The sheriff's gaze was concentrated on the young man's face, the serious blond features so devoid of any nerve play that a whip snapping in his face would probably not have made him shy. However, there was another dimension in his eyes. They were light brown, the color of walnut just split open. They kept a watch which missed little, and their calm did not come cheap.

"Yes, you used to bring us up, Duncan. I've seen forty thousand people stand up and yell when you began to run. I used to think I knew how you felt when the last white stripe went past."

"Not much different from winning an election maybe," said the other. "Though maybe it doesn't last as long. Not being so important."

"I don't know. Winning anything is good. I still remember how good I felt the day I won Miss Ada. You never did much in the war."

It was an accusation. The storekeeper laughed. "I did a great job in the war, Travis. I kept every juke box in Camp Shelby running with music and neon rainbows. I was so good at it they sent me out to Fort Sill, Oklahoma, to do more of the same."

"Never overseas, never an officer, let Jimmy Tallant come home from England with a hatful of medals. Now Jimmy's running that bootleg joint on the highway and paying me protection money. It's a crying shame. Once we wanted to put up a sign: 'Lacey: Home of Duncan "Happy" Harper.' Then we started to put one up: 'Lacey: Home of Jimmy Tallant.' But then you turned into a juke box engineer and now a groceryman, and Tallant went into bootlegging. Looks like we'll never get to point with pride."

"When I was in the Army," Duncan said, "they lost my papers twice. I should have gone to OCS, but the papers stayed lost for two years."

"Then you lost your girl," said Travis.

Had this been said? The young man seemed uncertain as to whether anger was expected of him. Then he answered, "Yes, I did."

Travis lolled back in the chair. "And now you're a family man, running your daddy's little grocery store."

"If you think I couldn't have gone anywhere else and done better, you're mistaken. Even after the war, there were plenty of people over the state that remembered me. The fact is I decided to stay in Lacey because I wanted to. My wife likes it here, and I like it. There's always been a Harper on the town square. You know yourself I've got property around here and there—the grocery isn't everything. The people I grew up with are all here, and all my father's friends that are left alive. I want my children to grow up here. I don't see anything wrong with that." His face gentled suddenly. A certain anxiousness in his own defense dropped away, and he said, smiling, "For a man who claims to be dying, you've sure got a nerve."

"Dying," said the sheriff, flatly. "I forgot about it."

At these words the day sank back toward dream.

The grocer, who had taken his seat on the counter in the space where he sacked purchases, propped up a knee and turned idly to stare out the door toward the courthouse. No one on the Lacey square would have had anything but a glass door. Through it, hundreds of times in the last five years, or leaning in warm weather against the door frame, Duncan had watched the routine of the town. He had seen how day after day at midmorning and midafternoon, the girls who worked at the courthouse crossed the street to the drugstore for coffee. They came always on high heels, in the thinnest stockings, with their suits neatly pressed and their earrings shining. The narrow iron gate in the fence funneled them through and later drew them back again. All the way across the street you could hear the clatter of their heels in the high crossed hallways.

Then there were the old men, who sat on benches under

the elm tree in the courthouse yard. They looked always to have been carelessly dressed and set down there by someone else. A fly was open, a shirt button missing, or a shoelace broken and retied low. Spring, summer, and fall, toiling uphill and down, they ventured out of houses where if they were loved they were no longer wanted, and came daily to this place that was theirs, a sort of no-place between the courthouse and the square because they had no business in either. Here they whittled and gossiped and spit and said Lord knows what about you. Even the politicians paid no attention to them: many a time Duncan had watched the sheriff striding by, and his heel struck past them like a hero's.

Duncan had seen funeral processions also, one so like another it was easy to forget, while the grave still yawned, just who had died. In the afternoons around four, eight yellow school buses eased past: it was about time for them now.

Look at it however you would, love it as much as you please: Lacey was dull.

Travis rose experimentally. "If I don't die today, I'm bound to sometime. What I came to say to you: I want you to take over when I'm gone."

Duncan laughed. "Preach your funeral?"

"You know what I mean. In a certain way of looking at it, I hold this county in my hand. It's better for Jimmy Tallant to be a bootlegger than for Happy Harper to peddle Wheaties. I haven't rested easy about you and I'm not the only one. Other people feel the same."

"My friends don't say so," Duncan returned.

"Your friends don't say so because it's true," the sheriff answered. He fished with a long copper-haired finger in his shirt pocket and brought out a fold of paper. "Right now I'm going home. You might as well start learning. Here's a list of country folks paid their tax today. You can go to the office and register them—somebody over there will show you how. I'll see you—"

The phone began to ring. Duncan turned aside, and as he did so he glimpsed the Negro delivery boy again. His eyes had bugged, he popped up from the feed sack like a released spring, struck the floor running, and shot out the back. Duncan wheeled.

Travis Brevard had lunged toward the counter for support, grasping as though it tried to escape him, had missed and was falling. He went to his knees. When he tried to rise, his head went down, too, and his forehead dragged the floor. He seemed to be broken in the middle. Duncan rushed to catch him, and another man, in full stride, burst through the door to help. Between them, with a slow turning motion they brought him upright. Step at a time, heavily weighted, the two of them gained the small chair, where they lowered him.

A crowd had gathered at the door; it may have been there for some time, for the man who entered had broken from it or through it. Someone was running to the drugstore for the doctor. Others were pressing into the store. As they approached, Duncan and the man who had helped him exchanged a glance. It seemed unlikely that the person with the least chance of getting there—he had had to drive in from a roadhouse two miles out on the highway—had not only made it to the scene but had also got the jump on everybody else. Whenever the story was told, his name would be mentioned. It was a name often mentioned anyway: Jimmy Tallant. It figured in most stories worth repeating and came easily off the tongue.

He spoke quickly to the grocer. "Will you be at home to-night?"

"Yes."

Then he smiled. His features were sharp and quick. In

comprehension, too, he liked to stay one jump ahead. "So he wants you."

"Wanted," Duncan corrected with sudden sorrow at Travis's passing and a lash of resentment against Jimmy Tallant. Already the political picture had begun to shift and re-form in this shrewd head.

Duncan thrust the tax list into his pocket. The telephone was still ringing. Somebody asked if he wanted it answered, but he shook his head.

the
sheriff's
women

3. Far into the early winter twilight Duncan Harper remained in the store and the store was full of people. They wanted to hear all the details of the death. For a while they talked in low tones, but gradually they spoke louder and, toward the last, one or two had cracked a joke and there had been a little scuffling, quickly dropped not so much out of propriety as because their hearts were heavy. When a silence fell, they left the store altogether, as though a program had been concluded. . . .

On a hill just at the outskirts of town, a Negro woman was sitting in a rocking chair on the front porch of her house. She was dressed in her best silk dress, the dark one she wore to church. Her hands, resting in her comfortable lap, held a handkerchief and a folded fan. She was Ida Belle, for fifteen years Travis Brevard's Negro woman. All around her front porch and the steps, other Negroes were gathered; they talked a little in low voices, or lounged silently against the porch, staring outward toward the town. Bone-white grass fringed the gullies, and in the clean winter leaflessness the white houses, the courthouse and church steeples and Confederate statue appeared to be quite close, both to one another and to the hill. Ida Belle would not go to the funeral, though she would dress for it as she had dressed today and would sit on the porch in the rocker. The other Negroes, all dressed too, would bank against the porch and fill the yard. . . .

Down in the town, in one of the larger white houses, Miss Ada, Travis's wife, lay on the bed in a darkened room. A cold compress covered her eyes and the single light bulb which burned near the dresser had been shaded with a newspaper. Two Negro girls stood one on either side, fanning her. Her cries had been silenced by hypodermic: word went out that she was "resting easier." Food had begun to arrive twenty minutes after Travis fell; there was enough of it now to last for a month. Two ladies, working hard, entered the back hallway from opposite doors. One was carrying a newspaper full of damp fern, the other a pitcher of ice.

"Hot," said the first, and pressed a sodden handkerchief to her upper lip. "It would be hot."

"And me with four to feed when I get home," said the second, pushing back a wisp of hair.

"Why don't you just go on home now, honey? *I* can manage here."

"I wouldn't dream of it! Leave poor Ada? Not for anything in the world!"

"Poor Ada!"

"Poor thing!"

Raising their eyes to heaven, they parted and swept to their imperious labor with a sigh. For women bear the brunt of everything, always. . . .

4. Duncan Harper stood saying goodnight and locking the store. The lights had come on, but since his was one of the store fronts where an old-fashioned shed roof extended to the edge of the sidewalk, the larger angle of the doorway was shadowed. It was from out of the deepest plunge of the dark that the voice said, "Mister Harper?"

"Who called me?" he asked.

"I did, Mister Harper."

This time he caught the underlying negroid quality of the voice and smelled the smell. "What do you want?"

"You employ W.B. Liles?"

"No, I don't employ anybody. You've got the wrong— Oh, W.B. You mean the grocery boy? Yes, he works for me, but he—"

"Yes, he ran off. He got scared by what happened in your store. Now he's afraid you might fire him for running away. He's nothing but a child."

"No, it's all right. Tell him it's all right."

"He ran nearly all the way home, then he remembered—"

"Yes. Tell him to come in the morning as usual." Duncan turned away.

"He said there was—"

Duncan walked away. He had to get to the courthouse before the janitor left. The tax receipts were still not registered, but he could at least leave them locked in the sheriff's office. He was tired, filled with the event; perhaps for these reasons some assertive quality in the Negro had irritated him.

He crossed the street in the dark and went up the courthouse walk, past the empty benches under the elm tree. Inside the sheriff's office, he waited while the light flickered on. He looked all about him: at the dusty calendars on the walls and the rows of tax registers that reached to the ceiling, the hand-cuffs hung on a nail, the mounted deer head, and Travis's old suede jacket, alone on the hat tree. The wood floor was worn wavy around the stove; though they had gas now, the old building was still hard to heat, and this was where men had always stood to talk. The news of the county came here first, also the talk on a lot that went on everywhere. He looked toward the high dark windows with their carved wood moldings. It was a beautiful proud old building: it had been built before the Civil War.

The current tax register lay open on the high desk. The office force must have walked right out as soon as they heard the news. Duncan opened the register and turned a page or two, feeling the weight and smoothness of the paper.

He looked up, straight into the eyes of the same Negro man who had stopped him on the sidewalk. He had followed ever so silently inside, and was now studying Duncan with as much interest as Duncan had shown for the tax register.

The Negro was frail, thin as though he had just come out of the jungle, but he had lost the savage's wiry drive. The force in him—and he did have it, far beyond the simple sur-prise of his presence—might have been mistaken for the force of a sick person who orders things to be done for him and people to do them just because he is not able to do them himself. You could not imagine his long face and high fore-head undertaking to smile. He was, instead, already equipped with the kind of humor he fancied. It emerged clearly enough in the first thing he said.

"You want somebody to deliver those groceries, or don't you?"

"I forgot that order," said Duncan. "You're right."

"You certainly did. I walked three miles in to tell you. I been lecturing W.B. to do his job right ever since you hired him. He's crying now, scared you'll fire him, and scared to come back in where sheriffs can pick him out to die in front of. So I set his mind at rest. I said I'd come in."

"It's good of you," Duncan said. "I—" He pressed his hand to his brow. "Don't worry about the order. I'll take it myself. I'm late getting home as it is."

"It's W.B.'s job, Mister Harper. I intend to see that it's done."

"I'd have to go back and open the store for you."

"But if I has to go home and tell him—"

"God damn it!" Duncan burst out.

"I admits," said the Negro, after a pause, "that it was not altogether a sense of duty that got me to walk into Lacey after a hard day's work. It was in part a sense of curiosity. One sheriff dying means another sheriff coming in. I expect that means you, don't it? Mister Duncan Harper, the new sheriff?"

"It's no business of yours," said Duncan.

"It's a fact they never say a word to me. My acquaintance is not cultivated. My vote is not sought after. The truth is I got no vote to seek. If I had a vote, my acquaintance might be cultivated."

Methodically, Duncan straightened from leaning on the high counter, circled the counter, and approached the Negro. He put his hands into his pockets and went back on his heels a bit. He was never in any doubt of what he could do physically, and so he could behave gently: it had been noted, in the old days, that he could bring off a tackle with a kind of politeness. His children obeyed him. He came close, and looking down on the Negro, saw in the open throat of the blue work shirt that a tendon moved stiffly at the collarbone.

"That kind of talk's no good," he seemed to be merely remarking. "On your way, boy."

The Negro withdrew from the shadow of the big white man, but he was still erect when he stopped in the door and said, "My name is Beckwith Dozer, Mister Harper. When I was a small child, my father was shot to death upstairs in this courthouse. I never been inside here before tonight."

"Oh. I see." Their eyes met and though they were alone in an empty building, and no one knew they were there, it seemed that the world listened, that a new way of speaking was about to form in an old place. They were a little helpless, too, like children waiting to be prompted. What should the words be? "There aren't many people you ought to talk this way to," Duncan said.

The Negro almost smiled. "I know that."

"It would help you to say 'Sir.' "

"I realize that."

"On your way," said Duncan.

"I wish you luck, Mister Harper," said Beckwith Dozer, and passed into the quiet dark hall. Duncan heard the words in his head for some time, and savored them there like the taste of something new, trying to decide if they mocked him, or spoke sincerely, but he could not.

an evening
at
Duncan's

5. When Jimmy Tallant reached Duncan's house that evening, he was aware even before he stepped inside that someone had got there ahead of him. He saw the rear bumper of a car parked around the corner of the hedge, as though whoever had driven it there had considered concealing it altogether, then had decided not to. The left wing of the house where the little boy and girl slept was dark. The hall was empty, but light was coming into it from the sitting room.

He let himself in quietly, preparing to say that he had nearly beaten the door down, but no one would come. He passed into the hall at an angle that allowed him to see deep inside without being seen. He avoided the spot where the old floor moaned, and stood in the dark, watching.

The room that he spied in upon was his favorite of all in the world—the place where he cared most to be. That it was another man's living room was ironic, and of this he was all too fully aware.

It was a room whose thoroughly old-fashioned proportions had not been altered: it had a ceiling that vanished in shadow, and windows that dropped to the floor. Though scarcely pantry-size by the old standards, it was far too large for small company. Yet the woman who had touched it had understood both its own nature and what she wanted from it. She had gathered it toward the fireplace, faced every modern sort of softness and comfort into the mantelpiece. Only this part of the room was lighted, and the light did not go high. She loved to have a fire and would bring in wood for it by herself, if no one was there to help. A fire seemed to put her into some kind of timeless mood, the way it does a cat, except that she watched it, and a cat doesn't. She could not take her eyes off it, as if for fear of missing some new subtlety. She was watching it now.

She was within full view of him, curled in the armchair as usual, a small dark warm woman of unextraordinary beauty. She had no right to knowing what to do for an old house, for until she had insisted on buying this one and fixing it over nobody in her entire connection had ever had anything, and her father's family was common as pigs' tracks.

But it was not her gift for interiors that made the man in the hallway pause. He would have given her equal attention if she had been sitting on an empty Coca-cola case in a filling station.

Duncan was seated opposite her—Jimmy could see his long legs stretched out before the fire. The third person, tucked away in a deep chair, showed only a pair of bony knees crossed in oxford gray trousers. But the town of Lacey was such a size that a few inches of a person were all that was necessary to make out who it was. The only person Jimmy Tallant knew who would want, out of some quirk of youngness, to sit like an old man was Kerney Woolbright, Lacey's only gift to the Yale law school in twenty years. His voice, which had been trained to carry, carried very well indeed: Tallant realized they were discussing him.

"He's the only one who might beat you," Kerney was saying.

"But he's a bootlegger," Duncan's wife objected.

"Doesn't matter, Tinker," Kerney said. "They'll vote for him because he shot down twenty-three German fighter planes, just like they'll vote for Duncan because he set the national all-time touchdown record for a single season. Besides that, country folks like law-breakers, and besides that, he married a Grantham and is kin to half the county. The Granthams will vote their hound dogs if you get them riled."

"I wonder," Duncan said, "if it was really a shotgun wedding."

His wife nodded placidly. "Didn't you see her uptown? She's begun to show."

"I wonder how he feels about her," Kerney said.

"Ask Tinker," Duncan said. "She knows."

"You see him as often as I do," Tinker returned.

"Yes, but I didn't date him every night for five years."

"To tell the truth," said Tinker, "I'm a little bit hurt with him for marrying her."

Kerney laughed. "This sounds serious."

"It is," Duncan said.

But Tinker did not smile. "I love Jimmy," she said. "I really do. I always will."

"You see, Kerney," said Duncan, "how serious it is."

"You can make her jealous, remember," Kerney said. "Marcia Mae Hunt is home."

Canny as he was, he could not have helped knowing, even before he spoke, that he should not have said this. But perhaps he could not stop himself. He was so crazy in love with Marcia Mae Hunt's little sister, the one they called Cissy, that he schemed up ways of bringing her in.

"How *is* Cissy?" Tinker asked flatly, and gave him sweet relief.

He was going thoroughly into this subject, when Jimmy Tallant decided to walk in.

"Are you deaf? I nearly beat the door down."

Tinker brought him a drink from the kitchen.

"To the memory of Travis," Jimmy said, and raised a solemn glass.

"Will they have the election right away?" Tinker asked.

"No, regular time, August primary."

"Then who's the sheriff now?" she wanted to know.

"One of the deputies," Duncan said.

"Follansbee, of course," Jimmy said. "He's done all Travis's bookkeeping for him for years. Travis never cared for the paper work."

Kerney Woolbright laughed. "If you want to know who the sheriff really is going to be, Tinker, child, you'd better ask Woolbright."

"Then who?"

"Miss Ada. Herself."

Jimmy said, "Well I be damned."

"A courtesy appointment by the board, customary, and I heard a couple of the members say that's what they planned to do. It gives Miss Ada the fees, nothing more. She turns the job over to whomever she wants, probably Follansbee."

"That's funny," Duncan said, "Miss Ada being the county sheriff."

"Only for six months, of course," Kerney said. He grinned and added, brash as a bad little boy, "Then you two can fight it out."

"Call his mother to come for him, Duncan," said Jimmy Tallant.

"I feel like it," Duncan said.

"Junior," said Jimmy, "just because they give you a drink of whisky, it's no sign you can shoot the twelve-gauge and borrow the car."

Kerney continued to grin. "I'll let you in on a secret of my own. I'm coming out for the senate this summer."

"Senate!" Tinker stared at him. He looked so young.

"Duncan," Jimmy Tallant said, "it is my deepest conviction that the stripling has reference to the state senate, but I stand in awe before the size of his conceit. I could be wrong. Have you got your eye on Washington, boy?"

"Eventually," Kerney returned without batting an eye. "But not right away."

"You barely got into the legislature, you know."

"I know," said Kerney, "but I did get in, and I've been in for two years."

"It was a fluke. Anybody can tell you. Jenkins and Storm started fighting amongst themselves."

"And Brer Rabbit got away," said Kerney. "I know. But I also got enough votes to win, don't forget that. I'll go to the senate, too, Jimmy. They'll vote for me. If you ran for anything they'd vote for you the first go-round because you've got a war record and for Duncan because he used to tear up a football field every Saturday, but they'll vote for me for the rest of my life because I'm a politician. It's a fact."

"This makes me so unhappy," Tinker said suddenly.

Her voice fell among the three of them, sweet, unreasonable, and urgent—it was as though she had thrown something down which they all looked at for a moment before they turned to her. There were ways of associating her with unhappiness which were not pleasant to think about.

"Unhappy, darling?" Duncan smiled. He was sprawled low in the chair, elbows at equal rest, and hands clasped around his glass. A very gentle feeling for her had touched his face.

"You're so silly," she said. "All of you. Who else in Lacey has a good time besides us? You know what they do. They go to the Rotary Club and the Garden Club or church parties, or else they play bridge and gossip or else just gossip. You know the ones who stay sloppy drunk all the time, and the ones who keep nosing around after each other's husbands and wives. But all we want to do is sit around the fire and have a drink or two and talk. There aren't many things nicer to do, and you know you like it, because you come here all the time. But if you all begin running for these little two-by-four courthouse jobs in Winfield County, you're going to fight with each other and have all sorts of grudges. You aren't going to want to come here or anywhere else and talk any more. You aren't even going to want to have a drink together any more. If Duncan gets elected sheriff, I guess I'll have to go sneaking off by myself somewhere to have a decent drink. I don't like to think about it."

Her voice trailed away toward the end; in fact, her whole

speech was more of a swan song than a plea, and they were not so much persuaded to deal with it as they felt how nice she was to have thought it. It was usual in her to feel that anything bad she anticipated was accomplished and should be adjusted to rather than resisted. This bitter tinge had worn her smile a little crooked, and made it very dear.

Duncan, naturally, was the first to shake away from her. "If I do run for sheriff, Tinker, it will be for better reasons than wanting the corner office in the courthouse."

Kerney was quick. "For certain things the office can be, you mean?"

"Yes, that's it. Of course, I liked Travis same as everybody did and more, but his standards were easygoing and after twenty years in office, this county has run down till it's a grand mess."

"That's true," Kerney said.

"I'll be damned if it is," Tallant objected. "I can't agree with you. Why, Duncan, ask anybody in Mississippi what the quietest county is and they'll tell you Winfield County."

"That's on the surface. That's what Travis was good at. He could keep order at a dogfight because every dog there would be in mortal fear of him."

"All about order," Kerney said, leaning forward; "nothing about law."

"That's all right," Jimmy contended; "it's a fact that every sonofabitch black or white, east of the creek or west, thought twice before they picked up the razor because of who we had in that corner office."

"Fine," Duncan said, "but still on the surface. Under the surface, Jimmy, the sinkhole has been eating away, and you know what I mean. When Tinker and I were on the coast last spring, everywhere we went they said to us, Don't see why you folks had to come down here when you've got the neatest little Gold Coast in the USA up in Winfield County. Why, Lacey in Winfield County used to be known as the home of two senators and a governor."

"And a football star," Jimmy grumbled. "Can I help it if people like to drink? You've said yourself time and again, Duncan, you and this prodigy here, that the dry laws in this state are nothing but damn foolishness."

"Sure I have. I'll say it again, and publicly. But if prohibition is what people voted for, then I say give them what they want."

"But it isn't what they want. It's just what they voted for. Can't you get it through your head what they want? What they want is *illegal whisky*."

Kerney nodded. "I figured it all out years ago, and I think Jimmy is right. In order to get the maximum kick out of a thing, you've got to be absolutely certain it's a sin. Everybody's been led to believe in the course of a proper childhood that sex is a filthy, degrading, bestial business, and look what a lot of fun it turned out to be. Everybody has likewise been instructed that whisky is a filthy, degrading business, but half the fun of it (exactly like illicit sex) turns out to be all the maneuvering, the slipping around, the dark back doors, and the whispering: Naw I ain't got none, but Joe has. So we flock to the polls to keep the old tradition alive. Really, Duncan, it keeps everybody happy:

"Preachers are happy because everybody on the church roll has signed the pledge; mothers and grandmothers and aunts are happy because not a drop of it has ever been allowed in the house; the bootleggers are happy because they are collecting from twenty to fifty per cent markups on standard brands; the state highway patrol is happy because they get up to half the markup in the shakedowns; the county sheriffs are happy because they make enough on protection money rake-offs to send their daughters to fine Eastern schools and buy Stromberg-Carlsons for their nigger mistresses—"

"Did Travis really do that?" Duncan inquired.

"Sure, he did it."

"Hush," Tinker said suddenly. "He's not in the ground yet."

"That's right," Jimmy Tallant said.

Kerney and Duncan glanced at the two who had spoken so quickly, and then their eyes met. The gesture was so involuntary, so slight, an outsider could not have discerned it. It was Duncan and Kerney's recognition of belonging to a class somewhat superior to the others, though Duncan would not have claimed any superiority even if Kerney might.

"I feel so sorry for Ida Belle," Tinker said to Jimmy.

"I do too," Jimmy said.

"She had the easiest life of any nigger woman I can think of," Kerney said. "She didn't even have to pretend to take in washing."

"That's not it, Kerney," Tinker explained. He did seem so young when he came out with things like this. "She lived with him so long, she's bound to be grieved, but she can't even go to the funeral. You know how they feel about funerals."

"It's a shame," Duncan agreed. "I thought about it at the time."

"*Couldn't* she go?" Kerney inquired. He would not stay reproved.

They looked at him.

"I'm only curious," he went on. "What would happen if she went? Would anything happen?"

"I don't know," Duncan answered thoughtfully. "Before the war, I could have said for sure, I think, that she would take a big risk to go. Since the war, I don't know."

Tallant said, "I know. There'd come a knock at her door

before midnight. We would never know who knocked. But it would happen."

"What would happen?" Tinker asked.

"I don't say they'd kill her. She'd just vanish, probably."

"Well," said Kerney, "we could all go up and protect her."

Tallant laughed. "They always told me to protect Southern womanhood. I'm just now seeing what they meant."

"Whoever knocked at the door," Kerney pointed out, "he would be protecting Southern womanhood."

"Namely, Miss Ada," said Duncan.

"The sheriff moreover," said Jimmy.

"And my second cousin," Tinker said, and they all laughed, thinking not without affection of the thin, nervous, excitable little lady. In the face of the most remarkable resemblance, she refused to believe that her own cook was the daughter of a gentlemanly old doctor. "He died nursing a sick baby," she would say, "and nobody's going to tell me he would do such an awful thing." Whereupon she would open her fan and flutter it at her breast, frail weapon against a hot flash.

"I'm still not sure," Kerney said. "I'm not sure anything would happen to her."

"I tell you one thing, son," Jimmy said. "Ida Belle is not going to give you a chance to find out."

"But if she did go," Duncan said, "and something did happen to her, I bet my bottom dollar that somewhere along the line she would have dared it to happen."

He spoke with a certain anger, out of tone with the pleasantly speculative nature of their conversation. They turned to him and waited. He shifted in his chair: thinking was apt to make him uncomfortable, yet he would go off into it when he had to, like wading into cold water. This was part of a fateful simplicity in his character, something that went along with his curious absence of any purely sensual awareness— his face was a collection of matching planes. He had listened to the teacher and the scoutmaster, and later to the coach: the coach always said that was the true secret of his great career, that he could listen.

When they said in the Sunday supplement that he was unique among college athletes in that he not only made good grades but also read books, he joshed about it with the boys; but he felt secretly ill at ease until he had gone to the library and read the books the reporter said he liked. This was the first article that appeared about him, when he was only a sophomore. Later the lies and exaggerations made no difference to him. But the reporter had had good taste. It turned out that Duncan liked the books—he could listen to what they had to say, too—and when he finished these he read some more. When the word got around that this activity actually engrossed him, it was a matter of concern to responsible persons. He had, by then, a nationwide reputation. The coach called him in. "I don't know whether it's true or not," he said, "but you have to watch that sort of thing. Back when I was up at Kentucky, they had a basketball star went off on music. No harm in the thing itself, of course. But when he started meeting with some other fiddlers—well, frankly, there's always a lots of queers among people like that, and you have to watch out for them. The wrong kind of word got around. I just drop the hint to you, Harper: if you must go in for this sort of thing, keep it to yourself and mind you stick with decent people. That's all, boy."

Duncan had read far enough into the books to know this would be ridiculous to the people who wrote them; nevertheless, he saw the coach's point. So he shook hands cheerfully and departed, being mild by nature. That was why his sharp tone now brought them up.

"Dared it to happen?" Kerney repeated.

"They try to aggravate. They try to work themselves into a position where you can't do anything but get mad, cuss them out, fire them, knock them down. I don't like to think about them that way, then every once in a while—well, one made me pretty mad today. He was little; I would have felt like an s.o.b. if I had hit him, and he would have been glad to make me feel like one."

"Who was it?" Jimmy Tallant asked.

Duncan hesitated. "I don't remember. Uncle of my delivery boy."

"Was it Dozer?" Jimmy pursued.

"Dozer. Yes. Beckwith Dozer."

"Beck Dozer," Jimmy said. "I know him well."

There was a silence. Some line had been crossed; a crack in the sidewalk had been stepped on. There was no exchange of glances.

"Why didn't you hit him?" Jimmy asked.

"Oh, now, don't start talking about hitting niggers!" Tinker cried. "I won't stand for it."

"Travis would have hit him," Jimmy said to her suddenly, and she answered at once, "But not Duncan."

"If I'd hit him he would have been glad," said Duncan.

"I don't get that," Kerney said.

"You don't deal with them every day in the week," Duncan said.

"If you had just hit him hard enough he would have forgotten to be glad about anything," Jimmy pointed out.

"I don't see it like that," said Duncan.

"Travis would have hit him," Jimmy Tallant repeated.

"Yes," said Duncan, meeting him, "and that was a bad thing about Travis."

"Bad thing? The niggers were crazy about him."

"They had to pretend they were," Kerney put in.

"What kind of talk is this?" Jimmy demanded. "Travis was the only white man I know they would ask to nigger weddings and funerals."

"That's right," Duncan agreed. "It's also true that he let a nigger man bleed to death on the floor of the jail."

"That's right too," Jimmy said.

They were silent for a moment, knowing in common with all Southerners that when the knot got too tangled it was just as well left alone.

It was just as well to tell a story.

"I was with him the night it happened," Jimmy said. "We were playing poker. The jailer's boy came over and told him. He crept up and whispered it to him and Travis said out loud, 'What nigger?' Somebody asked him what the matter was and he said, 'The boy says the nigger's dead.' Then he said 'Oh.' Flat, just 'Oh.' He had drawn out three for the discard and his hand stopped in the air. 'I never knew I hit him that hard,' he said. Everybody waited. Matt Pearson was waiting to deal. 'I had clean forgot about him,' he said. Somebody sitting outside the light said, 'You don't know your own strength, Travis,' but I don't know if he heard it. 'God have mercy on my soul,' he said. He brought down his fist with the cards and flung the cards away. 'Three, Matt. I'll take three.' "

"That wasn't all that happened," Duncan said. "Just a couple of months ago there was a wreck on the highway. A wagonload of colored people were smashed up, and five of them killed."

"I heard about it," Jimmy said. "Mighty bad."

"It was hushed up," said Duncan. "And I think I know why."

"Of course you know why," Jimmy said. "Wagon without lights—the same thing that's happened a hundred times on 82, 51, every highway in the South."

"I don't know who didn't have lights," Duncan said, "but I know where the car was coming from."

"What are you trying to say, Duncan? If you think you

can lay those five niggers at my doorstep just because the fellow was drinking at Bud's. . . ."

"I didn't say I blamed you with it. I just say it's more convenient for you if the word doesn't get around that five people got killed by a man who had been drinking Grantham-Tallant wet goods."

"In other words," Kerney said, "Duncan means that protection money covers a lot of things."

"If you want to know the truth," Tallant said gloomily, "it costs a lot and covers too damn little. The only reason I'm tempted to run for sheriff is because I'm tired of seeing five hundred dollars a month checked out to profit and loss."

"Just five hundred?" Kerney asked. "I've heard that Travis alone pulled down that much."

"He didn't," Jimmy said. "However"—he grinned suddenly—"if business expands and things ride along, there's no reason why it wouldn't be worth that and maybe more—to the right sort of person." He looked at Duncan and deliberately closed one eye.

Duncan colored swiftly. "You'd better be joking."

"Sure, I'm joking." Jimmy got up and stood with his back to the fire, empty glass in hand, warming himself. "Haven't we all been joking tonight?"

"As a matter of fact," said Duncan, "no. It's a fair warning from the start, Jimmy. If I run for sheriff and if I win, I'll shut you and Grantham down first thing."

Jimmy chose not to answer, but rather to leave him sitting there with his seriousness upon him. "It's turning a little colder." He examined the ice at the bottom of his glass. "Tinker, child, it's been a long dry day."

She uncurled and stood. "I'll fix you one, you and everybody. But if there's any more fussing, I warn you: I'll go straight to bed and read a murder mystery."

Jimmy Tallant followed her through the dark dining room and into the kitchen. "What's got into Duncan?"

She frowned, breaking out ice into the sink with annoyed rapidity. "He and Kerney. You haven't been here in a while. They sit and talk by the hour . . . niggers, politics, Truman, the South. . . ."

"Duncan's not pro-Truman?"

"No, I don't mean *that*. It's something called the 'new South.' Kerney thinks the day of the liberal is at hand. He thinks all you have to do is get a few people in a few towns to take a great big risk of being martyrs, only it will seem like a bigger risk than it actually is because people know deep down but won't admit that the old reactionary position of the South has played out to nothing but a lot of sentiment. He thinks the Dixiecrat movement was the last gasp of it."

"What big words you know, Mrs. Harper."

She laughed. "I've learned them by heart. Kerney's not interested in a solitary thing but politics. It's worse than hearing girls talk about their babies all the time."

"He's pretty interested in Cissy Hunt."

Pouring whisky, she glanced up sharply. "Sure, that's the whole thing."

He looked mystified, so she explained, though she obviously thought it was like adding two and two: "Because Duncan used to go with Marcia Mae. That's why Kerney comes here." She emphasized the last word by striking the bottle stopper in place with the palm of her small hand, a childish gesture like many of hers. It was hard to believe how shrewd she was. She gave special attention to matters of love. "Kerney *would* have to have Cissy Hunt."

"Why?"

"It's the best family in town for him to marry into. They aren't in politics, but they have influence."

So she would have her terse say about every match and marriage, driving in the slender accurate nail: she knew the reason for love was seldom love. Still, what she hardly believed in had snapped up her life—she had never loved anyone but Duncan Harper. She had known this always, from the time they were in high school.

Jimmy Tallant never had to recall that she was his first girl. He had gone with her for five years. He had taken her to dances, had parked with her on dark side roads and twisted his long intelligent limbs in every possible way around her body, which seemed so resistless. At the end of embraces incredibly extended, she would ask him to take her to the drugstore before it closed because she wanted a Coca-cola.

She had cast him into a long agony; he tread water in a lake of fire. He told her so, and she only said it wasn't her fault. Nightly, he passed from rage to tears and back again. He grew so irresistible that all the girls in the eleventh grade (to mention one group) lost their virtue to him, but nothing did him much good.

One thing: Tinker always liked to talk to him. She could even tell him about Duncan. Thus one falls in love with unhappiness, not through choosing it or wanting it, but through having to live with it. He did not know quite when she ceased to be a passion and turned into a state of mind.

She still was. He could lounge near her, against the kitchen cabinet, smoking, watching her move around and mix the drinks and hear her talk; he could remember that he had taught her to dance and smoke and kiss and drink; and he could still be moodily satisfied that she had finally got the man she always wanted. So be it ever, he thought, when suddenly she was close to him and her hand lay on his arm.

"Jimmy, don't run against Duncan."

He hesitated.

"I've never asked you for anything," she went on. "Have I?"

He saw instantly the forty ways in which this was absurd, unfair, and beside the point.

"Tink. Ole Tink." He touched her hair. "Are you happy?"

"I will be, if you won't run against Duncan."

"Whatever you say."

"You promise me?"

"I promise."

"You won't say I asked you?"

"No."

That quick, she was gone. She was telling him which drinks were whose, so he could help her take them in.

two
old friends
meet

6. The next day Marcia Mae Hunt and Duncan saw each other for the first time since she had jilted him. She had run off and married an Irishman who everyone in town insisted was a lumberjack because he was from Montana and wore a plaid shirt.

Her meeting with Duncan occurred at midmorning in front of the post office. She saw that it was going to happen before he did. He was coming alone out of the post office, tearing open some circulars, sorting out a bill or two. She had parked her convertible, gathered up her bag and gloves and had one foot out of the door when she saw him, and knew she could not turn back. The square seemed empty, but she knew from old experience that it was not. In Lacey someone was always watching, and by no means could she lack courage. She drew a breath, and her heart, which had paused, rushed to beat again. It had to happen sometime, she thought. She set both feet in their expensive well-buffed leather loafers on the pavement. She was glad that she habitually did a careful make-up, that the white collar of her blouse was clean above the beige cashmere sweater. She advanced in the mild winter sunlight, across the old brick paving before the post office.

In a moment he would look up, and see her coming toward him. It was not unlike, she recalled absurdly, the first time they had met, back when they were children.

That was the time he had happened across her back pasture with two other boys. They had been shooting jaybirds down by the branch, and carried .22 rifles with them. She was playing with the cook's little boy, making him swing her. The swing was hung from a high limb in the oak tree and the oak tree grew out of a rise, so with high swinging the flight could be perilous. She loved high swinging. That day she was going higher than ever before. "Again!" she kept screaming at the panting little black boy, knowing that when he took a notion he would quit and say "I ain't" when she wanted him to start over. But today he did not quit. He was growing and could push harder. She soared on, entranced by the dip and rise and great outward plunge.

A dreamy time elapsed between the breaking of the rope and the end of the fall. She knew what had happened. Up there, cracked aside like a whiplash, the good end of the rope snatching itself from her hand, she felt her small body take the rise anyway, without the swing to send her, and at the crest she rocked a little, sleepily. Down below she could see the creek and the place where the branch ran into it, and, over across on the bluff, the sawmill, sending up a puff of smoke. Just below there were three boys who seemed to be talking; then one of them threw his gun down and ran. She wondered where he was running.

Duncan said later it seemed to him too that she stayed up a long time. It was long enough for him to watch the broken end of the rope riding in a slack S against the sky, and to conclude when and where she would stop going up and would begin to come down. He did not know who or even what she was. The only impression he had as he threw down the gun and ran was of a positive quality of blondness—total blondness, not just a color of hair.

Then she hit him. She fell into him from above and to the left, shooting neatly into his arms. He thought at first that she had buried him so deep in the ground he would never see daylight again; the fact was that she had knocked him out and broken his collarbone. The only thing he had failed to estimate was her velocity. Otherwise, he had succeeded. She rolled safely out of his arms, and began to bellow.

Her parents came, running down the hill, and after them four or five Negro servants, and finally her brother Everett at a walk, holding his finger between the pages of a book. He did not come down the hill; being lazy as mud, he calculated he would have to climb back up it. He almost got caught in it as it was, for they kept yelling back that he was to call the doctor; but he pretended not to hear and the yard boy passed him at a run, heading back to the house to do the errand. Mr. Hunt, holding his baby close, took time to speed a look of disgust up the hill, then, turning, said something to his wife, who nodded. Everett believed they had spoken of him. Raging, he turned away. He wished that his father would die, and he called his mother a bitch. As for his sister, he wished for her simply some sort of disappearance, something that would sponge even the memory of her out of his mind. Wasn't she always into things that did not interest him, though plainly they should have done so? Last week, running to the bluff to watch the Rabbit Foot Minstrels parade into town, she had stuck a dark thorn, smooth as walnut, in her foot. Another time, greedy, she had climbed to the top of the scuppernong arbor and taken grapes right out of the sun until, reaching too far, she tipped over and fell through, flat on her stomach. Her screams were wheezy; everybody's nap was broken up. She climbed trees, had to have a pony, and went fishing with Negroes. Someday, when she got married and left—or at least when he went off to college—he was going simply to appropriate her past. He had saved the thorn and taken Kodak pictures of the pony and the fish strings. All this he thought while he sat in the double swing in the side yard reading, and refused to look up when they passed in procession with Duncan, guiding him toward the doctor's car. "Stop twisting your hair," his mother called out, and he raged again; the page before his eyes grew actually red. The only reason he had gone even to the top of the hill was because he hoped she was dead.

He stole a glance. The Negroes were ahead, carrying a lot of useless things including blankets and a hot-water bottle. His parents and the doctor were helping Duncan. The two little boys with the rifles trailed behind, and at the very end his baby sister Cissy was hopping along on the sides of her bare feet because the sidewalk burned them—she was trailing her diaper behind her and had on nothing at all, but nobody noticed. Marcia Mae had slid in close to Duncan. She was a messy little girl, fidgety, full of reactions to everything, some-times three or four at once, such as right now, she was happy the accident had happened, was wondering how she could work her way in to watch the doctor set the bone, she wanted to go tell the cook all about it, and she was dead to go to the bathroom. But the bone came first, being the most unusual, and she was sticking as close as she could to the boy who had saved her. He walked slow and held his arm with contemplation. He was blond too, Everett noticed, and half a head taller than Marcia Mae. Maybe they'll get married, he thought hopefully.

He was the first to think it, but in a couple of years everybody thought it. For they grew to be a fine-looking couple, fair, beautifully built, alert as a brace of hunting dogs, mettled as a young carriage span, and always going somewhere. With them on the horizon you could do two things: join their procession or go sit over with Everett in the swing, because they were It. Later, on the noble Saturdays, Duncan's football feats traveled over clicking wires to every newspaper in the world, but to Lacey this was merely a proof of something known all along: namely, that he got the best because he had the best already, that unfair way it says in the Bible that things ought to be.

What had happened to part them? Everyone gave a different answer. She had run off with a Yankee, a redheaded Irishman named O'Donnell who had got killed in the war. Nobody would ever call her by her married name. She was still Marcia Mae Hunt, the girl who was Duncan Harper's girl. An image had been violated; they were left with a sense of unease.

That morning before the post office, so many years later, the image was restored: the few who saw it would be glad to describe it to the rest, then all would have it back again, the thought of the two fair heads.

Duncan and Marcia Mae knew this, and came together with a certain stateliness in the sun—without haste. They stood talking for a while (it was, as if anyone could hear, a ritual language), parted once, turned, spoke again, walked away a second time, turned a second time, and waved goodbye. These were the gestures they had known always.

She drove through town with a steady profile. At home her mother called from the sitting room. "Is anything happening uptown?" She paused, calculating. Then she said, "I ran into Duncan." "Where?" "In front of the post office." Her mother came out into the hall. "How does it seem, after all this time?"

The two women regarded each other.

Mrs. Hunt understood that her daughter had had an unhappy time of it because she had never learned anything about men. She felt that she had failed Marcia Mae by not finding some way to impart a knowledge she herself obviously possessed in quantity, as witness the darling dazzling time she had had as a girl, the foresight she had shown in selecting a man who would amount to something, to say nothing of how wisely she had weighed her assets when she had made her choice. She had judged to the dot how much her family name (Standsbury) would mean to him, and how much beauty and charm would have to be added. She had had enough, naturally.

Admirably controlled and considerate to the limits of her subtlety, the mother never mentioned her daughter's shortcomings in these matters to her face; in fact, she believed that Marcia Mae did not know what she thought of her. She was given to mentioning when she spoke of other girls who had failed to make a proper match: "She could have had so-and-so, but she didn't play her cards right."

As for Marcia Mae, she had long ago in a chill crystalline hour faced the fact that she was the daughter of a Southern belle. That meant, beyond a shadow of change, that exactly to the extent of her own attractiveness she was her mother's enemy. As she had felt the necessity of a stage presence before the post office, she felt it now, in the house she was born in.

She said, "How does it seem? We recognized each other, so I guess we haven't aged too much."

"No, I didn't mean that. I meant—"

"You mean, did my heart turn over? How could it? I never loved anybody but Red O'Donnell."

At this time it was being said on the telephone by one lady to another: "You can't tell me she ever loved anybody but Duncan Harper . . . why, she doesn't even go by her married name, nobody calls her Mrs. O'Donnell . . . and one or two people I won't name go so far as to mention she never was married to that man at all, but I don't believe that. You know, Sally Ennis's niece saw her eating a hamburger in San Diego with another man in Marine uniform who wasn't red-headed in the least. I've always understood Marcia Mae was a nice girl but, even so and notwithstanding, will you tell me why she felt compelled to elope? And if she loved that Yankee and he got the medal they said he got when she went to Washington then why wouldn't she talk about it . . . you ask her and she stares a hole . . . no, I don't believe *that* for a minute, I think she's a nice girl, but all I want to know is *why did she come back home?*"

Upstairs in her own room she closed the door. All her old things were around her—the cherry furniture, the quilt her grandmother had pieced, the radio she had got for graduation, the silver dresser set they had mailed to her when she got married. It had been dented here and there—a shame. When she looked in the mirror she wanted to surprise a child's face, lurking inside. She wanted a moment to examine that face, to ask what it had been that was so different from what everyone had assumed it was. Instead, a woman's eyes regarded her with level clarity. They had seen a great deal, had remembered it all, and told nothing, not even to herself.

Suddenly she felt like crying. The eyes were slightly surprised, they refused even to consider tears. She put her head in her hands to block out their cool regard. At this her knees shook and her wrists, as though after hard tennis.

"Why did I come back home?" she asked. "Why did I?"

And Duncan that day had questions to ask himself, too, and asked them more than once, conscious that nobody uptown mentioned her name to him. "Why did she leave me?" he wondered, and then, "Did I fail her? How?" He went to no mirror, but perhaps he was seeking after all no more than a clear look at himself.

an hour
at
the Hunts'

7. The firelight was sunken as comfortably deep into the silver coffeepot as Kerney Woolbright in the armchair.

"Of course," Mr. Hunt was saying, "I don't know what the boy will do, but the last thing we need to discuss openly in this county now is the Negro question."

"I don't know that he means to discuss it openly," said Kerney.

"You don't know," Mr. Hunt returned. "I like Duncan, always have." He laughed. "And I've seen a lot of him. But you know his family."

"Good people," said old Mrs. Standsbury, his mother-in-law. She wore a blue sack and was crocheting bootees. She had got to the age where her descendants were multiplying like rabbits.

"Good people," Mr. Hunt agreed, "but you know back during Roosevelt's first term people used to go in that store for a nickel's worth of kerosene just to hear old Phillip Harper cuss the New Deal."

"Duncan's father?" Kerney asked. He had not been brought up in Lacey.

"No, his uncle. Great-uncle, really. He was a Hoover man."

"Yes, and too hard up to buy kerosene himself to build a fire with," said Mrs. Hunt in her cool, amused voice. "But then we were all poor then. More coffee, Kerney?"

"Please, Miss Nan." He watched with pleasure the movements of her sure hands with the big veins and the rings, the practical trim of the nails, the emphatic visible contour of the bones. This was how a mature woman's hands ought to look—he had known this always. He heard the touch of silver against the thin china, and the coffee was his.

"We're poor now," said Mr. Hunt. "We just don't know it. Income tax is just around the corner."

"Everybody says that," said old Mrs. Standsbury, laying aside her work to scratch her back, "but I never notice any difference."

"Of course *you* don't," Mrs. Hunt returned, glancing at her husband.

"Well, I eat the same food you do," the old lady said without rancour and continued her work.

"Bought your new spring hat, Miss Tennie?" Kerney inquired, raising his voice a bit. Old Mrs. Standsbury's hats were beautiful, expensive, and famous. "At her age!" people said, marveling with delight, and agreed they had never seen anything like her.

"Not yet," said the old lady, "but I hope to get to Memphis next week. Nan is going to take me when she goes to the dentist."

"Dentist?" Kerney inquired. "That really sounds like hard times."

"Another inlay," Mrs. Hunt told him. "I wouldn't dream of letting Dr. Neighbors touch it."

"Old Neighbors has hammered in a many a one in his day,"

said Mr. Hunt. He liked to pretend it was the women folk who had torn his country loyalties.

"In his *day*, yes," returned his wife.

"Where is Marcia Mae?" Kerney inquired.

Mr. Hunt pulled himself out of a reverie. "Marcia Mae? Gone to dinner at the club. Thank God." He came out so strongly on this last that his wife glanced at him.

"Heavens, Jason."

"Well, she's worrying me to support Duncan in the sheriff's race. I seldom take a hand in local politics; too many friends here. And I certainly don't want to support the boy if he's going to make a fool of us."

"I don't think he's radical," Kerney said. "He merely wants to try out two things: enforce the liquor law and apply justice equally for black and white."

"Half the niggers will be in jail, too," said old Mrs. Standsbury.

They looked at her. They had a way of forgetting that she listened, or if she listened that she had opinions of her own.

"Oh, no, Mother," said Mrs. Hunt. She read liberal papers and always, without offending anyone, tried to see the Negro's side.

"*I* didn't say it," the old lady said. "Old Black Jonas said it a long time back. He's a nigger and ought to know."

"He was trying to please you," said Mrs. Hunt.

"He never tries to please me the way he transplants my bulbs," Mrs. Standsbury returned.

"This likker thing," Jason Hunt resumed, "you take this likker thing. Duncan's right about that. It's gotten bad in this county. There's at least one wreck on the highway every Saturday night, and there must be plenty of them we never hear about. Winfield County is notorious all over the state. This Tallant-Grantham partnership—"

"What about that, sir?" Kerney inquired.

"Well, you tell me. What about it?"

"I can't say. Jimmy's a friend—at least, I guess he is. But I have heard one or two people say it may be that he and Grantham control not just that big highway place, but pull the strings for a whole dozen others."

"And—?"

Their eyes met. Kerney grinned. "You're making me say all this, sir. You aren't running for anything; why don't you say it?"

"You're among friends," Mr. Hunt said, smiling.

"You mean there's more?" Nan Hunt was leaning forward. Men never told her anything.

"This goes no farther, Nan," her husband said. "It has been talked, however—I don't know if it's true—that some of the New Orleans syndicate that Kefauver closed down are behind the Highway 82 mess we have now in Winfield County. You take Jimmy Tallant. He's no fool. He is also no man to be shoved into a shotgun wedding. But he married Bud Grantham's daughter because Bud threatened to cut him out of the business if he didn't. Jimmy Tallant doesn't do that for a small-time bootlegger's partnership. Of course, nobody knows the straight of this. Travis Brevard didn't know it; he said all his life—"

"Toting that wad of protection money in a belt next to his skin—" Kerney put in.

"That's right. Said that Jimmy Tallant was a good Winfield County boy. Travis lived by a country code. He trusted Tallant to do the same. But Duncan now—"

"That's a different thing, isn't it, sir?"

"It is."

"I've always thought Duncan was a clean-minded boy," Nan Hunt said.

"Yes, ma'am," Kerney agreed instantly. "You are right."

"He's never amounted to much," Mr. Hunt said.

"I don't care," Nan burst out. "He's kept the store his father left him; he's stocked the things I'm used to buying; he hasn't 'renovated' and made his store front look like the inside of a bathroom; but he makes a living and lives in a quiet way, so you say he's never amounted to much."

"Yes, and where will he even get the money to make the sheriff's race, unless he asks his wife or his mother?"

"Does his mother have anything?" Nan asked.

"Plenty," said Jason Hunt, nodding. "Stashed away."

"She never spends a nickel of it on her back," said old Mrs. Standsbury. "She's worn that one dress to prayer meeting and that one old blue sweater for twenty years."

Nan smiled. "With that old long black flashlight with a head this big. Does she still have that, Mother?"

"If you'd go to prayer meeting sometime, you'd know."

Nan winked at Kerney.

"How about a drink, Nan?" Mr. Hunt inquired.

"Speaking of bootleggers—" She rose. "Soda for you, Kerney?"

"Plain water, please, Miss Nan. Can I help you?"

"Keep your seat, boy," said Jason Hunt. "Jonas is back there somewhere." He went to call the servant.

When he stood before the fireplace, glass in hand, he laughed boyishly—you saw in little flashes like this why Nan Standsbury had found him winning. "Whisky is pretty damn good at that."

"Duncan will agree with you," Kerney said. He was busy finding every chance to put a word in.

The older man became more serious. "No, and I agree with Duncan, Kerney. He's quite right. Until we can have whisky legally, people will turn drinking into an indecent and messy business. Most people, that is."

"We certainly don't," his wife said. "Not in my house."

Kerney remembered hearing of certain parties Marcia Mae

46

was said to have thrown back in the old days, but he said nothing.

"It's still whisky," said old Mrs. Standsbury. "Whisky is whisky. I don't care who drinks it."

"Don't mind Mother," Nan said to Kerney.

"Oh, I don't care what you do," the old lady said. She never made anyone uncomfortable, because she had told the simple truth: she did not care what they did.

The Negro man left the room, shutting the twin doors carefully.

"Kerney," Mr. Hunt asked, "who is sheriff now?"

"Why, Miss Ada, sir."

"Right. Miss Ada. And does Miss Ada know that Travis's last request was for Duncan Harper to be sheriff?"

"I don't know, sir."

"Well, don't you think it would be a good idea for somebody to tell her?"

"Me, sir?"

"Well, you, me, anybody."

"I think it would be a fine idea for you to tell her."

There was a long silence. Kerney said, "You are thinking, sir—"

"I am thinking that the likker stand is a good thing, that the Negro stand is a good thing too, but we gain nothing—we might lose a great deal—by saying so in public. I am thinking that Duncan has no experience in politics, that we do not know what he will do. I am thinking it would be much better to let him have experience for six months before he loses a race or before he wins one and gets stuck with the job and gets us stuck with him for four years."

"Oh!" Kerney scratched his head. He wondered that he had not thought of this before.

"I am saying, in other words, that I don't care to elect a man whose mistakes may have to be paid for in blood. You say Duncan wants to experiment—to try something out, I think you said. I tell you, Kerney, no one should experiment with dynamite."

"No, sir."

"Yet on such a platform he wants me to elect him."

"He didn't send me here—" Kerney began.

Nan Hunt's cool voice interposed. "I think, darling, that the voters will elect Duncan, not you." It showed at such times that she felt she had married beneath her. A tiny line of pain appeared between her eyes. Compulsively she touched her fingers there; everyone remembered her fierce headaches. But suddenly, radiantly, she relaxed. A light broke over her face. A dash of cold, stairwell air entered the room, and in the middle of it, clouding it with her perfume, a young girl was rustling, approaching. Kerney tried not to turn too fast, but he could no more keep the radiance from his face than could her mother.

"Cissy." Her father caught her hand. "You've kept this boy waiting for two hours."

"I have not, silly." She bent to touch her grandmother's forehead with a kiss. "He'd rather talk to you all than take me out in the cold anyway. Hadn't you, Kerney?"

"Well—"

"No fair, is it, Kerney?" Mrs. Hunt laughed. "Turn around, honey. Your skirt—there."

"It's six-thirty now," Mr. Hunt said. "You'll be late, Kerney. Nice to see you, boy. I'll pay that call we mentioned. But not a word of it, remember—least of all to Duncan."

"I quite understand, sir. I think it's a brilliant idea. Goodnight, sir. Coat, Cissy?"

They walked together down the long walk in the chill dark. He let her in the car, waited while she drew in her full skirts, then closed the door. She sat in the cold, settled deeply in her fur coat, waiting for the door to open, for the nice smell of cigarettes and whisky, the weight of him on the seat beside her. Kerney was so nice: he smelled nice, he talked nice, he met people well, he was going to amount to something, he was fun. Yet—

"Hurry, Kerney. We're late."

"Kiss me first."

"Oh, my lipstick, no!" But it was only a small kiss, and for just a second, his eyes looked watchfully into hers. "Hurry, hurry!" Then, to please him, she slipped her hand through his arm. "What a silly old boy you are. Silly, silly, silly! What a funny. . . ."

She could go on like this for hours, without even thinking about it. She thought it was disgusting, but it pleased him immensely. And he was supposed to be so smart, too. She could never figure it out.

Miss
Ada

8. Miss Ada was still in bed, where her husband's death had hurled her.

She was very thin and her face, devoid of make-up, had cast all its wrinkles. It was a sensitive, high-strung face, long, with well-set cheekbones and a crooked patrician nose. The eyes, luminous and somewhat exalted, fixed upon Duncan, who had come at her summons, with the misplaced fervor of a young girl reading from the Bible at a "program."

"I was so happy to learn, Duncan, that Mr. Brevard's last wish was for you to be his successor. It proves to me he was functioning right up to the last."

"Yes ma'am, he was," Duncan said. "He was as clear as ever."

"Semper fidelis!" The long thin hand swept delicately upward. "You understand me, Duncan. We cannot have the class of people Mr. Brevard *generally* appointed taking over in the Lacey courthouse, can we?"

Duncan did not answer. Class seldom entered his head; he was sure it had never entered Travis's.

"Those deputies! That office! Those spittoons! That Willard Follansbee!"

Duncan immediately recalled, by the force of Miss Ada's tone, the rich black hairs that covered Willard Follansbee, Travis's favorite deputy, down to the last finger joint.

"How could *I* be expected to deal with such people? No." Looking down, she drew circles with her forefinger around each tuft on the pink spread. "No, I think when Travis—when Mr. Brevard stopped by your store that day, he was thinking only of me."

"You do?"

"I do. Because how could *I* be expected to deal with people like Willard Follansbee? Can we have that class of people taking over in an office that is responsible to *me?*"

Duncan had a sudden wild moment of wondering if Miss Ada thought her appointment was for life. He remembered Tinker once at the store, snatched back just in time from throwing a whole wad of invoices into the stove. Her excuse, which she seemed to find adequate, was that nobody had ever told her what invoices were. More total confusions have never been rendered than by innocent women.

However, Miss Ada soon set his mind at rest.

"I realize, of course, that my position is merely titular." She colored faintly. "Just the same, they say I can appoint anybody I want to." She gave him a coy glance.

Not till then did he understand. It had taken him, he realized, uncommonly long to catch on. Because it seemed unthinkable to him that this outdated, inadequate, ridiculous old woman should have anything to say about what happened to him. Yet if she had been different, would Travis Brevard have come into a store to die?

He approached the bed and took her hand. He felt the bones slip loosely together under his hand's pressure. Could the substance under the blue twisted ridge possibly be blood?

"I'll have to think it over," he said. "I'll have to talk to—to my wife."

"Bless her heart," Miss Ada said. "That was a wonderful cake she sent over to the funeral. Not that I could eat a bite of it. But everyone said—" Suddenly her eyes fell shut. Gently, but insistently, she pulled her hand backward from his grasp. "I'm rather tired, Duncan. If you'll forgive me."

"Yes, of course."

He hesitated for an instant at the door, and it was then her eyes popped wide open and a look of distaste hastened him out.

So she had seen the weight of Travis clamped in a box and dumped in the ground; she had flicked off the hairy thought of Willard Follansbee like something nasty on her hand; now she wanted shut of Duncan too. He took his hat from the dark-stained hat tree in the hall with its mirror and side drawers, and retreated into the sun. Miss Ada's front door framed an oval of sanded glass with a flowering trellis design; it was flanked by matching rectangular sidelights. He closed the latch gently and remembered the fall of the surprisingly large eyelid, coarse as leather. Behind that door, behind that eyelid, lived the clearest conscience in town, clearer than the tiny silver bell beside the bed. He half expected to hear it ring for the colored girl, but it didn't. Miss Ada had probably gone to sleep.

a
deal

9. In the sheriff's office the next day, along about ten, Mattie Sue Bainbridge, the secretary, wrapped up good in her coat and went across the street for a cup of coffee. Willard Follansbee, mouth partly open, rared back a little more in the split-bottom chair by the stove. It had turned off freezing cold, and sound traveled far: all the way inside you could hear the iron chatter of the gate on the sidewalk when she passed through.

Willard said, "They wrap up the top part, but what do they do about the bottom?"

"Nothing," Jimmy Tallant said. He had just come in; the room was still smoking with his coldness. He spread one long raw hand quite close to the stove top. In the other he held a pair of expensive tan leather gloves.

"You know," Follansbee went on seriously, "there's a bare space that long between the top of their stockings and the bottom of their pants."

"So they tell me," Jimmy Tallant said.

"That is," said Follansbee, "if they wear pants. You think Miss Mattie Sue wears pants?"

"I never looked into it," Jimmy Tallant said. "Have you?"

"Never looked into it."

There was a long silence. Jimmy Tallant turned to warm his back, then turned again. "Well, Willard. I hear that Duncan's in the saddle now."

" 'Swhat I hear too."

"You moving out?"

"No. Staying in to help him. Duncan's all right. I got nothing against him."

52

"I got nothing against him either. Except he thinks he's Jesus Christ."

"Does he?" Willard glanced up.

"He does."

"Travis"—Willard burst out, and Jimmy turned his back to the stove because Willard couldn't mention Travis without choking up—"Travis never meant what he said to Duncan. I bet you anything in the world you want to bet he thought he was talking to me. I bet you anything you *name* he was out of his head and thought he was talking to me."

"Only he wasn't," Jimmy said coolly. "He was talking to Duncan Harper."

"Duncan Harper. What did he ever do for Travis? Listen, whenever Travis couldn't run for sheriff by law because by law he couldn't succeed himself, I ran for sheriff for him, but it was him that was running and it was him that was always sheriff, and everybody knew it. I never grudged him."

"Yeah," said Jimmy, "and when Travis needed a nigger woman, you found a nigger woman for him."

"I went there that day," Willard recalled. He was nearly weeping again. "It was the first hot day that year, along in April, going to take the refrigerator back or make her pay for it. She was on the front porch in a purple kimono and nothing else, and it broad afternoon, drunk as a coot. 'Send me the high shurf, white man,' she said. 'Hit's the high shurf I wants to see.' I came back and told Travis, 'She's tender as cream,' I said. 'To hell with that,' he said. 'I'm going up there and get Clem Gates' refrigerator.' The next morning he paid Clem Gates for the Frigidaire, out of his own pocket."

"What's Ida Belle doing these days?" Jimmy asked.

"Nothing," said Willard. "She plays nigger blues on the Stromberg-Carlson Travis gave her. There those that have been up there. But nothing doing. Nothing. Never will be. I'll bet money on it. It's the way Travis was. Never another one to fill his bed, or his shoes either. Duncan Harper can kiss my ass. I wish I had me a Stromberg-Carlson to play. Instead, I got to show a groceryman what to do with a poll-tax receipt."

"I wouldn't be surprised you'll be doing a few more things than that," Jimmy Tallant said. His tone had not changed, and Follansbee did not look up. Only in the way his hands and face stilled was it apparent that he knew that Jimmy Tallant had stated his business.

"I might," he said at last. When he looked up, through the silence, Jimmy Tallant was holding out his hand.

Willard did not take it. "I was just thinking the other day," he said to Tallant, "that now I'm going to be doing a good many things Travis used to do, and it don't seem right not to be getting Travis's check."

"You might have something there," said Tallant.

"Might ain't do," Willard returned.

"I'll say this," Jimmy offered, "if you really do Travis's job and yours too, you ought to be getting more. Say twenty per cent more."

Willard paused. He let out his breath slowly. "Ought ain't do either.

They stopped at the clack of heels in the high hall. Mattie Sue Bainbridge returned, hugging herself with cold. Behind her, relaxed and silent as a thought of himself, came Kerney Woolbright. He shook hands with Follansbee and Tallant in turn.

"When's Duncan coming over?" Kerney inquired.

All sorts of spiteful things occurred to Willard, but he only said, "Tomorrow, I think."

"Don't seem right in here with Travis gone," Kerney said.

The two men eyed him. They knew what he was up to,

he a college man, a Yale law graduate, going to marry Cissy Hunt if it killed him, going around shaking hands and saying the commonplace thing. They didn't fall for it, but somehow they didn't challenge it either. Perhaps the reason was the uneasy feeling he gave them that he was as sharp about them as they were about him. Maybe a little sharper? They doubted that. He thrust his gloves in his overcoat pocket and warmed his hands over the stove, a little too exactly like anybody else. Tallant especially surveyed him with the eye of an old actor for a young one.

It was Mattie Sue who answered him. She said that it certainly didn't seem right, that every few minutes she caught herself thinking that was Mr. Travis just shut the outside door, and once she looked up thinking she actually saw him come in—she was all by herself with nobody else in the office, and it actually scared her. She actually thought about closing up and going home, but somebody came in.

Kerney heard this through with such sober attention that she wished there were more to say, and suddenly thanked him for the coffee he had bought her at the drugstore. She observed the two other men watching her and blushed, then began to type rapidly.

As women said of some books, there was something in Kerney for everybody.

a
phone
call

10. Cognizant of the merits of the dial system, Kerney went home and telephoned Duncan.

"Anybody in the store?" he asked.

"Nobody but me and W.B. I'm closing for lunch."

"I'd get rid of Follansbee," said Kerney.

The wire was silent for a moment. "I can't," Duncan said.

"Sure you can."

"I can't add insult to injury, Kerney. He loved Travis like a hound dog. I told him he'd be staying on to help me."

"Yes, and what thanks do you get? He's in there this morning conniving with Tallant."

"What about?"

"You *know* what about, Duncan. You wouldn't take protection money from Tallant."

"Willard knows my policy."

"Do I have to bore a hole in your skull? Do you think Willard's going to respect your policy?"

"I don't know. I have to give him the chance."

Kerney could see Duncan as plainly as if he had gone to the store (which he hadn't wanted to do because the eye of the courthouse would follow him as certainly as God's own): Duncan warming his hand on the cat's fur, and the colored boy across the room like a maharajah's lackey, cross-legged on the sack of chicken feed, probably picking his nose. Didn't everybody know instinctively the decent thing to do? Why must Duncan Harper have the gall to insist on actually doing the decent thing?

Kerney knew within an ace what Follansbee would do: the thing that irritated him was that Duncan knew it too. Still, he was for the moment compelled to see what Duncan saw—the Follansbee so ugly, so poor, so unimportant, the aging drugstore cowboy, the third best shot at the pool hall, for whom life, like a lucky throw, had suddenly added up—its soundlessness suddenly filled with the roar of privileged cars, the rattle of handcuffs, the glamour of guns, all because Travis Brevard had looked at him one day and known what he would like. And Travis in death now stood present with

Willard, bright as a saint in his simple and adoring heart. A man with his capacity for devotion must have his chance. For what? For honor?

"Okay," said Kerney. "Okay, okay, okay!"

He hung up and that was when he saw her, his mother, standing in the door with that proud little smile which said how well he looked in the gray suit.

"Good God," Kerney flared. "I thought you were shopping in the Delta."

"I changed my mind," she said.

"You heard everything I said. You could have let me know you were there."

"I don't have to let anybody know I'm in my own house," she returned, passing by him, her feelings hurt.

He caught her. "If you repeat one single damned word of what you heard just now, it'll be your own house for sure, all by yourself, because I won't be living in it any more. It was that important, do you understand? No college campus doings any more. I make you a promise: if you tell this, I leave."

"I'm not going to tell anything," she said. "I didn't hear anything you said anyway. I wasn't even listening. I was thinking how well you looked"—her voice caught—"in your gray suit."

"A likely story," Kerney said. "You didn't lose two husbands over nothing."

"*They* didn't leave me; you know very well what happened. I left—"

But he had gone upstairs and slammed the door. He gave himself a ten-year limit to be in Washington, and no eavesdropping woman who thought he was a clever child was going to keep him down.

If that was love, he hoped Cissy Hunt would never love him, just so she married him. She would. Duncan had lost

Marcia Mae, but Cissy would marry Kerney Woolbright. Whom did she know that was better? Nobody. And on the heels of his confidence, fear came and touched a finger to his heart.

the
raid

11. Tinker did not know a thing about politics, as she kept on saying, but she did know that one night two weeks after Miss Ada turned over the sheriff's office to Duncan, the National Guard came up from Jackson to Winfield County to raid the Grantham-Tallant roadhouse. It was misting rain, and cold. The jonquils were in bloom and the flowering shrubs had put out; but now everything would be nipped.

About ten-thirty Kerney knocked on the door. She heard him stamping on the doormat and, switching on the porch light, she marked the rime of white on his shoulders and hat brim, and beyond him, outside, the sparse wet white dots lancing down the dark. "Snow!" she cried out with delight, and ran past him, out into the yard, lifting her face skyward and holding out her bare arms. Kerney watched her, smiling, and started to follow, but she came right back in, running with a slightly mannered little gaiety that was nonetheless attractive.

"It won't stick," she said. "The ground's not frozen."

"It never does."

"Sometimes. Once when we were children there was a big sleet and snow here for three days. I expect you were too young to remember, Kerney. They turned out school and none of us went home that I remember for a week. We made sleds and skis and played everywhere. Everything was different. Duncan and Jimmy and Marcia Mae Hunt and I went out rabbit hunting together and all got lost from each other. Come on in, Kerney. Duncan's not here, but he'll be back."

"It's as bad as being a doctor's wife for you now, I guess," Kerney said.

She shivered in front of the fire. She had put on, to keep her spirits up, little gold lounging slippers and velveteen slacks. She was practically positive that Kerney already knew where Duncan was.

"It couldn't do any harm to tell you now," she said. "They're raiding the highway place tonight."

"Who?"

"The National Guard." She spoke with confidence, though she had no idea on earth whether there were five of them or five hundred, whether they had come in convoy trucks and dressed in olive drab with guns at their feet, the way you used to see GI's moving toward maneuvers during the war, or whether they were in policemen's uniforms, riding in long black patrol cars with the slender aerial whipping sinuous and bright from the left rear fender. She decided on the black cars and imagined their soft pneumatic shimmer through the dark, the glimmer of the snow that melted when it touched the black metal. "You don't think anybody will get hurt?"

"Hurt? I wouldn't think so. Was Follansbee along?"

"I don't know. Duncan wouldn't tell me anything at all until just before he left. Let me get you a drink."

"No thanks."

"I'll have one then."

The drink was half gone when Duncan returned. There were no long black cars with him, no men in uniform, not even Follansbee. His Chevrolet sedan skidded and gave an angry snort entering the drive.

He came in laughing.

Tinker was cross-legged on the floor before the fire. Only

her eyes moved to him. He stripped off his overcoat and shook hands with Kerney.

"How did it go?" Kerney asked.

"It seems," said Duncan, "that everybody has got Tallant and Grantham wrong. You know how they make a living? They sell Coca-colas, Orange Crush, Dr. Pepper, and hamburgers, and they charge a little bit, a dollar a couple, for people to come and dance to the juke boxes. Do you know how much whisky there is in all of Winfield County? One half-pint bottle belonging to old Mars Overstreet who runs that little country store. He keeps it there for a cold. He's a deacon in the Baptist Church and was right embarrassed that we caught him with it. And he really does have a cold."

Kerney's mouth tightened. "I knew this would happen. I told you."

"It was worth a try," Duncan said. "I had to give Willard a chance."

"You didn't owe him a chance. You didn't owe him anything."

"Well," Duncan said mildly, "he has more stake in the sheriff's office than anyone I know."

"He's no more than the hired help. Travis tolerated him. It's no more his business than anybody else's what you decide to do."

"I think it's probably more his business than it is yours," Duncan said.

"You don't know anything about politics," Kerney said. "You're trying to play this out like it was a football game. You want to give everybody a break and play it clean. Did anybody ever offer you anything to throw a game?"

"Hundreds of people."

"But you never took anything. Nothing. You think you can work politics that easy."

"I knew it!" Tinker said. "I just knew you'd all be fussing."

"As a matter of fact," Duncan said, "I did take something once. A wrist watch. When I found out it was meant for a bribe, I gave it back."

"I'm sure you did."

"Kerney, there's no use getting worked up over this."

"I'm sorry, Duncan. It's only that I'm for you. I'm tired tonight. I've been straining myself all day to keep out of work, and it's worn me to a nub. For God's sake, don't take me seriously. If you and I don't stick together here, we'll both stand by ourselves, because there's nobody else we can stick with and be sure of."

"I believe that," Duncan said. "I'm tired too. Let's shake on it that way and forget it for now."

Kerney met his clasp with a good grip. "I best get home," he said. "I'm Mother's baby boy and she waits up with the porch light on."

Duncan turned back from the door, saying to his wife, "He is a baby, you know. It would be too much if it didn't dawn on him every once and a while."

He came to the fire. Tinker's head came level with his knee and he pressed it close against him, moving his hand caressingly through her short dark hair. But he was not thinking of her. He was still out there on the highway where exciting things had been going on for the first time in maybe too many years, and she knew it. She tried again to see it all: black cars, men in uniform, neon reflections on the wet gravel, and the occasional glint of snow. The men in uniform were heavy and handsome and she asked him suddenly, "Was Marcia Mae out there?"

In her hair his fingers stopped still. "Yes. How did you know?"

"I just thought she probably was."

. . . He did not dare at the moment, considering Tinker's mood, to remember fully the sight of the Cadillac convertible on the outskirts of the parked cars, or the arm in the window, propped straight up with the hand against the car roof, that way she always put her arm when she was behind the wheel and the car was standing. Then the bare length of wrist between the sleeve and glove, white as the snow—the sculpture of it jumped at him and said it was she. He got a remarkable thrill of pride, not thinking she had stopped on his account especially, but thinking how game she always was, to be curious and not ashamed of curiosity, to happen along and then not pass by. She was game and she was, in her curiosity, ageless: little girl, woman, old woman, with the bright interested undemanding eyes that missed nothing. In that moment, looking toward her from where he had stopped in the lighted door of the roadhouse, he was overcome with a delight that was all innocence. He was glad that he had known her and loved her and that she had loved him, and for the first time he could take the thought of what she had done without resentment, could step right straight into it and toward her, quickly crossing the gravel, threading among the cars. As he approached, the white shadow back of the arm grew as firm as the wrist. He leaned against the window.

"Nothing here," he said.

"Nothing!"

"Nothing. It will be the same everywhere."

"Follansbee," she said.

He shrugged. "Never mind. He loved Travis so, I had to give him a chance. It's no surprise."

"I see how you felt."

"He would have been sheriff if it weren't for me."

"I see."

"Marcia Mae, I came over to tell you that it doesn't make any difference to me any more that you ran off and married somebody else."

"It was an awful thing to do to anybody," she said. "I just couldn't help it. There was nothing *personal* about it, though."

"Well," said Duncan with a wry laugh, "I don't know how personal you can get."

She laughed too. "I mean I would have done it to anyone, for"—her chin lifted—"for Red."

"I'm sure he was a great guy. And I'm sorry, Marcia Mae, about—"

"Thanks."

The short silence that followed was certainly the time when he should have gone away. But she was saying, "I'm glad you don't hate me. I couldn't stand that."

"Hate you? Listen, I don't even dwell on it any more. I think you're just a hell of a fine girl, that's all. I came to tell you—"

"You cared the other day," she said. "That day uptown. I could tell it. You resented—"

"I know."

"Then when—?"

"Just now, when I looked up and saw your arm in the window. I knew it was you. You always stop that way. It came over me that I didn't care any more. Why? I don't know why. Because I was glad to see you. That's all."

"Glad to see me?" she repeated.

"Yes, glad. Mighty glad."

"Oh."

In the second silence, he knew he should have gone away during the first one.

But a narrow face had joined them.

"I got a complaint, sheriff," Jimmy Tallant said. "One of them big soldier bastards tilted my Miami Beach Bathing Beauty Contest pinball machine and all the lights on the breasts went out. I think you ought to go have a look at it. I heard you was pretty good at fixing up radios, juke boxes, that sort of thing. You might as well accomplish one thing during the evening."

"I'll get you yet, Jimmy," Duncan said pleasantly. "You know that, don't you?"

"I'll lay money on it," Tallant said.

"I don't make big money," Duncan returned, "so I can't afford to win big money. But this is just one time I missed, Jimmy. There'll be other times."

Tallant leaned his face down to Marcia Mae. "Where do you stand on this, old buddy?"

"I side with Duncan," she said. "He'll get you, Jimmy."

"Is that gratitude? After all the whisky I've got at cost for you. Tell you what, Marcia Mae. Soon as these folks hit the road, let's you and me have a drink up close to the stove. If Duncan won't bet with me, maybe you will."

"I might have a drink with you at that," she said.

"It's snowing," Duncan remarked.

Marcia Mae held out her hand. "Snowing." She smiled with sudden charm. "Do you remember the time, Duncan, when you and I got lost out in the woods that big snow we had when we were in high school?"

"What do you mean, you and Duncan?" Jimmy demanded. "I was there and so was Tinker. We all got lost, from town and from each other."

"That's so," said Marcia Mae, "but who found us? I forget."

"We found each other," said Jimmy. "I found a nigger house I knew, and Marcia Mae hollered her way toward me with Duncan not far behind."

"And I went back and found Tinker," Duncan said. "She was crying, down by an old stump."

"I remember now," said Marcia Mae.

64

"Yes," said Jimmy, "we found each other. . . ."

So it now seemed to Duncan that every time in life he came on Tinker she had contrived to get herself below knee level. Maybe she looked cute and felt right on the floor, but it made him feel like a fool. "Get up," he demanded.

She came up quickly, like the good dancer she was, rising further than her feet, all the way to the tips of her toes, with that startling quality of lightness she had, as though she had shot up through water. Her eyes were dutiful.

"Tinker," he said, "we are not going to start quarreling about Marcia Mae. I've seen her exactly twice in the last ten years. The first time was the other day in front of the post office. She happened to be uptown. The second time was tonight. Why she was there I don't know, but I ought to know her pretty well and I can guess. She saw something was going on and she was curious and—"

"And brave." She said it instantly, and it made him mad.

His jaw tightened, but after a moment he forged ahead. "As for what she did to me, it was terrible at first. It would be for anybody. Later it all boiled away and cooled. There was nothing left but a scar in my mind somewhere. But tonight when I saw her—this is important, Tinker—I knew that I didn't care any more one way or the other. I knew that as the person I used to know, she just didn't exist any more, not for me."

"Not an attractive woman any more?"

"Attractive woman? Oh, now, that's different, Tinker. And not fair. Lots of women are attractive; I can't help knowing that. The other way around too. Tallant, for instance. You aren't ever in any doubt—"

"Tallant! He's got nothing to do with this."

"Well you started it, honey. You brought up Marcia Mae. I only thought I'd get it said once and for all, so things wouldn't pile up before we knew it."

"I didn't start anything at all, Duncan. All I asked was if Marcia Mae was out there tonight. You could have answered yes or no."

"All right then. I thought you started it. I thought you had more in mind than that. I was mistaken."

She sat curled in the chair now, the big soft one: she could get as much out of its comfort as a kitten. She was fiddling with a little steel puzzle that had come in a box of Crackerjack: she liked to eat Crackerjack. She was also observing his rather monumental efforts at complete honesty.

Tinker's father and stepmother lived in south Mississippi in what Tinker called "the most expensive pigsty in the world." They had a swimming pool and several long cars and a station wagon with the name of the estate written on the door. They gave drinking parties and so did all their friends. When they were all together, they told dirty stories, and when they separated the men talked oil production and cursed the Fair Deal and the income tax, while the women gossiped.

Tinker's own mother had left her father back in the days when people thought all the oil was in Oklahoma and Texas, and when instead of being filthy rich he was filthy poor. Not that she wanted him back. She had returned to her girlhood home, which stood empty, one wintry fall afternoon, leading Tinker by the hand. There was a red glow among the trees, which stood black and wet against the horizon. Every pane in the bay window was drenched in red. Tinker's mother hoisted her in through a window and she unlatched the front door.

Indomitable, she called a Negro in off the road to build a fire, and after that sent him, protesting and laboring as though against a physical force, into town for some groceries from Harper's store. She cooked cheese crackers and toast in a Dutch oven and made hot chocolate on the hearth. There was molasses too, so thick and cold a knife could slice it.

Nothing had ever tasted so good. Later they sat on the floor before the fire and played crokinole.

The house was not really hers but nobody could stand to move her out, and she was still in it when her ex-husband's oil money bought it for her. She was in it now. She was a tall thin woman with no figure at all, and heavy hair as dark as the day she married, wound in a rope around her head. Her eyes were gentle, clear, and somewhat vacant: people said she was "off."

If there was anything Tinker did not want to do, it was to go live with either of her parents. At the same time she knew, while she sat in the chair and solved the Crackerjack puzzle, that she was closer to it than she had ever been before.

Jimmy Tallant's wife

12. "Whisky and sex," said Jimmy Tallant to his wife. "That's all there is. Whisky and sex. Not even money. Nobody cares about money, only the best way to throw it away. The best kind of whisky. The right kind of sex. You don't believe it? All right, take away whisky and sex and tell me the history of Lacey, Mississippi, since 'seventy-five. *Eigh*teen seventy-five, that is. The year we ran the damn money-grabbing Yankees out so we could swig our likker and f— our women in peace. But hell, you don't even know what happened in *seven*teen seventy-five, much less anything that's happened in Lacey in the last seventy-five years. You been living here all your life in Winfield County, but I bet you don't know one thing about it. Do you?"

"Did they find anything down at the Idle Hour?" she asked. "Did they make you pay anything?"

"You are the dumbest woman I ever saw," said Jimmy.

"Here I make you a speech that Kerney Woolbright could ride to the senate like coasting in on a pair of angel's wings, and all you have to ask is whether the governor's boys rated any cash. Well, I'm not going to tell you. You don't get out that easy. You got to tell me that one thing. One historical fact." He raised a finger. "Historical."

She tried not to laugh. She ground her swollen body down under the pile of blankets and, lips quivering, put the magazine she had been reading when he came in (a detective magazine full of pictures of beauties like herself who had been murdered) in front of her face, up close. She thought he was the cutest, funniest thing she had ever seen in her life.

Then, before she knew he had moved from across the room, his long steely fingers closed painfully on her hand. "You know what your daddy said about you? He said, 'Bella ain't really a bad girl and Bella ain't really all that dumb. I reckon the fact is Bella is just silly.' "

Bud Grantham, her father, had really said that. As if to prove him right, she went off into giggles. Jimmy hitched up his pants legs and sat down on the edge of the bed as impersonally as a doctor. Then he bent her hand backward into her wrist. Her laughter ended in a gasp. "One fact I asked for. One fact I get."

"The Monroe Doctrine," she said, wild-eyed. This hurt. Didn't husbands sometimes murder the beautiful women?

"About Lacey, I said. Who the hell you think wrote the Monroe Doctrine? Old Judge Standsbury? Come on. One thing." He increased the pressure.

"You're killing me!"

"I may."

"I remember one time Daddy said—*oh!*—said that there were twelve niggers shot one time in the courthouse upstairs. In the courtroom, he said. Twelve."

He dropped her hand. "Right." He returned across the room. "But it's a hell of a thing to remember. Why did he tell you that?"

"I was little. It was cold and in the wintertime, back during the depression. We didn't have much. We went to school in the buggy."

"I remember all that."

"So he said if anybody at school ever laughed at us, or asked me why I didn't have but one dress to wear, not to say anything back, but just to leave. Then he said that about the niggers being shot in the courtroom, and said to remember when they laughed that it was their daddies or granddaddies that did it, and that they weren't all that hot themselves."

"If anybody had thought to invite him to that party," Jimmy grumbled, "he would have been up there pumping bullets in every belly he could aim at. He was mad because he got left out."

"Daddy's a good man," said Bella. "I think Daddy's just a real fine man."

"Ummm," said Jimmy Tallant.

. . . A real fine man. He remembered the old cropped bur head hunched down low and the leathery face, which was exactly the same color as his khaki shirt, bent frowning toward the floor, for it always embarrassed him to talk seriously about any woman to another man, much less about his daughter who was already an embarrassment to him. "Bella ain't really a bad girl, and Bella ain't really all that dumb. I reckon the fact is Bella is just silly. I know you never wanted her kind, but I tell you as a matter of personal experience: these high-class women can give you a lot of trouble." What Bud Grantham had in mind when he said "high-class women" was his second wife, a high-heeled, swivel-hipped woman from New Orleans who claimed to be a Creole and draped herself in a fake French accent and, on occasions, not much else. She had disappeared one night—come closing time they couldn't find her—though she had waited on some plush customers from California headed for Florida, and there was not much doubt what had happened. It seemed a funny way to go to Florida, up 82, and Jimmy kept an ear cocked for quite a while, but he never heard any more. He idly recalled that he had slept with the woman, and reflecting on the ways of sex which always lay like a senseless tangle of roots below the surface of the ground, he thought wryly that if he had known Grantham's first wife he might have to be wondering not only whose child Bella was carrying, but whose child Bella was. It was a hot day and he was getting drowsy: his head felt thick. He asked suddenly, "Bud, is Bella your own daughter?"

"What!" Grantham bellowed and jumped up.

"No, now wait a minute," Jimmy said, telling the truth. "I was thinking you might have adopted her from your brother, the one"—he paused delicately—"the one that's in Atlanta."

"Oh." Grantham sank back. He was sitting on top of the desk in the office, right back of the roadhouse. "That there was a grudge fight they fetched Herman up for. They had no call to meddle in it."

"They will do that," said Jimmy.

"Yeah." Grantham was getting sleepy too: he yawned, rubbed his eyes, then righted himself decisively. "I ain't going to shoot you."

"That's good," said Jimmy.

"She's my daughter, but that ain't to say I don't know how she is. All I got to go on is what she says, and all she says is that it's yours. If you won't marry her, how do I look? I won't turn her out, no matter what. If you won't marry her, then you're leaving me, selling out to me for good. Take till in the morning if you want to think it over."

"How much will you give me?" Tallant inquired.

"Ten thousand."

"What! I can get five times that out of you in court, Bud, and you know it."

"Go to court then," said Grantham. "We'll both be down in Atlanta with Herman."

"You wouldn't—"

"Wouldn't I? My friend, I was better off than this when I made my living grubbing for cotton and hunting coon. The penitentiary can seem like a right quiet place to be compared to what I've had to listen to at home for the last month. Oh, I could go out to California and fetch her back one of them movie stars; they'll do anything for enough jack. But I know ain't nothing going to settle her but you. She's my little girl, Jimmy, and I'm your best friend, boy. Where're all the fine ones you growed up with in Lacey? What did they do when they got through admiring the chest full of decorations you brought back with you from across the water? Did anybody offer to take you in as partner? Nobody but ole Bud—"

"Oh, cut it out," Jimmy said. They were both well aware that it was Jimmy's father who thirty years before had led the gang who shot the Negroes down in the courthouse.

Jimmy never knew when people were thinking about this and when they weren't. All his life it lay in the back of his mind except during the war when he flew the planes and did the heroic things. He had a scorn for the good families in Lacey because he figured his father had done their dirty work for them once, and then they had turned on him. The Tallants had had a most uncertain status since—or was it all settled and nobody had thought to tell them? Jimmy didn't know. He knew that he and his brother and sister had run with the nicest people who sooner or later had told them what had happened. He was aware of vital statistics: his parents had died; his brother had been killed early in the war;

his sister had married out of the state and moved away. He had rented the old house, ignored his aunts and cousins, drunk too much, and never cared for any girl but a nice little no-body—Louise Taylor, the one they called "Tinker," old Gains Taylor's daughter. He had cut a path for the bombers over Germany, and thousands died. He had returned a hero, but his girl was already married. She had gone to Duncan Harper with the soft tan hair and the smile and everybody's love. When Marcia Mae Hunt had deserted him, Duncan had only to turn his head and call Tinker's name.

So what better was there to do, he asked himself, than to go into business with a man he had always liked, a man whose family had been for generations bootleggers, hunters, trappers, owners of small country stores and tiny crazy-shaped farms. He judged wryly that this was where he belonged; he would say to anybody that the Granthams were the cream of Winfield County. So the match with Bella was a natural. Was it, and everything else in his life, an outgrowth of what his father had done? He didn't know. He saw it in any case as a joke on Jimmy Tallant, and as such he could accept it.

"Cut it out," he repeated. "I'll give you the business before I'll start crying. I'll marry her, sure. Why not? . . ."

"Listen, Bella," he said to his wife, "don't you ever mention those niggers to me again. It was my daddy that led the gang that did it." Her eyes got big. "You didn't know that?" he asked her.

"Seems like, now you mention it, I did hear something about it, long years ago."

"You mean folks don't talk about it now?"

"I don't know." She was honest as an animal. "I don't know any folks that would."

"I reckon not."

"I always say," she said, "let bygones be bygones."

He did not hear her.

"In the army, overseas," he told her, "I been known to drink with niggers. Some would be together with us at the same party, or maybe enlisted men too, shut up in a pub together during an air raid. That would be a kind of party. We'd get to talking and shoot the bull. We'd take a razzing sometimes, the niggers and me, from the Yankee boys that would always be bringing up the Civil War. 'Don't fool with me,' I'd say; 'my daddy shot twelve niggers dead in one afternoon between two and two-fifteen.' Then they'd all laugh, black and white together, thinking I'd strung the long bow again, because if you talk to Yankees they never hear you; all they hear is the accent, so they figure nothing you say could be important, or even true. If it was Yankees he'd shot instead of niggers, they'd have a statue to him in the courthouse yard and I could put on my string tie and lay a wreath on it, every Memorial Day. But let it pass.

"One night in a pub during the buzz-bomb raid, I said those words, 'Don't fool with me,' I said, and the rest of it, and from way out in the corner there after they stopped laughing, just when the next close one began to sing, a voice a whole lot flatter than mine said, 'It's the truth. His daddy shot them dead.' I said, 'Where you from and what's your name?' He said, 'I'm from Winfield County, out on the old Wiltshire Road near the covered bridge. My name is Sergeant Beckwith Dozer.' Then everybody hit for cover because it was going to be a near one, and just when the silence came I walked to the door and outside. They yelled after me, but I was tight, and the way it had all turned up that way, sudden and sharp, I wanted to be right under the damn thing when it fell. If he hadn't said that about the old Wiltshire Road and the covered bridge. But he knew it, too, see? Knew what would get me where I lived. A nigger always does know how to work you. He knew how to get me through that door; though the rest of them shouted after me, Yankee voices in with the Limeys', his voice I never heard. The earth rattled and shook me down flat, so I thought I was dead. But I woke up in the night, not even scratched, and walked on back home. The next time I saw him was on the Lacey square and the war was over. But he remembered and I did too, and the bastard grinned, remembering the time he nearly killed me. Do you think if it had worked *he* would have lost any sleep? Not Sergeant Dozer."

"Beck Dozer, is that who you mean? The one who's all time hanging around?"

"He's a good man to have. Don't ever get the man who claims to like you to do your work; get the man who hates your guts, because he'll see you in hell before he'll show himself to you as anything less than the best. Sure, he hangs around; he does whatever I might happen to need him for."

He hung his shirt and tie on a hook in the closet. "Pull down the shade," he said. When she leaned to do so, she screamed and jumped out of bed. "That nigger!" she cried.

He was across the room at once, taking his revolver from the desk drawer. She caught hold of him and clung to him, pointing back toward the window. Her knees were literally knocking together.

"Turn me loose, Bella. What nigger was it?"

"That Dozer nigger. The one you were just talking about. Quick. He's going, don't you see?"

"What was he up to?"

"Walking close by the window. Looking back over his shoulder."

"Did he stop?"

"Yes. No. I don't know. Quick and you can catch him."

"Not if you don't let go of me." He steered her to the

bed and set her gently down. "Take it easy. You want to lose the baby?" He went to the window and cupped his hand to his eye, peering out. He called Beck's name twice, then lowered the shade, returned to his desk, and replaced the gun. She was quaking under the cover, making noises like a puppy. He began to laugh.

"You wanted me to shoot him, Bella? You actually did, didn't you? You wanted me to shoot a nigger. All for you."

"It was scary. It was so. It scared me half to death. I don't like niggers. I'm here alone so much of the day, way out here in this house by myself, way out from town, way out on the highway. There's niggers everywhere. Anything can happen. Look at me shake."

"I'll see him tomorrow," he said. "Get over. Tonight I'll sleep by the window." He covered her with another blanket and tucked it round, all she needed to make her happy. . . .

The next day when he saw Beck Dozer, he asked him about the incident. "I crossed through your back yard, Mister Tallant," Beck said. "It happened to be the shortest way home."

"Don't do it again," Jimmy said. "We don't like strangers in our yard at night."

For some reason he had not said niggers. But then his mother had brought him up never to say nigger to a nigger's face.

part two

Jimmy Tallant
drives
south

13. A week later Jimmy Tallant was driving southwest toward Vicksburg and the River. The snow and freeze had staunched the spring: he drove through misting rain, swamps, and advertisements. The heater smelled. The windshield wipers kicked like a weary dance team. He played the radio until he couldn't tell a cowboy song from the lady interview with the dress designer. He wished that Tinker was right there next to him, riding in front of the cigarette lighter.

At Yazoo City, after many miles in the flatland, the road veered due south, rising nobly into the hills. Along the highway now, nearing Jackson, there were many new houses. Some were regular government, FHA styles with the carport, the empty picture window open on the highway, and nothing inside the whole house, it would seem, but the "Gone-with-the-Wind" lamp right in the center of the window. Bella had bought a lamp like this and put it in the middle of her picture window. "It's a real imitation colonial antique," she had told him. Other houses were larger and swankier: imitation Southern colonial, imitation Georgian, "ranch type." They had probably cost a filthy lot of money. For this was oil country now, and what wasn't oil was cattle. All the front yards of the new houses were mushy and sparsely covered with grass. The trees in the yards stood hardly tall as a man and had been planted in pairs.

He passed some places he liked to see, houses low-set and deep in porches, screens, and tacked-on rooms that country people always add because they live from the inside of a house outward and hardly ever think about how a thing will look to themselves, much less to strangers going by in a car. Theirs was the opposite impulse from the picture window.

Heavy trees belonged to them, bare pecan whose intricate branches collected a blue, wet intensity out of the cold, and disheveled old cedars. Chairs on the big front porches were propped face to the wall to get them out of the damp.

He was glad for places like these.

Yet actually he had no desire to know the people who owned them, any more than to know the people who lived in the new imitation houses. Less, in fact, because in the new ones he was liable to find somebody he had been in school with or known in the war, he was liable to be offered a drink. But nothing on earth lured him toward the old places. In Tinker he could have made peace with them. She got on well with country people and she liked country places. She was interested in what went into the soup mixture, how long it took to hook a rug, and where an antique highboy came from. The talk would mute and fade and come again—old talk you didn't have to listen to any more because you know it by heart already. But Tinker was gone, his link was broken. He sometimes wished now that he had not relied on her so much, or left behind him the road that would take him to the front yard, the shaggy tree, the screened porch, and the big Sunday dinner. Yet left it he had, and he could not go back. The very thought of it bored him to death. He would rather be riding the leaky gray monotony of highway, listening to the windshield wiper and the cowboy song, pursuing his own illegal business.

Beyond Jackson, before Vicksburg, he began to look for the station and café. He found it right where they said, an ordinary white frame building, trimmed in red, pitched out on a swath of gravel. He was the first to arrive. But the others were prompt. He had not entered the café before a black Cadillac rose over the hill from Vicksburg and slid into place beside his Ford. Its plushy wheels pressed the gravel tenderly, and its motor purred like a kitten.

Three men got out and went with Jimmy into the café. They sat down at a table covered with a red checkered cloth which matched the curtains in the windows. The windows were sweated over from the gas radiance which had over-heated the upper air of the room, though the cement floor, sweating also, was chill. The proprietor came in from the station and said he thought it was too hot in there. He turned the gas down and blew his nose. He had a bad cold.

One of the men put a pint bottle of whisky on the table and asked for four glasses. He was chewing on a broomstraw. It seemed unlikely he had been near a broom on that or any other morning.

"Hear you got rid of your sheriff," he said, and shifted the straw with his tongue. The skin of his face was extremely thick and of a yellowish-brown color, the consistency and depth of discoloration often seen in sideshow barkers or men from the Southwest—it seems to come not so much from the sun as from exposure, and exposure not so much to weather as to every kind of strange affair and person and injury. He wore a dark wool shirt, a brilliant tie and a light gray hat of extraordinarily fine felt. When the glasses came he poured out a scant inch of whisky for himself and took it quickly, then drank a little water. He shoved the bottle toward the second man, who did the same. This one was dressed like the first, and looked a good bit like him, except that he had a squat face that seemed thoughtful but may only have been stupid. His hair was jet-black and very coarse, and grew in spikes out from the crown, each hair making its separate break for the open. He might have been sitting under a little plate. He looked Indian, just as the burnt-faced man looked Mexican: but then you usually thought men like them were part something else.

"Excuse me," the second man said, and pushed the bottle on to Jimmy. "Hair of the dog, you know."

Jimmy shook his head and passed the whisky on to the third, who was young, just a boy, and who wore his coat very roomy. "I'll jest wait till I get me a Coca-cola," said the boy, and grinned. There was no doubt whatever where he was from. Jimmy Tallant was probably kin to him. So this was who they got to carry the gun for them. How important were they, then, or how important did they think they were, or hope they were?

"Yeah, the sheriff," said Jimmy. "He took a notion to die."

"Just took a notion, huh?"

"Natural causes," Jimmy said. "It's still being done every once in a while."

"Yeah, so what about this new fellow?"

"That's a different thing," said Jimmy.

"What is he? A Baptist? A Jesus boy?"

"He's a sheep dog," Jimmy said. "He's going to cross the Delaware if he has to swim through the light brigade."

The second man, the thoughtful one, woke up and looked suspicious.

"I don't get you," he said.

"He's a football star," Jimmy said. "He's trying to make a touchdown."

The second man turned to the first. "If I don't get it, how is Sam going to?"

The first man took the straw out of his mouth and winked at Jimmy. "That's right. He was a football star. Won five hundred cold cash for me one time in the last thirty seconds of play. Against LSU in '39. You remember the day?"

"I remember them all," said Jimmy. "But the word I came to bring you is, he might be better in football than he is in politics."

"I understand you've been shut down for two weeks. He must be doing all right. Ain't that what they want up there, the Sunday-school class and the Epworth League? Ain't that what they vote for up in them hills? Wallace here, he's from up in them hills. Ain't that the way they are, Wally?"

The boy in the loose coat grinned. "I ain't from Winfield County. Winfield County, tha's a crazy county. I wouldn't be from Winfield County for nothing."

The thoughtful man leaned forward. "How'd he do it? We heard you had a inside man—a deputy."

"I have," Jimmy said. "He's all right and he's working. He tipped me off when they brought the National Guard up. They scoured the county and they found one half-pint. But what Harper did two weeks later he did by himself. Nobody knew it. He just drove out in a strange car with his hat pulled down to his nose and ordered a fifth from the carhop. When the boy brought it out, he had us cold. Slapped on the biggest fine in the books, confiscated ten cases of bonded whisky, and fixed it so we can't even sell beer for six weeks."

"One man walked in and did you that much damage? What did he have with him, the atom bomb?"

"I can't hurt him," Jimmy said. "It's still my place, goddam it, you haven't moved your wheels and tables up there yet. I got my reasons and I stick to them."

"The thing we came to say is, we may not move the wheels and tables up there at all. So Sam says."

"Tell Sam," Jimmy said, "that by September this man will not be in the way any longer. We have an election in August. When there's an election Harper goes."

"How do you know he will?"

"I'm going to see to it, that's how I know."

"You running yourself?"

"We're running Travis's deputy. And I'm fixing it beforehand so he can't help but win."

"How? How are you fixing it?"

"It's my county and my neck of the woods. I know better how to handle it than anybody else. If you want to get somebody else up there—"

"That's not it. Just tell us a little something."

"Something we can tell Sam."

"That's right. Just a little something we can tell Sam."

"All right," said Jimmy Tallant. "This joker, this Harper, not only wants to purify Highway 82 from one county line to the other; he's got principles drawn up about treating the niggers right. He's had the gumption not to mention this out amongst the constituency. He thinks he can do a quiet job along those lines without anybody much noticing how liberal he is. I intend to smoke him out."

"So then?"

"So then it takes care of itself. Ask the kid here. Nobody with one solitary idea on the Negro question has got a chance in the world of getting elected to public office in Winfield County."

"Tha's right," said the boy cheerfully. "They ain't got a chance. Nor in Tippah County either."

"So everything's under control, Mitchell," said Jimmy. "You can tell Sam."

Mitchell sneezed. He went and stood by the gas radiance, and stared at the sweat-covered windows. "God, what a joint. You couldn't pay me to live in Miss'ippi."

"There are plenty more just like it," Jimmy said gloomily, "in Alabama, Georgia, Louisiana and Texas, Montana, Utah, Idaho and Kansas. To name a few."

"It's the truth," said Pilston, the Indian-looking one. "I wonder why Mitchell picked this one."

"I remembered it," Mitchell said, "because they got a alligator out back."

"A alligator!" the boy repeated.

"That's right. There used to be a sign up: ten cents to see the alligator. The sign's gone, so I don't reckon he's still got the thing."

"Did you ever see it?"

"See it? No. I never seen it."

"Maybe he never did have it," said Pilston.

"Why would he put a sign up about a alligator if he didn't even have one?" the boy asked.

The proprietor came in. "Hey," said the boy, "have you got a alligator back in the back?"

"Sure," said the proprietor; "back in the back yard. Go on out and look at him if you want to. I don't charge nothing in the winter."

The boy got up. "Sure enough? Can I?"

"Sure. I'll show you."

The other three men for a moment seemed about to follow the boy and the proprietor. There seemed to be something awful about not having in the room with them a person curious to see an alligator free of charge.

Mitchell said, "They have them all out West, you know, these roadside zoos and things. They put up signs all along the way about what big Gila monsters and rattlesnakes they've got. I remember one time I was driving out to Tia Juana with a young fellow something like the boy here and we stopped to get some gas and a hamburger at one of those zoo places. Wasn't a soul around. Just a lot of yellow and red signs about what a hell of a fine place it was—I can see them yet. The kid went back to the zoo, but he couldn't find a soul. He came back and said the animals were all starving and some of them were dead. They didn't have any water. It smelled to high heaven back there, he said. A Mexican came along and said the man that owned the place had died and the woman had hitch-hiked off and never did come back. So the kid couldn't stand it. He went in and shot the snakes and the wild cats, and opened the other cages for the things to get out. That's how come I remembered this place. Everytime I see anything like a zoo place, I think of that other time. This kid here, he had to see the alligator too. They're all alike, kids like that."

"Wonder why they don't charge to see him in the winter," said the Indian-looking man.

"Alligators get cold in the winter. They ain't up to much," said Mitchell after a time.

The Indian-looking man thought it over, then said, "How the hell do you know what a alligator's up to in the winter?"

"I don't know. I'm just guessing. It stands to reason, don't it? Don't it, Tallant?"

"Sounds all right to me," Jimmy said.

"I bet he's 'sleep right now," said Mitchell. "Cold and sluggish and 'sleep. Lay you four bits on it."

"If this keeps up we'll have to go back and look at the damned thing," said the Indian-looking man.

"No we won't," said Mitchell. "We'll just ask the kid. He'll tell us."

"Okay then. We'll ask the kid."

When the boy came back, Mitchell asked him, "How was the alligator? Wasn't he cold and sluggish?"

"Mighty sluggish," the boy said, "and he looked cold."

"Was he asleep?" the Indian-looking man asked.

"He was when we came out, but then he opened his eyes. I couldn't tell if he was looking at us or not."

"See, so I don't owe you nothing. He wasn't asleep."

"He was asleep till they woke him up."

"No, we didn't wake him up. He woke himself up. Maybe he wasn't asleep."

"See, you can't tell. I don't owe you nothing. Not a dime."

They were still arguing when they got into the Cadillac.

14. Beck Dozer would not tell his wife where he was going.

"It's best you don't know. If something happens and they ast you, it's best you can just say, He never said."

"Next time I going to marry me a field nigger," said Lucy. "Somebody too tired at night to go out and get theyselves in trouble."

"Whar you goin', Unker Beck?" asked W.B.

"Blow your nose," Beck Dozer told him. "You been running like a sugar tree all this blessed day."

He put on his town-cut coat, and English-type tweed jacket, ordered by measure from Sears Roebuck. In overalls he was apt to give the impression of being not exactly skinny but skimpy, as if there had been just enough material to make him. But in this coat, and especially when he shined his glasses on the sleeve and put them on, he brought to mind a college classroom and himself with a notebook, ready to walk in and lecture. He took a swallow of whisky from a pint bottle on the mantelpiece, then he went to a large mirror in a gilt frame and examined the knot in his tie, firming it.

Just across the room in a matching gilt frame, hung an enormous daguerreotype of Beck's father, Robinson Dozer. He had a thin face, large eyes, and wore a string tie. If Beck Dozer looked professorial, his father's face brought gentlemen to mind, and a gentleman's household, and how gentlemen liked their own kind about them, never mind who brought the whisky in and who drank it. Robinson Dozer had been one of the twelve Negroes shot down in the Lacey courthouse in 1919. He had been the emissary to the blacks, the one who had said, You all come on in; they wants to talk this thing over. Beck Dozer had been four years old when it happened: his father's murder was his earliest recollection of childhood.

"You ain't going to wear your good coat out in this rain?" his wife asked.

"Lucy," said Beck, "I gots to wear my good coat tonight."

Back in the kitchen where W.B. had gone there was a sudden lot of racket involving a tin bucket top, a pan that had been set under the leak, and a scuttle of kindling. Lucy went back and yelled at W.B. "What you thank you doing? Jest tell me that!" She returned with the baby on her arm, cleaning its face on her dress and hushing it. Beck was putting on his GI slicker.

"Don't go out in this, Beck," Lucy said. "Hit's way too bad a night."

Beck Dozer took the baby from her and set it on a pallet down before the fire. He caught her arm and pulled her after him through the door to the hall, then through the hall and front door to the porch.

Lucy was thin as a railroad track, a real nigger gal in a straight-cut cotton dress, with big bare feet, black greased hair, and a world of softness on the bone. In the big room, through the open doorways, the raining sounds talked loudly. W.B. forgot about his troubles in the kitchen. He ran into the hall and back, then leaned over the arm of the rocking chair by the fire where a pile of petticoats and skirts and an apron lay like an old soft quilt.

"Granny," he said. "Unker Beck hugging Aunt Lucy. Out on the poach. I seen hit and I knows hit."

The pile of clothes shook. A hand like a daddy longleg's foot came out and groped for him.

"He's Granny's Jesus chile," said the old woman. "He's Granny's man."

"I'se a little bitty ole black nigger," said W.B., and got the silly giggles.

Beck Dozer heard this as he left, and had the impulse to go back and tell W.B. that he was in reality half British. Nobody could have told him except Beck Dozer, nor that Beck was not his uncle but his father. As he double-buttoned his slicker high at the throat and went down the steps into the rain, he wondered now if anybody would ever know. It made him sad to think about W.B., never knowing whose he was, and sad to think of the plain little English girl who wouldn't leave a Negro Yank alone, and sad to think of himself who no matter what he argued or said had always wanted a white woman. He thought of his father too, the gilt frame being all he could do to please that gentle face, and he thought that dying should not be a public thing. He saw that everything most clear to him was sorrowful, full of Negro sorrow. He included himself in his sorrows, for he always suspected that, like his father, he was going out to deal with white people someday and never come home again.

Some hours later, both his hands were bleeding and he was standing on the hill outside a white man's house. The hill was narrow at the flank, scarcely large enough, it appeared, for the house to rest on it, so that where Beck Dozer stood at an angle back from the lighted windows he had to watch out that he didn't fall off in the gully, down amongst all the vines and varmints.

The room he could see into was a bedroom, a children's room, with an iron white-painted single bed and a crib. A young white woman with dark hair was moving about, putting two children to bed. The older one, a boy, with hair so blond it was white as his skin, turned over the wastebasket meddling in it and got blessed out for it.

Beck Dozer circled the house and gained the back door.

15. Tinker kept insisting she heard something until she went to the back door to see for herself, and there stood a Negro out by the steps in the rain.

"Duncan," she called. "Duncan! There's somebody here to see you."

Her husband was beside her quickly, leaning out. The Negro had not knocked, but had stood saying, "Mister Harper? Mister Harper?" over and over, and now that they saw him it seemed they had heard him for certain all the time, for no telling how long, for it is part of the consciousness of a Southern household that a Negro is calling at the back door in the night.

"It's Dozer, isn't it?" Duncan asked, shielding his brow and squinting against the rain.

"Yes, Beckwith Dozer."

"Come on in out of the wet." Duncan held the door for him. He raked the mud from his shoes on a steel mat.

"Watch out for the floor," said Tinker.

"A little mud," said Duncan.

"Not mud; he's bleeding. Don't you see his hands?"

"Good Lord, what have you got yourself into?"

"I got in a fight. That's how come I'm here."

"You wait right there while I get a towel," Tinker said. "Don't they need to be bandaged, Duncan?"

"Looks like it," he called after her. "Do you need a doctor, Beck? Are you hurt anywhere else?"

"Just my hands," said Beck Dozer.

In the kitchen, Tinker made him wash in a basin she kept put aside for the children when they hurt themselves, then dabble on some medicine while she cut strips of gauze and adhesive.

"Looks like to me," said Duncan, looking at the curiously jagged cuts and scratches, "you got mixed up with some woman owned a crosscut saw. Who've you been scrapping with?"

"Bud Grantham was who it was," said Beck Dozer. "I went out there to buy some whisky."

"He can't sell you any. I shut him down."

"That's what you think. It's going out the back door to anybody comes along. He sold some to a white man just before me—I seen him leaving with it in a newspaper—then he said he didn't have none for me. I said, I gots the cash money, and it's just as good money as that one just now bought a fifth from you, Mr. Grantham. He spit and says, It's nigger money; don't fool yourself, nigger, it ain't never good as white money and it ain't never going to be. He threw in a word or two I wouldn't repeat before Mrs. Harper here, then I said a GI word or two back and he hit at me, but I ducked him and hit back."

"You hit Bud Grantham!" Tinker exclaimed. The idea of this Negro hitting anybody was more than you could have expected of him, as if a soggy, thin little firecracker, long after the explosion of the pack, had taken a notion to go off. But she saw his face and did not laugh. Beck Dozer blinked behind his glasses. "I had a razor," he announced.

Duncan whistled.

"He picked up a butcher knife he had there with him opening a crate of whisky and came at me with it. He started yelling for Jimmy Tallant. That's when he hacked into my hands—they was up like this to save my face from him. So I outs with my razor and gave him the quickest cut I could"—

he made a nasty motion with his bandaged right hand—"and ran."

"Where'd you hit him?"

"I aimed about here." The hand moved to the side of his neck, below the ear. "But you know you can't tell when a razor goes in and when it don't. It's so fine and sharp and slices so smooth—"

"That'll do," said Duncan sharply, as Tinker shuddered.

"As I say, I aimed there."

"Yes."

"But I missed."

"That's good," said Duncan dryly.

"I got him on the shoulder instead, right between the arm and the collarbone. I heard his shirt when the cloth split, but about the flesh, like I was saying—"

"Then you might have hurt him pretty bad?"

"I might have grazed him, sure enough," said Beck Dozer, studious behind the milky shield of his glasses. "On the other hand, I might have missed him completely."

"Umm," said Duncan. "Bad. Either way. Where's the razor?"

"I threw it away in the woods."

Tinker stepped back. Beck Dozer looked down at the snowy bandages and nodded to her. "I thank you, Mrs. Harper. But whatever I done"—he turned back to Duncan— "is done. And whatever it was, a Grantham won't forget it."

He moved to sit by the stove, the way Negroes coming into the white kitchens always did in the old days when the stove burnt wood and dried them while they smoked like bread, and warmed them, too, clean through to the bone.

"If I no more than nicked Bud Grantham, if I no more than fanned the air in front of him, it's enough for him and all them other Granthams to want my black hide. I'm scared, Mister Harper. I came to ask you for custody."

"It might have been better, seeing that it's Granthams we're dealing with, if you had left town instead of coming to me."

"That's the old-timey way," said Beck Dozer. "Getting out of town never solved anything. If a Negro never takes advantage of what legal rights are open to him, he can't hope to enjoy those that ought to be open and ain't. You are the law, Mister Harper. I have come to you."

"That's all very good reasoning," said Duncan, "until a Negro picks the toughest white man in Winfield County for fancy razor work. If you're so damned philosophic about this, you should have done about two seconds of thinking beforehand."

"But I didn't," said Beck Dozer.

"It looks that way," said Duncan. He went to telephone the Idle Hour, Grantham's house, and Jimmy Tallant's, but received no answer to any, whereupon he called the Woolbrights' and discovered that Kerney had taken Cissy Hunt to the picture show in Stark. He reentered the kitchen carrying his hat, his GI slicker slung over his arm, one pocket heavy with his gun.

"You don't agree with me," inquired Beck Dozer, "that a Negro must use the law in good faith wheresoever and whensoever the opportunity arises?"

"Except for all the soevers, you might be quoting me," said Duncan. "Okay then. We'll go to jail."

"Jail?" said Tinker at once.

"I may be late," Duncan told her. "I'll try to call you. Lock the house up good. If Kerney calls in, tell him to come up to the jail."

She had been scalding the basin at the sink. Now she went anxiously to him. "Jail?"

Duncan smiled. "He asked for custody, darling. That's

what custody means. I have to put him in jail to keep him safe from the Granthams."

"It's my legal right," Beck Dozer explained to her kindly.

"I'm sorry you're mixed up in any of this," she said, helping him with the slicker.

From the back door, she leaned out, calling after them, "Duncan, look for Jimmy."

He turned at the car door. "For Tallant?"

"Yes, he—he'll *know*."

The rain rustled between them. "You're right. He will." The car door closed.

the
jailer

16. Upstairs, the jail was so black you could not even see the iron bars. From below, Mr. Trewolla, the jailer, at last found the switch; a bulb that hung from a dusty cord shed a thin light about them. All the cells stood empty with the cold, sweaty black iron doors slightly ajar, and when the big door that closed the stair ceased to send forty kinds of echoes walking amongst the shadows, you could hear the coal dust near the stove smashing unpleasantly beneath their damp shoes. But this was an ordinary sound, better than the big door. At the touch of the key, at the pull of the hinges, almost at the brushing of a sleeve, the door's voice stirred; a little more and it might have formed a word—the very one you never wanted to hear.

The only person in jail was a Negro woman named Lu, sitting over in the corner on a broken chair.

"Oh, Jesus, Brer Beck," she said, "I never thoughts to see you here."

"What you doing in here?" he asked her.

"I had to eat," she said. "Anybody ought to eat. How you do, Mister Harper!"

Duncan remembered her well. She was a slump-shouldered Negress who wrapped her head in a rag and carried her chin low and to one side, angling a sour eye at the world. Tinker had hired her, being unable to get anyone else, right after their second child was born. She did not steal or tote, but was of a complaining nature. She had nothing, she said; her children had nothing; they had to go to school barefoot over frozen roads; her mama and papa lived with her and should have furnished her a little from the old age, but they couldn't get the old age because they had the law title to that old pieced-together house that all of them lived in; and her husband should have helped her at least to raise the lawyer's fee to transfer the title of the house so her mama and papa could be legally penniless and get the old age, but her husband took up with a yellow. About this point of hearing the story for the fifth time, Tinker raised up suddenly in bed and told her, "There's a ten-dollar bill on the mantelpiece. Take it and buy those children some shoes and don't you ever come in this house again."

"The cawn bread ain't done," said Lu.

"Then it'll just have to burn up," said Tinker.

Lu thought. "You firing me?"

"I certainly am," said Tinker.

"Oooo!" said Lu, and woke up the baby.

"If I goes on relief next," Lu told her, "I has to say how come."

"You can say you talk too much," said Tinker, and fell back, exhausted.

Lu thought again. "Does I?" she asked.

"Your sister has got food," said Beck Dozer to Lu. "To my personal knowledge."

"You needn't think she's going to give me none," said Lu. "What you done done to your han's?"

"Why won't she give you none?"

"She too stingy. Me and her's twins and she was bawn sucking on both tits."

"You're not going to want to stay up here long," Duncan told him, "unless you can find some way to hush her."

He went downstairs.

Mr. Trewolla was an old man with liver spots on his hands and a hernia which he thought about tenderly, all the time. He had been the jailer for twenty years, for longer than Travis Brevard had been sheriff. He took a dim view of all sheriffs and town marshals. A deacon in the Baptist Church, he had considered Travis a loose character, and had felt comfortably backed up by God when Travis died. He thought of Duncan as a boy who had a lot to learn, but since he understood around town that Duncan would "take a drink," and that his wife "took a drink" with him, he felt the chances of his learning anything were small indeed. Mr. Trewolla honestly believed that anybody who would "take a drink" would do "most anything." Nobody could tell him: every Saturday night he saw plenty of the kind of thing whisky could do. He held complicated opinions on every arrest, but these opinions, like tortuous country roads that all led to the same dreary hamlet, invariably ended: "Whisky, you know. Whisky."

Mrs. Trewolla, his big fat wife, cooked turnip greens and sowbelly for the prisoners every day on the wood stove downstairs. Then after she took a bath and powdered, she would go uptown in the afternoons, walking around visiting, telling everybody exactly the things Mr. Trewolla had already said. "Daddy says," she would begin, then she would quote, all the way through, "Whisky, you know. Whisky. Just like Daddy says." She did not have the imagination to alter anything.

Duncan stood in the hall of the jail and looked through into the living room where a hooded metal lamp was burning beside the armchair. Mr. Trewolla, in his green eyeshade, had gone back to reading the newspaper. Behind him the high old-fashioned windows rattled in their frames when the wind sluiced the rain against them. Duncan had recently read about a man at the university who had made a study of jails and had come up with the information that only five jails in the state of Mississippi took an unskilled person of average intelligence more than twenty minutes to break into or out of. He did not think that the Lacey jail was one of the five. It was among Mr. Trewolla's duties to make a yearly report on the condition of the jail. Mr. Trewolla had done this faithfully every year, but every year had always said the same thing—that the jail was sound as ever.

Duncan entered the living room and laid Mr. Trewolla's keys on the table.

"Have a seat, have a seat," said Mr. Trewolla. He laid aside his newspaper.

Duncan felt too rushed to sit down, but he did it anyway.

"Looks bad in Korea," said Mr. Trewolla.

"Yes, sir, it does. I'd hate to be fighting in all that mud and ice."

"They ought to have done what MacArthur told them. It's enough to make you sick. That fool Truman. Trying to tell the finest general of our time how to fight a war. Trying to tell us down here in Miss'ippi what we got to do for niggers."

"He's got his faults," said Duncan.

"Faults! Name me one virtue he's got. You can ask Mrs. Trewolla what I've said about him from the beginning. Ha!"

"Mr. Henry, about this boy upstairs—"

"Drunk?"

"No, sir, I want to tell you. There may just possibly be trouble. He says he's been in a scrap with Bud Grantham. He came to me for custody. Grantham and Tallant would bend heaven and earth to give me trouble. They may come for him—you can't tell."

"What was he doing at Grantham's?"

"Trying to buy some whisky."

"Then it's dog eat dog," said Mr. Trewolla. "The best thing you could do was let Grantham handle him. They've got their ways, those fellows. They deal with rough cases all the time."

"He asked us for nothing but his right. That is, if he's telling the truth. We're going to give it to him, even if they try to take the jail apart. You see, if I can prove they're still selling whisky, I can throw the book at them."

"You can what?"

"I can ruin them. Confiscate everything."

"Nothing is going to stop them, in my opinion," said Mr. Trewolla. "Don't think you've cramped their style. There's just as much going out the back door as ever went out the front. I been knowing that. Said it at the time."

"Mr. Henry, the only thing I want you to do is keep that nigger safe."

Mr. Trewolla's nervous old man's hand with the yellowed nails fumbled with his eyeshade. He scratched his forehead where the mark of the shade showed red across his indoor skin.

"You'll never get a conviction. You going to carry a nigger's evidence in front of a grand jury?"

Duncan rose. "I'm trying to carry out one step at a time what the law says is the right thing, Mr. Henry." He smiled. "I never heard of a law against the law, did you?"

Mr. Trewolla followed him to the front door. "And what's that nigger trying to do? Commit suicide?"

"I don't claim to understand it all so far, Mr. Henry, but I hope to before the night's over. Let's just keep him safe and don't let anybody in unless they've come from me. Don't you think that might be best?"

"If that's your orders, why then—"

"I'd think it might be better for Miss Annie to go over somewhere else."

"I'm staying right here with Daddy," said Mrs. Trewolla at once from the other side of the kitchen door.

"Whatever you think. Goodnight then, Mr. Henry, and thank you. Goodnight, Miss Annie."

"Goodnight, boy."

"You heard it all," said Mr. Trewolla to his wife the minute the door closed; "what do you make of it?"

"What do you make of it, Daddy?"

"There's something funny about it."

"That's exactly what I said, Daddy. There's something funny about it."

"You remember Duncan's uncle, old Philip Harper. He was a Hoover man. The only vote cast for Hoover in Lacey and Winfield County in 1932 was Philip Harper's."

"But Duncan is sweet," said Mrs. Trewolla suddenly, with flat conviction. "He sat down and talked to you. He thought about me staying here. You know that was sweet, Daddy."

"I'm telling you right now," said Mr. Trewolla, who was far more alarmed by an opinion from his wife than by anything Duncan had done, "there's funny politics mixed up in this. You'll see. I never thought I'd wish for Travis Brevard back in office. I *know* what whisky is, but funny politics—!" He shook his head, readjusted his eyeshade, and shuffled back to the rocking chair, the lamp, and the newspaper.

a call
to
Kerney

17. Duncan felt the need of Kerney so much that he telephoned the movie house in Stark from the pay station in the drugstore and had him paged.

"There's a nigger in the woodpile," Duncan concluded, "in addition to the one in the jail. I think Tallant is back of it."

"Then there's a hook in it somewhere," said Kerney, "at the very least."

"I can't get anybody I can depend on," said Duncan. "Trewolla is set in his ways and thinks I'm still in knee britches, and Follansbee is off God knows where, though I certainly don't want him."

"You can deputize, you know."

"But it makes me look a fool to deputize over nothing."

"Then what are you planning to do?"

"Go look for Tallant and Grantham first, and try to get the straight of it."

"Suppose you don't find them?"

Duncan paused. "Then I'll go sit in the jail with the nigger, I guess. What's the matter, Kerney?"

"Nothing; I was laughing. Can't you lock him in the jail and leave him there?"

"The jail is nothing," said Duncan. "You could break into it with a can opener."

"Look," said Kerney, "I'll take Cissy home now and come up and check with you. Maybe we can figure something out. Duncan?"

"What?"

"It's raining too hard to lynch a nigger. It's too cold."

"It's what?"

"It's the wrong time of year, too. These things are supposed to happen in the middle of September after it hasn't rained for forty weeks, after all the cattle have died of thirst and their stench rolls in from the country and there's so much dust the sun looks bloody all day long. Isn't that right?"

"I don't know," said Duncan. "I never saw a lynching."

"I never did either," said Kerney. "All I know is what I read in William Faulkner. Duncan?"

"Yeah?"

"I just thought. I never heard of a Negro that would make a farce out of a lynching, let alone his own."

"You never met Beck Dozer," said Duncan.

"No, I never did. See you later, Duncan."

"See you later."

the
squaring
off

18. In Jimmy Tallant's house on the highway a little light burned through the rain; it seemed a friendly sight in an otherwise doleful, chill, muddy, self-centered world.

Inside, in the bedroom, Jimmy Tallant's wife Bella was sitting on the arm of the easy chair with a magnifying mirror in her hand, pulling out her eyebrows. Jimmy stood in the door watching her for a while, wondering why she was doing it, until he remembered that if he asked her she would probably tell him.

"What are you trying to do, get rid of all of them?"

"It said in this magazine article," Bella explained, in her care not looking up, "that I'm the age to do it this way."

"What age is that, and what way do they mean?"

"Well, they said that back in the 1930's Marleen Deetritch and Jean Harlow used to know how to make their faces look more sophisticated by refining the line of their eyebrows, but that women finally revolted from that fashion and went in for the natural look. They said that was still all right for young girls up to when they got around twenty-five, but after that that a woman owed it to her maturity and poise to use every device to give herself more sophistication—"

"Yes, but Bella, are you absolutely sure that when you get through there you are going to have a sophisticated look?"

She put down the glass and thought it over. "If you don't ever try anything, you don't ever change at all."

"You best stop that kind of changing before you start it. Turn around and look at me. Lord, Bella, you're going to scare the doctors when you go to the hospital."

"I ain't done yet," she said, and picked up the mirror sadly. "I read another article. It was written by a doctor, an M.D., only he's a famous psychiatrist too; I forget his name. Anyway, it said that at this particular point when you're pregnant, husbands ought to be especially considerate and thoughtful. This doctor said that in his personal opinion husbands were personally responsible for one-third of all miscarriages, and that all that the husbands caused were pure and simple psychological cases. That's what it's called: The Psychological Miscarriage. I saved it out for you to read. It's over there on the dresser."

"God," said Jimmy, "if everything's so damned psychological, suppose I have a psychological miscarriage? Had you thought about that?"

"There is such a thing," she said earnestly, "as a psychological pregnancy. I know because Elsie Mae Henderson had one, remember?"

"Just so you didn't read it in another article," he said.

"I haven't got anything to do but read articles," she said; "that and *True Detective*. Just waiting for my time to come."

"You might try washing the dishes. I bet you haven't touched them."

"You never did send me the nigger," she said.

"I tell you every goddamned time it comes up. I can't get the nigger since the joint shut down."

"You could go and get the nigger!" she shouted at him, and began to cry.

"You've got so damned important since you're really going to have that baby there's not any staying in the same house with you. I never heard of a baby taking so long to get here. Seems like you've been pregnant for at least a year. You better not give me one of those psychological run-arounds, miscarriage or otherwise. I'll have this marriage declared so null and void I'll not only swear you're a virgin, I'll even believe it. The kitchen is full of coffee grounds and rotten orange peels. There's bacon grease all over the sink and a whole raw egg busted in one stove eye. The living room is full of dirty glasses from three nights ago, and there's a washtubful of cigarette ashes turned upside down in the middle of the rug."

"My back hurts me all the time," she said. "It hurts me so bad sometimes I think I'll just die. And I'm all time wanting to wee and then I can't."

He advanced on her. "I'm not going to live in filth. I hate it. There are women who keep their houses straight with pains in the back, pains in the head, no help, a husband and two or three children to cook for three times a day, seven days a week. You don't have much to do. So for God's sake, do it!" He took a swat at her, but whether he intended it to land was not clear to either of them, because she began to giggle as though it were a romp and caught his hand, dropping the mirror, which broke on the floor. It was a ten-cents-store mirror, the kind that magnifies on one side. She spent many hours a day with it, doing minute things to her face.

"Stop, stop. Stop, silly. There's somebody at the door! Don't you hear them? Somebody at the front door."

He did hear. He let go her arm, which she began to nurse. He stared at the broken pieces of mirror for an instant. "Seven more years' bad luck. Well, clean it up."

He shut the bedroom door behind him and crossed the living room. Out on the doorstep stood Duncan Harper, his slicker gleaming with rain.

"I've been trying to call you," he said. "Your phone out of order?"

"Not that I know of. Come in."

"I'm looking for Bud Grantham," Duncan said. "You haven't seen him?"

"As a matter of fact, I have," said Jimmy Tallant. "He can't see anybody, now or later. He had an accident tonight."

"It might have been a fight he had," Duncan said.

"It might have been."

There sounded a wail from the next room. "My daddy's hurt and you never told me!" The door clattered open—the damp had swelled the wood, so that it stuck on the jamb.

"Get on back to bed, honey," said Jimmy. "You know you oughtn't to be up. It's nothing serious or I would've told you." She hung in the door, mouth open, wrapper drooping about her shoulders, eyebrows mismatched, and in all her pregnancy so honestly uncomfortable that Duncan felt sorry for her. "Good evening, Bella," he said.

She looked just like one of her cousins who used to sit in front of him in one grade and comb her hair over and over with a pink comb. She had the bobby pins all piled up before her open book and a little mirror propped in the pencil rack, and when the teacher asked her a question all she heard was her name and all she said was, "I don't know."

"Hello, Duncan." She looked around the living room. In truth, an oversized ash tray lay upside down in the middle of the carpet, and ash had tracked away from it on either side. "Isn't everything a mess?" she said.

"I know how it is," Duncan reassured her. But even as he spoke he could hear in his head Tinker's slow laden steps around the house, up to the minute of going to the hospital, putting clean things into orderly dresser drawers.

"Sure," said Jimmy. "He knows how it is."

"No, he doesn't," she said quietly, and closed the door between them.

"Come on back here where she won't hear us," Jimmy said, and led him into what Bella called the "dinette," where he lighted a large gas radiance. They stood near it, warming. The rain beat a steady drum. They found it awkward to be alone together. "Well, sheriff?"

"I want to see Bud Grantham."

"All right. I'll tell you what you do. You follow the old Wiltshire road for ten miles till you get right this side of Black Hawk, then you take off up a hill without any gravel. There's a bob-wire gap about a half a mile on, that's how you'll know you got the right road. About another half mile you have to ford a branch. After that it's only two more miles to where Bud's gone to."

"He couldn't have got back there in this rain. Nobody could."

"His brother came for him. You see, Granthams are like that, Duncan. Every time one of them gets sick, they figure they're going to die, and they got to die on the old homestead or they won't go to heaven. So Bud heads home if he has to swim the branch with galloping double pneumonia."

The gas heated quickly. In the living room Jimmy drew out

chairs for them both and offered Duncan a cigarette. "How about a drink?"

"No thanks."

"If you want to go back there, Duncan, you'll have to go without me. I tried to get him to stay here—"

"He must have had a doctor; that is, if he's so bad off he went home to die."

"That's another funny thing," said Jimmy. "Bud don't hold with doctors. Bud's a herb man. He's got an aunt who stirs all this stuff up in pots on a stove out in a little outhouse about the size of a pantry. She doctors every Grantham in the county—no, Duncan, it's true. You haven't been out in those woods, I bet, since all of us used to rabbit-hunt. You haven't kept up your connections. How should you know?"

"You aren't convincing me of much," said Duncan. "I've got my doubts that Grantham is so much as scratched. Still, there's a nigger come to me for custody. I've put him in jail and now I'm answerable for him."

"There's no answerable to it. A nigger that jumps a Grantham is answerable to the other Granthams. That means me."

"Then you'll have to deal with me first. There are two types of mess I'm not going to stand for in this county. The likker traffic is one, and nigger trouble is the other."

"It's widely known," said Jimmy Tallant, "how you feel."

At the scorn in his tone, Duncan rose impulsively. "You've got no right to play with important things like these. They reach out to be bigger than us or Winfield County. Bootlegging isn't like having a still out in the back pasture any more. It pulls a lot of wires all over the country. I've heard that you're going to put gambling in, that a New Orleans syndicate is backing you. What are you trying to make out of Winfield County? You're big-talking now about lynching a Negro. Maybe you don't mean any real harm to him, but suppose the thing gets out of hand? There's a national press that stands ready to jump on all such as this, and they never get the straight of things. They make us all sound like a bunch of barefoot morons who love to smell black meat burning."

"I'm not what you'd call a public-spirited citizen, for a fact," said Jimmy. "I care about as much about the national press and the nigger organizations as they care about me and the niggers. And that, as you know, is exactly nothing."

"At least you could care about your own people."

Jimmy narrowed the lids of his foxy eyes. "I've appreciated your hospitality from time to time. I've taken right much pleasure from your drinking-whisky."

"We've always been glad to have you. Tinker's devoted to you, Jimmy."

"In your place I wouldn't have stood for it," Jimmy said.

"Now you're after saying I don't care much about her. If that's what you mean—"

"I even named her," Jimmy went on. "Her name was Louise. Louise Taylor. I started calling her Tinker because she was counting off some buttons on her dress one day at school. She said tinker tailor, and I wouldn't let her get any farther. Every time I would say, Who? Who's Tinker Taylor? till she got mad at me and cried. She was a true old compass, Tinker was, and every time I took her out and looked at her, the needle pointed north. Every time I said, Who do you love? she said Duncan." He rose and went to the window.

"It's true things never worked out for us the way we thought they would," Duncan said earnestly. "But what's done is done. I don't think our private lives should have anything to do with the nigger in the jail, or the bootlegging business, or the sheriff's race. I think you've got to face public things in another frame of mind."

"My father did a public thing," said Jimmy Tallant. "He

shot Robinson Dozer, among others, and that's Dozer's son that's sitting in the jailhouse. You'd be surprised how private it makes me feel."

He had been looking out the window while he spoke—Bella's picture window she'd had to have, to be like everybody else; the imitation colonial antique Gone-with-the-Wind lamp was not lighted. So when he said what he did about his father and turned away from the rainy dark toward Duncan, who stood near the mantelpiece, he looked out of certain long shadows and seemed a greater distance away than he actually was. His face, so sharp when the mind sped, held now a touch of the hound's sadness, but above all it was a lonely face, pulled in like the rain off the wild stretches. He made you think of telephone poles leaning infinitely on along a highway that went forever toward the mountains. You could no more talk to him than you could talk to a song.

"I hate to say this," said Duncan, going toward the door, "but until this election is over and I've won, or you've found some way to lick me, I don't think you'd best be dropping by the house again."

Jimmy Tallant did not answer him or protest. He did not bat an eye. It seemed that his face darkened slightly, as though dark had come strongly between them through the front door when Duncan opened it.

"I might drop by the jail and get that nigger," he said.

"I'll be ready for you," said Duncan.

19. "You gots a long time to wait," said Beck Dozer. "It's not but ten o'clock."

"If it's much later maybe they'll be too sleepy or too drunk," Duncan said.

"But in the earlier hours, or so I have read, they still have got their daylight minds. It takes the midnight mind to do the black deed to the black man."

"Oh, Jesus," said Lu. "Don't make it sound so *true*, Brer Beck."

Duncan laughed. "All you niggers ought to be preachers with a carload of nigger women saying Oh Jesus don't make it sound so true, every time you paused to mop your brow. You could preach them in and out of hell all day long, stop long enough to go outdoors and eat fried chicken, and take a different one home every night."

"And you think that would be the end," said Beck Dozer, "of the so-called Negro question."

"They call it bread and circuses," said Duncan.

"Why, so they do," said Beck.

"This is the first time I done ever darkened a jail door," said Lu. "And now look."

The two men were seated in cane-bottom chairs on either side of the cold stove. The Negro woman had retreated into the corner of the nearest cell and had begged Duncan until he had locked her in. She wanted to make sure that an iron door stood between her and whoever might arrive. Duncan had tried to make her go home as soon as he had returned from Jimmy Tallant's.

"S'pose I meets 'm on the stairs?" she had asked.

"But you can't now," said Duncan.

"Why can't I?"

"Because they aren't there."

"S'pose I meets 'm at the do'?"

"But nobody's outside. Look out there; it's empty."

"S'pose I meets 'm on the road?"

"You can see the road, too, in the streetlight. You can see nearly all the way around the courthouse. Nobody's there."

"But when I gets to the *turning* of the road, what if I meets 'm there?"

Duncan had not answered. It would be just Lu's luck to meet a pack of drunk Granthams, sure enough, and get hurt by mistake.

"With they bob-wire whups," Lu went on, "and they fat pine kindling wood. With they coal oil and they blow-torches—"

"Hush up, woman," said Beck Dozer. "It ain't you, it's me, and anyway I understand that kind of thing is out of date. I hope somebody has told them so."

He sat angled a bit forward in the stiff little chair, keeping his weight off the corner where the cane had worn through. He had placed his hands one on either knee and the white bandages showed annoyingly clear in the dim light.

He said to Duncan, "Why don't you go downstairs with Mister Trewolla?"

"Mister Trewolla's bedtime is nine o'clock. I let on I was just coming up to check on you, then going along home myself."

"You don't want Mister Trewolla to think you're casting aspersions on him, in other words."

"No more than I can help," said Duncan.

Lu had found an empty cigarette package in the corner, had spread it out carefully and was dismembering it, piece at a time, with her long picky fingers. You could hear the cellophane come apart at the seams, then she moved on to the printed paper, then the tinfoil.

"I wonder where is Mister Kerney Woolbright," Beck Dozer asked.

Duncan did not answer. He got up, took a restless turn back past the cell doors, looked up the narrow circular stair that led up to the death cell, the cupola of the jail.

"There ain't a soul up here to help you," said Beck. "In past time, or so I hear, white folks could raise a number just like each other to stick together on these things, but you can't even find one honest deputy. Either you is the only man around with principles, or everybody else is stitching their principles together out of a different bolt of goods."

"It so happens I'm the only man that's sheriff," said Duncan, "and that I haven't tried to deputize. Now shut up. If there's anything worse than Lu talking every minute, it's you talking every minute."

He looked down through the narrow barred window into the jailyard, the streetlight glow of the hollow square, his own grocery an obscure ridge in the store line along the farther side.

He was wondering himself what had happened to Kerney Woolbright.

the
attack

20. It was twelve midnight, as Beck Dozer had predicted, before they came.

From the windows Beck and Duncan watched them get out of the car, which had arrived stodgily, slushing through the puddles. They piled out endlessly, like the old clown act at the circus, and milled about, turning their big shoulders to the rain's slant and swapping a word or two until a familiar figure came up wirily from behind the ignition and led them through the gate. By count there were only seven.

Lu began to wail, like something way off in the woods before dawn on a clear spring night. The sound, mounting, became less mysterious and more like Lu.

"Shut that up," Duncan said. "I can't hear anything that's going on."

But all she did was change pitch. Beck crossed quickly to Lu's cell and stuck his face halfway through the bars. He spoke roughly.

"It's that kind of noise they wants out of a nigger. It's what they're waiting for you to do. It makes them feel good when you sound like that. It tells them they got you where they want you for another fifty, hundred, two hundred years. I says to shut up because I personally can't stand to listen to it, Lu Johnson. Nobody studying you. You think Jesus done forgot you?"

"Jesus," said Lu, and hushed suddenly. "He ain't never forgot me yet, Brer Beck."

"Then set there and think about Him till I tells you you can quit."

In the quiet, voices rose to them from the hall below, brushing now and again a tender spot in the iron. Mr. Trewolla was at the door in his bathrobe, trying to explain things without his teeth.

"Orders ith orders," said Mr. Trewolla. "He'th told me not to let you in."

"I just want to talk to him," said Jimmy Tallant.

"Don't you let him through that door," Duncan called out from above. "I've talked to him once tonight already. If he wants to talk again, I'll come downstairs."

"You thee?" said Mr. Trewolla.

"Some things have come to light since I saw Duncan. Grantham's willing to settle the whole thing with no harm done to anybody. I have to see the nigger too. Five minutes will settle it. Okay?"

Mr. Trewolla sneezed.

"Okay," said Jimmy Tallant.

A large young Grantham boy beside him laid a shoulder to the door which Mr. Trewolla had cracked open to talk. The screws that held the chain-bolt locks fixed in the old wood wrenched free, splintering.

"You better go put some socks on, Mr. Henry," Jimmy Tallant advised, as he stepped inside. "You can catch cold mighty quick like that, especially this kind of weather."

"Duncan!" Mr. Trewolla called toward the ceiling. "In thpite of everything I could do—!"

"That's okay, Mr. Henry," Duncan answered, this time from behind the iron door at the head of the stair. "Just get on back in the back."

"You come back here to me, Daddy," Mrs. Trewolla called. "You leave those awful people alone."

"It's dog eat dog," said Mr. Trewolla, going to obey Mrs. Trewolla. "Nothing in the world but likker-heads. If I'd had my gun, now, but whisky'th, whisky, just like I always say."

"It's a mighty brave man," said Jimmy, "would come to meet six Granthams without even a beebee gun. Not to mention a Tallant."

The Granthams stood politely about in the hall like Granthams invited to a party in a stiff house. One said, "You wouldn't of thought he would of come to the front door without no gun. But he sho' did do it. He didn't have no gun at all. None I seen anyway."

"Turn that light out," Duncan said rapidly to Beck. "Here's the key. That little winding stair there leads up to the death cell. They can't shoot at you there. Lock yourself in good."

He checked his automatic, and took his stand behind the door. The bottom two-thirds of the door was solid iron, plated and bolted like the sides of a battleship, but the upper third was barred. Through the bars, looking down the stairs, which from the first landing upward narrowed to the width of a ladder, he saw Jimmy's face surface toward him, pale against the dull iron gloss around about, and with the same distance in it he had noticed before, so that, rising steadily toward him, its distance increased—just as a star falling seems to be palpably near the earth the instant before it vanishes in space, or as a car hurtling out of a highway gains a point in the glittering light where it seems to still and then reverse, or as a dying face still retreats the closer down you bend to hear the words and stay the breath, or as a man turns from a rainy window to say, "My father did a public thing." Then Beck switched out the light.

Granthams came up the stairs, banging and clattering, and by the time the noise died Duncan could make out Jimmy's features again, now nearer than ever in the dark. Down near the bottom two Granthams were talking to each other. They used to be just that way, Duncan recalled, when he went to school with them. They were always five grades behind and had never been known to finish out a school year, because they came to school only when cotton picking was done and before spring plowing started, always provided the hunting season was poor. So when the teacher lined the classes up after recess to march them inside through the halls, she did not even try to quiet the Granthams. They were at the end of the line shoving each other, marveling at the size of their great big fists, bigger already than most men's on the town square ever got to be, and the misery and terror of anything not Grantham or Grantham kin that crossed their path was the misery and terror of the Pygmy who got in the giant village by mistake and walked down the street apologizing all the way. A Grantham by himself could be docile, and sometimes discovered sweetness and grew so good it would seem his own goodness was the only thing that amused him. So Granthams who got separated from other Granthams during the war came back from the Army sometimes leading fine girls who looked proud to be their wives, and so they moved into town or into other towns, and so the tribe had thinned. But Granthams together were another matter. Somebody had wronged them once—perhaps a British king had gone too far. Whatever it was, it wouldn't happen again. Granthams were good as a king; they were better than a nigger. Nobody ought to forget it. The proud "high-white" servant made them spit. Granthams left living back in the woods now had few friends except each other; yet a man like Jimmy Tallant, who had shown those foreigners over there how to fight a war, had known who he wanted to be home with when they got through pinning the ribbons on him.

Duncan recalled, too, that the day he had entered Camp Shelby, in the same bunch with himself was a boy who happened to fall in beside him after the sergeant had dismissed them. "I think I'll go back to town," said the boy. "Town!" Duncan said. "Didn't you hear what he just said? We can't go outside camp for two days." "Yeah, well I just thought I'd go in for a little while. I thought you might want to come." Duncan stared, then laughed. "But you can't! Don't you know this is the Army? You have to take orders." The boy was mild, but there was flint in him. He regarded Duncan and a mild spark fell. "You don't want to go, I'll go ahead on by m'self," he said, and walked away. They had considerable trouble with him before he would make up his bed the way they had in mind, or keep his effects the way the diagram wanted. It wasn't that he didn't understand them.

Jimmy Tallant said, "Y'all boys shut up down there."

"Y'all hush," the Granthams said to one another.

"I should have picked up the keys from Trewolla," said Jimmy.

"He hasn't got them," said Duncan. "They're all on my side of the fence."

"I was prepared for that," said Jimmy. "Hey, Lewis! Are you ready with that blowtorch?"

"I'm ready, Cud'n Jimmy."

"I've got a gun," Duncan said, "and I aim to use it on the first person tries to burn that lock."

"Whereabouts is your gun?" Jimmy Tallant inquired.

"Right here in my hand."

"Everybody knows that Duncan Harper tells the truth. It's why he made so many touchdowns. Are you ready there, Lewis?"

"Ready, Jimmy!"

"Okay, then, shoot!"

A single brilliant flare illumined the whole interior, and Lu shrieked once from the cell.

council
of
war

21. The night that Duncan Harper felt duty-bound to go sit in the jail and protect that nigger that had been in England during the war, naturally nobody wanted to get mixed up in it. Still, along about eleven-thirty with the town as quiet as snow, a good many people got restless and drove up to the jail. They stopped in the street where they could watch from a distance, and sat in their cars; and some rode by time and again, asking what had happened. Probably nobody thought that there would be any trouble, else they would not have brought their children with them.

When Kerney Woolbright got to town, he took Cissy Hunt straight home. Marcia Mae was out on the porch swing in the cold, and insisted on riding up to the jail with him. Cissy was prevailed upon to come inside the house, but it was accepted in the family that nobody could do anything with Marcia Mae. She wore loafers and a slouchy raincoat with a hood and sat in the corner of the back seat. She had been walking in the rain, she said, and was wet. She assailed Kerney with certain remarks.

"Wonder what his wife is doing all this time?"

"Whose wife?"

"Duncan's."

"Oh, Tinker, you mean. She's home with the children, I'd think."

"Has she changed much?"

"You haven't seen her?"

"No."

"I expect she's just as she always was."

"A real cute girl," said Marcia Mae.

He drove around the corner without replying.

"You see her often, I guess," Marcia Mae went on. "What's she like?"

"She's like herself," said Kerney. "There's nobody quite the same."

Marcia Mae would have thought that out of all the average American-looking girls she had ever seen, Tinker Taylor was the most average American-looking of them all, but she recognized the rebuff and took it. Maybe Cissy ought to marry

Kerney, after all, she thought idly. He had spoken up like a man.

They drew up across from the jail, on the side of the street next to the courthouse, at a little distance from the other cars. Watching across the rainy yard toward the jail, they saw when the windows blazed blue-white, heard the woman scream, and saw the windows light a second time. . . .

As a matter of fact, the light was a flash bulb. Duncan recognized it instantly for what it was, because they had once gone off in his face all the time.

Duncan Harper's life had taken an unusual course mainly because his nerve centers enjoyed a remarkable balance. Under extreme pressures toward action, he could reason through any number of possibilities and choose one with as much leisure as he might choose lunch from a menu, and all in the five seconds it was said to take a good tackle to rush the backfield. They said that from the stands he seemed not to be moving at all, that he looked dazed or maybe just lazy, as if he might yawn. Then the pass would be aloft and landing, or you would glimpse his heels rounding right end.

So when he was standing back of the door with the gun in his hand and Jimmy Tallant said "Shoot!" and the flash bulb went off, he realized he had the best opportunity anybody could ask for killing Jimmy Tallant. He could have said for the rest of his life that he had thought the flash was gunfire. He knew now too that Jimmy wanted himself shot; he understood now the strange distances he had noted before in the face which as the light glared pressed upward closer to the bars with a look like a high diver's plunging toward twelve inches of water in a dishpan. But Duncan did not fire. He would hardly have killed anybody, even someone he despised, and he did not despise Jimmy. A second bulb went off. When Lu's cry died in the iron, there came the splintering of the tiny bulbs, dropped on the hall floor below.

After that, they all went away. They filed out the jail door in the dark, tramped through the cinders, and loaded into the muddy car. When they entered the square from the jail drive and saw cars massed silently in the rain, one of the Granthams leaned from the window and fired a pistol. He may have thought he was shooting straight up, and the car lurched, or he may have had his wrist deflected by the narrow opening of the window; however it happened, the bullet went low and broke the ventilation window in one of the parked cars. In passage it sang a tune in several ears and, dying, it angled a scar into a brand-new Pontiac fender. The Grantham, when he fired, had sounded the high-pitched exulting yell that some people say is the old Rebel yell. If anybody had asked him why he fired the shot, he would have said that something came over him.

Anyway, before whatever it was came over him and he leaned out and yelled and fired, the people in Lacey who were watching were as ready as Mr. Trewolla to speculate unfavorably on the subject of Duncan Harper. But then the bullet made its little music, and they remembered what dangerous people Granthams really were. The man who got his ventilator window broken had his wife and grandbaby with him. Granthams were lawless and bad.

Nobody left. They all sat waiting after the load of Granthams had screamed away through the rain: you could hear the gears mesh a half mile away on the long drag running outward toward the highway. Still they waited. When Duncan's car at last drew out of the jailyard, some of the townsmen alighted to stop him. He stepped out and stood hatless, talking in the rain. Lights in the nearer cars flashed on, and he was plain there in the crossbeams, his fair hair feathery under a bright crust of rain.

He had won again.

It was easy to idealize Duncan Harper. He was never

proud; you could not spoil him. He was fine yet familiar-looking. He seemed to present no complicated problem. It seemed he always felt just what a person ought to feel.

That night when he stepped out into the eyes of Lacey, ranked behind the black car-hoods and rain-glazed windows, he stepped for a second time in heroism.

Then Kerney Woolbright had crossed the street and was drawing him aside.

"It's time you came," Duncan complained. "What in hell happened to you?"

"I had to get hold of the Humphreys County sheriff and talk him into coming over. I figured if nobody in Lacey would take sides, we ought to have help from somewhere."

"When I was up there waiting for God knows what, I doubted you were coming at all. I'm sorry, Kerney." He put out his hand impulsively, and Kerney grasped it.

"What did Tallant want?" Kerney asked. "What was that light?"

"They took two pictures," Duncan said. "That's all."

"Pictures? Of you, of the Negro, of what?"

"When I heard them coming inside, I told the Negro to get himself upstairs to the death cell and lock the door; then there was so much racket I didn't hear him go. When the flash went off, I noticed him standing there by me, just a little to the back."

"Then you think it's one of Tallant's concoctions."

"Yes, and I half suspect the Negro of being in on it. He was nervous, but not scared enough. He kept talking too much."

"But what will they do with the pictures?" Kerney asked.

"We'll have to wait and see."

A car roared round the square and drew up short beside them, splashing mud. It was McCutcheon, the Humphreys County sheriff, enormous in his custom-built trousers. He heaved himself out of the front seat and struggled erect to meet Duncan. Standing, he propped himself up on a stout short walking stick. Two deputies were with him. They remarked that in time past Travis would have asked them in the office and offered them a drink, but they understood everything was changed. They said people in Winfield County had to pick a nigger fight every once in a while these days in place of getting drunk.

The Lacey crowd had thinned by the time they drove away. Duncan followed Kerney to his car and sat inside for a moment, out of the rain.

"So what about the Negro?" Kerney asked.

"It's custody he asked for, and he's going to get it."

"No excitement after all," said Marcia Mae.

Duncan had not noticed her before and he started, turning, and saw her emerging from the dark bundle on the back seat which he had not even taken for a person. She was shaking back the clumsy raincoat hood from her bright hair.

"Since nobody else will lynch him, let's go lynch him ourselves."

The men were silent. Her confident Hunt voice, with the smoky tint it had always held, framed now and again a Yankee crispness on a word, reminding them of her life's distance since ten years ago—no, nothing that happened here could seem important to her.

Duncan pointed toward the courthouse whose upper story rose whitely into the rain, while out beyond, whiter still, the inevitable Confederate soldier's statue held a stern guard toward the North. "Upstairs there," he scolded her, "twelve Negroes were shot down in cold blood."

"When was that?" she asked.

"Nineteen-nineteen," said Kerney, "or was it twenty? Somewhere along in there."

"Oh," she laughed. "I thought you meant last year."

"You've heard about it," said Duncan, "all your life."

"Yes, now that you mention it. I've heard it and forgotten it because I don't care. If I don't care nobody cares. I'm no different from anybody else. Nobody our age in town could say offhand who was there or why."

"Jimmy Tallant's father was there," said Kerney, "for one."

"Yes," said Duncan, "and Beck Dozer's father, for another."

Kerney whistled.

"They both knew it," Duncan went on. "Tallant would do a toe dance around a volcano. I could have shot him by mistake tonight when the flash went off in my face. It looks to me he's been trying to die for years."

"I wish," said Marcia Mae, "that I was anybody's secretary in some big city. And that every morning I got up and put on a gray suit and a clean white blouse and went to work in a beautiful soundproof air-conditioned office one hundred and one floors up, with streamlined filing cabinets and a noiseless electric typewriter. I wish I had a little apartment with a view from the window of nothing but skyscraper tops. Then I would be happy."

"No, you wouldn't," Duncan said.

Now all the cars had gone away but theirs. They were left with the old square. The two streetlights bleared in the wet. The last car, disappearing, jolted in a rut by the filling station. Its tail-light described the corner. Then it was nothing.

"Why wouldn't I be happy?" she demanded.

"You'd have to get up early every morning, for one thing. For another, you'd get bored."

Kerney felt that the two of them were alone in the car, that he was not there at all.

"So many things are boring nowadays," she said. "Why is that?"

"It's part of getting old," said Duncan.

"I take it hard. Harder than most people do."

"I don't know whether you do or not," he answered.

a path
leads
backward

22. If any one household was most afflicted by the new law enforcement principles in Winfield County, it was Duncan Harper's. On Saturday nights, as Tinker had predicted, people no longer wanted to stop and talk. Wednesday-night trips to the next county for bingo had to go as well. And Jimmy Tallant never came.

After the heavy rains, the sun had come out and discovered a jungle. To human beings it seemed that their bodies had got involved in the rich growth; thinking went laboriously— the mind seemed to work like a motor under too great a dredge of oil. Vines drew the fences down to earth, and the leaves on every kind of growing thing looked too large, like an elephant ear. It had also become suddenly hot.

Down on the terrace just back of the house, Tinker found that grass had forced up overnight between the bricks. She went down on Sunday afternoons with her trowel and scissors, working on her knees until the sun lowered. Her little girl Patsy, freshly out of her winter overalls, ran minia-ture errands for her, talking a blue streak. The work seemed an excuse for getting out of doors and for meeting Sunday by doing a thing that was not everyday.

For Sunday, whether you have a hangover or not, is a restless time. There is the thing that Saturday night held out to you and never quite gave, but there is no use complaining to Sunday. It is stone deaf, and does not even know your name.

Earlier, Duncan had taken his son for a walk in the woods.

The boy, who was around ten, had hair so blond as to be white, and for this reason they all called him Cotton. He was sailing comfortably into the future under his father's banners; it had been impressed upon him early that he was not to talk about football outside the family. Usually nobody in the family wanted to talk about it either, but at the moment he was enjoying a day of grace and had felt encouraged to reveal, while crossing a barbed-wire fence, that he had changed his life's ambition to being a big-league baseball pitcher, instead of a football star.

"Why? Do you like baseball better than football?"

"No, I still like football best. But there's already a Harper that's an All-Time Great in football. I want to be an All-Time Great in something else. I thought baseball would be the next best thing. Then when Patsy grows up, she could be a girls' tennis champion. If Mother has another little boy, he could —let's see, what could he do?"

"Track, maybe?"

"I don't like track. It's not a game."

"Swimming?"

"That's no game either. Maybe basketball. Lightweight people are good in basketball."

"Why is he going to be so lightweight?"

"Because he'll be so little."

"What makes you think Mother wants another little boy?"

"I don't know. I thought maybe she might."

Duncan sat down. They had gained the middle of a roll of pasture underneath a bluff. The cows had cropped the grass short there. He leaned back on the hillside in the sun.

"Mother wouldn't let you do that," said the boy. "You'd catch cold."

"But Mother isn't here. Won't I still catch cold?"

The boy caught on and laughed. "I don't know."

"We used to find Indian arrowheads on this hill."

"Who did?"

"Oh, your mother and I."

"Was she your girl friend, Daddy?"

"Of course she was."

"Your girl friend all the time?"

"Most of the time."

"You had another girl friend besides Mother!" But these matters did not really interest him. He had begun to tumble about on the hillside like a puppy, making foolish noises.

"Don't act silly," said his father. "Let's go down to the branch."

"Can I carry the shotgun?"

"You know I've told you a hundred times. You can not carry the shotgun."

"Maybe Mother could have *two* more children," said Cotton.

"Oh? What's the fourth one for?"

"Well, ice sports are real important some places. Not around here because there isn't any ice, but up North they are. This would make a good ski jump, if there was ever any ice on it. It would make a good place for a swing."

"A swing! Who told you that?"

"Nobody. I just thought of it."

"That's funny. There used to be a swing here. Right from that big tree limb."

"Let's build one here again sometime."

"We can't. It isn't our land."

"Whose land is it?"

"Let's go down this path," said his father.

A bank of plum bushes and willows screened the branch from the pasture. The path down to the watering ford was cleft two feet deep or more into the bank, chopped in slowly by the hooves of cattle. A muscle of current curved into the shaggy bank. Duncan and Cotton jumped to an island of sand, then across the stream. They sat down on the sandy farther bank. The small sound of the current filled the open space between the stream and a thicket of willows.

"We used to build dams here," Duncan said.

"Dam is an ugly word. You said an ugly word."

"Would you like to build a dam?"

"You said another—"

"Cotton, I told you to stop acting silly."

Stricken by his father's sudden change of tone, the child tried hard not to cry, and finally succeeded. They often said to him on such occasions: "Be a man, don't cry." He now said this to himself, and found it worked.

"I'll tell you something that's true," said Duncan. "When you want to stop acting silly, start doing something. Now think of something you can do."

"All right, I've thought of something."

"What is it?"

"Go wading."

"Good, we'll both go wading."

They both removed their shoes and socks, and laid them up on the grass, away from the sand. Duncan unloaded the gun and put it down on his coat. The water was chilly and only the top crust of sand was warm. The boy's feet were still tender from having gone shod through the long wet spring. His toes curled at the touch of the water. Duncan rolled up his pants legs and splashed across and slightly upstream to where an old fence post lay on the higher bank. He loosened it from one end, lifting it as though from its grave, for an outer strip of it had rotted into the earth. Black bugs shot away into the brush and a few maggots made a sluggish, agonized gesture at the sudden sunlight. Duncan observed this for a moment, then he laid the post in the water, across the narrowest neck of the branch.

"What's that for?" asked the boy.

"Go on and wade," said Duncan. "I'm going to build a dam."

He scooped out a ditch in the stream's bed, laid the post there and leveed it in place with dripping handfuls of sand. Then he began to bring heavy damp sand from the bank.

Presently the water downstream ceased splashing. Cotton was standing near him to watch. Drops of bright water fell from his fingertips. Little drying rims of sand had formed on his legs.

"Can I help you, Daddy?"

"No, thank you."

"Please, Daddy."

His father straightened and they grinned at each other, understanding the game. "I thought you didn't want to build a dam. I thought you'd rather wade."

"I changed my mind."

"All right then. You can help me."

They both began to carry sand in double handfuls, holding it out before them like bowls too full of something. The water backed up gradually behind the dam. It hunted patiently, found the weakest place, and struck through.

"It won't hold," said Cotton, staunching it desperately.

"I saw some rocks over yonder a little way. And some chunks of log from an old pigpen." Duncan pointed.

"Oh, boy! We could build a big dam with those."

"Sure we could."

"Let's go." Cotton began to run.

"Wait a minute. Listen. This will be good. You get the

rocks and the wood and build one up here and I'll go down the branch a little piece just around the corner there and build another one. When it all backs up good and strong, you can break this one and make a real flood. Then you can run down to where I am and watch the water break the other one. Won't that be fine? That is, if you don't mind working hard."

"I don't mind working. I like it. I can beat you finished."

"Don't forget to leave your spillway running right up to the last. You saw what happened before."

"I won't!" He ran again. "When I'm almost through I'll holler."

"Holler loud. And wait till I answer you. You hear?"

"Okay. I'll holler real loud."

He was hard at work already, trustworthy, concentrated, and happy. Under the sun that fell on the ruined pigpen, his white hair grew hot as glass. A tuft would not lie down at the crown. He did not hesitate to tackle heavy loads of rock and logs. The big thing was that he and his father were working together. This knowledge, like the sound of the branch, filled the open space he moved in, and more than the sunlight, shadow, or greenness, made its quality. He did not feel it when his legs and arms got tired. He enjoyed majestic securities.

He laid the last stone, sealing the spillway. The dam was an austere production, tough with stone and thatchings of wood, packed in with wet sand and firmed across the top. He had worked for an hour.

He stood straight and called his father. After he had called several times, he realized the truth. His father was playing a joke on him. The water mounted imperceptibly behind the dam, which was holding well. He ran downstream. When he burst through the plum thicket, a new reach of the branch curved before him. There was another ford, muddy and pocked with hoofprints, and far over to the left a fence corner and a wet brown field beyond, empty and taking Sunday. Besides these, there was only a confusion of new leaves up the bank to his right, and a silence full of birds. There had never been the start of a dam.

"It's ready, Daddy; come out! It's ready; stop hiding!"

He did not know how many times he raced back and forth, people being always foolish as children when they are betrayed and children being very foolish indeed. He was suddenly frightened, and returning at a walk through the thicket, he began to cry.

Then he stopped dead still. His father was sitting on the higher bank beside the path that they had followed down from the pasture above. He was staring at the boy. The dam still held, but the water had backed up behind it in a pool and begun to swirl. Duncan sat with his head lowered. There was green stain on his cheek and pressed into his hair, and his clothes were twisted strangely.

"Were you there all the time, Daddy?" There was no answer, and Cotton wondered for a terrible minute if this man was his father at all. He pulled a weed and began miserably to peel it.

The water struck free, first a trickle, then a loud gush, which faded.

"I built it real good," said Cotton.

When the water made the noise it made, the man seemed to come to himself. With an athlete's decision of movement, he jumped from the bank and cleared the stream and, bending, swung the child affectionately against him.

"It was a wonderful dam," he said. "It was the best I ever saw."

"But where was yours, Daddy?"

"You know when I went down around the corner? Well, there was a man came by who wanted me to help him head his cow back to the pasture. We had to climb all up through the woods. I'm sorry I had to leave you by yourself. Let's go home now."

They put on their shoes and walked back. Duncan shot the gun twice to amuse him. On the way they stopped by Duncan's mother's, the house that was low in the front but tall in the back, with a long wooden flight of steps dropping down into the back yard. They all three sat together on the steps and ate teacakes out of a crock. When they reached home, Tinker was not long in discovering that Cotton had fever and had to be put to bed.

"You shouldn't have let him go wading," said Tinker.

"It's May," Duncan said.

"I know, but you know what a late spring we've had, and the water was still cold, I bet. I bet you let him sit on the wet ground too and probably let him get too hot dragging all that stuff around in the sun. You ought to think about things like that when I'm not there."

The little girl began to sneeze.

"I guess that's my fault too," said Duncan.

"No, it's my fault. I took her down with me to weed the terrace, and the brick is still damp." She turned away from the sink. There was a cup towel, as usual, tied around her small waist and she dried her hands on it, found a piece of Kleenex and blew the child's nose.

Later, after she had put them both to bed in the twilight, Duncan's mother telephoned and told her how Duncan had come by with Cotton and they had sat on the back steps eating teacakes, what Duncan had said, what she had said, what Cotton had said. She lived alone and appreciated every little attention, and she was always wanting to remind Tinker of this.

Tinker hung up the phone. The twilight in the house, wide open to the outdoors, had just passed gold. The free Sunday quiet of the light called up the love of innocence in her heart, and with it the ritualist's faith in the innocent trappings of the day: a walk in the woods, playing at the branch, a visit to Grandmother's, children. I'm foolish and wrong, she confessed to herself, not to trust what I know I can trust. Duncan, she thought, and at his name tears sprang at once to her eyes.

She looked in on the children. Tired from the day outside, Cotton slept already, an arm flung wildly out, and Patsy whispered something, as she was apt to do, and shut her eyes again. Tinker closed the door softly. She moved through the filmy light in the hallway and saw how every pretty thing she had cast its long graceful shadow. From the threshhold of the living room she saw Duncan on the couch. His sleeping hand hung toward the floor.

She knelt and unbuckled her sandals and, stepping free of them, went and sat on the bit of couch beside him. She unbuttoned his shirt and was about to lay her head down when she saw the red mark in the skin itself, and beside it the lipstick stain.

From long habit, out of even so deep a sleep, he threw his arm up around her, and she dropped down to the floor with a little moan.

picture
in
the paper

23. "It's happened," said Kerney Woolbright.

He stood in the door of the sheriff's office. Duncan was alone, Mattie Sue Bainbridge having gone across the street for her morning Coke.

He looked up from the desk at Kerney once, then taking greater care, he looked again. "What's happened?"

"It's come out," said Kerney. "After two months. I kept wondering. I guess you have too."

"I don't know what you mean. What are you talking about?"

Kerney tossed a newspaper open before him on the desk. It was a Chicago paper for Negroes; the outer pages were pink. Negroes were always sending the white people's laundry back wrapped in pages of this paper, or others like it, as if they hadn't thought what they were doing or there wasn't any other paper around the house.

"There's a picture of you inside," said Kerney, "in quite a prominent position—the one they took in the jail. You've got a gun in your hand and Beck Dozer is behind you. You look real good. Handsome."

"That's nice to hear," said Duncan.

"Also," Kerney went on, "there is an article here about you. It tells how proud everybody ought to be of you, born and raised in Mississippi and yet defending a Nee-grow. Nobody can understand it, but they all think it is wonderful. You are a champion of civil rights, you are a defender of the black race. In Chicago, friend, you are solid. In Winfield County you'll probably be everybody's least favorite grocer till the day you die."

" 'Lone hero,' " Duncan read, " 'in a gallant defense of a hapless Negro—' "

" 'Nee-grow.' "

" '. . . falsely suspected of a minor offense against a local café owner, Sheriff Duncan Harper of Winfield County, Mississippi, successfully turned away from the cell door an angry lynch mob. . . .' "

"I always said," Kerney remarked, "that you were everybody's hero."

"Oh, shut up, and try to figure out who might have sent them this article."

"They have reporters all over the South," said Kerney. "Tallant may have written it himself."

"It's signed 'Cuthbert Owsley.' What a name! It sounds like a Tallant-type invention. How else would they get the names, the dates, all the details? But we can't go on guesswork. We have to know."

"The trouble with this is, it takes time, and we haven't got the time to waste. The first thing to do is to hit back good and strong. Buy space in the paper, or print a handbill and show Tallant up for what he is."

"I can't accuse him without knowing."

"You don't have to accuse. You can insinuate. I'll write it, or rather we can do it together. You can suggest that Tallant bribed the nigger to pose for the picture, then sent the story in. You know that's the size of it. But you've got to say it quick."

Duncan shook his head. "I've got to know first. When I walk back across to the grocery store, I want to go with my shoes clean."

"You got in trouble before by not listening to me," said Kerney.

"You weren't born and raised in Winfield County, Kerney. You wouldn't know a lot of people around here as well as you do if it hadn't been for me. The Hunts, for instance. I gave you a good name with Mr. Jason."

Kerney stood undecided. "You're saying we ought to stick together."

"I've always thought we had the same feeling about things. If I'm wrong, why then—"

"You aren't wrong; we do."

"I'm willing to risk losing a race to—"

"But that's just it!" Kerney cried with a sudden lost wild boyishness. "It doesn't matter to you!" His picture, labeled Candidate for the Senate, Third District, had just appeared on the telephone poles. He recovered quickly and, stepping toward the desk, laid his hand palm down between them. It was a long-fingered, thin hand, the kind that held the pen that was mightier than the sword. "I've got to have this county's record, Duncan."

"I want to see you win," said Duncan. "I'll do everything possible to see that you do, that we both do."

"If Tallant and Grantham get back in the saddle—"

"Are you sure you've counted all my cards? Tallant is the brains there, and I wonder if he really wants to lick me."

They looked at one another, and both of them thought of Tinker.

"Meanwhile," Duncan continued, pointing to the paper, "I'll have to work this out in my own way, Kerney."

Mattie Sue Bainbridge came back. "Miss Winfield County Courthouse," said Kerney, "of 1950." He laid his hat across his heart.

Mattie Sue wrinkled up her mouth and blushed. "You're the craziest thing!" she said.

"Give me a piece of tablet paper, Mattie Sue," Duncan said, when Kerney had disappeared.

He bent over the paper at the small desk by the window, writing laboriously with his left hand.

"dear Mr. Editor: I am a negroe in Wingfeeld county, Mississippi, who wish to get in tuch with the man who sent in the peice which tell about mister Duncan Harper our sherriff. You say the man is name mister Cuthbert Owsley, but there is not a man of this name in Wingfeeld. It is important to some of us negroes because we have made up a club (secret) for our civil rites and wishes to find all who will help us. Yours truely, A. P. Abbott."

He sent Mattie Sue to the post office with the letter along with a note to the postmistress to put any mail for A. P. Abbott in the sheriff's box.

Three days later an answer came. "Cuthbert Owsley is the nom de plume of one of our valued correspondents in your area. His name is Mr. Beckwith Dozer. We wish you great success with your civil rights organization."

Duncan read it over twice and a pair of eyes seemed to be regarding him out of gold-rimmed glasses.

"This doesn't make any sense at all," he thought and, catching up his straw hat, went out to find Beck Dozer.

**Beck
thinks it
over**

24.   Duncan drove to the tie plant, but it was shut down for the day, so he followed first one side road, then another, until he reached the mailbox with "Dozer" written on it. The ink had bleared under the "Z." He left his car on the road, close in beside the bank, and climbed the narrow dusty path where a child had been playing with spoons and snuff bottles. The house was a plain two-wing country house with a hall down the middle and a gable to the right. Once at the top of the bluff above the road the ground was flat as a pan and went flatly back into the wood behind. The fence around the front yard was fancy calf wire that had seen better days; the front gate was weighted with a plowshare. No one was in sight, yet the sense of human presence lay strong everywhere, as in the old story of the ship that is found empty at sea. Duncan minded his country manners and stood by the gate, calling.

"Anybody home?"

" 'Home?' " said the wood behind the house.

A tiny black boy scampered across the open hall. Someone moved inside the gabled window. In the back yard a dog barked and would presently trot around the corner of the house, stand in the front path, and bark again. Duncan waited.

After so long Beck Dozer emerged into the hall and came directly down the steps. "Git away," he said to the dog. He wore new overalls and an old work shirt that clung to his small shoulders.

"I've come to ask who Cuthbert Owsley is," said Duncan. He held the Chicago paper in his hand.

"You already know," returned Beck. "Don't you?"

"Then I have another question too."

"Go ahead."

They talked across the gate, standing equal distance back from it, not lounging against it as two white men might when they talk together, but looking straight into each other's eyes, and Duncan commenced to see the advantage of Beck's glasses.

"What crazy streak makes you do business with a man like Jimmy Tallant who doesn't give a damn if all the niggers in Winfield County get wiped out one way or another as long as he has a free hand on Highway 82?"

"Mister Tallant and I are tied together on account of what his daddy did to mine. He wouldn't lose me, nor let me come to harm for anything in this world. He's my main protection in this life. That and he pays me for what he gets me to do. He's paid me high as two hundred dollars for some jobs. You take that night I was up at the jail with you. That's what he gave me for it."

"So how did you really get your hands cut?"

"That was the only hard part. I did it myself on some-body's new bob wire."

"These Chicago articles—what are you trying to do with them?"

"They pay pretty good too. I gave you a good enough name, didn't I?"

"You gave me such a good name you as good as lifted me

out of the sheriff's race, and you damn well know it. If you're trying to help your people—"

"I don't run in pack, Mister Harper. I'm not trying to help anybody but me. I said that when I came on back down here to live after the war was over. Any Negro with little enough sense to choose to come back to Mississippi to live, had better hew his own road and not look to right nor left."

"Is that what you call yourself doing?"

"It's what I does."

"I don't believe a word of it," said Duncan with such force the Negro fell silent.

"You've seen a light these days," Duncan went on. "All of you have. You keep casting around for the best way. You want to deal equally with white men but you don't know who to trust. You'd rather have Mr. Willard Follansbee in office instead of me?"

"To be honest with you, Mister Harper, I prefer the status quo. You can climb the status quo like a step ladder with two feet on the floor, but trying to trail along behind a white man of good will is like following along behind somebody on a tightrope. As he gets along towards the middle his problems are likely to increase, and soon he gots to turn loose of me to help himself."

"I stayed with you at the jail," Duncan reminded him. "I didn't like it, but I did it. You were the one cheating that night, not me."

"I remember." He stood blinking for a moment, then he opened the gate. "If you'd care to step inside the yard a minute, Mister Harper, there's something I'd like to show you."

To their right, tall althea bushes framed a path that led down to a house scarcely larger than a privy. Beck unlocked the door and pushed it wide. Duncan looked in on a square room where two long hand-hewn benches and two tables faced a raised platform with a desk and chair. Behind, a blackboard was set neatly into the wall. The three remaining walls were lined with bookshelves, these giving way only to the windows. From an iron stove in the far corner came the scent of coal dust.

"I lights a fire in here every so often during the winter. They tell me damp is not good for books."

Duncan glanced over the shelves. They held mainly leatherbound sets, perfectly arranged. Many titles were in Latin with authors he had heard of somewhere; memories stirred in him of vague desires he had once felt to know what these very books said. His own reading had been largely in the English and American books his professors had talked about most, and later in modern books that Kerney was apt to like mentioning. And he remembered, too, one night in summer sitting in the porch swing with Marcia Mae, how Nan Hunt had come out to bring them coconut cake and fresh peach ice cream she had taken for them ahead of time out of the freezer, saltpacked for Sunday. They begged her to stay and talk to them, and somehow the talk turned to reminiscence—somehow she had come to say, her voice very sweet, "I wonder what happened to the old library Senator Upinshaw gave to Robinson Dozer when he died? I suppose they must have destroyed it when they killed Robinson. A thing like that knows no bounds."

"They left the library, then," Duncan said to Beck. "And the school too."

"I used to say that to myself," said Beck. "At least they left his books the Senator gave him. At least they couldn't touch the books. But you know, Mister Harper, it finally came to me why they hadn't done it. You know why? They didn't do it because they didn't care."

"Can you read these books?" Duncan asked.

"No. Can you?"

"No."

"You are the first white man I ever showed the inside to."

"You're the first Negro I ever invited to my house to talk business with. I need your help."

"Help for what?"

"I want to expose how Tallant got that picture. I want you to be in on it."

Halfway to the gate they stopped. The Negro grew cold right in the sun and shook. He could not answer the white man with any poise, so he stood noticing the sights of the season. The chickens shuffled for worms on the spring ground; wood smoke came from the washpot out back along with the slap of a sheet being pounded on the board; jaybirds screamed in an oak tree down near the road. The dog slept, sprawled in the sun. A little naked Negro boy came out the door and halfway down the front steps, where he squatted like a savage.

"Git back in the house," Beck told him. "What you mean outdoors without your clothes?"

He turned finally to Duncan. "I tell you, Mister Harper, you are the only white man to see inside my papa's school, but Mister Jimmy Tallant knows it's there because he asked me once what it was. I think maybe he's thought too, So they left the books, and then I think maybe he's gone on to think, They left them because they didn't care. Mister Tallant and I, were yoked up together, you might say. There isn't anything one of us thinks that the other one hasn't thought too. They say a nigger's got to belong to some white man."

"You believe that?"

"No," said Beck, and sighed.

"I won't force you to come," said Duncan, "or pay you anything for doing it."

"Lord knows, the Granthams will have my hide on the door before night come, if I do this."

"I count on Mr. Tallant," said Duncan. "I don't think he'll let them hurt you."

"You don't *think!* It's not you, it's me!"

"It might be me! It could be me! Don't you know it might come to that?"

"All right then. I'll come."

When the gate stood between them again, Beck asked him, "Why you wants to act like this, Mister Harper?" and one of his dark cheeks gleamed wet, smeared down from the gold rim of his glasses lens.

"No reason," Duncan returned. "I want to do what's right, I guess. That's all."

The slight Negro stood watching the big genial figure of the white man descending the steep path with paced, confident control of motion, and he felt his unease deepen. In a country where the motives for doing things are given names like honor, pride, love, family, greed, passion, revenge, and hatred, "right" had an odd inadequate sound. Beck shivered again in the smooth sunlight and thought that he had warmed the books so carefully and now needed warmth himself. He entered the house and there sat his wife's grandmother, Granny (Aunt Mattie, the white folks called her), drawn up to a little low fire.

"Granny, are the Harpers Yankees?"

He had struck a moment when her mind was clear.

"No, son, dey's here all along. Dey's cu'us, dat dey is, but dey ain't Yankees."

"Cu'us how?"

"Jes' cu'us. Jes' like I say."

25. "Looks like Duncan's done him a do," said Jason Hunt.

They had sat out on the lawn since supper and now it was dark, and their shapes in the wicker chairs scarcely impressed another shadow. But they saw each other clearly, through long knowledge. Kerney was there, his long legs stretched out in the grass, elbows propped on the chair arms, fingers laced. From time to time, with the toe of his shoe he scratched his leg where a mosquito bit him, or a gnat. The gnats were getting worse. Nan Hunt kept a Flit gun beside her and sprayed every few minutes. It was the only time of year, she said, when she approved of her daughters' smoking. "But you smoke yourself," said Marcia Mae finally. Everybody had waited so long for somebody to say this, there didn't have to be any answer.

Old Mrs. Standsbury, sitting erect with her thick short legs crossed, said, "Yes, she certainly does." She was wearing her sack against the night air and kept her hands thrust in the folds. She wore a diamond pin low at her throat, which was soft as a girl's.

"You tell them about it, Grand," said Jason, using the children's name for her. He had had in him a love for her growing many years. There would never be any need to mention it. He sometimes thought of it as the most satisfying force in his life.

"I never wanted any of my children to smoke," the old lady said, "but they all did it anyway."

"Just like Cissy," said Kerney, wanting her name in it.

"Huh?" said Cissy, who had not been listening. She knew she was sitting just beyond where Kerney would have liked her. He wanted to hear her breath, or graze her arm as though by accident when he raised his hand. A little out from the rest, in a loose peasant skirt, one knee hugged against her, Marcia Mae sat low in a canvas beach chair, a huddle, darker than the others.

"You approve of how he's handled it, sir?" Kerney asked.

"Duncan? Yes, I approve in general. I think he might have done it quicker. I think he might have talked to me, to somebody older."

"*I* talked to you, you remember," Kerney said.

"I remember. But Duncan—he never comes to me."

"Must he?" Nan Hunt inquired. The edge was in her voice.

"Apparently not," said Jason, dryly.

"What did he do?" Cissy asked.

"I've told you three times," said Kerney. "You don't listen."

"I'll listen now," she said. "What did Duncan do?"

"Oh, Lord," said Marcia Mae.

"You don't ever read the papers?" her mother asked her.

"I read the funny papers," she said. They laughed. "Tell me," she insisted. "Grand doesn't know either."

"Do you know, Mother?" Nan asked, raising her voice.

"Know what?" She was a little deaf.

"About what Duncan did."

"The piece in the paper, you mean?"

"That's right."

"What did she say?"

"I said *yes. The piece in the paper.*"

"Certainly I know. I read the paper every day."

"She keeps up," said Jason.

"Well, you children won't let me cook or work in the yard with Jonas. I have to do something. I can't crochet all day long."

"There, Mother. You're exactly right."

"Of course, she's right," said Jason.

"For crying out loud," said Cissy. "Will *some*body tell me—"

"Yes, somebody will tell you," said Jason, "but where do we have to start?"

"You'll have to go back to when Duncan was born," said Marcia Mae.

"Then you'd better tell her," said Nan. "You'd know more about that than anyone else."

But Marcia Mae fell silent, and Kerney at once commenced relating:

"It was just after Duncan closed up the highway place— now you must remember hearing about *that*, Cissy—there was a Negro named Beck Dozer came to him and asked for custody, claiming he'd got in a fight with Bud Grantham and Bud was sure to get him. It was raining like hell and Duncan couldn't locate anybody but Jimmy Tallant, who claimed they'd taken Bud back up in the hills, maybe to die. Duncan shut the Negro up in jail, but old Trewolla's not the most forceful character in the world, and Duncan wasn't easy in his mind. He didn't want either to sound the alarm over nothing, so he just stayed up in the jail with the Negro. Sure enough, the Granthams came and Tallant with them, walked right by Trewolla and were heading upstairs for the Negro when Duncan stopped them. At that point, they shot two pictures with a flash bulb and went away.

"That was the night," said Jason, "that one of the Granthams fired a gun out of pure devilment and almost hit old Morris's grandbaby."

"That's right. And the night I brought Cissy home early from the picture show in Stark."

"I remember that. It was raining."

"Yes. Then finally, the picture of Duncan and the Negro in the jailhouse comes out in a Chicago Negro paper, the kind they're sending out all over the South now, with an article saying Duncan is a defender of the colored. Come to find out the whole show was a put-up job—there never was a fight with Grantham, and Dozer was paid a fat fee for his part in it. This lays the carpet for Follansbee to walk into office. It was a stunty way to do it, but Tallant is that kind."

"He likes to play games," said Jason. "It amuses him."

"Why couldn't Duncan just tell everybody how it all happened?" Cissy asked.

"Because in politics," said Marcia Mae, "everybody agrees to confuse a perfectly simple issue that everybody understands."

"No," said Jason, "that is eventually what Duncan did do, Cissy, but he had to tell it in some forceful way, in print. He came out with a paid political statement in last Sunday's paper, containing along with his own statement a sworn statement by Beckwith Dozer. Is that nigger still alive, Kerney?"

"So far as I know, sir."

"He won't be living here much longer, then," said Jason.

"Duncan also stated," Kerney continued, "that he was not the willing subject of comment from any outside group, that as long as he was sheriff he was managing things for the constituency and nobody else."

"So that's the size of it," said Jason. "I suppose he'll run it again when the campaign heats up and they start circulating that picture and the Chicago article as handbills."

"There's going to be money poured in against Duncan," Kerney said.

"From who?" Cissy asked.

"Who indeed!" Nan said. "People who want to sell whisky in Winfield County."

"Then Duncan will have to circulate handbills," said Jason, "reprints of *his* article, and the whisky people will go in with the Chicago Negro people to circulate more handbills denying Duncan's handbills, and the beer people will go in with the Baptist Church, only the Baptists won't know it's the beer people, and circulate handbills saying Keep Whisky out of Winfield County, and Tallant will still make money because somehow or other on election day with everything shut up tighter than Dick's hatband, everybody is going to continue to get"—he slapped a mosquito—"Goddam it—dead drunk.

"I have my objections to Duncan," he went on, "and always have had; still he's a decent sort of fellow, and I hate to see him get lost in this sort of mess."

"Isn't there a chance he won't get so lost as you think?" Nan inquired.

"He seems some way," Jason reflected, "always to go in over his head. I've noticed that about him."

Marcia Mae stirred restlessly. For a few minutes past, heat lightning had been flashing in the west.

Kerney said respectfully but firmly, "I'm not sure that's true of Duncan, Mr. Jason. I see a lot of him. He thinks the time has come to progress a little, but he wants to do it in the right way. Doesn't that always make people seem slow?"

"Jason means to say you can't be right unless you talk to the right people," Nan Hunt said.

"God knows, Nan—!" It sometimes seemed to Jason that his wife had turned into evil.

The front screen door slammed, and brought them all to notice that Marcia Mae had left them.

"So now, Cissy," Kerney asked, "do you understand?"

"About what?" asked Cissy.

Later she followed him out to the car where it sat under the cedars in the drive. They sat in the car and had a cigarette and she let him kiss her a few times. Then she drew away and laid her cheek down in the window, against the metal of the door. Honeysuckle smelled so strong you could not even smell the car.

"I know about Duncan and Marcia Mae, Kerney."

After a long silence, he said, "How did you know?"

"She goes back in the woods to walk sometimes, and one day I was out near where the path goes down to the tennis court when I saw her coming up through the trees. She looked pretty and happy and she was singing something, then she saw me. She got mad, and mean—goodness! She said I had followed her. It made me so mad I could spit. I went and told Mother on her and Mother said we all had to be patient, that Marcia Mae acted peculiar because her husband had got blown up and she went off by herself to be unhappy. Then I thought, She sure wasn't unhappy when I saw her before she saw me. But I didn't say anything to Mother and then I knew about Duncan. Goodness!" She laughed. "A scandal in the family. You guess everybody knows it?"

"People have been waiting to know it ever since she hit town," Kerney said.

"How did you know?"

"I went by the office to find Duncan a couple of weeks back. He wasn't in, so I went to his house. Tinker was sitting out in the back yard with the lawn mower, trying to make up her mind to get up and use it. Then she looked up and saw me and I knew I'd better not say, Where's Duncan? God bless her."

"You feel all that sorry for her?"

"There's nobody like Tinker."

"It's funny. Men always feel that about Tinker, but she doesn't have any girl friends at all, does she?"

"You women are such snobs, that's the only thing. You think, Oh, Tinker *Taylor*. The one that chased Duncan Harper till he finally married her. She's nobody but old Gains Taylor's daughter."

"I don't think anything of the kind. I just think she's hard to talk to. I tried to talk to her at the garden party last summer, but she wouldn't say anything."

"She probably felt uncomfortable in stockings and heels," said Kerney. "She's the original woman. All the rest of you are playing paper dolls."

"Well I like that!"

He held her back from opening the car door and they scuffled a moment. "Want to go for a ride?" "No." "Want to go get a Coke?" "No." "Want a drink?" "No." "Want a kiss?" "No. No, no." "Cigarette?" "Umm. One more."

"What do you think about it?" he asked her. "If it's true?"

"About Duncan and Marcia Mae? It's their business, I guess. It's her own life. That's the way she's always acted."

"But what do *you* think?"

"I think she's crazy," said Cissy. "Where's the future in it?"

Kerney shrugged. "Maybe they still love each other. Maybe he'll leave Tinker, and they'll get married."

"She wouldn't have him. She wouldn't before and wouldn't again." She said this in her chill proud little voice.

He put his hand under her chin and turned her face to his. "But if he wasn't married and if you were she, what would you do then?"

"You wouldn't catch me on a deal like that. I used to have this awful crush on Duncan. I still just think he's wonderful. But you know what I'd tell him? I'd tell him to go jump in the lake."

"But suppose—suppose it was me instead of Duncan? What would you do then?"

She stared at him a moment and then burst out laughing.

"Why, Kerney Woolbright! If you aren't the craziest thing! Do you think for one minute—Kerney!"

"Hush," he said. "Stop laughing."

She stopped finally and put her cigarette out, snuffing it carefully in the ash tray. "I've got to go in." She turned to him. Her face, serious, lovely, melting, came lifting toward him, and to herself she knew exactly how she looked in her young softness. She saw herself better than she saw him, how her eyes were velvet, her mouth tender, and her dark hair all intricate with the swelling night.

So he kissed her and as they drew apart his hand, in mid-impulse of caress, fell short and touched her cheek instead. He saw how slight such moments were, and wondered at love's terrible deflections. That night he lost more than his usual quota of sleep over her, twisting on the crumpled sheets, eluded continually by a mosquito.

Cissy, meanwhile, quarreled with her mother about having to go back down and latch the screen, played the radio awhile, filed her pretty nails, and went to sleep.

the
rejected
ones

26. The blue glitter of Tinker's little Chevrolet, coming out of the east, was marked by Jimmy Tallant long before he saw her inside or knew she was going to stop there. He stood with his hands in his pockets out in front of the roadhouse, which was now no more or less than a filling station with a couple of gas pumps, a Coca-cola cooler, and a snack stand. He or Bud opened the place just enough to keep up their license with the gas company. As a matter of fact, Jimmy liked to be up there by himself. He had his morose side, and alone he watched endlessly the trucks come snorting to the crest of the hill to the west, admired the triumphant boom in their descent, or from the long shimmering eastern approach the razzle-dazzle of the new cars in the sun, making such a little sound when they passed, exactly like an ounce of air pressure being released from a tire, and there went a ton of sweet metal, lancing at eighty toward the Mississippi and beyond. It was not the cars themselves that intrigued him, though questioned at any moment he could have said instantly what make, what year, and what model, but the sense of the linked immensities of America, the feeling that he and his two gas pumps and roadhouse were all another flicker in the eye of the traveler who found nothing there out of place. So the long hot hours passed, one after the other: Charleston, Atlanta, Birmingham, Meridian, Shreveport, Dallas, Houston, El Paso, Tucson, San Diego: the sun blazed on them all, and everywhere a man stood before a roadhouse, near two gas pumps, arms folded, and watched the highway.

Then he saw the car that looked like Tinker's and he forgot the U.S.A., for she was slowing down, a quieter dazzle tossed about the blue hood, and the gravel crackled beneath the tires.

"Well!" He leaned into the window. "If it isn't herself. The rich man's beauty and the poor man's dream. Get out, lamb child. I wanted to see you most in the world."

Beneath her dark glasses her mouth smiled. She wore, as always, a true lipstick color. For coolness her dark hair was caught up from the nape by a black grosgrain band.

"Where've you been, honey?" he asked.

The red mouth talked to him. "Over to the picture show in Stark."

"The picture show? Right after lunch on a day like this?"

"Well, I got somebody to keep Cotton and Patsy for a

change. I walked right out the door when she walked into it."

"What was on at the show?"

The mouth hesitated. "Isn't that silly? I can't even think—Jimmy, I wanted to ask you if you knew a Negro to do my wash. Duncan is wearing about a dozen shirts a day. I don't know why shaking hands with people should get so many shirts dirty."

"Everybody asks me about niggers since Duncan shut me down. But hell, I can't even find anybody to wash dishes in my own kitchen. You might try Beck Dozer's wife, though. She'll take in a little sometimes if she needs the cash."

"I'll drive by there now."

"You know how to go. It's the old Wiltshire road, the first cutoff past the covered bridge."

"I remember. Yes." She did not move to turn the ignition.

"But you couldn't remember the name of the show." He still could not see her eyes. He did not need to.

She put both small hands on the wheel and laid her forehead down on them. "Oh, Jimmy. What am I going to do?"

"I don't know, baby. You've just got to ride out the storm, I guess."

"They'll never come apart. Only she—if she'd been any kind of woman she never could have left him before. How can he forgive her now?"

"How can you forgive him?"

"I don't forgive him. I can't stop loving him, that's all."

"Then there you are."

"You remember how she used to play tennis when we were all in high school? All afternoon; I can see her yet. In white shorts and a black leather belt and a white boy's shirt. She could hit a ball as hard as a boy. She'd throw everything behind the racquet, leave the ground. Grit her teeth. I bet when she's in a rut she gets like that. I bet when she—"

"You'll make yourself sick," said Jimmy. "Come inside out of this sun. There's a room in the back where it's cool."

She opened the car door. "We'd better drive it around to the back," he said. "Lacey is another name for the Gestapo."

"You think I give a happy damn? Let them see the car. Let's make it all more interesting for them."

But he shoved her gently over and took the car around to the back himself. Just off the office was a bedroom where he and Bud used to take turns about sleeping the morning through when the business was on the boom, and they didn't shut down till dawn came and bled the neon. It was neat, this room, with a linoleum rug, a brass bed, a cane rocking chair with a cretonne-covered cushion, and a pair of straight curtains in the window which the Negro cook had made himself out of a pair of flour sacks. There was an old-timey Victorian bowl and pitcher, soap-dish and chamber-pot set stacked up on the dresser. A Negro had once offered it to Jimmy in exchange for a fifth of whisky. Jimmy had no use for it, but he pitied an honest thirst. Later it came in handy, for Bud had been known to rent the room to couples when the little houses out at the side were all filled.

Jimmy raised the window and propped it in place, then turned on the electric fan.

"It's shady back here now. Lie down, honey. It'll be cool in here in a minute."

He brought back two Cokes from the cooler and packages of Nabs. She took a few thirsty swallows and then sat holding the bottle, forgetting it.

"Jimmy, what am I going to do?"

"My theory is that you work this kind of thing out so that you live it one day at the time. You don't see things in big blocks of months and years, or what awful thing is finally going to happen. You just say, Now let's see. What am I going to have for supper?"

"I've said that already. I already know."

He saw her neat kitchen where there were no gadgets: the smooth marble slab she rolled the biscuits on, the grease-blackened pans she cooked her muffins in, and the big butcher knives, not bought out of a store, but the kind the Negroes made out of scrap steel, the hickory handles steel-hammered in place, and she had a whetstone too. One time during one of her summer parties when they had all gathered down on the terrace she had been slicing some ham in the kitchen and had cut herself. Duncan, who had been drinking more than usual, had picked up the knife. "Look at the size of this thing," he kept saying. "Her hand is about the size of a baby's. You wouldn't think she could pick it up, you wouldn't think—" He held it out before him. "You're letting her bleed to death," Jimmy remarked, so that Duncan's hand went tight on the hickory handle. They all knew each other too well. She, meanwhile, had stopped the blood herself, having recalled something she learned in Red Cross class about a big vein—she forgot its name.

Jimmy turned her wrist and there lay a small white line.

"The thing is," she was saying, "no awful thing is going to happen. They can go on like this forever. She doesn't want a husband, she just wants a man. You think she wants to cook and keep a house? You think she'd love a child if she had one?"

"I think it's possible that she might."

"She doesn't love anything, she wouldn't know how. She doesn't know what love is."

"Let's get off this one, Tinker. Everybody knows about love. Men, women, children, and coon dogs. They all know. It's the big old wide-open secret of the world, honey. I've loved you all my life, for instance. You think I ever have to tell you or anybody else?"

"Oh, Jimmy." She began to cry a little and he sat down by her to comfort her, holding her against his shoulder. "It should be after a high-school dance," she said, even smiling a little.

"Except I never got you on a bed before. I suppose I neglected to mention it."

They remembered his long agonized speeches, the times he used to break out laughing at himself.

"Yes, you did once before. The night Marcia Mae's and Duncan's engagement came out in the paper. I went to Memphis with you and went up to the hotel room with you."

"And then got drunk and then got sick and then passed out. You never gave me a chance."

"I'm such a common girl. I do such awful things. You didn't think less of me?"

"I never thought more of you."

"How do you manage, Jimmy? Duncan always says you like to be unhappy. That if you were happy you wouldn't know what to do."

"Duncan pursues happiness and I don't. That's the whole difference. He needn't talk smug. Right this minute I may be a sight happier than he is."

She sighed and dropped her head. "Men like to talk."

"You think it's all her fault, don't you?"

"Of course it's her fault. She left him, ran off with that lumberjack."

"Honey, he wasn't a lumberjack."

"All right, what difference does that make? The minute she came back she started after Duncan again."

He was silent.

"Well, whose fault do you think it was? His?"

"I don't think she would have left him if he hadn't failed her someway."

She stiffened to make some wifely defense, but thought better of it. "We can sit here for hours and say nasty things about them."

He smiled. "Well, let's do."

"Let's be mean."

"I hate blondes, don't you?"

"Despise them. They tell you lies."

"And they're dumb."

"And stuck up."

"And mean and—"

"*Jimmy!*"

The shout from outside the empty roadhouse struck them both silent.

Jimmy said rapidly, "It's Bud. I'll put him off. The door there goes into the rest room and it opens out the side. You can watch your chance and get out that way."

The next instant he was through the door to the office, and she could hear Bud Grantham calling again, and Jimmy answering.

a
hasty
conference

27.   They met in the office door.

"Have they come yet?" Bud asked.

"Has who come yet?"

"Who's back there then?"

"Nobody. I was taking a nap, for Chris'sake."

"Don't give me that. There's a car out back."

"Oh yeah, I know. Hanley sent his nigger in the Chevvy demonstrator. Somebody told him his new hog-wire fence was broken down back in the bottom. The nigger left the car up here in the shade."

"I thought they might have come."

"Who might have come?"

"Sam called this morning. I left word at the house with Bella."

"I haven't been home."

"You didn't eat at home?"

"I ate uptown, at the café."

Bud said, "You ain't doing right by my little girl, Jimmy. And her with a chap to care for."

"Listen," said Jimmy, "there ain't a woman living in this world don't say Praise God when her husband can't make it home to dinner. I was only being thoughtful. You think any man likes to eat in a café when he could put his feet under his own table? Now come on. What about Sam?"

"He called from New Orleans, or rather got Mitchell to call for him. He—"

"*Jim—meee!*"

The door far up toward the front of the roadhouse slammed and they heard the drag of loose heels on the concrete floor. It was Bella. They both lowered their eyes, like boys caught in something. Neither one of them ever really wanted to see Bella. As a matter of fact, Jimmy liked her better than Bud did. She frequently amused him; he sometimes pitied her; and when he felt both of these things at once he became quite fond of her and could make her happy for weeks at a time by letting her know it once. But the only thing she ever did to Bud was make him nervous.

She stood in the door where Bud had moved out of it. She was wearing the flowered wrapper, the one they had told her when she bought it looked enough like a dress to wear it up-town and she had believed them, and a pair of high-heel sling-back white shoes, grass-stained, with the heels broken inward and the strap that was supposed to hold them up lying under her instep. She wore the baby at her waist as if it were a big bow tie.

She said to Jimmy, "Are you back here?"

"Looks like I am. Doesn't it?"

She giggled. "Silly! Daddy come by the house this morning. He said to tell you there was a man from New Orleans called— Daddy! Are you back here too?"

"Wipe his mouth," said Jimmy.

"I didn't bring nothing for it." She caught up the hem of her skirt.

"I should have worn a tie," said Jimmy. "We could use that." He looked at the child. "God damn, what a face. Come here, Buster." He took the baby and held it folded together under one arm in a manner unorthodox but firm. The baby grew extremely happy and began to sputter.

"Miss Annie Miller uptown," said Bella; "she told me yesterday he looked exactly like you."

"She must have lost her eyesight," said Jimmy. "He looks more like an Apache Indian chief than he does me or you or Bud or half-dozen Granthams all put together." He thrust the baby suddenly in Bud's face. "You notice a resemblance?" he inquired. "See anything you want to claim?"

The baby was indeed uncommonly dark. He had a thick crop of spiky black hair that stuck out around his brow, saucer fashion. "Koochee koochee," went Bud, wiggling one tough old brown finger. "Koochee koochee koo. Don't give him to me, Jimmy. Fannie had seven but I was ever a-scairt to hold one. Koo, baby. Koo, baby. Koo."

"Whose car is that one I saw out back?"

"Huh? Oh, car. Is it still back there?" Jimmy craned out the window. "Hanley's nigger he sent up to check the fence down in the pasture. Left it up here in the shade."

"Hey, *Tallant!*" The door of the roadhouse banged again and a man's voice rang.

"Old home week," said Jimmy. "I think it's the Candidate."

"I called him," said Bud. "Sam will want to see him. That was all right, wasn't it? They aim to put the skids under this Harper thing. We might as well put all we got behind it."

Jimmy sighed. "Sure, I know. It's just that Follansbee is my personal nomination for the man least calculated to put me in a mood for weaving daisy chains." Willard appeared in the door. "Well," said Jimmy, "if it isn't the white hope of Winfield County. Only you look more like the black hope than the white one. Christ a'mighty, man, don't you know if you're running for office you've either got to look like a one-gallus tramp and slobber tobacco juice, or make a half-hearted pass at looking like a gentleman? When did you shave last?"

Follansbee touched his chin. It was not really a chin, only a gable on his neck. "This morning," he said. "I shave every morning. It just grows so fast, that's all. Means I'm virile, Jimmy. Full of sap and spark."

"That ain't the way I heard it," said Jimmy.

"How'd you hear it?"

"It means you're going to grass. For a fact it does. Didn't you know that dead people's hair keeps growing, growing, growing. That's all *they're* busy doing. Going to grass."

"Oooooo!" said Bella. "It's the truth. I read it in a magazine."

"Bella, my heart," said Jimmy. "Why don't you get the hell on out of here? There must be a whole pile of things the mother of one has to do around the house."

"Travis's hair," said Willard dolefully, settling back on his head the hat he had lifted as Bella left (he lifted it now about a million times a day). "I reckon if that's so what you said, his old red hair must be a yard long by now, with five months to grow in."

"It's laying all around him in the coffin," Jimmy said. "All around his shoulders."

"Hush up!" Bud Grantham said. "You're tempting the devil, Jimmy, you and Willard, talking about the dead. It ain't fittin'."

"Well, we've all got to join him someday," said Willard.

"It's a fact," said Jimmy.

"I don't dispute it," said Bud.

"Jimmy, about those folks that are coming up here—"

"Talk to Bud. He caught the phone."

"You both know what they want. They want to put money back of Willard."

"Money, yes," said Jimmy. "But why come up here?"

"Well," said Bud, "to see where the money's going to go to, I reckon, just like anybody else. They've had experience in these things."

"That's just the trouble," said Jimmy. "They've had too much experience. I don't know if I like it much."

"We've got to have their money to fight this Harper thing."

"That's what they want us to think," Jimmy said. "That we've *got* to have it."

"Well, don't we have to?" Willard asked nervously. He was at that point in a race—about six weeks before the election—that comes to every political candidate whether he is running for the Presidency or justice of the peace in the smallest crossroads in west Texas: he had to win. It had become a total necessity.

"I don't like the way the wind's blowing," said Jimmy. "Look. They come up here, they offer to pour money in. How much do you think they'll offer?"

"We mentioned five thousand," said Bud, "the first go-round."

"But they're making a special trip. Suppose they mention ten thousand, fifteen? What then? Do we take it?"

"We'd look silly not to," said Willard.

Jimmy turned on him. "Will you keep out of this? What do you mean *we?* You don't own a stick of this place. It's Bud's and it's mine, and what we say you abide by."

"I never meant to meddle," said Willard.

"What do you think we ought to do then?" said Bud. "You got to hurry up, Jimmy. They're on the road and traveling."

"I'm thinking maybe we shouldn't take anything."

"Nothing!" Willard squeaked.

"Look," said Jimmy, "I planned the right way to throw this thing our way and there's no reason on earth why it won't work. All you got to do is keep it up and keep it up and keep it up that Duncan Harper is a nigger lover. The keystone is the picture we took: we embroider from there, we quote him, we tell stories about him, and maybe none of it is quite the truth, but we've always got to lead back to that picture which is down in black and white and nobody can dispute it.

"On the other hand, if we get scared and take this money, what then? We win the race, but we've sold ourselves. We've sold our right to say how much gambling equipment we want to put in, who we aim to hire and why; pretty soon we won't even be allowed in the room when they count up the cash. They can sweet-talk all they want to about there aren't any strings on this money, but you know and I know, Bud, that there are always strings. It's exactly like taking federal funds to build your houses, to plant your land, to buy your cotton nobody else wants. No strings on that either except pretty soon the government owns your soul and you sit and cuss it till you're blue in the face, but if somebody mentions taking that precious parity away from you, you squall like the last of a noble line threatened with imminent castration. I'm sorry but I'm too much of a states-righter to see this any other way. If you're subsidized you're sunk. I've got a natural love for the business Bud and I had built up here together, and I'm enough of a Winfield County citizen to want to tell those sons o' bitches to go back where they came from."

"It's your business and mine," said Bud, "for a fact."

"I don't know," said Willard gloomily. "All that talking is all right, Jimmy, but when the time comes you haven't been coming down the line."

"What do you mean?"

"You pulled that one off after I tipped you the National Guard was coming up: they didn't find a drop. Okay. But two weeks later Harper comes out singlehanded and shuts you down. There were those standing by to cart him off neat and quick that night, but you stalled. Then up at the jail, okay, you wrapped that one up, picture and all. But two weeks later Harper gets the nigger to come out and say it was a put-up job and what then? You don't lay a finger on the nigger. You don't let anybody else tend to him either. It ain't like you, Jimmy. There are those that keeps on saying you're just projecking around, that you don't want to win this race at all. They say that Harper's wife's got the Indian sign—now, I never said it, Jimmy. I never even thought it. But if people are saying it, then you ought to know about it, is the way I feel. I honestly do."

"He sho' don't lay a finger on that nigger," said Bud. "And won't let nobody else."

"Seems like it's you that's the nigger lover," said Willard. "If a nigger double-talked me that way I'd have me a show-down before nightfall."

"All right then, run it without me," said Jimmy. "I'll get out right now. Walk out of here and never come back. Bud, you can write Willard's speeches. Willard, you can bargain with Sam and his crew. Both of you can decide how much money you want, how much share you're willing to give for it. I'm tired anyway. It's time I took a vacation. Every morning I say to myself, Here I am thirty-five years old and I've never seen Niagara Falls or Mammoth Cave. Or maybe I'll go West. There's things to see—"

"Jimmy, for God's sake," Willard said, "I think I hear the car. Whatever I said, I take it back."

Bud Grantham hauled his shoulders together. "It's nothing to prank about, boy. Old Bud wouldn't know his own name without you to tell it to him."

The screen door far out front slammed and numbers of footsteps sounded and stopped. There came a murmuring, but this time no one called.

Jimmy went out to greet them. He hoped to hell that Tinker had seen her chance and taken it, but he had not heard the car.

the gang
visits
Lacey

28. This time there were four of them. There were Mitchell again and the Indian-looking man, Pilston, and the boy who carried the gun for them. And there was Sam himself. Sam was a gentlemanly-looking man who did not weigh very much, and though all the men were taller than he, he did not seem short either. He wore a light blue Palm Beach suit, crisply pressed, a white shirt, and a navy tie with a maroon figure. He was bald with a benevolent rime of white hair, and his eyes were a clear blue. He gave a sort of definition to the two older men who were with him: Jimmy had not thought of them as thugs before. But he failed somehow to define the boy who carried the gun. He only made him seem younger than ever, and chewing gum that way made it seem a toy pistol that he wore beneath his arm, probably one that had come full of candy.

Jimmy shook hands with the boy heartily. "Hello, Wally. Still like your work?"

"There ain't any work to it," said Walter. "All I do is ride around in the car and look out the window."

"You mean you ain't used that thing yet? There ain't been anybody mean enough to shoot?"

"It looks like it," said Walter. "Only it ain't shooting anybody they got in mind. No more than a policeman shoots people. I'm kind of like a policeman, see?"

"That's a new one," Jimmy said. "What about that, Mitchell? The kid here says he's like a policeman."

"We explained it all to him," said Mitchell. "We talked it all over with him and we all came to that conclusion. That's right, ain't it, Wally?"

The boy grinned, shifting the gum to the other jaw. "'At's right."

"This boy here," said Sam to Bud Grantham with pride, "can shoot a gun better than anyone I have been privileged to observe. I've had some idle time in recent months and I've spent pleasant hours watching the kind of mark he can strike. He doesn't miss, that's all. He simply does not miss."

"Is he really that good?" Jimmy asked Mitchell.

"He can shoot all right," said Mitchell.

"How good are you, Wally?" Jimmy asked. He liked Wallace. He felt he knew him by heart.

Wallace grinned. "Well, up in Tippah County where I'us bawn, that's where I learned to shoot, from my Unker Chollie Klappert—up there they usta say I could take the middle claw off a killdee's foot on the far side. It always come easy to me, shooting."

"Chollie Klappert your blood uncle?" Jimmy asked.

"Sure is."

"I'm kin to them myself. That makes us cousins."

"Well I swan," said the boy. He was pleased.

Sam said, "I dislike to change the subject, but I think we'd best get down to business. This office is all right, but it's rather small, don't you agree? Now if we could have some light out in your main room and pull two of the tables together . . . ?"

He gestured toward where Jimmy sat in the window, blocking the larger part of the view with his shoulders. "Sure," said Jimmy. "We can do all that and we can serve you a drink of whisky for real hospitality. But we better tell you first off that Bud and Willard here and me been talking this deal over and we've decided that we're against it. We've got this election sewed up anyway; there's no need for outside help. As for the business we do with you after the election, we've discussed that months ago, before Travis Brevard died, though I never got to sound him on it. Willard here has been sounded and is agreeable provided certain interests of his own are protected. Bud and I, we deal with Willard, and we deal with you and we deal with Duncan Harper. We do the dealing. Now if that's clear we'll have a drink on former contracts and call it a day. I've got—"

"*Jim-mee!*"

The screen had banged again and the heels were sounding

on the concrete. Bella was back. She would have the baby with her, Jimmy knew. He took advantage of the moment to look out the window, and he could stop sweating, for Tinker had got away.

Bella stood in the door. She always wanted to look at people up close. She used to meet everybody that stopped even long enough to use the rest room back when the road-house was open, and now she was lonesome, and to add to it she needed a certain number of people every day to tell her how cute the baby was.

She had on make-up this time and a proper dress. Jimmy spieled out the introductions without even uncrossing his knee. Sam was smooth as butter—it was enough to make you cry; and Mitchell got clumsily to his feet. The boy from Tippah County took Bella's appearance as the most natural thing in the world—it would seem that women carrying babies had showed up in most situations of his life. So the turn passed round to the fourth, the Indian-looking man, and Jimmy still could not remember his name. It was the name that stopped him, and while he was still staring trying to think of the name, he found instead that the face he was looking into, framed with spiky black hair, was more familiar than it had any right to be and still be on a man whose name he couldn't call. He saw that the face was muting like the coils in a juke box from scarlet to purple, the way a baby's face colors when it screams its head off at night for nothing but pure unadulterated meanness.

The room had grown deathly silent, until at last Bella, who had apparently been hard put also to remember the man's name, burst into a smile of innocent delight.

"If it ain't George! George Pittman!"

"Pilston," said the Indian-looking man, and swallowed.

"Pilston. Sure. What on earth made me say Pittman? I declare, I said to Jimmy the other day that I'm alltime getting—"

She trailed off, seeing that they were all silent and downcast, and at last her face burned (for memory walked as slowly into Bella's brain as a solitary hen in midafternoon deciding for some reason to climb the crosswalk and hop into the henhouse). She looked wildly from Pilston to the baby, who were staring at each other in primitive horror, the baby's face unfortunately reflecting not only Pilston's every feature but his emotions as well. Then she said, "Oh." It was a little sound uttered in a little girl's honest voice, and on it she turned and fled.

After a time Jimmy Tallant gave a short laugh and walked out of the room.

Every so often things happen to a person which are like others that have happened, and in these things, even if they are bad or foolish or disgraceful, the person finds his identity is reaffirmed, and so he is at peace. He had grown up in the shadow of what his father had done—all his growing indeed had been raising his head closer to that knowledge. Tinker had not chosen him. Even in the blind senseless dark of poor Bella another man's seed had contrived to run home and lock the door against his own.

But not being really a bitter person, it was not that he thought so much about it as that he felt cast back again into his old lonely freedom. So as he went down through the field to the woods back of the roadhouse, having recalled an appointment to meet Beck Dozer, he went whistling absently, and once picked up a stone to see how far he could throw it.

Back up the hill in the roadhouse office, Bud Grantham at last straightened from where he had been leaning against the desk with his shoulders hunched to let his old tough brown head sink low between them. When he stood up he looked gravely around him.

"You folks make yourselves at home. I best go and see about my girl. Her mother died when she was scarce the size of that one with her and I was never the one to raise a pack of little chaps, as time over and again it's proved to me I was never the one for it."

Leaving, he drew out a great handkerchief, and from outside they heard him honk his nose.

Sam, all the while, had sat cleaning and paring his nails with a nickel-plated gadget. His hands were white, clean and firm, like a surgeon's and he cut the hangnails cleanly free on all ten pure white, without a trace of blood. He at last folded the gadget back upon itself and dropped it into his coat pocket. He dusted his knees. Then he looked at Mitchell.

"Ignoring various family complications which have arisen, I conclude that Mr. Grantham and Mr. Tallant do not wish to do business with us today."

"It looks like it," said Mitchell.

"Well," said Sam, "we have a long hot drive ahead, and before someone or other of them decides to come back and shoot Mr. Pilston here, I suppose we had best be on our way." He made a gesture of rising, when Willard Follansbee, who had been thinking in the corner for some time, said, "Wait" in a tone of despair.

"Yes?" said Sam.

"He don't want to win the race," said Willard. "He ain't going to lift a hand to win it. Everybody knows it."

"Not want to win? Why on earth not want to win?"

"I'll tell you, but don't you say I told you. He's crazy about Duncan Harper's wife. She can turn him any way."

Sam sat thinking. "That clears it. I thought myself, he does not want to win." He straightened. "Go get him, Mitchell."

"Where from?" Mitchell asked, rising.

"His house, I would think."

"He didn't go home," said Wallace, the boy, who had been sitting where he had a glimpse out the window. "I seen him head down that field and towards the woods."

"You go with Mitchell then, Wally. And quickly, please."

the
point
of panic

29. As Duncan had once before, Tinker came to Beck Dozer's house, saw where the "Z" had run on the mailbox and drew her car into the shallow curve out of the main road. She ascended the path to the gate and stood outside it.

"Anybody home?"

" 'Home?' " said the wood.

A young Negro woman, thin and straight as a broomstick, dressed in a straight-cut gingham dress, came down the steps and out to open the gate for her. Her head was wound in a white rag and she wore straws in her ears.

"Come on in," she said to Tinker. "The mosquitoes gits bad out cheer this time of day."

Tinker accompanied her to the house. The Negroid effluvium touched her round, mingled with a drift of wood smoke from the back, and the scent of spring water which draws itself clean out of the earth and brings with it of all earth only its black odor.

"Does Aunt Mattie still live with you?" she asked.

She had suddenly, by the smell of the house, remembered the old woman, though she had not thought of her for years. She had been very sick once when she was a child, and Aunt Mattie had invited herself in and stayed with them and nursed her. When the fever left her, she was weak as a baby and had to learn to walk again. Aunt Mattie would take her up in her lap and sit near the window with her. It was April and the spring was just turning to a deeper warmth—this was a new time and Tinker felt herself new again. With fever's sensitivities she had heard them talking it that she would die and seen them looking it too, but Aunt Mattie had not wavered and had had no time for them: the spoon with the food in it had come at her in the black hand with the nails blue-gray like the silver spoon, had come at her, and come again. Her mother cried in the kitchen, "You put bacon grease in it again!" and wept she was so vexed. In bed Tinker heard it and her tongue came out and licked. That was why it had tasted so good and strong and black, not because it came off the blackness of the hand with the spoon. When she sat weak in the window and Aunt Mattie held her feet together under an old piece of cotton blanket, she thought she had been born out of Aunt Mattie's lap. Aunt Mattie was not a bit modest. "Mattie done save this precious," she told her. "Hadn't been for Mattie you'd be gone from here. Yo' mama don' know nothing about dis chile like Mattie knows her."

Lucy said, "Yes'm, Granny's here. You wants to come and speak with her?"

Tinker followed her inside, through a dim hallway where a door led off into a large room with a bed in the corner and chairs grouped around a cold fireplace. In the far rocker, the largest, Aunt Mattie was waiting out the time under an old pile of quilts. Her thin hands kept together on her lap, and her head leaned to one side as if trying to catch a little light from the window. The hair was gray, kinky and very short: it hugged the old skull and made a neat fitting of itself, all the way around. The wrinkles ran downward and were cleft deep; Aunt Mattie had not played around with age. She was so nearly blind she was aware only of strong sunlight. Yet she could hear well enough.

"Here's somebody come to see you, Granny," said Lucy.

Tinker put her hand on Mattie's. "I haven't seen you in a long time, Aunt Mattie."

The old hands moved caressingly, exploring the fingers and wrist with a fine tremulous dry touch.

"I doan' know you, chile, but doan' tell me. Talk twel I hears your family voice."

"When I was sick one time you came and nursed me."

"They ain't a chile in this town can't say I didn't. White folks doan' know nothing about they churen."

"I'm married now myself, Aunt Mattie. I've got two children of my own."

"I hears your voice now. You's Emmie Taylor's chile."

"That's right."

"I mind the mawning they tole me you's sick. I was down by the branch at the ole place, boiling sheets. They come down the heel and say to me, You know Miss Emmie Taylor's little girl? They had to keh her home from school today she took so sick. So I says right then, Take this clothes-punching stick. Miss Emmie Taylor cain' keh for no sick baby. So that's when Mattie come, honey."

"You saved my life, Aunt Mattie," said Tinker, kneeling down so that her hand rested comfortably between the fingers that held so lightly, pressing now and again to emphasize a word. She had not meant it so, but when she knelt tears came easily, rushing, and fell warm on Mattie's hands and her own. Mattie did not question her. "There, baby. There. Hit's going to be all right."

Her head sank then and she cried all over. Mattie groped across her head, her shoulders, caressing her. "There, baby. There, baby. She Mattie's chile."

She rose when she was done and found her bag for a handkerchief. Lucy had retired, who knew when, or would ever know? She was a Negro, and her tact was of this quality.

The room rested deep in twilight. Tinker walked into the open hallway. She glanced back fondly toward Aunt Mattie, but did not return. She knew that Mattie now perhaps thought she had come yesterday or last year, and would not know her if she spoke again.

The tears had left her exalted and hushed. She thought with a gratitude as immense as a clear sky that today there had been Mattie and Jimmy to ease her. She sat down gravely on the porch steps.

A man ran into the house from the back steps. It seemed that Lucy had entered the hall from some side door the instant that he was calling, "Lucy! Lucy!"

Tinker sprang up and saw him say, "I gots to run, Lucy. It's Mister Jimmy Tallant. Somebody shot him—"

"Lawd, Beck, was it you?"

"No, but they'll think so. They thinks so now."

"Who thinks? How come they thinks?"

"I was coming along the path, hoping to see did Mister Tallant have any little job for me, when I heard some talking and a shot, right close, but I never thought nothing except it was somebody out hunting, till I looked over in the edge of the pasture and there was a man laying and nobody else near. I come up close to see who and there was blood running out and I says, 'Oh God, it's Mister Tallant!' "

"Was he dead?"

"I don't know. There wasn't time to see. Then's when I saw two white men walking away up at the rise of the hill toward the highway, and I thought I better get away from here, but one was coming back already, pointing at me and hollering, 'You can say what you want to, but we know you did it, nigger. We saw you and we know and you sure better run! You better get lost, nigger!' "

"Oh Jesus, Beck!"

"What chance I got, Lucy, if they say it was me? What can I do? I gots to run, Lucy, as fast and far as I can. . . ."

Tinker was running herself by then, back along the path to the woods that Beck had fled from. She was the first after Beck Dozer to find him.

Bud Grantham, some little time after the New Orleans car had driven away, had begun to look for him here and there, and so came upon them both in the dewy corner of the pasture just at dusk, she on her knees in blood beside him, tearing cloth from his shirt.

"Call an ambulance!" she cried across the field.

He ran at once to obey, not completely understanding. He felt that day that his tough old heart had been grieved once, and now again, beyond anything it had been fitting to expect. To Bud nothing seemed to be happening decently, and it was at this, as much as for fear that Jimmy was seriously injured, that he almost wept as he made for the telephone.

part three

30. Nan Hunt had a caller. The girls, Cissy and Marcia Mae, sitting out on the side porch where they had hurried and quickly shut the curtained French doors because they weren't dressed and had no wish to talk to anybody, could hear from within the murmuring rise and fall of ladies' voices. They did not make out the words.

Cissy was doing her nails. A manicure case waited on the floor beside her chair and she held a large open bottle of polish remover clamped between her bare knees. She wet bits of cotton with the remover and cleaned the old polish away in gaudy smears. The reek of the chemical was all out of proportion to the importance of the affair, but so, for that matter, was Cissy's degree of concentration upon it. Gunshot would scarcely have disturbed her. Her nails grew in firm ovals out of the moist pads of her fingertips; she enticed them to a shapely length with her emery boards. Marcia Mae, who glanced now and again over her plain hands, could not resist watching her sister's strategies.

Cissy was nineteen, and poised that summer at a moment of femininity so intense that her virginity seemed scandalously out of order in the universe. The flesh of her arm was soft as freshly molded butter; even the redolence of the bathroom when she left it held something all lazily like a sigh. She was not at all beautiful; perhaps she was not even pretty: she made everybody so nervous that nobody knew any better how she looked than Kerney Woolbright did, with her eyes like chocolate fudge still warm from the pan and her hair as glossy as a blooded chestnut's coat. If the fact of her innocence was disturbing, the question of her self-knowledge was worse: every touch of the file lured the little hands into a greater sensual alertness—was Cissy so unaware of this?

"If you paint them now," said Marcia Mae, "I'll scream."

Called up, Cissy questioned that she had been addressed. Her little uncertainties were charming. She touched her tongue to her bottom lip before she spoke.

"Didn't you ever like to paint your fingernails? When you were my age, I mean."

She had almost said, "when you were young," and Marcia Mae knew it.

"Some women, even at thirty, can still manage that sort of thing."

"Mother says you ought to quit it, though, after you're mature."

"You mean to say you admit you're immature?"

Cissy, like a plot of lush foliage reluctant to stir in the breeze, only yawned. Her voice, like her mother's, was seldom raised. But she was apparently not without kindness.

"I wish I had grown up when you did," she said. "You all had a lot more fun. I used to be jealous of you, always going somewhere with Duncan and Jimmy and Tinker Taylor. I used to wish I would hurry up and grow too. But it isn't all that much fun."

"We did have fun. But there were lots more of us than just four."

"You were the main ones. Things didn't happen without you."

"Yes, we were the main ones."

"You and Duncan always went in Jimmy Tallant's car."

"That's because Duncan never had a car of his own."

"No! I didn't know that!" In Cissy's time, for a man not to own a car seemed as bad as if he never brushed his teeth or shined his shoes. "But he was a big football player!" Her sense of shock increased.

Marcia Mae laughed. "Duncan Harper was the only All-American in captivity, I reckon, who never so much as owned a Ford, let alone a Cadillac."

"Is he still that way?" Cissy asked.

She did not look up, but in the ensuing silence she steadily painted a fingernail with a tiny brush.

"You'll have to ask his wife," said Marcia Mae.

Cissy painted another nail. "You know, Kerney is just crazy about her. He likes her more than he does me."

"There's something pathetic about her," said Marcia Mae. "She makes men think she has to be protected. God knows from what."

"She's common," said Cissy and dipped her little brush.

"Men don't care if women are common," said Marcia Mae.

"Look what she did," Cissy pursued, "when Jimmy Tallant got shot. She went all out, stopping the blood, getting an ambulance, crying right in front of everybody, sitting all night in the hospital. I'd just die before I'd do anything like that. It's like crying out loud at a funeral, or saying you're constipated."

"What a prissy little thing you are!" said Marcia Mae.

"It isn't just me. Everybody said that, said she ought to be ashamed taking things over like that when it was another woman's husband. Even Grandmother said so, and she never talks about anybody."

"Oh nuts. I don't like her either, but that's not the reason. I think you've got a right to get worked up over anybody's shot husband you want to."

"Then why don't you like her?"

Marcia Mae hesitated. "I didn't really mean I don't like her. I mean I didn't like her when I knew her best. That was nearly ten years ago."

"Well, why didn't you like her then?"

Marcia Mae set both hands into her waistline and, sitting

up straight as though weary from long traveling, flexed her slender back. "Well, she was always so little and cute. Her fanny bobbled when she crossed the room. She would listen to shady stories, but she wouldn't tell them. She went with Tallant for years and never gave an inch."

"Never did what?"

"Never slept with him, I mean."

"Should you?" inquired Cissy, who had taken root in her mother's virtuous advice that if you gave a man what he wanted he wouldn't want it any more.

"Should you, shouldn't you? I don't know. I think it's wrong to parade it like a bowl of cream before a cat. I think it's disgusting."

Cissy capped her little filthy-smelling bottle and spread her fingers out on her bare knees to dry.

"But maybe she's changed now," said Marcia Mae.

She lighted a cigarette and drew her knees up in the swing and circled them with her arms. She had really fine legs, better than her sister's, whose ankles were too round and thighs shapeless where the little-girl fat had not cleared away. But Cissy, if she lived to be a hundred, would never have an inch of flesh that would hold a candle to Marcia Mae. Marcia Mae's ankle shot down as straight and trim as a blade, and it was fleet: even in repose it ran and halted to make the stroke and ran again. A certain clean physical intonation of superiority—carriage, people say—she would have perhaps had anyway, being well-born, but the limbs' decisive justness, the back's subleties, the neck's pride—all these she had earned without knowing it, climbing high into the grape arbor, racing with Negro children to see the minstrel parade, swinging whole mornings through out in the pasture swing. When the yard and the woods and the Negro children fell away into a dream world (though they were all still there, the sense of them had vanished), she had gone on to tennis and in college spent more time in the swimming pool, they said, than in class. On her idle wrist now a round gold watch no bigger than a dime was bound by a gold snake chain. She glanced at it now and again.

Before the two girls the level side lawn spread away like a gracious open fan. Its grass was soft gray-green, rich this year by reason of the wet spring. The black shadows which embossed it fell where they would: feathery, but in grand possession, toward dawn, lightly sustaining the big dew, they shrank up tight and black toward noon, and swelled darkly on till five or thereabouts when the sun shot a glare through, this being the only hour you could not enjoy sitting out in the yard. Flowering shrubs flourished in their accustomed places, deep-rooted and assured as trees. There were a few flower beds near the porch steps and one or two far out, very far, there where the bluff dropped suddenly and Jason Hunt had strung a white-painted chain for fear someone might fall in the dark—he could even be sued. Not much was blooming now at this high point of summer with all its layered green and shadow. Roses were in bloom, and certain stiff common flowers like zinnias and marigolds, but none of these were on the lawn. It seemed to have had its own way about things, and if it had rejected roses, that was that.

The fact was, however, that the lawn took a terrible amount of labor. Nan Hunt talked about it so much nobody heard her any more. She was out every morning in a large straw hat, with shears and work gloves. She directed a Negro boy, who drove her to distraction. She wouldn't "get rid of him" because he had a "growing hand," but you had to "keep in behind him" because he was "not worth killing." He cost her a great deal of anguish, and after dinner every day ran the power mower, a wonderfully sleepy sound for napping.

His name was George, and right now he was sitting on the far side of the cedar tree out back of the kitchen, dozing. He was the same who used to play with Marcia Mae and had pushed her in the swing so many times, including the day the rope broke on the rise and slung her up so high and she looked down out of mid-air and saw a boy throw down his gun and run and wondered why he did it. A bumblebee warred twice against the porch screen; a green lizard ran across a flagstone.

With effort like rising out of deep waters, Marcia Mae re-heard her own last voice, and added, "Maybe I would like her all right now. Maybe I would like her just fine. I don't know."

"You could go call on her," Cissy suggested.

"Damn it, Marjorie Angeline," for this was Cissy's true outlandish name, "I'll go to see who I please."

Cissy yawned again. "I wish I had a Coke. I'm sleepy."

"So do I. Go get us one."

"My nails aren't dry. Besides, I can't go through the living room without speaking to whoever is in there with Mother."

"You could go around the house," suggested Marcia Mae.

"Umm," said Cissy, meaning that she didn't want to.

Marcia Mae stood up and, tucking her shirt into her shorts, caught up a wrap-around skirt from the back of her chair.

"Going for a walk?" Cissy ventured.

But her sister did not seem to have heard her.

"Now Mother will make me come speak to the company," Cissy complained.

"You'll survive," said Marcia Mae, and went off arrow-straight across the lawn. The path lowered her, gently at first, then quickly; her high bright head vanished downward among the trees.

a
rendezvous

31. Little by little, only as much each time they met as her pride would allow, Marcia Mae had told Duncan about her life away from Lacey. Slowly, she had brought herself to admit that this was why she had come home, to tell him everything. He was the only one to hear that behind the high proud look she had whenever Red O'Donnell was mentioned, lived the memory of a marriage that had not been a raging success.

The big handsome Irishman had loved to drink and party; he had loved the figure he cut in Marine officer's uniform. He thought his Southern bride was the prettiest girl he'd ever seen, and because he had always lived in California, he was pleased to be ordered to the San Diego Marine base. For the first few months he was charming, generous, and gay.

Then routine began to weigh on him. He was assigned to paper work at the base, which bored him; his opinion of his superior took hours to describe and he described it every night when he got home. On weekends he felt it necessary for them to go to parties with other young married couples of the service. He could whip a party together in no time, inviting along as his best friends in creation people whom he had met a few hours before in a bar. These people, Marcia Mae said, invariably seemed all right; they were attractive, well-dressed, well-paid, often amusing. She learned that after a certain point in the evening's drinking it was best not to enter any bedroom. Once after midnight she discovered that when looking for an ash tray it was more tactful not to walk back of the sofa. One night Red vanished for several hours with a movie bit actress somebody had brought along; he claimed afterwards not to have remembered anything after ten o'clock. They had a terrible fight—it seemed he expected women to fight, and moreover expected her to be angry with him, but not for very long.

A day or two later, his ex-wife appeared. He had never mentioned that he had one. They still owned some property together in Los Angeles and what she had in mind was that he make over the property to her in lieu of back alimony. "I don't really owe her any alimony," Red explained to Marcia Mae. "I was just supposed to pay it till she married again and she married inside two months. But now she's got another divorce, so she claims I have to start paying her again. If anybody ought to have alimony it was me." And he would plunge into the long list of her faults. When she telephoned, however, which was often, he became as docile as you please and made appointments with her to discuss business or see lawyers. Marcia Mae put her foot down. "You either stay with me or go back to her," she told him. "Do you want to go back to her?" "Oh, no," he said dolefully. "She spends too much money." He was sitting on the couch in the living room of the duplex they lived in, and was heartily worrying about himself. Marcia Mae burst right out laughing. From that moment she stopped believing that she loved him or ever had. "You get rid of her," he begged. "You start answering the phone and say I'm out of town." She seemed not to be able to stop laughing. He was finally offended. "I don't see what's so funny," he said. "The joke is on me," she told him. "I left the best man in the state of Mississippi for you —for this."

She began to think of leaving him, but she was too hard-headed to do it right away; she hated the thought of the news going back home, of the people who would say "Uh-huh, I told you so." While she was still debating, she learned to be fond of him in a way, the way one feels for a child after taking care of it for a time. "Which only proves," she told Duncan, "that I never loved him. I was never hurt enough."

His orders came, and he was gone. On shipboard he wrote her two passionate letters in a style not quite illiterate, begging her pardon for everything and saying how sweet she was. She had to admit that she cried over them.

One day she came back walking from the grocery store to their duplex on a sunny California winter day and saw the telegram on the table where the cleaning woman had left it. She knew already what it said. She put some coffee on the stove first, thinking that if the coffee was going before she read it, then afterward she would have to do something about the coffee. Later she went to the beach in the car Red had left with her and walked by the sea for a long while.

Later communications filled in some details: the telegram had merely stated a fact. Finally a picture formed quite clearly in her head. There had been ten men gathered in a fringe of palms just off the beachhead at Tarawa. A grenade had come bouncing out of the jungle and rolled at their feet; it was seconds from detonation. Nine of the men had plunged to earth, face down, clutching into the ground, but the tenth had leaped deliberately upon it and had been blown to smithereens. She could imagine the island: palm trees rising in a proud disheveled way, strong sun, the sea and white curling foam, the square-nosed landing craft rolling in and every so often a bright flash of fire. And there at center stood ten men just before a moment of impetuous decision. She was linked back to the time she had first laid eyes on Red O'Donnell, a carelessly handsome man walking straight toward her the moment he set eyes on her at a soldier's dance, saying in his confident Yankee way, "You're not to dance with anybody but me," and thirty minutes later, "You don't know it yet, but you're going to marry me." It was his sense of freedom that had drawn her. Of course, he would jump on a grenade if he wanted to. Now he was a war hero.

The nine men he had saved appeared one at a time or in pairs, always in dress uniform, presented themselves with great formality and told her their stories, turning the Marine dress cap in their big hands and sitting forward on the edge of the sofa. Then, very likely, the man next door in the duplex would knock and say, "The Missus thought you might like this," and it would be an upside-down cake or a pot of Brunswick stew or half a lamb roast. Then the Marine would be persuaded to stay. Life for Marcia Mae at that point entered a kind of beautiful vacuum. The woman next door cooked herself crazy, the sun shone, the flowers bloomed, the men Red had saved all fell in love with her, the car Red had left ran like a dream.

She was out on the beach for a picnic one night with the ninth and last one. The sun had set far out over the ocean, and she said, "Now it will go on to Tarawa, and shine on the beach there and the sea and the little bit of jungle with the palm trees, just exactly the way it was shining when Red blew himself up." So the ninth man said, "Who told you the sun was shining?" She couldn't remember. "It was rainy," said the Marine, "with a heavy wind, the tail of a typhoon, we kept saying. Things were confused. I kept thinking I had forgotten something. It was hard to do the simplest thing. Salt water blew down my back. I was sitting by O'Donnell in the LCI coming in, and I said, 'There's salt water down my back, for Christ's sake,' and he said, 'Mine, too.'" After a time he said to Marcia Mae, "I don't see what difference it makes whether he got blown up in the sun or in the rain." She said, "I don't see why either, but it does." She asked him,

"When are you going home?" "It's like I told you," he said, "I don't want to leave you ever at all." "Yes," she said, "but think of what you've got back home," because she had heard all this from eight before him, and knew exactly how to impress it on him. "There *is* the wife and kids," he said. "I guess responsibility is what you might call it." "I think you might," she agreed.

With the illusion of the sunlit explosion, her last hold on a dream vanished too. Her husband's valor was extensively publicized and she found that the woman next door was not the only one eager to do things for her. She accepted a free business course, got good jobs one after another, keeping them only so long as they interested her. She was twice engaged, but her enthusiasm waned decidedly each time.

One day she came back to Lacey.

Now that she was very near the end of telling Duncan Harper everything she could remember of her years away, she wondered what would happen next. Walking, she came from the woods into open pasture, took off the skirt that had shielded her legs from scratches and some idea about snakes, and threw it over her head for protection against the July afternoon sun. As she came down to cross the branch by one of the many small fords the cattle made, she heard footsteps approaching from a path hidden in trees. She withdrew along the sandy stream, concealing herself in a thicket that came down into the water.

A Negro boy came into view, carrying a molasses bucket full of blackberries in either hand. She watched the innocent gliding white of his eyeball. The tin bucket touched sunlight. He stepped straight into the stream; water sucked and sloshed into the diamond-shaped cut-out places in his rubber boots. The rich black fruit lay piled above the buckets' mouths, but the boy's easy stride held every berry safe. She knew the way of a wood enough to know he could not possibly see her. How was it he made her feel that he knew she was there?

She waited till his footsteps died quite away on the roll of pasture behind her. Then for motion there was only a buzzard, high up, asleep on the air, and for sound a cricket that woke, wound once, then drowsed again. Every leaf, grass blade, and twigged arm of brush seemed hushed in contemplation of the heat, and motion went so against this prevalence that it took a penalty: she was wet with sweat and trembling when she gained the top of the bluff and saw the car waiting for her where the old road forked. Black spots danced before her eyes. When she saw no one inside, she gasped.

Then Duncan called to her. To escape so much hot metal he had gone a short distance away to the edge of the bluff and was sitting in the shade of an old beech tree. He had taken off his coat and rolled up his sleeves. Sun through the narrow leaves speckled his arms and turned the hairs golden. She came to him and he drew her down and close to him with one arm.

"You're shaking. What's the matter?"

"I thought I would have a sunstroke." Their voices had fallen at once to whispers.

They clung together; kissing, their heads sank against the tree trunk. At last she pulled apart from him and straightened, saying, "How awful in this weather. It makes me feel like a bitch."

"You looked worried when you came up the path. I was watching you."

"Cissy has been baiting me again, the disgusting child! You can't tell me she doesn't know I see you. Coming through the pasture I heard a colored boy and hid from him. Then when I saw the car without you in it, I thought at first it must be someone else's car and we'd be trapped."

"You're having a hard day."

She broke a twig between her fingers. "I don't actually feel guilty myself. I feel that other people are trying to make me say I'm wrong whether I think so or not. I've always hated that about Lacey. They all know how right they are. Anybody who disagrees is wrong. Why shouldn't I see you? Who else is there in the world I'd want to talk to? If we want to meet for dinner right uptown in the café and sit there till closing time, whose business is it to have any opinion about it?"

He did not mention whose business it could be said to be, but only observed, "It might be a little hard to convince anybody, sure enough, that the only thing between us was conversation."

She almost flared up at him; but the rueful humor in his tone was too familiar and dear, and what he said was true. She laughed in spite of herself.

"Oh, Duncan, I do love you. I know you love me, even if you won't tell me so."

A cricket wound a dry spiral of sound into the heat. She was forever coming at him in a new way with this question. She raised her eyes to his and caught him watching her with the worried, removed look people have for sick children.

"I knew you had to see me, Marcia Mae. I knew that all along."

"You're going to make it out you were only doing your duty!" She hurled down a handful of broken twigs. "You're the most dishonest person I've ever known."

"All right, just suppose I said, Yes, I love you, I'll never leave you! What next? What would you want me to do about it?"

"Well—" She hesitated. "I never thought we could be happy staying here. Beyond that—" She made a little gesture. "I don't want to try to run your life for you."

He laughed. "You just want me to leave my family and home and business. Beyond that I'm perfectly free."

"Nobody made you find me that Sunday in the woods! Nobody made you show up today, no, nor any other day!"

They fell unhappily silent.

She spread out her wrap-around skirt and lay on it face downward, propped on her elbows. She pulled up grass, clearing a little bare space to draw in with a stick.

"How is Jimmy Tallant?" she inquired.

"About the same. It's touch and go. I stopped by the hospital this morning and they let me in to talk to him for a minute. He still says some strange white man shot him."

"Everybody thinks it was that Negro. Even the Negroes think so. Jonas told me."

"Well, I don't think so," said Duncan.

"You think it was some white man Jimmy Tallant never saw before and nobody has ever seen since?"

"I think Tallant and Grantham were up to their necks in crooked business. It could have been any number of people."

"The first person there was Tinker, wasn't it? What does she say?"

"Just what she always said. That she was at Dozer's when he ran in and said Jimmy had been shot. Nobody was with Jimmy when Tinker got to him. But Grantham contends that Dozer did it, though he didn't see it happen."

Marcia Mae wrote "Tinker" on the bare space of ground, then erased it with her fist.

Duncan ground out a cigarette under his heel. "She'd tell me anything she knew."

"Listen!" said Marcia Mae and looked up from writing "Duncan" on the ground. "I thought I heard someone."

"There's nothing. You're nervous today."

"I always expect people to jump out of trees on us. I always feel better inside."

He stood up presently, knocking the dust from his trousers, and put down his hand to her. "We'll go inside then."

They walked together up a disused, shady path which gave on an open space with a deserted Negro house. The gate was broken in, the yard weed-grown; gigantic purplish-crimson Negro plants, the kind called "prince feathers," plumed above the steps and the floor of the sagging porch. Marcia Mae had found the house and had first brought them there. If they were happier going down the familiar path together than they had been so far that day, it was perhaps because they had come to equal terms in a common attraction.

Marcia Mae realized this, and wondered if he came with her only to give her, generously, this sense of an equality they had lost. The thought depressed her; she forgot it, but it returned again when she lay with a hand under her head on the little pile of cotton left over from last year's picking —they had found it in the only room of the house not full of wasps. The shadows had lengthened, streaking the bare dusty floor. They had not spoken for a long time; then Duncan turned abruptly to her from the window, demanding, "Why did you leave me? *Why?*"

There was finality in his voice; this time he would have to know. Looking toward him in surprise, she understood that his need to see her had been as great as hers for him. She saw his searching baffled eyes and knew that impossible as it seemed, she would have to try to answer him.

what
she
remembered

32.   At the time, ten years before, her reasons had all seemed
very clear, but now there was no one answer she could give
him. She could see what she had done only in terms of what
she remembered, and she did all she could, which was to
start remembering again.

"That summer," she said. "That awful summer."

"It was terrible, yes."

"My brother died."

"Everett. Early in June."

"We had to put off the wedding "

"I remember."

"There is one thing I have to say that nobody has ever
said." She sat up. "It's better Everett died. Nobody would
come out and say so, but everybody thought it. You wouldn't
say so either."

He winced, turning away. "If everybody does know things
like that, what's the good of saying them? It seems kinder
not to."

"Kind! Duncan, I saw with my own eyes how glad Daddy
was when Everett died. Mother felt it, and all the love she'd
had for Everett, the weak one, her only son, turned into hate
for Jason. She was left living with the man who'd killed
him—"

"Killed him?"

"Wanted him dead. People hear wishes as loud as guns."

"You think it was all your father's fault, the way Everett
was?"

"No, it was Mother's too. They pulled him two ways. He
was sensitive and lazy and clever and he never found himself.

Daddy bought him a gun. He made him go deer hunting. They stood on a stand together in the freezing cold and mist from before daylight on till ten and when the deer came by, Daddy shot and said 'Shoot' to Everett. Everett was funny when he told me about it. He said he knew the gun had to go off, so somehow or other he jerked the trigger. He said the miracle was that he didn't hit Daddy. He said he couldn't have come within a mile of the deer. But when it fell, Daddy, to cheer him up, said, 'You got him, Son, you got him!' Then he dragged him out to where the deer had fallen and was heaving to rise and run again with one leg shattered and the heart torn but still pumping out the hot blood. Daddy kept a death grip on Everett to keep him from running away, then he slit the deer's throat with his knife and shoved Everett down to bathe his face in the blood. The old hunter's ritual, you know. Everett saw the big soft eyes veiling over, and the shattered bone in the leg poking up and Daddy's hand coming at him with big globs of blood smoking on it. He began to vomit and say, 'I didn't do it, you did it, you did it!' He broke away and ran. He met some of the other hunters coming in to see the kill. They laughed about it. Daddy was humiliated. He told everybody that Everett was sick and he took him home that night. Everett did get sick, as it turned out. Mother stowed him away under hot-water bottles. He was sick all during Christmas. His fever nearly broke the thermometer. Daddy wouldn't come in the room. When Everett lay in bed recuperating, he cut out little bits of velvet and silks and taffetas from Grandmother's rag bag and made Cissy a wonderful doll. It was the prettiest doll I ever saw, a Turkish doll with long balloon pants bound in silver at the ankles and a wicked black mustache. And a fez. Daddy saw Cissy with it and said, 'Where'd you get that, Baby?' She said, 'Everett made it for me.' He reached out his hand to take it. 'Don't you touch it,' Mother said. I was there. I saw it all. I felt sorry for all of them, but I didn't understand. Now that I understand it, I don't feel anything any more. Once you know whodunit, you don't care about the book any longer. They killed him. I understand it. He was miserable. I think it's better he's dead."

"I had the impression," said Duncan, "that Everett died of bronchial pneumonia."

"Yes, but they had set up the pattern long ago. When anybody rejected him, he got sick. Mother would nurse him. The last time was your fault, actually."

"Me! What on earth do you mean?"

"He had finished college. He was supposed to go to work, find a job, *do* something. Life was closing in on him, tightening over him like a fist. He wandered out of one room and into another and read in stuffy corners. The summer got hotter and hotter. Daddy wouldn't look at him. I was too kind to him. Grandmother was knitting him some Argyle socks. Mother planned the meals just for him.

"He used to ride around in the car with us at night. I thought he enjoyed that. We'd make him quote us poetry. He never seemed to want to go home.

"He didn't want to leave us alone because he didn't want us to make love. He was in love with you, Duncan. Now don't deny you knew it."

He did not answer.

"He was out in the garden alone," she continued, "or out near the sundial beyond the cedars or in first one room and then the other where the sun had left for the day—there are lots of rooms in our house—I can't tell you just how many there are right off, because when I'm away I remember some at times and others at other times—but it does seem to me when Everett died he took with him some rooms I can't find any more. He had an imagination and it was always going —imagining, imagining. That's different from thinking. It pulls everybody off base, makes them nervous. When it's going on in one room, the room you're in looks dead and plain because that other one is so alive. So he drank too much, standing on the back porch sipping whisky through the long sweet awful dusks, and read every book not only in our house but in the library and all he could borrow from other people in town. I think it must have been the day he put down the last one that we had all gone away. I was in Stark for fittings on my trousseau, and Mother and your mother were up at the church to talk about decorations. The house was empty and you were in your empty house. He got up and went to you."

"I never told that to a soul, Marcia Mae, not even you."

"He told me himself when his fever got high. He kept saying, 'Duncan hates me now, I know Duncan hates me,' and I would say, 'Why, Everett?' and he would say, 'I saw him in his house and now he hates me.' When he died and I knew Daddy was glad, that was when I tried to get you to run away with me. Do you remember?"

"We were sitting in the yard," he recalled, "in that double swing where Everett used to read books all afternoon. My mother came up the walk and went inside. You said that was the fourth time she'd been to call since the funeral, then you said you weren't going to be nice about it, that the reason she came was that she loved being in with the Standsbury family. You said you were sick of everybody agreeing to cover up the plain truth by being nice to one another. Then you said we had to leave home."

"It was a day a lot like this one: hot, shady, beautiful, still. The lawn was lovely and the house was quiet. You could even think that death was something like poetry. When the swing went back I thought, With all this horror in people how can things look so beautiful? and when the swing went forward I thought, It is so beautiful maybe the horror isn't real, and then I put my foot on the ground and stopped the swing, because I saw them both, both together, the beauty and the horror, like one gorgeous rotten fruit. That was when I knew we'd have to leave. I had an absolute conviction of it."

"The only thing you didn't consider was that your having an absolute conviction of something did not mean that I would have it too. You threw it all at me at once."

"Just as it came to me, right in the swing."

"You wanted me to sell the grocery store and my property, and we would take the money and go West, take one of the coaching jobs I kept getting letters about, wait till my draft number was called. Then you would follow me around to army camps or, if I went overseas, you would get a defense job and wait for me to come back and then—and then what? I forget."

"Oh, just that we'd start from nothing but ourselves, clean, out West somewhere. We couldn't stay in the South and be free. In the South it's nothing but family, family. We couldn't breathe even, until we left. I explained it all. When I finished you said, 'Do you guess it's too soon after the funeral for us to go to a nice cool movie?' "

"At that point you jumped up, slapped me in the face, and walked into the house. From then on I never had any peace. You said we had to leave, that I didn't know a bad thing when I saw it."

"You were very patient. You said you were all your mother had, that your property was all here, that Jason had already turned over some of his business to you, that he would make over more in time, that we would have a house of our own—way across town all by ourselves—imagine! You said I was just upset over Everett." She paused until he looked at her. "If there's anything these ten years prove, Duncan, I hope at least you know now that *I was not just upset over Everett.*"

He did not reply to her vigor, her assertiveness. He came to her and held her close to him. "I failed to understand you. Is that what you're saying?"

"It wasn't only me you failed to understand. It was everything."

But she had softened. She studied the lines around his eyes, running back into the boyish fuzz of hair that his blondness kept, shading out a more definite hairline. She pressed up the skin of his brow and watched the long horizontal lines disappear, and then as her hand relaxed saw their inevitable return.

"Before he died," she went on finally, "Everett thought there were soldiers out by the summerhouse. They were in ragged clothes, he said, all gathered around somebody or something on the ground, and talking, until one left and ran toward the house. This was a hot afternoon. It had threatened a storm at dinner, but it blew over, then things seemed drier and stiller than before. Flies had come into the house. The soldier went past the corner of the porch. Everett kept asking where he'd gone. Grandmother said that her mother told how during the Civil War some soldiers had stopped on the lawn. One of them was sick and they were afraid he had cholera. They wouldn't bring him in the house, but one of them finally came to ask for water and food. She couldn't recall the rest of the story."

She said: "The day I really left you, I didn't have any idea I was doing it. I walked out of the house just before the afternoon broke. Those were long days after Everett died. It seemed that the heat would never climb high enough, satisfy itself enough, to start down again. Mother had to start taking shots for her headaches. Daddy kept right on calling you in to talk business. We had let them put the wedding off three months. There was a war in Europe. You said we couldn't hurt the family now, we ought to help them. Mother was asleep in a pitch-black room. I thought I was so nervous because maybe I was getting the curse. I walked down through the cedars and out into the sun. I had not walked to town since I was a child. People looked at me on the street without speaking, it seemed so odd to see Marcia Mae Hunt walking. I had forgotten how broken the old sidewalks were, with cow hooves printed in them. I thought I would buy a Coke at the drugstore and walk back home, then I saw at the drugstore that the Greyhound bus was in. It was going East. So I got on it and rode over to Stark.

"As I was drinking another Coke at the Stark drugstore, I saw a sign up that said there was a dance at Willett Hill for the members of the armed forces. It said the bus would stop at the schoolhouse at seven to pick up the girls from Stark. I drank the Coke and went to the movies and ate popcorn. Then I ate a hamburger in the café. And a piece of coconut pie. I was just on time for the bus to the dance. The other girls were all dressed up in low-cut peasant blouses. They had artificial flowers pinned in their hair and too much black lipstick on. They also wore fancy strapped sandals and had their toenails painted. But they were mainly country girls, you know, and hadn't done any of this in too wise a way. They seemed to feel sorry for me, because I had on a tailored cotton skirt and shirt and scarcely any make-up. Finally one of them pulled a spare artificial flower out of her bag and offered it to me. It was a red poppy and smelled of dime-store powder. I thought at first I would put it in my hair if it killed me, but then I knew I couldn't. Whatever I meant by going off like that, it wasn't for a pack of country girls to call me 'Hun' and offer me Dentyne.

"At the dance they all left me and herded in little bunches on one side of the room and giggled, waiting for the soldiers to come ask them to dance. All the soldiers, instead, began to ask me to dance. For one thing, I was alone; for another, I was blonde. It never hurt anything, being a blonde. The little soldiers were sweet, touching somehow, like Confederate soldiers are, and I remembered the soldiers Everett saw on the lawn, though you didn't believe he saw them. We argued and argued, you remember? It was Jimmy Tallant who said, 'For Christ's sake, Duncan, let her believe it if she wants to.' And you said, 'I don't care if *she* believes it; she wants *me* to believe it too.' "

Duncan recalled, "And Tallant yelled, 'Well, believe it too then, for Christ's sake!' We were all over at Stark at the café, and all a little tight on beer."

"Tinker said, 'I believe it, Marcia Mae.' " After a silence, Marcia Mae added, "She has a soft voice."

"Yes, she has."

"Will Tallant live or die?"

"They still can't say."

"I looked for you that summer, Duncan. I looked and looked. I trailed every scent like a bloodhound and bayed all night at empty trees. I wanted, passionately, for you to understand. If I could have showed you once why we had to get away, that they were turning our love into a complicated family thing, that they had killed Everett and oh, you kept going to talk business with Daddy and saying that Everett was out of his head with high fever, and you didn't, couldn't, wouldn't understand!"

"I suppose Red O'Donnell understood perfectly," said Duncan.

"That's funny," she said, "I never once expected him to. He was a Yankee."

She said: "He wasn't even supposed to be at the dance. He

was a Marine on a three-day pass from the Pensacola base, determined to hitch-hike as far through the South as time would allow, any direction he got a ride. He had waited an hour in Willett Hill for a ride and when nobody stopped he kept reading the sign for the soldiers' dance. Finally he thought, If nobody comes along for another fifteen minutes, I'll go to the dance. He went and there I was. We called it destiny.

"We left the dance. We went to an all-night café and tourist court out at the highway junction. We kept drinking whisky in a booth. I kept getting him to talk to me. He might have been a creature from Mars. He had no consciousness of families, small towns, roots, ties, or any sort of custom. I expected lightning to strike him. I had always taken so much for granted. I had never gone with anyone but you. I thought I knew everything, but here was someone unconcerned with everything I knew. I won't deny remembering anything about it, though some of it was always awfully vague, but I woke in a cabin of the tourist court at three A.M., cold sober, saying, 'Marcia Mae Hunt, what are you doing here?' I did exactly what I told myself to do and came straight home. On the bus. The driver let me off at the corner.

"It was a warm night with a moon, very sweet. I remember it so well. I was tired and the house had never looked so good. I thought, Well, what a crazy thing I did. White houses in the South in the summer at night, with all the big trees so dark and deep, they float, you know, and the sweet air that comes through the window and over your bed—

"Well, unfortunately, there was a light on upstairs. Mother was worried; she had thought I was out with you, but you had called around eight, then some lady in town called and asked Mother why I went to Stark on the bus and an old friend of Mother's from Stark called and asked what I was doing over there in the picture show by myself eating pop-corn. Then Mother called you back and promised to make me call you the minute I came in. All this that night. The next morning a cousin from Willett Hill telephoned to say she had heard but could not believe that I had come to the soldier's dance *alone*, and by afternoon you and Daddy had had a conference about just how upset was I really over Everett's death, and afterwards I saw you and said, 'Let's get out of here, let's go now.' You said, 'Marcia Mae, I'm pretty damn sick of your carrying on this way.' You said, 'You might as well realize that I'm not going one step anywhere, and you aren't either.' Mother was calling out of the bedroom to re-mind me for the fourth time that I hadn't been uptown to get the mail—she still didn't think it proper for her to go about. She had a great greed for sympathy notes and kept getting them from old boy friends. Daddy called at me from the library, 'Are you going to run uptown for your mother, or do I have to do it?' And I looked at you and knew you thought there was nothing on the face of the earth that ought to stand in the way of my going uptown for the mail. I de-spised you, Duncan, for the first and last time. It was an awful feeling.

"So I went uptown to get the mail.

"Red O'Donnell was standing out in front of the drugstore where the bus had dropped him. He had sweated out his only two shirts and had bought a plaid cotton sports shirt. West-erners are like that; they'll wear whatever they feel like wear-ing. They think it's nobody's business what they have on. I was never so glad to see anyone. He could have been in over-alls. I thought the best thing I'd ever done was get drunk and go to a tourist court with a strange Marine. I thought, At least he's free. I said to myself, I wish I were free like that. Then I thought, I love him."

It was not clear at what point twilight had commenced its serious summer ritual. Already the shadowy, dusty room seemed a reflected place and silence a spell impossible to break by any means close at hand. Then they heard the bump against the door.

They had already decided what they would do if anybody came along. They had discovered a small windowless room, a storeroom perhaps, or closet, set between the two larger rooms. Marcia Mae was to close herself inside there while Duncan got rid of whoever it was.

When he heard the sound he was instantly on his feet, bringing her up with him, and as she showed alarmingly no inclination to stir, he pushed her toward the little low door. The sound came again, but louder and with more intention, a thud and shove against the door's lower half, as if someone struck a knee there. Duncan walked directly forward then, removed the wooden peg from the latch, and opened the door.

It was a dog, a mongrel hound the color of the Mississippi River, whose hide was nothing but a coat of paint over the skeleton, and whose eyes were totally prepared for human life, understanding at one time both the giant succulent unplucked hambone and the dishpan full of scalding water. The hindquarters were set low at a bias, alert to dodge and flee; while one forepaw rested bravely, even handsomely, and the other was lifted in all the gentility of prayer. His nose had pushed the door.

"It's just a dog," he turned to call to her, but saw she had not moved to hide. He flushed with annoyance at her, but before he could speak they both grew suddenly ashamed; so he stepped outside and, sitting on the door sill, began to coax the dog back to him.

The animal came in low to the ground, the tail wagging between his legs. Speaking quietly, Duncan was at last allowed to stroke the low head. Marcia Mae sat down on the sill beside him, tucking her clothes together. "He's shaking all over, poor thing," she said compassionately, but when her hand moved the dog leaped away, and would not return, though he longed to.

"You frightened him," said Duncan. "You put out your hand too fast. Here, boy. Here." He whistled softly. "He probably lived here," he went on, "else why would he be trying to come into a house where there isn't any smell of food? Probably when the family left here to go to Detroit and work in the dee-fense plant, they had to leave him."

"Yes," she said, "only that would be so long ago."

"They say they don't forget," said Duncan. "It's the hound blood."

"We sit here mourning over a damn nigger dog," she said, "as though we had nothing better to bother us."

The dog crept halfway in and lay down, observing everything about them. A little more and he would have belonged to them. When it grew as dark outside as it had been inside the cabin, they walked back to the car. The dog hovered, following at greater and greater distances, until their departure left him alone with his hour's bewilderment of heart.

**the way
back
home**

33. When he drove back to Lacey, Duncan did not go immediately home. He noticed with relief that his mother's house looked empty, so he stopped there and went inside, walking into the unlocked hallway and back to his old room, the one she kept just as he had always had it. Duncan was an only child.

The room was almost dark, but he did not switch on the

lamp. He sat down in the straight chair at his old high-school desk, his head lowered. There was always with Marcia Mae the problem of her vividness: whether she fell out of the sky at him or climbed up a hill to meet him, it took awhile for him to right himself.

From the empty Negro house she had returned to the car with him and had sat for a time on the front seat beside him. At last she said, "Duncan, I cannot bear this sneaking and hiding and deceiving."

"You don't see how it is."

"No, I don't," she said. "One other thing I can't bear is to say goodbye."

She jumped out and ran away down the hill before he could say a word. His first impulse had been to follow her, but he did not quite obey it; then it was too late. He had watched her hair, combed simply back behind her ears, toss from side to side as she ran. He could see it still. She had not looked back once.

He faced it now, admitting that what they had had was over; that they had reached the end of what they had to tell. He wondered if he was any nearer answering what he had asked himself so often: "Why did she leave me?" She had told him, certainly, everything she knew.

He tried to bring all of it into one statement. She had left him because he would not run away with her and be free from the evil she saw in her family and in the whole South. It wouldn't do to think, Marcia Mae is just that way: emotional and sudden and proud. She did see something different from what he saw, and had tried in vain to show it to him; like pointing out something on the edge of a distant wood, the effort had come to nothing. He did not believe that the Hunts were worse than anybody else, or that you escaped from anything when you left Lacey and the South. Still it was what she saw and what he did not see that had torn them apart.

He remembered his father, a patient, soft-spoken man, trying to read the paper after supper while his great-uncle Phillip walked up and down the room saying that the New Deal was unconstitutional. "I tell you, Henry, I tell you," he had cried to Duncan's father, "I can endure poverty, I can endure starvation. Let ten thousand depressions sweep down upon us! I take my stand upon the Constitution! That man is promising bread, jobs, and easy money in return for our freedom! Do you realize it, Henry? Do you realize what this means?"

"How can you stand it every night?" Duncan heard his mother ask once while his father stood in his nightshirt, about to switch the light off. "If you try to stop it, he only gets worse," he said. "If you really cross him, he'll move out again." Uncle Phillip had done them that way once because Duncan's mother had twice forgotten to send his linen to the washerwoman. "Woman!" he had risen from the table announcing, "the same roof shall shelter us no longer!" He had moved down to the hotel. Duncan's father let him go, refused to discuss him even in the family, and three weeks later in the store asked him home for supper. He came meekly, this terror of children uptown on the square, possibly driven on by the strings the hotel cook left in the beans. Mrs. Harper, standing at the front window with her little boy, said, "Oh, mercy, your father's got him back. Look how well your father walks," she said with pride. "He's a gentleman." They watched while Henry opened the gate for Uncle Phillip, who leaned back on his walking stick and huffed a moment from the climb. "I do believe that Uncle Phillip's getting old," said Mrs. Harper wistfully. "Run put another plate on the table."

There was never any doubt that it was in Duncan's father's mild grasp that the stability of the family lay. He had died when Duncan was in high school, surviving Uncle Phillip by two years. Though he had married late, a much younger lady, he was still not an old man. It was judged that he had never been very strong. Their last two years as a family had been unquestionably happy. Released from the burden of Uncle Phillip, Henry Harper spread himself amiably among old friends. He was proud of his fine-looking boy who was attracting notice everywhere the way he played football. It amused him that Jason Hunt sometimes stopped in the store to talk. Though he never said so, he was conscious that back in the old days Hunts used to come to town on Saturday in a wagon, wearing shoes for the first time that week. But Jason had been a smart one: he had set out to marry a Standsbury, and he had done it. His daughter was pretty enough; everybody said how nice she looked with Duncan.

One day in the early fall Duncan had come home from football practice and been surprised to see his father's hat and cane on the hall tree. He found his father lying down. He lay in his shirtsleeves and suspenders, his button collar open at the throat. "I felt a little tired at the store, son. I wanted to rest a little before supper." "Do you need anything? Are you sick?" "No, just tired. Where's your mother?" "It must be Auxiliary day." "It always is," said Henry Harper, and smiled. This was a joke they shared. Duncan went back to the kitchen for a drink of water. From the back porch he looked out on a familiar calm stretch of yard, dropping down to a barn, a chicken yard, and a small orchard. He smelled the dusty stir of autumn in the twilight—it always said football to him and school opening—and there was that other quality beneath the eagerness and color that tried to speak and could not, so he had never known what it was, except that it was sad. He heard his mother come in, and presently she called him from the bedroom. His father had just died. So ever after he knew that the name of the other quality in autumn was death, and that it was sad, but only sad—there was nothing terrible about it. He did not believe that he and his father would ever have quarreled.

In what small light was left he looked about him, noting without further interest his cabinet of football trophies, the big handsomely bound book of newspaper clippings resting on a special shelf. In the closet he found another book he had suddenly remembered; it was really a large folder, and inside were crumbling samples of insect life, butterflies, moths, and such like, mounted on stiff sheets and labeled. This had been his Boy Scout project one summer and some of the lettering, he recognized, had been put there by Tinker Taylor, who had been helping him. "I declare," his mother said one day after Tinker had gone home, "that girl is just crazy about you. That child!"

Maybe football hadn't been such a good thing after all, he thought, taking comfort from the careful, loving uprightness of the lettering that she had done for him. He put up the book in its right place, switched out the lamp, and left, passing in the hall the door to the room where his father had died. His mother still had not come home. Maybe this too was Auxiliary day.

He considered that he knew himself by certain things, by their certain manner of being themselves that identified them with his deepest self. He wanted, positively now, to go home to his wife and children.

Duncan Harper was a citizen of Lacey, that was it. Just answering a question about love could not alter this fact. Just saying "Come away" could not change it. It was his strongest and final quality.

what
Tinker
knew

34. He found his family all together in the kitchen. Tinker was getting supper and talking to both children at once— they were forever carrying on conversations with her on two completely different subjects, each unaware that the other was speaking at all. Cotton, who was standing near the door, was interrupted in a long story by the sense of someone near him. He looked up and said, "Hello, Daddy."

"You're getting tall as I am," Duncan said. "How tall are you?"

"No, precious," said Tinker to Patsy, who was sticking her finger in the biscuit dough. "It isn't good to eat."

"Tinker, I—"

She glanced up. The wooden spoon continued to move rapidly. She was the instant before turning the dough out to knead.

"People have been calling you all afternoon. If you look on the phone table."

He lied automatically. "I was up at Mama's."

She stopped dead. "Why don't you move up there? Why don't you eat up there too? Isn't her cooking better than mine?"

"Hush, Tinker—the children. I want us to talk—I want to tell you—"

"Yes, the children," she said, louder than before. "See how they've grown. Can you think of their names?"

He crossed toward her, and at his approach she flinched and ran backward from him. It was when she released her hold on the spoon and pan that she seemed to turn wild.

"Tinker! Darling, listen—!"

" 'Darling!' You've got me mixed up!"

The next step forward he took, she snatched an empty preserves jar from the shelf and hurled it at him, and after that a potato, which struck him painfully, just below the eye. Her hand seemed about to pick up a large knife, but just then she gasped, whirled, and dashed down the back steps into the dark. Patsy shrieked and ran after her, but the screen door whammed to in her face. She started wailing. Cotton only blenched and clung to the wall exactly where he stood, as though the house itself had tilted. Something boiled over on the stove. "Turn it off," his father told him, pointing him relentlessly into the cloud of steam, then he too ran out into the dark.

Tinker reached the barn ahead of Duncan and fled up into the loft. He tried to follow but two steps broke under his weight and the whole structure quivered flimsily. She crouched in the dark above him like a small animal run to its den. He could hear her breathing and see what looked to be the glint of her eyes. He was forced to remember how people said her mother one day had picked up and left old Gains because he wouldn't stop driving the Model T around and blowing the horn. She had taken Tinker and simply repossessed the house she had lived in as a child, was still in it. The town had therefore judged Mrs. Taylor crazy; they said she was "off."

And Tinker herself had run away home from the playground at recess because they'd laughed at the suit her mother had made for her from an old "costume." It was navy wool with big pearl buttons the size of moons. They had worked on it together, her mother teaching her to turn a hem, baste, and square a corner. All for nothing: it would not "do." She had run from their terrible laughter, and on the sidewalks heard for a long time, before she would stop or turn, a boy's steps running and a boy's voice: "Louise. Louise Taylor. Don't run so fast. Wait for me." He had taken her to the drugstore and they had had a Coca-cola, and people told them they ought to be in school. She had looked along the straw, down into the glass where the ice was fading color. "I think your dress is real pretty, Louise." Still sipping, she raised her eyes full to his, and before the straw could suck in the glass she was in love.

"I'm not going anywhere, Tinker. I'm never going to leave you. Whatever there's been is over now—over for good."

He could hear her breathing going on from the run, but couldn't know what she felt or but what she might launch a rusty piece of pitchfork in his face—no telling what was up there handy.

"You ran away another time, remember? I ran after you. I bought you a Coca-cola, remember? And Tinker, you remember the summer you helped me make the butterfly book? It's still up at Mama's. I found it today. I could still tell your handwriting. You were a lot of help."

He had made her cry. He could hear her snuffling like a puppy; she never cried out loud. When she stopped he said, "Louise?"

After a while she crawled to the edge of the loft and looked down into his face. "Duncan, there's something I never told you. You know the day Jimmy got shot? I had stopped to see him and four men from New Orleans came there. They wanted to put money in the race against you. There was somebody named Sam in charge and Pittman, Pilston, something like that, and another name I can't remember, and a boy named Wallace who had a gun."

She told him all she could think of.

"But where were you? How did you hear this?"

"There's a bedroom off the office where they were talking.

Jimmy hid me in there." She shook some trash out of her hair. "I would have told you, but I thought it might help you. The last thing I've wanted to do lately was help you. I'm coming down now." She accomplished this without his help, straining every rotten step to the cracking point, though none broke.

"But Tinker, all this time, and you never told me. Don't you realize—"

"Duncan Harper, if you say another word about it, I'll go right straight up that ladder again, and I'll *never* come down."

When they returned to the house they found it tranquil. Kerney Woolbright, election-weary, thin as a string, was sitting in the living room.

"It sure gets my goat," he said as Duncan walked in, "that Jimmy Tallant, lying up in the hospital still having blood transfusions after two weeks and twice reported dying, has got more power in this damned election than you and me put together. He may be hiding Beck Dozer himself. I've shaken this county like a persimmon tree, and I can't find a single lead to who shot him if it wasn't Dozer, and you with everything you can do through the sheriff's office can't find out where Dozer must be hiding. That damn nigger-paper photo stares at me off every goddamn telephone pole. I tell you, Duncan, if we can't lay it on the line at the speaking Saturday, we're licked."

"It so happens something new has come to light," said Duncan. "I think I know who shot Tallant, and I think I can prove it before the Saturday speaking."

"You what? But who—?"

"I can tell you what it is, but not where I got it from. Relax while I call New Orleans, Kerney. I really think we've got this made."

Tinker discovered the children in the bedroom, being entertained by Bimbo, the colored boy who brought the buttermilk by in the evenings. He had found them sobbing in the kitchen, steam gushing up on the hot stove, and had not only saved the supper but had engrossed both them and himself in a long story:

"Man, he got the eyes like this here, and man, he got the long ole swored bill coming out like this, and all pebbled out with little bitty old fine sharp teefies—yo' daddy's razor *blade* ain't no sharper than what them teefies is. And he go zooming in the water when the big old fantail move—that's his motor— and every once in a while out of purey dee devilment he come up for air and he jump Ker-*flop!* and sound so loud that niggers picking cotton a mile off in the field looks up and says, 'You hear that? There jump that old mean garfish what's bigger than a mule.' "

Cotton, who was sitting on the floor listening with his mouth open, was relieved to see his mother appear in the door; but Patsy, whose eyes had grown enormous, whispered solemnly, "It's a great big garfish." She was seated on Bimbo's knee, and was staring into his face like a devotee before an idol, and indeed she was to worship him, all her childhood long.

Jason takes a hand

35. The next day was Friday, the day before the big political speaking, and Jason Hunt felt he had put things off as long as he could be expected to. From his office in the wing of his home, he put in a call for Kerney Woolbright and waited there for him, savoring the summer morning breeze and the smell of dew, which had bent the rich grass. He had a love for the country and could spend time with pleasure by watching simple details of it. This part of his property reminded him time and again of the country place where he was brought up. A gully was always a gully, but here and there vines mantled it: jackson vine, virginia creeper, ivy, honeysuckle, and at the rough points farther down the fall, trumpet vine and elderberry. Wisteria clothed his dying cedar; the mistletoe did not kill his oak, and storms, for all people told him of shallow roots, had yet to bring it down across his house. So when he closed his uptown office (he called it "retiring"), he had built an office here, adding one more wing to an already overgrown, haphazard house, setting himself above the wilder and least tended part of the grounds—the lawn his wife fretted over, where garden parties were held and guests strolled, was not visible to him here.

It was strange how his family, all within the same walls, had had a tendency to withdraw. Marcia Mae, her high room brooding abovestairs (he thought she woke at night and smoked), his dead son's room that nobody entered but guests, Cissy (he smiled) tucked away back of the side porch with her tester bed she had begged to have and a jungle of scented jars and jugs nobody dared to touch. And Nan, all silken, touching a glass stopper to her ears—she kept her room too hot in winter and must darken it when her headaches struck and took her off with them into suffering none of them would ever know. Only his mother-in-law's room stood free of all uncomfortable privacies. Her bed was covered with the patchwork quilt, the old-timey gaudy kind that he liked; her room was closed only for her afternoon nap. Otherwise, her doors were open all day long, and even at night, as long as the light burned and she lay propped on pillows in a lacy jacket to read first the Bible and then *The Ladies' Home Journal*, nobody stopped to knock.

Jason contrived to spend part of every day alone with her,

and sometimes they did not speak. In his younger days he had considered her a burden. Now he felt simply that he had won through to her, and not only to her but to his office with everything just as he liked it, and to his yard and trees that seemed blessed in an Old Testament way, they flourished so. He could think now of his son without bitterness and of his wife without anger. He had learned you could not rule. Neither, however, could you withdraw entirely so long as God left you about. From experience judgment grew, and must emerge to give the touch where it seemed needed most. This he believed.

From his vantage point at the window, he observed the young man hastening up the walk. His face was earnest and his step firm. Jason recalled that he had also watched Duncan Harper approach to his summons, and had always discovered a slight irritation in his big indolent bearing—as on the football field, Duncan never seemed to hurry. Facing Duncan's steady eyes wherein responsibility sat large, Jason had explained the intricate Hunt affairs and felt in the boy an even deeper lack. It was not that Duncan did not understand when Jason expounded business, only that he would have given Jason exactly the same attention if a country store or a sawmill had been at stake. He had no more sense of greed than a child had lust; not that Jason approved of greed, but to have at least the sense of it seemed a proof of manly thinking and developed a firmer hand on the reins.

But this second boy was a different matter. Cissy had played the family role where Marcia Mae had not deigned: she "kept him guessing" as every Southern family advises, and politics dazzled before him in the same maddening sort of game. The boy was thin and walked with a stoop and someday soon now the knife-blade wrinkle between the eyes would not go away, even when he smiled. The first hurdles were always the hardest. Jason felt, in short, a likeness to himself in Kerney Woolbright that he had never felt in Duncan Harper. Yet he wished to proceed with caution, for the two were friends and were known as running mates. What had drawn this up? Young political ideals, brave things to say about Negroes? Or love of his two daughters?

Jason stripped a cigar and pared it in the wastebasket. He had short attractive hands, browned by the outdoors, and he met Kerney's practiced political shake with as true a clasp as Winfield County could offer.

"Sit down, boy, and talk to me a little. An old man gets to feel all out of it nowadays."

"Sorry I'm late. I came from town as soon as they told me."

"It's a bad day to bother you, I'm afraid. Four days before the primary."

"The funny thing is, sir, I was coming by to talk to you today. I was about to call you up."

"Well, then! Great minds, and all that."

"Yes, sir, but I've been wanting to come for some time and talk things over. The trouble has been that Duncan has been busy and I've been busy, so we've had no time to talk to one another. I finally saw him last night. We're pretty well committed to taking a similar stand on things. I felt I had to talk with him before I could see you and know I had the right answers."

"And now do you know?"

Kerney smiled. "I think so. Yes, sir."

"It has seemed a little odd to me," said Jason, toying with a useless sea-shell inkstand from Coral Gables, Florida, which somebody in the family had seen fit to surprise him with, "that you and Duncan have insisted on this partnership, no matter how friendly you may be personally. You're running for the state senate, he for county sheriff. The territories are not the same, and the two offices are bound to involve different kinds of issues."

"That's perfectly true, sir. I've been aware of that all along. But Duncan and I agree there are certain large issues abroad in the state and that every politician had better face them. Duncan and I are the same kind of folks, you might say. We're young; we're college graduates; we think we represent a type that ought to get into Mississippi politics on every level. It would be natural for people to associate us anyway. We think we're only taking a fair advantage to join forces on every forward-looking policy."

"Umm. And the certain large issues you mentioned, Kerney. We're back where we were last winter, aren't we? Right after Travis died, I suggested we work Duncan in as the sheriff appointment. You said then it was Negroes and the prohibition laws that concerned you two most. You said that Duncan wanted a fair deal for Negroes, and that he wanted to shut down Grantham and Tallant. Is that right?"

"Yes, sir, it—"

"Well, Kerney. Tallant is shut down. There's no doubt about it."

They were silent. Kerney sat looking at his hands and his brow flushed slowly.

"Tallant is shot to pieces, sir. Is that what you mean to say?"

"I couldn't help thinking it," said Jason.

"Mr. Jason, if you're implying that Duncan's policies are responsible for Jimmy Tallant getting shot, I think you're being unfair. I—"

"I never meant to imply anything, Kerney. I merely remarked that one can not help thinking about Tallant now when prohibition is mentioned, just as when you mention Negroes now, one can hardly help thinking about the Dozer Negro who may have tried to murder him."

"Sir, there's one thing you may not know yet. This is in strictest confidence. Duncan and I have learned that some men from a New Orleans gambling syndicate were up here to see Tallant the afternoon of the shooting. We know there was a quarrel."

"How do you know that?"

"Duncan says he is not at liberty to say."

"Well, what is being done?"

"They will be located in New Orleans if possible, questioned and arraigned if possible for attempted manslaughter."

"A slippery question," said Jason. "Ferreting gangsters out of New Orleans to answer for a small-time fracas in the backwoods. Even if they were up here that day, what makes you so sure they did it?"

"The Negro—"

"The nigger ran. As far as I can see, Kerney, somebody has yet to run after him."

"But Tallant insists the Negro is innocent."

"He would naturally do that. It's always galled Jimmy that his daddy was the one that shot Dozer's father."

"Yes, and Duncan feels for that very reason that Beck Dozer would never have fired on Tallant. There's been a tie between them for years. Duncan says they've kept each other company about the past."

"Interesting," said Jason. "But now what?"

"Duncan believes that Beck will come in and give himself up for custody until he can be proved innocent. He believes that Beck will take the risk and have the trust. He thinks if Beck won't do this, no Negro in the world will. I'm tempted to defend him myself if the case should go to court." He stopped for breath; his eyes were eager. "If the New Orleans lead yields anything, then Tallant and Grantham will be ruined for good."

Jason said, "You're clear in your head, of course, what is going to happen to Duncan at the polls?"

"You mean he's going to lose?"

"People want to vote for Duncan, Kerney, but the fact is that this sort of thing is not going down. You know that, don't you, when you associate yourself with him?"

"You mean then, that I'm going to lose, too?"

"People want to vote for you, too, Kerney. They remember how you came out ahead two years ago in the legislature's race. You were clever to split the vote that way and win. They like clever bright boys. They'd like to vote for you again. There's nobody against you but old Mavis over in Wyatt County, and people are sick and tired of seeing his face on the posters. I don't know. Maybe you and Duncan have the right line on this business, gangsters and all. Maybe Dozer is worth the kind of sacrifice you're making for him. But I certainly think you'll have to give up entirely any idea of getting the office you're supposed to be seeking." He smiled, his tough-skinned face spilling instantly and graciously all its store of charm. "You'll forgive me speaking plainly, boy. I've seen enough of you around the house for quite a while to get to feel like you're one of the family. With a little urging I might have called myself talking to a son of my own."

Whatever Kerney felt about this did not reveal itself in his face. "Thank you, sir," he said, adding, "I have faced the idea of losing the race, sir."

"Faced it, yes. But have you thoroughly made up your mind to it?"

"I felt it might be worth—" He stopped. He did not look at Jason or avoid him either, and his face became even more deeply his own possession. Kerney Woolbright was neither ugly nor handsome, and though he had the features neither of

216

aristocracy nor of common folk, he might have been placed in either. But above every other quality his face was his own: the large pointed nose, narrow chin cleft in the center, and eyes sheltered deeply in brows and lashes belonged to no one but Kerney Woolbright, a fact that grew more positive every day.

"How old are you, Kerney?" Jason Hunt asked gently.

"Twenty-five, sir."

"As young as that! I thought as much, but it always seems impossible. A college degree, Yale law degree, two years in the legislature, and now—well, who knows? You carry it all well. I never thought before that you got ahead of yourself in any way. Some young men do. And some, of course, only sons with a mother alone who has enough money, would say they had responsibility enough and just sit down, if you follow me. Some stick one toe out in the water and see how cold it is and they've had enough for the rest of their natural lives." He laughed. "I was one of a big family. It was never left to me to decide. They snatched me up and threw me in over my head and it was sink or swim from then on. If any-body looked back to see which one I did, I was too occupied to notice. I've got a sneaking suspicion, though, that nobody looked. I hope I've never been the kind of fellow to say every-body has to do it my way or it isn't done right. You've had a big opportunity for going ahead, and you've kept the trace chains tight and the singletree riding level. If I had had the money to go to college, I'd have gone into the law, I always thought, that or medicine. The law is the right thing for stepping off into politics. I thought the other day, You must have seen politics ahead of you all along, Kerney."

"You're right, sir. I have."

"The same time I wondered that, I was sitting out here in the office by myself watching the cat out there watching a jaybird and the jaybird watching God alone knows what, and I thought, What is Duncan Harper doing in politics? Isn't this sort of a sudden idea?"

"He's been interested in politics for a long time, sir."

"Yes, so have I. But I'm not about to start running for something."

"Travis Brevard asked him—"

"So they say. Do you think if Travis had had even a sneaking suspicion that Duncan took liberal views, he would have asked him to run for dogcatcher, let alone sheriff? Travis was asking a football star, nothing else."

"Duncan knows that, sir."

"What is Duncan living on these days? The store can't be bringing in much with somebody else hired to run it."

"I don't know about his finances. He still finds time to write a little insurance. I think he has some property in town and maybe a place or two in the country. You know how it is."

"I ought to," said Jason, and they exchanged a smile. Nobody could name a business in Winfield County that Jason Hunt had not at some time been in it. "He has a nice house," Jason continued. "Of course, his wife's father has that oil money."

Kerney was about to speak again, though what he would say seemed uncertain to him, when Jason Hunt rose and spoke with swift strength.

"In my opinion Duncan Harper has no business in politics. He is not only inept, he may even be dangerous. You instead have every business to be in politics. He has no right to ruin your career, as it will be ruined, Kerney, in this race, for good."

Kerney had risen also. His face flamed completely red; that was all he showed.

"Duncan is my friend, sir," he said firmly.

"I have every respect for friendship," said Jason Hunt, and put out his hand. "Good day, my boy. Miss Nan and I are always pleased to see you. Come back whenever you can."

**beset
on every
side**

36. When he came from the steps that dropped from Jason's office to the yard, Nan Hunt called to him from somewhere within the house. It was a testament to the absolute charm of her voice that she could win his attention at that moment.

"I know you're busy, but can you come here just a minute?"

He skirted the corner of the house with its rich slumberous shrubbery, and hastened up the low steps to the front gallery. She stood near the turn of the porch, back of the green glider.

"We want you for dinner tomorrow night after the speaking," she told him. "Perhaps Cissy mentioned it."

"No—oh, yes, yes she did, I think. Excuse me, Miss Nan. The heat and politics together are too much for me." He came toward her, threading amongst the rocking chairs, but she stepped back from him saying, "Kerney," and he had to turn the farthest corner of the porch, puzzling, to find her again. She stood near the wall. The walnut just outside shadowed them; the sun had not yet struck through: they were as sheltered and private as if they had suddenly entered a little grove. Her hand held his wrist, and her face so swiftly near him had transformed itself on the moment. He had never seen her like this before. She was touched back into youth as startlingly as though she had just died; she seemed never to have had a headache in her life; she was more beautiful than both her daughters; and she said, "Whatever he advised you, don't do it. I don't know what it could be. He does not discuss his business with me; I have no notion. But if there is a murmur of your heart against him, then follow your heart. Oh, believe me, believe me, Kerney! You will never be sorry!"

Kerney's intellect was catlike; thrown into a tailspin, it had a tendency to reappear on its feet. He thought at once: Was Jason Hunt *this* bad? The hand on his sleeve, not small, more strong than weak, was still of an indescribable fragility, and the whole woman like a flower nurtured to that perfect bloom which, inexchangeable for any other, is flawed only by its surroundings: it is a trifle too heavy for its stem, and what climate yields its proper airs? Certainly Mississippi seasons were all too coarse for her. What man could ever pass the long trials of her indisputable discriminations? Jason Hunt had failed, and Kerney knew that he would fail too. There remained to her the exquisite intimacies of pain, and what subtle memories one could not even guess at. Thus he rapidly reasoned himself apart from her, and though he replied with gallantry and affection that would have seemed genuine to almost anybody, he left her lonelier than before, for if she seldom risked a gesture of the heart, she had not forgotten how to recognize one. Her diamonds blinked but she did not; she parted from him graciously.

The irony of his reaction to her was that he had already made up his mind to reject Jason's ideas before she suggested it. The scales had already tipped decisively; his step had been certain as a saint's. But her appearance in the matter had thrown Jason into unexpected light, and not so much Kerney's decision, but the whole apparatus of it was shaken. For if Jason was wrong about Duncan, and Nan unjustified about Jason, then Duncan might conceivably be miscalculating about Beck Dozer, which put Kerney Woolbright on shaky ground, and was not good.

To add to his confusion, Cissy appeared on the path before him.

"Silly," she said. "You almost ran into me without looking. All time thinking about politics. Silly."

"Cissy," he said, and put an arm around her. "Walk with me down the walk and listen to me a minute."

"Well, I'm listening. What's the matter?"

He could not begin. He had no way to explain. "Don't say I told you, but I may not win the race. I may lose."

"Is somebody else running besides old Mr. Mavis?"

"No, honey, that's not it."

"But who on earth would vote for old Mr. Mavis instead of you? You're just worrying over nothing."

He went a little way down the flight of wooden steps that led to the street, and sat down, drawing her down beside him. He had foreseen her among young Washington matrons, photographed on the White House lawn.

"You haven't even noticed my new dress." She spread wide around her knees a chambray skirt of yellow, paneled in white cotton eyelet. "You don't notice anything any more. We never get to go anywhere. You never tell me anything."

"Cissy, please don't tell this to anybody, but I—"

"You always say that! You know I won't tell anything!" But, alas, she told everything she knew to everybody she knew, and they both knew it. But he never challenged her when she insisted this way, and he did not now.

"What were you going to tell me, Kerney?"

He shook his head. "I just don't have time now, honey. I have to go uptown."

"I don't like the way you're doing me, Kerney. I meant to wait and tell you after the election. I just don't like it. I don't want anybody who's going to be all the time leaving me about important things they won't talk about. You never do explain anything to me. All I'm supposed to do is talk baby talk to you. I do it when I don't feel like it one bit. I think it's the silliest thing I ever heard of. I get sick myself sometimes. I'm not going to do it any more, either. I tell you that right now."

He got up and went slowly down the steps toward his car, which in his haste he had left in the road instead of ascending the drive. He entered the scalding sun and paused, turning back. There were tears in his eyes, but he judged she could not see them. She rose from the ankles, sturdily, without touching anything.

"You're treating me the way Daddy treats Mother. He never tells her anything. If your business is all that important, and you're all that important, then I've got to be important too. Either that, or I'm going to quit liking you. You needn't think I can't, Kerney, not for a minute."

He went away without saying anything. He felt like a small boy, unjustly injured, and wanted to go home and be called soft names.

It happened to Duncan, he thought. Now it's happening to me.

part four

37. Willard Follansbee, child of scorn, sat in one of Bud Grantham's hide-bottom chairs with his straw hat in his lap. He looked about as delighted with the world as the world was with him, but his abiding consolation was that both he and the world knew it.

"They don't want me. I don't kid myself none. They don't even like me. When they voted for me before they's voting for Travis, just on account of he couldn't succeed himself. When they vote for me this go-round they'll be voting against Harper. The thing I aim to make certain sure of tomorrow is that they get an earful of plenty to vote against Duncan Harper *for*. You know, Bud, I can't stand the sight of that fellow."

"I never thought he was such a bad type," said Bud Grantham. "I never felt nothing unkindly towardjuh him." He ran one tough old finger across three warts in the palm of his hand. He had been to the conjure woman a week ago, but so far they hadn't shed.

"Listen," said Willard, "I get to where I can't stand the sight of the hat on his head or the shirt on his back. I can't decide when I don't like him the most, when he comes in the door or when he goes out the door. I tried to decide it yesterday, but s'help me, I couldn't."

"Folks like him in general," said Bud, "or so I'm told."

"Listen," said Willard, "I been treading lightly over him when I speak. But did you realize before, Bud, that country folks don't care nothing atall about football?"

"I knew," said Bud, "that Bud Grantham don't care nothing for it. I couldn't care less. I don't even care at the time, much less ten years later. I don't even put a two-dollar bet in on the pool."

"You tell me honestly, Bud. How do we stand?"

"We stand to win, is my feeling. But you know my heart ain't in it so much, Willard, what with Jimmy laid up and the place shut down. I got nothing to do all day but swat flies."

"Yeah, it's bad, I know. How you figger we stand to win?"

"Because Harper ain't caught the nigger yet. Everybody thinks the nigger shot Jimmy. I don't think he's going to catch that nigger. If you want to trample on him when you speak, that's the ground you ought to trample over. There's a might of folks in this county just crazy about Jimmy, and it don't set well that a nigger can shoot him down and go scot-free. Tell the truth, it don't set well with me. I'd like to get my hands on the nigger my own self."

"God help him to stay lost, is the way I look at it. If I laid hands on him first, he'd never get to Duncan Harper alive. I think he knows too much. I think that's why he run."

"I think he done it," said Bud.

"If he done it, how come Jimmy won't say so?"

"On account of what his daddy done. Jimmy don't find the way of resting easy over that. Don't ask me how come. We all got our peculiarities."

"On the other hand," said Willard, "looks like he could have made up something better than what he did. Jimmy's been laying up in that hospital for two weeks with all them nurses singlefooting up and down for him, talking way down weak: 'It was a strange white man. Somebody out hunting. Never laid eyes on him.' I've knowed him to make up better than that to pass the time during a slow hand of poker."

"If you think the nigger didn't do it, who do you think did? You said Sam sent them boys back there to talk to

226

Jimmy. He didn't say nothing atall about trying to kill him."

"It's true," said Willard. "But how come them to give up the idea of talking to him that quick."

"Well, you were there, and heard what they said. I'd gone on up to the house. Run through it one more time for me, Willard."

"It was after you followed Bella back over to the house. Pilston and Sam and me set there in the office and didn't say much except I think Pilston did remark once on the temperature, that it was unusually high, and I said he was right. Then I heard a shot, but I didn't think nothing about it. I knew the kid they had with them carried a gun, but if I thought anything, I thought somebody was just pranking with it."

"I'm all time hearing shots off in the woods," said Bud. "It don't signify no more to me than a axe ringing. You take just this morning. I heard two right close together off down towardjuh the creek."

"That day," said Willard, "you never heard but one. But, like I say, I didn't think nothing. Wasn't a minute later that Mitchell come to the door and called Sam out into the main part of the Idle Hour to tell him something. Sam came straight back, polite and cool as a preacher in the cool of Sunday morning before the singing and the sermon and the fried chicken, and says that they've decided not to talk to Jimmy right now after all. Mitchell says he's back in the woods arguing with some nigger. He says he and Wally were headed on back when they heard a shot from down there. 'Naturally,' he says, 'we don't care to be involved in any local matter. We prefer to drive along now, attend to some business over in the Delta,' he says, 'and strike back here long about nine or ten o'clock.' Mitchell had already gone and got in the back seat with the boy, and Sam and Pilston took the front, with Pilston driving. They said 'So long till later,' and drove off west, toward the Delta. They never came back."

"They might have heard about Jimmy in time not to come back," said Bud. "News being what it is when it comes to traveling."

"All I said to myself at the time was, 'Well, Jimmy's finally decided to handle that Dozer nigger for double-crossing him.' I didn't want to meddle in his business, so I drove on back to town. It wasn't till I heard Jimmy was in the hospital that I seen the light. So that's how come they left so quick, I says. They done it themselves."

"I think they caught the nigger at it," Bud said. "I think, like they said, they never wanted to be mixed up in nothing of that type. If Pilston had gone into the woods, now— But what call for quarrel was there, Willard, between Jimmy and Mitchell?"

"The one toting the gun was that boy."

"If I remember right, him and Jimmy had just struck up a kinship right after they come."

"That wouldn't make no difference to folks like them."

"I think it was the nigger," said Bud.

They sat silently for a time in Bud's room with the old iron bed, the washstand, and the desk pushed over against the wall. The ledgers were there, for Bud, like a conscientious accountant, brought them home from the office at the Idle Hour and sometimes tried to figure out where he ought to enter his expenses.

"I think it was the nigger, too," said Bella, walking in.

"He don't talk to you, either?" Willard asked.

"No more than to anybody else since he's been up yonder in the hospital, but one time he told me a story about when he was overseas. He run into the Dozer nigger and the Dozer nigger tried to kill him. Did you know that, Daddy?"

"I don't know nothing about overseas," said Bud.

"Jimmy's funny about that nigger," said Willard, "for a fact. You'd think he'd bought him and paid cash for him. He's that attached."

"Where you going, honey baby?" asked Bud. "All diked out."

She had got herself up in a cool sleeveless summer cotton with big Hawaiian flowers on it, and her hair was brushed smooth, her make-up careful. She was not such a bad-looking girl.

"I'm going to the meeting, Daddy," she said. "I was hoping you could come go with me."

"I best stay with the chap," said Bud. "Is he sleep?"

"Lucy's coming to stay with him. You come on now, Daddy. I promised I'd bring somebody. They had it all divided off last night. You could get in the Tomorrow I'll Take Jesus As My Savior group, or you could choose the Tomorrow I'll Speak to Someone about Jesus group, or you could be in the Tomorrow I'll Bring Somebody Else to the Meeting group. So I picked that one."

"Can't you just speak to him about Jesus and go on?" Willard asked.

"No, because I promised this other one. It wouldn't be doing right, would it?"

"It's a fact I ought to go," said Bud. "Bella's mama never missed a night; we had our own bench saved for us, me and her and all the chaps. They couldn't open a meeting without us. My own mother went morning *and* night. I've seen the time she'd get up sick to go. I never seen a better woman. Not in all my borned days. You tell 'em up there, baby, that your old daddy's a sinner, but his heart's with 'em, and he aims to get there yet."

A voice called from out in the dark.

"Miss Bella? Oh, Miss Bella?"

"It's Lucy," said Bella. "Come on in, Lucy."

"That's Beck's wife, ain't it?" Willard asked, as the quiet, thin Negro girl entered from the back porch and halted just inside the screen door. She wore a dark, straight-cut cotton dress and low-quarter tennis shoes. She had wrapped the hem of an old pillow slip around her head, for she had straightened her hair that day, using the hair grease and the hot-iron comb, just as if something special might be about to happen. She was at once aware from Mister Willard Follansbee's glance that the white cone on her head looked attractive, but she did not remove it.

"Come here, girl," said Follansbee.

Shy, tall, soft, she moved to the edge of the lamplight.

"Come here!" he repeated, pointing to a straight chair, and when she hesitated he seized her by the wrist and flung her into it. "Where's Beck at?"

"I don't know, sir."

"Look at me." He jerked up her face.

"I said I don't know, sir. I ain't seen him."

"You ain't seen him," Willard mimicked. "It's going on three weeks. What's he doing—or is he doing without?"

Lucy turned her head aside. She was conscious of the white man's slack jaw where the stiff black hair roots were visible like punctures and the breath moved in and out. She went dull all over, animal, African, obedient to the forcing whip. "I ain't seen him," she repeated.

" 'I ain't seen him,' " Willard mocked. "Listen, nigger, you know the worse thing a white man can do to a black man, don't you?"

"I don't know, sir."

"You don't? You never heard what happens to a black man if he tries anything with a white woman?"

"Beck ain't done nothing. There wasn't no white lady."

"You tell Beck to stay gone from here. 'Cause if I see him it ain't going to make no difference if there was a white lady or there wasn't a white lady. It's going to be the same for Willard Follansbee. Willard Follansbee. That's me. You understand?"

"Yes, sir."

"What you going to do?"

"If I see him, I tell him."

"Tell him what?"

"To stay way from here."

"Stay way how come?"

" 'Count of what you'd do."

"What would I do? You tell me." He bent suddenly close to her. "You tell me."

"Willard," said Bud Grantham and put a stubby old hand between them, shoving the man back from her, "you done said enough, considering there's a lady present."

"Oh," said Willard, recovering, "damn if I didn't forget." He glanced to where Bella stood just out of the light, leaning forward in close scrutiny of Lucy's face. Willard ran his fingers through his long thin straight black hair, pulling it away from his wet brow. He turned his back on Bella and walked uncertainly toward the dark back screen door.

"Oo," said Bella, straightening up with something like a shudder, or maybe a rabbit running across her grave, "y'al' ought'n to do Lucy that away," and she added, though whether to make her feelings plausible to the men or to herself was not clear, "if you bother her, she won't look after the baby good, and it's time I was at church."

"Run on along, baby," said Bud Grantham. "It's all agoing to be all right."

"Can I tell 'em you'll come next time, Daddy?"

"You tell 'em that."

Lucy rose and moved toward the door of the room where Bella was staying.

"His bottle's in the icebox, Lucy," Bella called back. "Don't forget to heat it."

the
helpless
one

38. Beck never let Lucy work in white folks' houses. He made good enough money when he was foreman at the tie plant, before all these things started happening. Now when they sent for her she was scared to go and scared not to go. She hardly knew day from night any more, and moved from one thing to the next without being able to say what she was doing.

After she had fed the little baby and joggled him and changed him, she knew beyond a doubt what the white man was waiting there for. He was walking around in Mister Bud's room by himself, drinking Mister Bud's whisky. Mister Bud himself was out on the back porch in the dark, rocking and singing along with the white-folks tent meeting down the road.

> "There is a fountain filled with blood
>   Drawn from Immanuel's veins,
>   And sinners plunged beneath that flood . . ."

She accepted what would happen. A Negro, lowered past a certain line of misfortune, no longer counts on cleverness: she did not think how she could divert him, contrive to upset the baby, win the other man's attention. Some savage instinct made her scrounge down low in the corner between the window and the bed. She took off her white headwrap and laid it on the counterpane.

> "The dying thief rejoiced to see
>   That fountain in his day;
>   And there may I, though vile as he . . ."

Out on the back porch, Mister Bud was belling like a hound. The room was dark. When the door opened, and light entered, she turned her head low. If he didn't quit breathing so loud, he would wake up the baby.

She recalled the time she used to go down to the Sanders' house, the white-folks kitchen where Aunt Mattie used to cook. On the sidewalk one day by the hill up Mister Sanders' pasture, that old white man stopped her. It was spring and the iris blades felt cold on her legs. Aunt Mattie had raised her nice: she didn't know what he meant. She couldn't have been more than nine or ten. When she came crying into the kitchen, Aunt Mattie looked her over good, then gave her some coffee. The white lady, Miss Jessie Sanders, took on worse than Mattie. "That awful old man. He ought to be ashamed! I'd like to let him know exactly what I think of him." "Yes'm," said Mattie, "nex' time she know to run 'fo' he see her, stid of after." But Miss Jessie still took on. She took on and took on. She told her husband at the dinner table. "That awful old thing," she said. "To hear him pray out loud in church! You think he'd died and gone to heaven." "Did he hurt her, Mattie?" Mister David called back to the kitchen. "Naw suh," said Mattie, taking her own sweet time. "I reckon he too old." "Nasty thing," said Miss Jessie. . . .

When Lucy walked back through the woods, tears lay along her cheeks like scars. The days for running to Aunt Mattie were gone long ago. She couldn't even tell Beck what the white man had done. He would feel it worse than she did.

He might even do something crazy. Right after she first married Beck, the yellow boy she had been married to before kept shining around. He wanted to come sit on the porch on Sunday and talk. Beck wouldn't have it. Little as Beck was, he said he would kill that nigger if he kept on coming by. That was how she knew about Beck.

"He sound asleep, Mister Bud," she had said. "My own chillen ain't had they supper."

"You can go," said Bud Grantham. "Bella'll be home now in a minute. I hear they're singing the invitation hymn."

They sure enough were.

> "Just as I am, without one plea,
> But that thy blood was shed for me
> And that thou bid'st me come to thee
> O Lamb of God, I come! I come!"

Brother Simmons at the Bear Ma'sh M.E. Church used that one too, but Lucy felt too ill-used to take satisfaction from it. She followed a twisting, wooded path that led her beyond the field where Mister Jimmy Tallant had got shot, climbed through two barbed-wire fences and went over a stile. She passed a spring, set back deep in a hollow where the water winked and shifted like an eye, and there gushed out into the night air the deep earth smell of black loam. The night was thick with life: it sang or buzzed or chanted or chirped or jumped off into the bog or ran through the leaves, and a lot of it probably had no business out on this side of the grave. Lucy had never bothered much about ha'nts.

Not that she doubted them. Black people are night people, and you do not drive a Southern road at any unearthly hour without seeing them along the roadsides, going somewhere, or marking at a distance across the field the oil lamp burning full wick within the cabin. Sometimes, passing near a cabin that is totally dark as though for sleep, one hears break out again the low mingling of many voices; no crisis has brought them there, but the instinctive motion of their strange society has behaved like a current deep down in the river, and here they are. Savage, they came to a savage land, and it took them in. White people, already appalled by floods and rattlesnakes, malaria, swamps, tornadoes, mud, ice, sunstroke, and typhoid fever, felt compelled to levee out the black with the same ruthless patience with which they leveed the Mississippi River. They were driven to do what they did, not by any conviction of right or wrong, but by the simple will to survive. Meanwhile, Negroes married the land. Its image is never complete without them; if they are out of the picture, they are only just around the corner, coming or going, or both. They are not really as afraid in the night as most white people are. Whiteness is a kind of nakedness to the dark world, and Lucy, who had all the fear she could do with, went to no trouble to imagine more. She moved on in her blackness, and her heart, sick and numb, burned tender as the eye of a night creature, alive in the dark.

"Who?" she asked plain out when the figure appeared ahead of her, silhouetted down a little free length of path.

"It's me, Aunt Lucy." It was W.B.

"You ain't heard nothing?" she asked when they came together.

"Nothing from Unker Beck. Mister Duncan is at the house, though."

"Doing what?"

"He is setting by Granny. Claim she nussed his papa when his papa died, and laid him straight and all. Claim she cared for his mama after his mama birthed him. He done tole me all about it once befo'."

"What he coming for now? It ain't no interest of mine who nussed his daddy and eased his mammy. If Granny done it, look at Granny. Who's caring for her now?"

"We is, Aunt Lucy."

"We sho' is. Don't you tell that white man nothing, W.B. Ain't nobody to help Beck but Beck."

"I ain't tole him nothing."

"Ack like you dumb, ack like you crazy, but don't say nothing to a white man. Wall yo' eyes like you ain't got good sense. You hear me, W.B.?"

"Yes'm, Aunt Lucy. I hears you."

"Beck call hisself being so smart. Going to make first this deal with the white, then the next one better still. There ain't no dealing with white folks, this one *or* the next one. I reckon Beck know hit now. Turn aloose of me and hush, W.B. I ain't got time for you to be no baby. You gots to be a man."

"Aunt Lucy, Unker Beck never done it. Unker Beck never shot Mister Jimmy Tallant."

"No, he never, W.B. But when the white folks think you done something, you just well's to run."

"I run the day Mister Travis Brevard died."

"Then you knows about your Unker Beck. He done the same."

the
distances
between

39. "He must have his own chance to decide," said Duncan, speaking very slowly. "He must have his own choice. If Mister Willard Follansbee wins the election, he and Mister Bud Grantham will kill Beck if they can find him. You'll have to leave here, leave your house and home to go to him. The reason people say they don't want to vote for me is because I let Beck get away. If Beck will come back, I will protect him. You know I'll protect him because I did it once before, up at the jail."

"I don't know where he at," said Lucy.

"Me neither," said W.B.

"Yo' daddy had the prettiest ca'edge hoss I most ever seen," said Aunt Mattie. "The day you's born it come up a little whipping storm and Mister Henry Harper hitched his buggy up at the top of the heel and come walking for me. 'How come us walking, Mister Henry, and you with yo' spohty ca'edge?' 'I gots to spoht my equipage uptown tomorrow, Mattie, and you ain't gwy catch me splashing it up on no nigger road.' But Lawd, in dem days the roads in town was apt to slush up bad as any."

"We know now that Beck did not shoot Mister Tallant. We have a good start on finding the people who did. We may find them any minute now. The last I heard, the police had located them, down in New Orleans; it's just a matter of getting them to confess. If Beck will trust me and come give himself up, then everybody will know he wasn't mixed up in anything. Nobody can say he was."

"Mister Jimmy Tallant ain't going to let them do nothing to Beck."

"Mister Jimmy Tallant has had two weeks to call the name of the man that shot him, and he hasn't called it yet. It would bust his business if folks knew that New Orleans gamblers were putting money in this sheriff's race. You haven't got to do anything that will cause you trouble, anything to put you in danger. You just have got to get word to Beck exactly what I say and let him decide."

"I don't know where he at," said Lucy.

"Me neither," said W.B., who was watching the white man he used to work for. In spite of everything he was pleased to death that Mister Duncan had come to their house.

"W.B. could go," said Duncan. "I know W.B. well because he's worked for me. Folks said, That boy is too little to know where to take groceries, but I didn't think so. I said, He's a

237

good boy and a smart boy. He'll learn. I was right. Wasn't I, W.B.?"

Lucy saw the child grin from ear to ear, and his absence of fear scared her. "Git yonder in the kitchen and see what is the baby got in to."

"Yes'm."

He skipped past Granny to obey.

All evening, with the sound of children in the house, Aunt Mattie felt she was in heaven. She had just gone in and looked at Miss Edna Harper's new baby; he was grown and in the room here now—she did not mistake who was there, though all her eyes could see was the kerosene lamp flame they lighted for her every time it got dark. Mister Henry Harper had just brought her to the door, he had let her in the front, the way she always came in to her white folks, and she'd gone straight on back to where Miss Edna was moaning. In heaven you talked to whoever came to mind or into the room, it was the same, and did anybody know for sure this wasn't it right now?

"Hit was the prettiest baby," said Aunt Mattie, "the whitest white chile I done ever seen."

Lucy flashed Duncan a look of scorn. Her walls were dark walls and the old woman with her perfectly round, addled eyes and her cap of hair short and kinky as a man's (for all her hundred and who knew how many years, it was gray, not white, and never would lose its tenacity to color)—the old woman sat under a dark old quilt and even her fingernails were the rich deep amber color of old tree bark, and the andirons in the swept fireplace were black as old muffin pans. What was white?

"Beck got to do what he do in he own time," she said.

"That's exactly right," said Duncan. "But he can't do anything unless you tell him how things stand."

"In dem days," said Aunt Mattie, "ever'thing Miss Edna

Harper say do Mister Henry Harper done. But she couldn't do nothing atall with old Mister Phillip, po' lady. If he wasn't a caution! I'se hanging out that chile's diapers out on the back porch when I heard them scufflings under the steps. Dere dey was, Mister Phillip and dat black gal that toted the milk. 'Ain't you shame?' I says. 'It not but ten o'clock in the morning, and a baby just bawn yestiddy in this house. I gwy have you churched, nigger.' 'Go on away from here, Mattie,' Mister Phillip says. 'You tend to your'n and I'll tend to mine.' Hee! Hee! He never seed me afterwards he didn't mention it. 'Did you get her churched, Mattie?' Hee! Hee!"

"How I know where Beck at?" said Lucy. "Maybe he in New Orléans, maybe he in Memphis. I don't know. What I got to do with where he at?"

"You know," said Duncan.

W.B. came back. This time he stopped by Granny's chair. Her hand touched his arm, groping up and down his sleeve. "He's Granny's man he is. Ain't nothing gwy harm him. Nare a ha'nt come nigh, nare a cross-eyed nigger. He Jesus' lamb."

Duncan picked up the kerosene lamp from the table and crossed to where the large daguerreotype of Beck Dozer's father hung on the wall.

Robinson Dozer

40. The face in the daguerreotype was thin and severe and the hair the true woolly African neatness of fit, the texture of a good rug. The head was held rigidly high, but neither, it would appear, through consciousness at having a picture made, nor from the restraint of the high boiled collar. The eyes seemed concerned.

This man, or so the story went, had given up his job as

butler in the fashionable Standsbury house and had moved with his family to the country outside Lacey where he owned a little legacy of land. There was a good-sized Negro-tenant and free-farmer population in that area: Robinson Dozer founded a little school in his own front yard.

His parents had been slaves of a senator, John Lucian Upinshaw, "Senator John." The old man, living poorly after the war in a splendid house, had wished to spend his last years educating the children of his former slaves. Robinson Dozer had sat on a bench with the other Negro children out in the guesthouse in the front yard—the one the Senator had converted into a library. Robinson's eyes were big as a raccoon's; his mouth hung open long enough for a jenny wren to nest in it; and he remembered every word that Senator John said.

Senator John thought that Southerners should have started this sort of thing years ago; he felt compassion for these black innocents so violently kicked into freedom; he thought that only the educated mind was fit for American citizenship. His mind burned clearly. He thanked God for this calling here in his old age, his poverty, the ruin of his country. One frosty morning an hour before his class, he fell on the back steps and broke his hip.

He sent his niece to tell the Negro children, but what with all the excitement of the fetching and carrying, she forgot to go. The black children sat on the benches in the law office for forty-five minutes in hypnotized silence; then, as though someone had signaled, they bolted. They ran in terror across the lawn, dropping the tablets and pencils along the garden path. Propped high in a mahogany four-poster, his stout old leg intricately distended toward the ceiling by a homemade pully, the Senator announced he would continue his classes in his bedroom.

Next morning, he sent his grandson down to the guesthouse to bring the students in. When at last the boy came shivering back across the frozen yard and said that nobody had come, he became nervous and extremely irritated. He guessed the truth, that nobody had got to them the day before; he commanded that everyone in the house be marshaled to go out and search for them all over the plantation, to bring in every one of them if it took till sundown. After a while, his daughter came into his room.

She had a paper full of cornfield peas and she shelled them with jerking motions while she talked, casting hulls by the handful into a bucket, funneling the peas into a boiler. She was running the house now. Her husband had been killed at Shiloh. She used to cry at night and play songs on the piano at twilight, but now she did not have time for either one. Her bare arms were broken out in red spots where she had been out in the garden gathering the peas and turnip greens—that was all they had to eat now: first peas, then turnip greens and turnips, cooked with a bit of salt pork. She did not notice any longer that it was cold: a fire in a room was apt to make her say she was burning up, whereupon she would stamp out, as though mad at somebody. A Union officer and ten strange Negroes had raided the smokehouse three days before and left them with no meat at all. She had penned two shoats right at the back door, and said she would raise them if she had to move them into her bedroom.

"Papa," she said, jerking the hulls away from the part that was food, "Papa, I can't have the children going out of sight of the house. It's dangerous on the roads now. I have to take Holcomb and the shotgun with me when I go to town in the buggy. If those little niggers appreciated what you're doing they'd come back. The answer is they don't appreciate it. You're not teaching them anything," she went on pitilessly; "you're wasting your time and your strength, out there in that cold office. I don't know that I want them in here anyway, smelling up my house. Every child on this place is working; why can't they?"

"Working! Why, Liza, child, what do you call work? I've raised a sweat on the little rascals out there in the cold; you wouldn't believe how much they've learned. They know the alphabet, and how to cipher, the names of some few states, and can print a sentence or two on paper. They're learning the story of Thomas Jefferson and how he set his slaves free. Think of it, Liza! In a scant fifty years from savagery!"

"Savagery! They're animals, if you ask me. They aren't as good as savages. There's Nanny and old Luke and who else? Nobody. They come to the back door wanting something to eat. 'Go to the Yankees': that's what I ought to say. But I don't. 'All right,' I say, 'I planted that garden with these two hands, and I sweated down to nothing hoeing it, and when nobody else is around, who goes out and gets the vegetables? Me. But all right. Go cut me some kindling wood, go straighten up the back fence where that crazy cow got her yoke caught, go in the woods and get me a new hoe handle. Then you can come and eat same as we do, turnip greens and side meat, corn bread and potlikker, and if that ain't good enough for you, go to the Yankees and see what you get.' That's what I say."

"You poor child. Having to do all this work. I'm sorry, Liza."

"It isn't only work, Papa. It's danger, night and day. You never know what's going to happen next. They can start burning houses again; they can turn *us* into slaves; they're crazy, I tell you; they can do anything."

"Liza, don't get upset."

"Upset!" This was too much. She told him everything, tearing the hulls viciously apart, things that were happening in town, along the roads, at the capital, all over the South.

"Why wasn't I told?" he asked sternly.

"I didn't want to worry you. You couldn't do anything about it."

He knew then that he was old. Easing the leather-bound volume aside, taking off his spectacles, he agreed, "No, I couldn't do anything."

"You seemed happy enough, teaching little niggers."

Not only old, childish. He had to be humored. He sighed. What had gone with his daughter's gentle tongue? He was not used to being wounded by women. "Poor Liza. Poor little girl."

They heard Aunt Nanny scolding in the hall. "You say you wants to see him, well, go ahead on in and see him. I ain't got time to waste on trash like you is."

In the high white doorway, there appeared the Negro boy with the raccoon eyes in the small face.

"Why," said Senator John, "it's Robinson Dozer. He's come for his lesson. Get on out into the kitchen with your pea-shelling, Liza. I'm lying here worthless, but I can teach this boy."

The old man never walked again. He went about in a wheel chair for years till he died, and it was Robinson Dozer who pushed him everywhere, reciting Presidents. The family mocked him, sometimes to his face, walking to the chant of "Washington, Adams, Jefferson, John *Quincy* Adams, Madison, Monroe. . . ." They did this when they got him by himself. They didn't dare mock him in front of Senator John. He eventually moved into the house with the old man, slept in the trundle bed, and padded in and out with slop jars, water for shaving, trays of food, and books, books, books. The family said that all he could learn was the Presidents' names, just as they said that this was all the old Senator had memory enough left to teach him.

But one day at the dinner table one of the cousins said he

had heard them wheeling around in the back yard together speaking French. "French!" There was a silence. "Or maybe it was Latin," said the cousin. "Well, I hope so," said Eliza. "Teaching that black thing French. The idea!" "Granddaddy don't know any French to teach him," said another cousin, Davy, a great sarcastic boy. "Naw, he don't know French." "*I* didn't think he remembered Latin either," said Eliza. "Maybe he don't," said Davy. "I don't see how Vernon would know. Maybe Robinson was teaching African to Granddaddy." "It wasn't English," said Vernon. "Holler see's there any more bread."

When Senator John realized he was perhaps engaged in a dangerous thing, it was too late to stop. An intellectual thirst is impossible to sate. Waking in the first dawn, the old man would lie regarding with the tenderness of a parent, the frail boyish form outlined under the covers of the flat bed near the hearth. "What will happen to him?" he thought. "What have I done to him?" In his will he left a little farm to Robinson Dozer, from his holdings in the county. Also that part of his library which had no pertinence to the state.

By rights Robinson Dozer should have gone North.

Eliza told him as much, the day after the funeral. "I'll always be as good to you as I can because of Papa. But there's not going to be anybody else like him, not down here. As I said when Xavier got killed in the war, This is another life I've got to start, another person I've got to be. You can stay here as long as you want to—"

"I've packed already, Miss Eliza. With your permission, I'll be leaving this afternoon."

"Oh." She gave him a hard look but she did not inquire into his business. "If I were you, I'd sell the land Papa left you and find some place up North. I'll write a note to Judge Standsbury. Maybe for Papa's sake he'll write letters to that college in the East. Do you want me to do that?"

He had been laughed at in her house, and he would not, could not, ask for anything. "Whatever you would like to do, Miss Eliza."

She turned abruptly to her desk, pulling paper forward from the pigeonholes, drawing out blotter, inkstand, and pen. "If it weren't for Papa—" The letters came out blackly aslant, but the words, as always in letters or conversations "outside the family," were courteous and warm.

Judge Standsbury, seated in his law office near the fire, said "Ummm" three times to the letter. He had no idea what to do with Robinson Dozer. His air of benevolent learning imparted the impression that he knew everything practical as a matter of course. When he took off his glasses and pressed his brows between two fingers he seemed to be weighing a number of diverse possibilities. Actually he was provoked at this whim of old John's, educating a colored boy, and the way John had reached out and snagged him from the other side of the grave.

"What do you plan to do once you get up North, Robinson?"

"I should first like to acquire a college degree, sir, then possibly secure a position as a teacher. I might even look into the law."

"Ummm," said Judge Standsbury.

In the grate a lump of soft coal burst from within and two parts of it tumbled out on the floor. Judge Standsbury watched Robinson's appreciative handling of the fire tongs and shovel, as if the feel of the wrought iron pleased him. As indeed it did. Along with a taste for Latin prose, Robinson had acquired a tendency to feel at home under hand-carved moldings.

"These affairs will take a little time, Robinson, a little time."

"I recognize that, Judge Standsbury."

"You mean to go back out to Miss Eliza's?"

"Miss Eliza and I do not have too successful an under-standing."

"Then I think you'd better come down to stay at our place, Robinson, while we're waiting for these—er, matters to go through."

In the ten years that Robinson was the Standsbury butler, the matter of his going North was never mentioned again. Judge Standsbury sometimes woke in the night and thought with a twinge in the direction of the old Senator's grave that he had never written letters for Robinson. But Robinson had never mentioned the matter again. Well, he was a whole lot better off down here and probably knew it. Hadn't they taken him in? Easy, easy now, Judge Standsbury slid back into sleep.

The truth was, Robinson could never bring himself to ask for anything. In summer he wore a white coat; in winter a black one with a white boiled shirt, starched collar, and black string tie. If he was superior to all the Negroes, he was no less superior to all the whites, for the Standsbury household was a sociable one—not much given to books. Robinson lived gravely among silver, polished woods, and heavy glass de-canters. In his room off the kitchen he read the books the Senator had left him. None of the Standsbury children dared enter his quarters. He was the terror of their youth.

The first anybody knew that Robinson had a wife and two children was the day he left the Standsburys for good. He led his family into the parlor where everyone was assembled just following Sunday dinner, and introduced them all around. He was already packed, he said, and would be leaving within the hour. Then he led the way from the room.

"So that's how Robinson spent his Sundays," said Judge Standsbury after the entire family had passed ten minutes in silence, something of a record. He had not dared say this in front of Robinson.

Ever after the Standsburys remembered him and talked about him, for living with Robinson in the house was a memorable thing. A glance from him was worse than a beating from their parents. The parents, too, had felt supervised, and had been known to leave the house to quarrel so that Robinson would not overhear them. His opinions were never expressed; hence everyone worried all the time about what he thought. When guests came, Robinson gave the Standsburys great prestige. In fact, his service with them solidified them in the opinion that they were aristocrats; before, they had often suspected that they were not. Yet they were never really comfortable with him, and his departure liberated their spirits so much that things looked rather perilous for a week or so. Judge Standsbury came to the table once in his shirtsleeves, and the children were discovered romping barefoot in the best parlor. But nobody said they wanted him back because neither they nor anybody else ever really liked Robinson. The old Senator had loved him, and this love had emancipated him, had made him independent, learned, scornful, superior, and unkind.

When he left he went back to the piece of land the Senator had willed him, which had been what Judge Standsbury was asked to sell for him to finance his way up North. Here he took possession from the former tenant and began to farm. For the first time in his life he wore a pair of overalls, blue-black at first and heavy as sailcloth, bending harshly to his thin limbs' motion, but finally a blue as delicate as spring sky reflected in an old window, and as gently textured as silk.

Word drifted back to town that Robinson had started a school for Negroes. Soon now, he was seen in town on Saturdays, not in overalls, but in the old black suit and string tie. He had long been a story, now he was a "character." Negroes, who had never liked the "high-white" Standsbury butler, accepted him, and even white people treated him with respect, called him 'Fessor without joking, and sometimes gave him a small donation. It was believed that you could not really teach Negroes anything; it was reported that Robinson could not get them to attend classes any more than the town schoolmaster could, but even when Vardaman stumped the state with the message that "every nigger you educate is another nigger you have to kill," it was not said anywhere in Lacey that the school was a bad thing until the First World War was over and the boys came home.

Three of the boys were big black bucks from Robinson's part of the county. They had learned a thing or two in France, they felt, and they called on Robinson to tell him about it. Later, they started taking lessons from Robinson at night. One of them had contrived to lose an arm in France: he got a disability check from the government, and the other two borrowed from him unmercifully, so they did not have to go to work. They were often remarked uptown on the square and not only on Saturday. There was something sinister about them: their togetherness, their size, their not working, their swagger, their watchfulness. It was hoped that Robinson was not putting any ideas in their heads. "Or vice versa," a man like Acey Tallant might say, flipping his cigarette into the open grate in the chancery clerk's office. He "traveled" during the week, gave the impression of statewide political connections, and was wont to check by the courthouse on weekends to see what was going on.

The three Negro veterans wore their uniforms, woolen shirts and khaki peg-top pants with wrap leggings that tapered to their wide army shoes. There was talk that Negroes would try to push for the vote since the war ended, that veterans would organize to this end; some said that Negroes had volunteered in order to get to France and sleep with white women; now that they were back, people said, they were crazy for more of the same. An automobile dealer ordered them out of his showroom because they had got in the habit of coming in and loitering all afternoon around the stove. Henry Harper said they always came into his grocery store after dark along about closing time and would not say what they wanted for an unaccountable long time. His uncle, old Phillip Harper, chased them out one night with his walking stick. They seemed determined to make people nervous. White people had been glad to listen at first to their experiences in France, but now they were tired of it; the same story four times over would not work any more; Negroes, if worthless, were at least supposed to be charming or funny. Robinson Dozer, as a matter of fact, had got tired of them too. He was still trying to make them stop talking about France so they could learn something, when the troubles started.

In quick succession a white farmer's cotton house was burned down, another had his pigs let out, a third was driving to town when the wheels of his buggy came off. White householders began to feel uncomfortably far from town, indeed from one another, and count themselves greatly outnumbered by the Negro farmers and renters. Unfortunately, at this time a white farmer's daughter drowned in Petticocow.

It had been a season of dry weather and she was found in the shallows of the deep hole where she had died. Or perhaps she had not died in the water, but had been thrown in afterward. She was heavily bruised about the head and face, and there were said to have been signs of violence on her elsewhere, but since the family would on no account allow her to be examined, all descriptions of them conflicted. The path that led from Robinson Dozer's house to the country road ran along the creek bank for a time—it ran, in fact, quite near the deep hole.

The father of the girl at first, in his grief, got out his gun to go and kill the three Negro veterans. His neighbors restrained him. Negroes outnumbered them three to one, but relations had always been peaceful, even pleasant. The families of the boys were "good Negroes." There were surely better ways to handle this.

After the funeral, the white men met and talked far into the night; the next day a sober wagonload drove ino town, calm in the sense of having reached just decisions without resort to violence. They had two demands to make: first that the three veterans be arrested immediately on suspicion of murder and, even if they appeared innocent beyond doubt, that they be made to leave the county for good; second, that Robinson Dozer's school be closed. "You see what happens," they said, "when you try to educate a nigger."

The three Negro veterans said that the first they heard of the girl's death was when they were arrested on the town square. Following the arrival of the latest disability check they had spent several days pleasuring themselves over in the Delta at a Negro settlement known as Coontown. Several hundred Negroes there must have seen them and remembered them, but though they sent urgent messages not one appeared to say so. The sheriff locked them up in the jail, the farming delegation turned homeward in the creaking wagon, the town passed uneasy nights.

Robinson Dozer was exercised; he made several patient trips between town and his home. He called on the sheriff, talked with the veterans, was closeted with Judge Standsbury for an hour. Secretly he did not so much care what happened to the boys; he did not want his school to be closed. He gained permission, at last, to assemble a black delegation: the parents of the boys (it then emerged that two of them were brothers), two leading Negro freeholders, and himself. The white delegation promised to return, and Judge Standsbury himself agreed to preside. Though tired, Robinson supped in the evening with dignity, spoke little with his family, and composed himself early for bed. The time had been set for two-thirty; the place was the courthouse.

Robinson Dozer with his delegation arrived at the courthouse an hour before the appointed time. He arranged this purposely. He did not want anybody saying that the niggers didn't care. The white delegation had been in town since morning. They scarcely ever saw town except on Saturdays, so they made a picnic of it, ate a box lunch, bought one thing and another, and jawed a good bit in the stores. In the drugstore they saw Acey Tallant—he had just come back to Lacey from a trip out of the state. He asked a lot of questions but his only comment was that "things had certainly gotten out of hand." He was seen later in the newspaper office, and again in the café, whence he crossed decisively to the pool hall.

Up at the courthouse, the sheriff sent the Negro deputation upstairs to the large courtroom to wait. He sent a man with a shotgun to stand at the door. He had the windows open for the first time that spring, and the flies were about to run him crazy. Around two o'clock he sent two armed deputies to the jail for the three veterans. A tubby, jolly, rather simple-minded man, his theory was that Negroes should be kept intimidated by a big show of handcuffing and guns. "You can do anything with 'em," he said, "as long as you keep the hell scared out of 'em." Playing solitaire at his desk, he heard the step of the three prisoners and the two white men resound in the big halls and pass up the staircase.

Judge Standsbury spent a calm morning, ate a good dinner, and settled for a little nap before going up to the courthouse. Several times the phrase, "Friend of black and white alike," occurred to him, for he had gained the age where what they could not escape saying in the newspapers when he died wandered pleasantly through his mind. He felt gratified that Robinson had had at last to call on him about something. Robinson had made all of the Standsburys feel uncomfortably that things would someday be the other way around. The judge napped with the Memphis paper on his chest and his feet covered by an afghan. At two-fifteen he rose, put on his coat, buttoned his vest, adjusted the heavy gold chain which caught the sun so skillfully, selected his handsomest silver-mounted walking cane and, wishing to be not more than a few minutes late, started briskly toward town.

The chubby sheriff, hearing the trample of a dozen men in the hall, came out of his office to see what was going on. The men were all from town or nearby; none of them had any personal connection with the matter in hand. They looked pleasant enough, however; the only noticeably sinister thing about them was that they were all of about the same appearance—tall, active, with weathered faces, neither young nor old—you might have thought that somebody had chosen them. The sheriff knew them all, and that they were part of his constituency.

"Where you boys going?" he asked.

"Just upstairs. Just to see what's going on."

The man who had answered was Acey Tallant. Everyone had expected him to be the spokesman. He looked like the others, only more so—he was always in some slight way different from any group he was discovered among. And he was discovered among them all. He hunted with men richer than himself who liked him well enough but said he would never amount to very much. He was not originally from Winfield County, but had married into a good family there. He talked about property in neighboring counties and in the Delta, sold a bit of insurance, managed some real estate for his wife, and was known to hold some sort of intermittent job with a state office in Jackson. If you asked what it was he would tell you, but five minutes later it would seem you were no clearer on it than before. He was attractive to women. Always, when he talked to anyone he managed to make it seem that he was wasting valuable time, and for this subtlety to make its perfect stamp required a man like the chubby sheriff, holding an uncertain grip on a small job, hoping he was popular with everybody.

"Y'all not toting guns or anything?"

"Of course we ain't."

"I don't want any trouble, you know."

"Trouble? Who said anything about trouble? We're just curious."

"Okay then. If you promise."

"Sure we promise."

The chancery clerk around the corner blew his nose on a large white handkerchief, went back into his office and shut the door. "I think you'd better go home," he said to his secretary. "In fact, I think we both better go home."

Upstairs, in the courtroom, the windows were open on the warm February day. Somebody had had the forethought to build a fire in the stove that morning, but now in the steady early afternoon warmth, the heat was superfluous and formed a visible sleepy glaze on the air.

Robinson Dozer had selected, with a teacher's instinct, a chair at the end of the table where the court clerk sat when court was in session. He now wore round gold-rimmed glasses before his round 'coon-dark eyes; he kept his hands folded on the table before him and his face showed nothing. The three Negro veterans, from the habit of standing around stoves to talk about what they had seen in France, were standing by the stove now, albeit they were running sweat down the collars of their khaki woolens. They had got sluggish in the heat and their mouths hung slightly open. Their three pairs of eyes saw three directions of nothing. The four older Negroes, their parents, had taken a bench together and were sitting now facing the empty judge's stand as though they had come early for church. The two freeholders sat on the front row near the table. The men wore their best suits, with ties. The women wore silk dresses and hats; one took snuff and another fanned herself. Over in the far corner of the large room, another Negro couple were sitting. They had come to see Judge Standsbury about getting a divorce, had been mistaken for part of Robinson's group, and had been sent upstairs by the sheriff. Now they wished to leave, but when they went to the door to explain, one of the deputies ordered them back. Awkward, obedient, ignorant, hoping only to please, they did not attempt to say more, but repeated, "Yes suh, yes suh," and drew away. They would not say anything now until somebody asked them something. Frightened, sitting close together, they began to think they did not want to get a divorce after all.

When the crowd of strange white men appeared in the center aisle of the courtroom, Robinson Dozer did not at first turn his head. "It looks like the niggers done taken over," said Acey Tallant. Robinson seemed to be looking them over, but the light glazed on his lenses and no one could tell but what he was contemptuous.

"We are expecting Judge Standsbury," he said.

"When you talk to me, nigger, you better say 'Mister.'"

"I don't know your name, sir."

"Then I'll tell you something funny. You ain't ever going to know my name. My name don't matter. I'm white and you're black, that's all that you and me need to know."

The delegation of farmers, seeing that Judge Standsbury was approaching the courthouse doors from the opposite side, gathered away from where the wagon was hitched by the iron fence and started together across the lawn. They were halfway to the door when the firing started and had to break apart and scatter when one of the Negro veterans, jumping from the upstairs window, nearly fell on top of them. It was the one-armed one who, ever since he had had his narrow escape in France, was apt to panic at the approach of danger. He had simply run out of the open window as though he would run on the air, and was still running with his legs and the one arm pumping perfectly together, when the white men saw him and scattered. It was thought the fall killed him, but the men were warned to stand aside while someone fired into his body from above.

Judge Standsbury was just entering the courthouse door when the shots began echoing and resounding. Plaster fell around him as he ran upstairs, but they would not let him in. He wept openly and called for Robinson and at last was carried home, completely broken up. The family reassured him until he died that nothing that had happened was his fault, and he tried to go on with his law practice. Yet it seemed to him that to the extent he would not let what had happened in the courthouse stop him in his work, the work was vitiated, and to the extent that he would let it stop him, not only the work but he himself ceased to exist. "He'll never be any good any more," the family said to one another. "Nothing named Tallant is ever coming in this house again." Yet one of his granddaughter's best friends was Acey Tallant's son. "Wouldn't he just die?" they said to one another, but by then he was dead already.

Beckwith, Robinson's youngest son, could still remember that they waited past sundown that night for his father to come home, that nobody ate anything all day, that when he giggled once his mother slapped his face, and that no lamp was lighted.

Then the car came jouncing, rattling down the dry-rutted

country road, and in its yellow approach the shadows walked like giants, paused, heard the silence, then the sound, and walked on. Then it was dark again. His sister clutched him by the shoulders and he held on to her knee. Finally his mother, who seemed to have it all in her head exactly when to do things, went out into the yard with his brother and together they carried in his father's body.

They washed him and dressed him in his other black suit, the old one, put on a clean boiled shirt and starched collar with the black string tie, and laid him out in bed. He lay straight and frail under the covers, and his head on the pillows was small as a child's. You would have thought he had died right there, decently. That was what everything they were doing seemed to be trying to pretend. But his mother said, in front of them all, though talking to Beck, who was the littlest:

"It's this they taken him up for, so's they could cast him down. Say Yes suh and No ma'am and You sho' is right, and don't ever say nothing else. What face you got, keep for the black. Yo' daddy never learned it. You see what done happened to him."

an
impulse
restrained

41. Duncan Harper lowered the lamp from Robinson Dozer's picture, and turned to Lucy. They each in their own way knew the whole story, but whether they had been told it or not or by whom would never be clear. Southerners hear parts of stories with their ears, and the rest they know with their hearts.

"If Beck will come to me," said Duncan, "I swear to do everything for his own good."

Aunt Mattie's rocker creaked. "I says to Mister Henry Harper many's the time, 'Mister Henry, how come you is such a gemman and yo' uncle so triflin' a man?' Said it right in front of Mister Phillip. But Mister Phillip he jes' giggle. 'I'll have you churched, Mattie, don' watch out. Sho' gwy have you churched.'"

"I don't know where he's at," said Lucy.

For an instant Duncan's eyes met W.B.'s. Then he set the lamp on the table and took his hat.

"Dey always tell it on Mattie, When Mattie got any sass to say, Mattie sass you to the face. But Mattie loves her white folks. What dey gwy do 'thout Mattie? Who gwy love 'em like Mattie do?"

The white man's step was in the hall, on the porch and path. They heard the plowshare scrape against the gate, heard him stumble once going down the hill; then the car door slammed and the starter touched the motor.

Lucy looked down for where W.B. was standing, but W.B. had vanished. She moved instantly to the far corner of the room and was back in the kitchen with W.B. by the collar and the buggy whip raised over his head before he could lower the foot that he was putting the shoe on.

"Where you think you going? Answer me that! You think you going to be the smart one, doing what the white man say. You think somebody going to buy you a ice cream on Saddy. You well's to learn right now, boy. You's a nigger, and you ain't never going to be nothing else. You don't learn it now you ain't going to live to learn it tomorrow. If I don't learn you, who is?"

The whip was keen, and her thin arm drove it terribly upon him. He danced at first, then threw up his hands and fought the blows like wasps, cried for her to stop, squirmed free and ran. He might have got away from a man, but she brought him down before he had gone two steps, and never missed a stroke. She tore his shirt to shreds and brought blood out of him, and kept right on till the whip broke, teaching him, the only way she knew how, the things she thought he had to learn.

"Nigger! Nigger! Nigger!" she cried, beating him, and her throat shone wet with her tears.

Jimmy comes home

42. A few minutes after Willard Follansbee had left Bud Grantham's house, another car pulled up before the front, and Jimmy Tallant himself alighted gingerly. He saluted the young doctor who had driven him there from the hospital.

"And take it easy," said the doctor through the window. "You got everybody's blood in Winfield County in you now. You've about drained us dry, to tell the truth."

"They lost blood and you lost sleep. I know I put you over the jumps. Thanks for everything, Doc."

"Goodnight. If you need anything, holler."

" 'Night."

Wobbly, he felt as tall as a telephone pole, and assailed the steps to the front gallery like an old man. From the room he peered out to the back porch where Bud still rocked and sang away, though in a calmer style than when the meeting fired him:

> "Shall we gather at the river
>   Where bright angel feet have trod,
>   With its mighty waters ever
>   Flowing by the throne of God?"
> "*Yes*, we'll gather at the river . . ."

"Well, I'll be damned," said Jimmy to himself.

He entered the room where he knew Bella would be staying. He propped a pillow against the headboard of the bed, and let himself down with a sigh. He switched on the bedside light to see the time. In the crib, the baby opened its eyes and regarded him in Indian silence from under the spiky jut of hair. "Hi, Buster," said Jimmy. The baby knotted its fists to yawn, squirmed, and went back to sleep. Jimmy turned out the light.

"Is that you, honey baby?" Bud asked from the porch.

The more Jimmy thought about answering, the less he seemed to find the strength to do it.

"Your old daddy's been setting here thinking tonight, sugar foot," said Bud, through the window. "I'm going with you to the meeting tomorrow night. I'm tired to death studying about this election, and I don't want dealing with them New Orleans fellows, no more than Jimmy did. I'm weary of this wicked earth, and if that preacher don't watch out I'll rise and tell it right out in front of everybody. Bud Grantham was raised to know left from right good as any. My mother was as fine a woman as ever walked the earth. I'm going on to bed now, baby."

"Well, I'll be damned," Jimmy said to himself again, hearing Bud's steps pass down the back gallery toward the bathroom.

The bed where Jimmy lay stood near the front windows of the house, and when the shade was raised one could watch the highway down the distance of the gravel drive. Bud's house had stood there long before they had straightened the roads and paved them. It had once been a country place, hard to get to as any other, but known to be worth the trouble for what you could get wrapped in a newspaper by driving around to the back and blinking the lights three times.

In those days there was every size of child around the house to play with, and every kind of dog to hunt with. As a boy, Jimmy used to go home with Granthams from school, spend the night or the weekend, hunt for 'coon and 'possum. There had been a well in the back yard—you let a tin pipe down for the water; at night in winter you could hear the dogs under the house when they scuffled for comfort, bumping the beams, or dreamed about a rabbit, or yawned with the high *Iiii* sound. In summer there were peaches like gold to eat, all off three or four old trees that grew on the slope where you went down to the still. And the still itself, all bowered thick in green brush, vine and secret path, was the place of rite and the hushed tone: with solemnity—pride and humility unlikely to occur again—Jimmy had learned its mysteries.

Now there was the highway instead of the old crooked road (which the supervisors had at least graveled better than any other road in the county), and water came in pipes; the still was gone in favor of the Idle Hour, and whisky, though wrapped in a newspaper the same as ever, bore a bonded government stamp and a different flavor.

No wonder Bud Grantham was weary of this wicked earth. Jimmy Tallant got pretty sick of it himself.

A car eased off the highway, and approached the house so slowly that when it stopped at the front steps the wheels scarcely turned at all.

Bella's voice came distinctly, the instant the motor died. "How in the world did you know where I was at is what I can't figure out."

Another voice, a man's, was not so clear.

"Oh," said Bella. "They told you because they'd seen me go past to the meeting."

The man talked so long then that Jimmy had given up

hearing any more, though Bella kept saying over and over, "Well, I think you're just the sweetest thing." Then she said, "But you just don't know how crazy I am about Jimmy. He's the sweetest thing in the world." Then she said, "I feel right bad about the baby myself, that is, if favor means anything. I'm not for sure. Some say it does, some say not." And finally she said, getting out of the car, "But I think you're just the sweetest thing in the world, Mr. Pilston."

"Well, I'll be goddamned," said Jimmy to himself.

When she tipped in and closed the bedroom door, she switched on the light and nearly shrieked.

"Hush," said Jimmy. "Bud's asleep and so's the baby."

"Were you wake? Were you there all the time?"

"No, I been asleep too. I just now woke up. Why?"

"Well, I been down to the tent meeting. There was a man drove me home."

"Who was it?"

"One of them Moreheads from over in Leflore. He was at the meeting."

"Which one? Angus?"

"Not him. It was one I never have seen before. Funny, I can't call his name. He asked about you."

"That right?"

"I thought maybe you heard the car and all. I just didn't want you to think nothing."

"I see."

Suddenly, she beamed. She came to him and gave him a great big kiss. "How you feel, darling?"

"Mighty puny," said Jimmy.

"Can I get you anything? How about a glass of sweet milk?"

"I was aiming to tell you soon as you got back, Bella. I think I best go down to sleep in the Idle Hour. The house is probably in a mess, and there's not but one bed up there anyway."

"You can't sleep with me!"

"I'm too stove up, honey. You know that. We couldn't have any fun anyway."

"Oh. Well, how long's it going to be, Jimmy? Before we can?"

"I don't know." He loosened a hangnail with his thumb. "Doc says a year or two."

"A year!" Her mouth seemed to have fallen permanently open.

"How's the preacher?" Jimmy asked. "Any good?"

"I just can't stand it, Jimmy. What on earth am I going to do? I never heard of such a thing as that. The doctor told me the bullet went through the lower part of your right lung and the upper part of your stomach, and that the most delicate operation he ever performed was getting it out of you and sewing you back up again, but I don't see why your lung and stomach's got anything to do with what you want to do with the rest of you."

"My injuries," he said, fending her off, "are my own business. Don't mess with me, Bella. You know I had three hemorrhages in the hospital, doing no more than lying flat on my back."

"Yeah, I know, Jimmy, but a year—!"

"At the least. Maybe two."

She sat with her hands knotted in her lap.

"You remember that Mr. Pilston?" she said suddenly.

"Sure, I remember him."

"Well, if there ever was anything between him and me, which everybody thought there was on account of the baby took a notion to look like him—I ain't saying there was, understand?—but *if* there was, then it was mainly your fault."

"*My* fault! I don't know how in the hell you figure that."

"Well, it was because I was so crazy about you, and first you'd pay attention to me and then you wouldn't. If you got drunk you'd dance with me, tell me how pretty I was and all, but sober you wouldn't look at me twice except to poke fun at me. It was then I got frustrated."

"You got what?"

"Frustrated."

"You're still reading those blooming magazines."

"Well, if it's true, does it matter whereabouts I found it?"

"I reckon not, honey."

"I got to feeling like if you wouldn't pay me any mind, I wished somebody would come along who would pay me some mind. The word they use for that is frustration."

"I think you're a nice girl, honey," said Jimmy, and kissed her on the forehead. "I don't blame you for anything you've done. Now you find me a blanket or two because I'm so weak I'm liable to get cold even in this weather, and fetch me the flashlight. It's time I got to bed."

Nothing would do but that she went down to the Idle Hour with him and made the bed for him.

"I meant to ask Bud," he said. "Has Follansbee been around?"

"He was out here tonight before I went to the meeting."

"What'd he say? Anything?"

"Lucy came to look after the baby for me. He was trying to get out of her where Beck was. Said if he found Beck he was going to treat him the same as if Beck had raped a white woman."

"God," said Jimmy. "What a scummy joker that Follansbee is."

"Jimmy, darling, just let me stay down here with you a little old while."

"I'm tired out, honey. I'm so weak I'm folding up."

"Well." She plumped the pillow and laid it straight, but

he propped it against the headboard and lay down as he had in the room at Bud's. She kissed him goodnight, and picked up the flashlight. At the door she turned. "You don't love me," she told him quietly. "That's the whole thing."

She went away behind the flashlight beam, through the dark.

stain
of
the past

43. He stayed for some time without moving to undress, twirling a penny box of matches between his thumb and forefinger. He tossed it aside, pulled himself up, and went through to the office, where he found first the light switch, then the telephone, and dialed a number.

"Hi, Tink," he said happily.

"Jimmy! Where are you?"

"Back home."

"But you weren't supposed to be out till next week."

"There was some woman having twins across the hall. They decided I'd be better off at home."

"Do you feel all right?"

"Sure, I'm fine. Oh, Tinker, thanks for the transfusion."

"Don't mention it. Duncan tried to give some, but he wasn't the right type."

"I'm having cards engraved to mail out. You'll both get one."

She giggled.

"How are things, Tink?"

"Okay. Everything's okay."

"Then I guess Harper must be home."

"Yes, he is. You want to talk to him?"

"Please."

A moment later Duncan's clear voice was saying hello. What don't I like about him, Jimmy wondered, all aside from hating his guts for marrying Tinker. There's something else. . . .

"I appreciated you offering me some of your blood, Harper."

"I tried," said Duncan, "but it wasn't the same type."

"They tell me," said Jimmy, "that I've got the commonest damn blood there is."

"What class does that put me in?"

"The blue class, probably. Say, Harper, you know you kept deviling me up at the hospital to tell you who it was shot me? Well, I've thought it over. Follansbee's out to get Dozer. I was afraid of that all along. I don't like to do this on account of Bud. But all things being considered I'm ready to turn everything I know over to you."

Duncan said, after a moment, "What kind of a deal is this?"

"No deal at all. I'm on the level. I can't locate Dozer for you, but I can fix it so everybody will know he had nothing to do with it. If you want to drive out here, we can fix up a statement."

"A statement on what?"

"You may not know. There were some gambling gentlemen from New Orleans by to see me that day—"

"I had a very good source of information about that. In fact, she was just the other side of the door."

"Let's keep her out of this."

"You listen to me, Tallant. You been lying up there in that hospital keeping shut-mouthed for two and a half weeks while this thing of Dozer got good and hot from one end of the county to the other. What happened could happen; you were sitting back to let this election fall right in your lap. As long as Woolbright and me were on the spot you were willing to watch us fry. Now you've got word the tide has turned. As a matter of fact, I'm at home waiting for New Orleans to call any minute. You needn't think you can jump on the band wagon and good as say to everybody, Look what I did! Kerney and I broke this thing and we're about to break you and you know it. You've had your chance. You've got less sense of public good than any man I ever saw, and if you ask me—" He stopped.

"Finish it," said Jimmy. "You were going to say I came by it naturally."

"I didn't say that," Duncan returned, his voice cooling. "If you'd come around sooner it would be different. But here at the eleventh hour— We don't want your help, Tallant. That's all."

Jimmy replaced the telephone, switched out the light, and closed the dusty office. When he gained the bed and sank down again, he was shaking.

He remembered what Bud Grantham had said through the window: Weary of this wicked earth. But Bud could do what Jimmy couldn't. Bud would rise in a meeting someday, if not this summer, then the next one, and tell his sins and let Jesus save him. When all the doors were shut, a lot of folks knocked at that one. They claimed it always opened. Well, I'll never know, Jimmy thought.

I even tried to get that boy to kill me, he thought, hardly believing it all himself. Even that didn't work, though it might have if Tinker hadn't come . . . Tinker Taylor . . . cowboy sailor. . . .

He raised up the matchbox to read what it said on the cover, when his hand grew tired as death; he let it fall, and presently he slept.

part five

44. In New Orleans, in the summer, the early morning is apt to have a false freshness, as if somebody had sprayed a big black stevedore with cologne. About ten the city begins to sweat: the sun is like a red-hot stove lid, only nobody looks at the sun, the heat being a condition in which one exists, and is not to be seen any more than air or the grace of God. All the subtle diplomacies of civilization enter into circumventing the heat: it obviously cannot be met on open field. There is air conditioning now for everything from movie palaces to dim little bars, but there are patios too, and latticed porches, shuttered windows, and polished hallways deep down the stairwell with old glass shielded from the glare. In Audubon Park the swans drift to the shade as it blackens, and down on Tchoupatoulos Street women go about all day in their slip and houseshoes, and an electric fan looks at them with one big eye from head to toe, toe to head, while they nap in the afternoon. With a car, you can take the shore drive along Lake Pontchartrain, though there is no shade and sometimes even the breeze off the water is hot. Down in the French Quarter you can buy tall frosted glasses with minty mixtures, cold as snow, though alcohol is always heating and will give you an awful wallop when you go out again. Then there are the oyster bars.

The oysters come in every day out of the beds in the river and the lake, and it is supposed to be dangerous to eat them in the summer, but they are kept directly on ice and are so good, especially when you have a hangover, that to many people it is worth the chance. A man takes them off the ice and breaks them open with an oyster knife and serves them by the dozen on a plate of ice. You can mix yourself a sauce out of catsup with a little Worcestershire sauce, lemon juice, and a dash of horseradish, though for an uneasy stomach lemon juice alone is enough. These, along with a tall cold glass of beer, will go a long way toward fortifying the soul to endure the heat of the day.

There is not much crime in New Orleans in the summer. At night, on weekends, Negroes carve each other to fancy bits with a razor, but if you put all the Negro crimes in the paper there would be no room for international affairs. Down on Bourbon Street, which burns at night like a pool of oil, homosexuals sometimes make nasty petulant scenes in the bars. But a people so earnestly concerned with keeping cool do not find the materials of crime ready to hand, and nothing about the young man who was eating oysters and drinking beer and the older man who had joined him would have told the waiter that one was from the intricate society of the underworld and the other a plainclothes man from the city detectives. Their conversation looked casual, not even businesslike. It might have been about the weather, how hot it was.

"You seen Sam?" the older man asked the young one. He picked his teeth with a match stub and watched the other lift an oyster till it severed from the shell.

"Not since last night. I won't see him either. He fired me."

"What you plan to do now?"

"I'm fixing to go back home, I reckon." The oyster glided down his throat. He took a swallow of beer. "It ain't nothing like New Orleans, but maybe that's a good thing."

"What is home at?"

"Up in Mississippi. Up in Tippah County."

"Well, there's one thing certain."

"What's that?"

"You might go back to Tippah County, but you sure got to detour by Winfield."

An oyster actually paused in the boy's throat. "Sam," he said, and swallowed. "That's how come he fired me. The son-ofabitch. He told on me. If they was to tell on each other, they'd start shooting. It just goes to show you, I ain't one of them. They knew it and I knew it. I never was."

"There aren't any charges I know of. You're just wanted to give evidence." The detective ordered himself a beer, then, on second thought, a half-dozen oysters.

"There couldn't be any charges, because I never tried to do nothing. It was completely accidental. It was the first shot I missed since four years ago when Unker Chollie Klappert said, 'If you'll go real easy you can shoot the marker off that hen's foot.' But she lifted her foot up somehow or 'nother and the bullet nicked her on the leg, so Unker Chollie said we was obliged to have her for dinner."

"Yes, and what about this other little accident? Just how did it happen?"

"I never hated anything so bad in my life," the boy said. "I always did like Mr. Tallant, though I never had met him but one time before, but the time we drove up in Miss'ippi to see him, we found ourselves to be kinfolks. Sure did. He was one of Unker Chollie's cousins, the one I was just now talking about with the hen. I don't know which side of the family, so maybe we was only connected. Anyway I sure did like him. If I was just ranking the folks I know I'd rather shoot by accident, I'd put him closer to the bottom than anybody outside of Unker Chollie Klappert and Aunt Darr. And Mama, naturally. Never seen him but twice. But that's how I feel about it."

"Yeah, so how did this get to happen?"

"Sam and Pilston and Mitchell went up there to Franklin

to see about farming out some gambling equipment. They were going to put some money into the sheriff's race so it would be safe to operate. But Mr. Tallant didn't much want to trade with them about the election. About that time Mr. Tallant's wife come in toting a baby which Sam said later was Pilston to the life, though I couldn't notice much resemblance. Don't never seem to me a little baby looks like any*thing*, let alone any*body*. Yet there's them that claim to see it. I don't reckon that's got the world and all to do with anything, except then was when Mr. Tallant got up and left the room. Sam sent me and Mitchell after him to bring him back and settle up about the election."

"So then?"

"So then we followed him on back of the roadhouse across a pasture and down a hill, back to the edge of a field where some woods started. We hollered to him to come on back, and Mitchell said, 'You better do like we tell you; this boy here's got a gun.' He turned around and started laughing. Real friendly and easy, like he was every other time. He said, 'You better take the gun yourself, Mitchell. You'll never get that boy to shoot me. I wish you could. Me and Wally's kinfolks, and what you asking for ain't done. But then I tell you, Wally,' he said, 'I hone to see how good you can shoot. You take this four-bit piece and when I thumb it in the air like that'—he thumbed it—'you see can you bring it down for me.' He thumbed it up again and when he stopped talking he looked at me and stopped laughing. He had the saddest face I ever saw. It was mournful. It called to mind a song Unker Chollie said he used to get on the old earphone radio set out of Shreseport, went 'Look down, look down that lonesome road before you travel on.' I always liked that song and thought it many's the time traveling round in the car with Sam and Mitchell and them. Then he was holding the fifty-cent piece on his thumb and saying, 'How good can you shoot now, sure enough? It must be a sight to behold.' So I said, 'It is a sight.' Then he said, real soft, 'Then shoot for me, Wally,' and he thumbed the coin, but where it had been sailing up free towards the trees it missed that time and only went about a foot high; I guess it never cleared him. Then was when I shot, having made up my mind to it. I don't know if you know anything about shooting or not, but once your mind tells your finger to pull that trigger it don't make no difference if a elephant gets in the way, you're going to shoot.

"It must be laying somewhere around there still, that four-bit piece, plugged. For I hit it, and him too. The minute I saw what had happened, I started to run towards him, but Mitchell grabbed me and got the gun out of my hand. 'You get on back up that hill,' he said. 'Don't, you'll stay down here and keep him company.' Mitchell taken charge of everything. He seen a nigger down the hill, down in the bottom, and went on back to scare him away so he couldn't tell he seen us there.

"It was later we heard from up there that Mister Tallant wasn't dead. I was mighty glad to hear it. Glad! I was downright thankful."

"It squares with what Mitchell says," said the detective, "almost word for word." He dusted the cracker crumbs from his mouth and polished off his beer. "I got to go send a wire up to Winfield County. Seems they had all decided that nigger you say Mitchell scared off had done the shooting, and some boy up there is having a hell of a time getting elected sheriff when he couldn't find the nigger or you either."

"I can't say how it happened, except by the way he was looking, so solemn and sad, his eyes pulling at me. You believe in himotism? Maybe he himotized me."

"Where you going to be?"

"Right here."

"Not going to hunt up Sam?"

"That bastard better stay away from me. Him and his talk about the 'code.'"

"He never told you to hit Tallant. What accident you had was your accident. I think Sam's played it straight. If you'd done it *for* him, he'd have backed you."

"He could have told me. Talked to him an hour last night. All he said was he couldn't afford me any more. Never mentioned Mr. Tallant, Winfield County, Miss'ippi, or Highway 82."

"I reckon he was scared anybody that could have one accident like that could have two."

"Two. I already had two. You remember I told you about that old hen. I never ought have got mixed up in this kind of business, but I always thought you ought to put your talents to use."

"I'm counting on you to wait here for me, Wally."

"Glad to," said the boy, and smiled at him gently.

the
fugitive

45. Earlier that morning, up in Winfield County, Beck Dozer walked in the back door of his own house.

"Lawd, Beck," said Lucy, "is it sho' nuff you?"

"It's me," said Beck. "You going to give your baby a kiss?"

"I sho' is."

He swung her around and set her down again. "What time is it, Lucy?"

"I don't know, but it's early. Granny ain't off the slop jar yet. Lord to God, Beck, you scared me half to death."

"Got any coffee?"

"There's some on the stove. Us had a scontious time in this house last night. I most had to beat the stuffing out'n W.B."

"How come?"

"Mister Duncan Harper come out here again makes the third time since you been gone. He got on W.B. to make him go find you."

"What for?"

"Tell you how-all he going to pertect you, how-all he got the chance to win the 'lection if you shows up, what-all he aim to want to do. W.B. ain't got a grain. Time Mister Duncan left he out in the kitchen wif one shoe on reaching for the other one."

"How come you not to let him go? You think I can't do my own thinking?"

She went on mixing corn batter in an enamel pan, now and again dipping water in from the bucket on the shelf, beating it with a flopping sound that seemed to be part of what she said.

"I think you don't git yo'se'f right straight on back over to Humphreys County, you going to land in a peck of trouble. Mister Duncan ain't the onliest one got the word for you. I seen that other'n running for shurf, Mister Willard Follansbee—*he* claim do he see you first he going to do you like what they does when a nigger get with a white woman."

"Unker Beck," said W.B., coming in in his shirttail, "Aunt Lucy done frail the life outer me."

"You think you telling sump'n," Lucy said. "Well, you ain't."

"Come here, boy," said Beck. "Lord, Lucy. You'd think he was mixed up with a wildcat. Time going to come, W.B., when you going to go wheresoever you feels called on to go, no matter who tries to stop you. Is that right?"

"Sho' right, Unker Beck."

"Don't call me uncle any more, W.B. I'm your blood daddy, son. You are my own natural child."

Lucy stopped still with everything. She did not understand all she knew about Beck, but every time he brought out something fresh, he gentled her more. "I been knowing it all the time, Beck. But he ain't. W.B. ain't."

"I sho' ain't," W.B. said, in soft self-contemplation.

"Where his mama at?" Lucy asked.

"She in England, where she always was. In London. You don't have to know all about it, Lucy. She wrote me a letter saying she couldn't work and keep him too and that her husband was working too and wanted shut of him, since he was black. She said if I'd send her the money there was an American woman getting a divorce and coming back to the U.S., and she could get him in by her. Either that or she'd put him in a home over there. She would have done it too. All them folks over there in England, they take their children when they ain't no bigger than W.B. and send them to school, then they're shut of them, they don't have to see them much more. So I wrote her to send this child to me. That was the time I went up North. It all worked out. The woman brought him to a hamburger and beer place in Harlem, and left him by himself, sitting in the booth. We had it all planned on the telephone. She didn't want me to see her, or be seen with me. She was scared about the law, somehow or other."

"His mammy just give him away, never thought no more of it?"

"They're not like us. Don't seem they care for chillen like we do."

"Sho' don't," said Lucy. She took down a black iron griddle

with a handle like a loop of string, lifted an eye from the stove, and set the griddle over the flame.

"You glad I'm your daddy?" Beck asked W.B. "Want to, you can say Daddy. Go on. Say Daddy."

"I can't, Unker Beck," said W.B., overcome with the shyness of names. He put his face in Beck's shoulder.

Holding the spoon firm in the cup with his finger, Beck drained off his coffee and set it aside. He pulled the boy closer to him.

"You liable to have a little white baby one of these days, black boy. Don't giggle. What you laughing for? Turn your face around here, and listen what your daddy tells you.

"If a child of yours want to go North, you let him go along; that is, if you're not already North yourself. If you marry light enough, your children might cross the color line, but if they do, you tell them to make sure when they marry a white girl that she's really one hundred per cent pure white, because if she's not she's apt to wind up with a black baby and that might not go down so well with her folks. That is, if anybody still cares much by that time. In another thirty years or so, Lucy, they might just think it's cute to have a dark child. Look how they all gots to have a sun tan. You ever thought about that? The day of the white skin might be near about over.

"I read up on all such as this, son. Your Aunt Lucy don't know, and most white folks don't either, but if you're going to mess around on the color line you just as well to understand it. I never exactly meant to mess with the white, but the British women came running to the black skin."

Lucy spread bacon grease on the griddle with a rag swab wrapped on the end of a little cedar stick. The grease spit like sleet. "Was she a real white lady?" Lucy asked. She portioned out the batter in cakes on the hot griddle.

"W.B.'s mama? She wasn't any prize. She looked like she was about half-starved, just like you."

"That accounts for that big old boat W.B. been talking about ever since he got here."

"I remembers hit jest as plain," said W.B.

"Don't say hit. Say I remember it."

"I remember it."

"That's right." He rose and reached down three plates from the safe, then the molasses bucket, and went to the back porch to bring the butter in from the icebox.

"Don't you use up all that butter," Lucy said. "There ain't no more."

She set the first of the batter cakes on the table. Beck helped himself, thrusting his fork in to the hilt. He smiled.

"You know I told you my sister brought W.B. in a boat across Lake Michigan. How come you so dumb? Granny knows better than you. I bet she knows folks don't cross Lake Michigan in a boat."

"Granny don't know nothing. She don't know no more than me."

"Anybody knows that."

"I can't help it if I'm dumb," said Lucy. "You want some more coffee?"

"Just a tap. Mind how you pours that sorghum, W.B.!" He spooned sugar into his cup.

"The city of London," he resumed, "is what I would call the white man's city. It is cold and dark and dirty. Sometimes they have the fog and sometimes they have the rain or maybe a little wet dirty snow, or then again it might just be cloudy. But there is always *some*thing, summer and winter, all mushy and run together. They sit in little steamy café-looking places and drink tea. The tea is the color of dishwater, but it tastes good, or maybe everything else tastes so bad you just think it tastes good. They all sit and read the paper or look straight ahead of themselves. They don't talk to one another much, except when they're drinking in the pubs. They don't notice the girls that wait on the tables. You take and let the door fly open and a big black good-looking GI walk in with a great big smile and an eye for the ladies, and every girl in that place is going to want to follow him down the street when he goes out again. It's only natural. Our white boys, they had an easy time in London. There's girl after girl there that nobody has ever yet told they were pretty. Maybe they *ain't* pretty, understand, but we all come to feel that this was partly the reason. We had to step careful and gather with the Yankee boys for company in the pubs, but when it came to women—man! we were all over that town.

"Such as it was. It is, as I was saying, the white man's city. You don't hear the jazz along the street like in New York, or the blues like in New Orleans. New York is getting to be a nigger town, and New Orleans always was. I knew a fellow in the Army that came from San Francisco. He said his town wouldn't be nothing atall without the Chinaman. I'm inclined to believe all this because if ever a city was in need of color it was London. You leave the white man to himself, I said, and this is what the white man does.

"The Negro city, on the other hand, rests on the Equator by the Ocean between the Mountains and the Sand. It is a pure-white city with little shade trees all along the streets and an artesian well on every corner. The men dress all in clothes white as sheets, which looks good because they are so black. The women are black too, but they dress in different-colored clothes, yellow and red and bright blue, with all different kinds of skirts, some long and tight and switchy, some short and tight, some short and pleated. There's no such thing as this year's style or last year's style. They can choose how they like it. Then they wear gold earrings in their ears."

"And in they nose," said Lucy, and refilled his plate. "I done heard about it."

"That's one style that's gone out," said Beck. "They changed all that."

"Whereabouts is this place?" asked W.B. "Is it close as Memphis?"

"It's in Africa," said Beck, "on the west coast."

"Where is Africa?" asked W.B.

"It's too far to walk. Don't you know about Africa? Don't you learn anything in school?"

" 'Cose he know," said Lucy. "He just showing out." She scratched between her plaits with a hairpin. "Watch these here hot cakes for me, W.B. I gots to go get Granny up. She be done gone to sleep again on the pot."

When she had installed the old woman in her chair for the day, had smoked and aired the room and let the light in, and put the baby on his pallet in the kitchen, giving him a cold biscuit to gnaw on, she ordered W.B. without any fooling to go and get his clothes on, and began to get out of Beck what she wanted to know.

"You ain't going into town?"

"Whatever I does, Lucy, you ain't stirring a step out of this house. You stay here with Granny. They all time claiming up in town how they love Aunt Mattie, done saved their lives, birthed their children, laid out their dead, mingled with the smallpox for them. Well. Maybe they love her and maybe they don't. Maybe they'd shame to come in the house where she is. You stay indoors. It's a speaking day, and our race must not be conspicuous. You don't know what that word means. I got nobody to talk to. My daddy had a senator. All his life he could stay right quiet, after twenty years of talking about Cicero and Plato."

If he was blaming her, she didn't know it clearly. She could not hear him well, but whether because her ears had dulled or his voice had weakened, she could not say. He stopped speaking and looked at her, and the way the light fell she could see right through his glasses to his eyes. She knew why he had been talking such a blue streak, and why he couldn't think of any more to say. She saw his fear begin. She saw it climbing toward hers like two people about to meet, and from that moment she believed he would die that day. She thrust her hand out before her, as though she fended something away. She felt her hand grow cold in the outward strain of the muscles, and saw below the gold rim of Beck's glasses the scorch of tears, and around the edge of his hair, the gray rime of sweat.

"You still can catch the train. Go on up North. Go to Chicago. Ain't nobody coming to look for you. You can send me word. When Granny dies—"

"Granny dies! You couldn't kill Granny with a machine gun."

"Beck, please go on up there. Take W.B. if you want to. You can send me the money to come. I'll bring Granny with me."

"I came home to change to my good clothes," said Beck.

"Beck, go on back to Humphreys County! The white ain't for us. They ain't for nobody but theyselves. It ain't for us to mingle."

"They gots to learn," said Beck, rising. In the catch of light his glasses were opaque again, and luminous. "They can't learn off nobody but us. All these years we been backing up, and you see they never have learned anything."

"It don't have to be you that learns them!"

"It's got to be somebody," he said. "Might be some nigger with half my brains, somebody who'd make a mess of things. Papa never made a mess of anything. That's how come they don't rest easy about him till this good day."

He went to find his Sunday clothes. When he came out,

W.B. was all dressed up too and stood alongside of him, both of them in their coats and ties, like wanting her to send them off somewhere, and it as hot as it was going to get.

"Where you think *you* going?" Lucy demanded.

"*He* taking me," said W.B.

It struck Lucy that they were doing her wrong.

"I ain't about to walk into Lacey all by myself. W.B. knows how to do. I told him. We going through and across the creek, over in back of Mister Mars Overstreet's store, out there where all the gullies are. I plan to wait there while W.B. circles into town, to the back of Mister Harper's house. Mister Harper can come out and get me, if that is what he wants so bad."

"You just as crazy as you can live," said Lucy, getting mad. "All them white folks in town today, all drinking. If you had to get hold of Mister Harper whyn't you stay over in Humphreys County and talk to the shurf over there? Whyn't you call him on the telephone from somewheres way off?"

"Because it's not just Mister Harper to think about. It's that town I think of. It's where my papa died."

"You just determined!" Lucy cried. She was really mad now. "Any day but this one you could have picked. Oh, no. W.B., don't you go a step of the way. Yo' Unker Beck think he smart, but he acting downright crazy now. You needn't think you going to get any big fun'al outer me. I don't care what your policy cover."

"We gots to go on now," said Beck, "before it gets too late."

Tremulous, half in tears, she stood for some time sulking near the stove. She felt ill-used, and thought of her first husband, that limber, yellow, shiny boy, all the time joking and joshing. If he ever went off it was for something like a woman; he never got determined where white folks were concerned. Then he left her mind like steam out the window. "Beck!" she cried, and ran after him. "Beck, Beck, Beck!" She was headlong on the path, crying outright.

She saw them down at the bottom of the hill, where the path crossed a footbridge over the spring-branch. They were walking hand in hand. "Beck!" He turned and W.B. turned. Beck lifted his hand. She halted on the slope.

"You go on back to the house, Lucy," he told her. "Look after Granny and the baby. Don't go outdoors."

Down near them, the branch made its clear small running sound.

She turned without saying any more and walked away home, just as he told her. She felt suddenly at peace, doing exactly as he said.

the
all-day
speaking

46. Hot weather clouds, voluminous, processional, pearly, rode high over Lacey. Out in the county the crops were laid by; nobody traveled in the fields. The country stores were all locked up, and so was farm machinery in the sheds, with the tanks and crankcases drained and spare parts locked in the houses. Bad dogs were chained to run on a wire. Good dogs pursued the cars a little way, gave up, and turned back home. In the old days they could have gone too, trotting just behind the wagon, or underneath it, for shade. In lots of ways it seemed like a Sunday; in others not so much.

Tinker dressed in her navy that she had not had on since June. She smoothed the white piqué collar before the mirror, wondering if a bit more starch would have brought another vote to Duncan. Whatever her collar, the children were shining triumphs of her hand. Sometimes it happened that soap and water, fresh clothes, damp-brushed hair, and shoes produced two marvelous creatures, docile to tears, too good for the human race, apt to glow in the dark, their eyes full of the secret that would set the world free. "Look how pretty Mama looks," Patsy whispered to Cotton, who gazed up at her in guileless adoration. "You all go get in the car," said Tinker. She was too well acquainted with their hellish moments to be unduly swayed.

Duncan, too restless to wait for everyone to dress, had gone ahead to the school grounds where the speaking would be. Driving through town, Tinker saw Kerney in conversation with a group on the drugstore corner. She stopped almost in the middle of the street, the way people always would do in Lacey, and honked to him. He glanced her way twice before he crossed to her.

"One look at these two," said Kerney, admiring the children, "and Willard Follansbee himself will vote for Duncan."

"I scrubbed them within an inch of their lives this morning and now they're in a coma. They haven't been this clean since last Easter."

"What I need in this race is a pair of those."

"It isn't hard. Happens every day."

"So they tell me."

"Kerney, has Duncan found you?"

"I haven't seen him, no."

"He wants to tell you that he talked to New Orleans again this morning. The police were expecting to get the straight dope on who shot Jimmy within the next hour or so, and were going to wire the minute they knew. The boy at the telegraph office will run the wire over to the speaking, and if he finds you first he'll give it to you. Is that straight?"

"Letter perfect," said Kerney, and smiled at her, leaning

in the window. "Tinker, you're the prettiest girl in Lacey."

"Watch out. I'll tell Cissy."

"I don't care if you do. I've told her myself. You're the prettiest, and the sweetest. I've never known anybody as sweet as you."

"It's meant a lot to me, the way you've stuck by Duncan. It's made all the difference to him."

He did not stir. "You have such pretty eyes," he said.

She reached over to pat his hand. "We're blocking traffic. Good luck!"

She drove on. She had seen in the rear-view mirror the handsome nose of the Hunts' convertible, and the two girls, Marcia Mae and Cissy, riding with the careless poise of people going to the beach. Marcia Mae was wearing a straw field hat to keep off the powerful sun, and she and Cissy both were half-masked in dark glasses. Tinker's smoothly groomed dark head was bound in a strip of white piqué—her summer hat—and she had even put on hose and carried short white gloves.

The convertible in turn pulled up beside Kerney Woolbright.

"I've come to hear you make a speech," said Cissy, immensely pleased with herself. "Tell me what it's going to be about, so I can look intelligent."

"Little girls shouldn't bother their pretty heads with nasty old politics," said Kerney.

"He's going to lose," said Marcia Mae. "I've been telling her all morning, but she won't listen. Duncan's going to lose, and Kerney is too."

At the school grounds, Duncan located Tinker and came to sit with her in the car. Patsy sat in his lap, put his straw hat on over her ribbons and curls, picked up his large hand as though it were a puppy and gave it a passionate kiss.

"She's discovered kissing," said Tinker.

"I thought politicians kissed babies. Seems it's the other way around. Did you tell Kerney about the wire from New Orleans?"

"Yes, haven't you seen him?"

"He should be here by now."

"He was up on the drugstore corner."

"They're all telling me I've got to explain about the Dozer case. Follansbee is distributing handbills of that damn picture Tallant had taken at the jail. He's written a lot of crap to go with it. You can tell he did it, instead of Tallant. There's not a correct sentence in the whole thing."

"What does it say?"

"Same old thing. I'm a nigger lover, protecting Dozer at any cost because he works for the nigger papers. Thank God, Kerney speaks in the morning. He's going to lay it on the line for me."

"He seemed upset this morning. I thought he was going to cry. He kept telling me how pretty he thought I was."

"He can say that again."

She laid her two small hands with the expertly lacquered nails side by side on the Chevrolet emblem in the center of the steering wheel.

"I think everything's all right between us now. I think it always will be."

He flipped the soft end curl of her hair with his finger. "I know it will be. I'm sorry anything had to happen. Do you know how sorry I am?"

"I think it had to happen. I always thought it had to, in the back of my mind."

"I thought so too, I guess."

And quickly as though he had told her a joke, she had turned and smiled at him.

"What had to happen, Daddy?" Cotton asked. He was standing on the floor of the back seat, leaning reflectively between them in that satisfying way children can make use of a car as though it were a house.

"Daddy had to run for sheriff, darling," said Tinker.

"You mean you're sorry you had to run for sheriff?"

"No, not exactly, but Daddy doesn't like to make speeches."

"*I* think Daddy means he's sorry he made you hit him in the face with a potato."

"*I* made *her*—well, see whose side he's on."

"There's not any side to be on, precious," said Tinker, and smoothed his hair.

"I want some ice cream," said Patsy.

Parked off at an angle down in the shade near where the bunting trailed down from the outdoor speakers' platform, Marcia Mae did not turn her head but saw just the same from her mask's corner the family group in Duncan's car.

"Isn't Duncan too bucolic for any use?"

"What does that mean?" Cissy asked, who thought maybe it was an illness like dropsy.

"Oh, so damn family-group. Little curly-haired cherubs, little home-grown wife. Thank God I'm not tied down that way."

But just the same her heart ached.

"Why would Kerney nearly cry?" Tinker asked.

"He hates the thought of losing. But you can't tell. He may make them see the truth. How can you ever know how deep a fake nigger-issue goes? We don't even know for sure how deep a real one goes any more. And Kerney's a good speaker, which I'm not. I had a lot of good friends around these parts, and I sold them on Kerney. His name has got around."

"How did you sell them, Daddy?" Cotton asked.

"Well, talking to them. I knew them all from the old football days."

"From when you were an All-time Great," said Cotton.

"I want some ice cream," said Patsy.

"If Kerney speaks in the morning, when do you speak?" Tinker asked.

"Not till afternoon. Kerney's running for district office—that puts him before lunch, a good spot, right after the gubernatorial candidates. I'm with the locals, later on. By then we're sure to have heard from New Orleans."

"Ice *cream!*"

"They've been so good," Tinker explained, opening the door. "All right. You all come on."

Over at the long table under the sycamore trees, the Garden Club ladies in their flowered voile dresses fanned flies away from the chicken salad, potato salad, fried chicken, ham, deviled eggs, rolls, pies, cakes, and relishes. Tinker spoke to all the ladies in turn and bought ice cream sandwiches for the children. She told them each separately to lean over when they bit it and to hurry and finish it before it melted. She straightened from explaining this to Patsy, and there was Marcia Mae. Seen by so many they could not do other than greet each other, and stand talking for a while.

Soon now the white collar of Tinker's dress would wilt, what with children and the heat, just as her white cotton gloves would acquire a streak of grease somehow, and grass stain would mark her spectator pumps. Marcia Mae presented a more unfenced appearance, as it were, in her ribbed cotton skirt and tailored linen shirt, her loafers soft as gloves on her narrow naked feet: a political speaking was no more worth dressing for than a soldier's dance.

Both these women, by turning their heads, might have seen across the level school grounds to the spot beside the seesaws where Marcia Mae Hunt had looked at Louise Taylor's made-over coat-suit with pearl buttons the size of moons, and said, "That's the funniest-looking dress *I* ever saw," in her voice that was always a little rough, like raw silk—she had never been known to lower it. Looking aside together, they would have seen the past as one turns to see a person who already stands at the elbow. For in a small town, in a society whose supreme interest is people, the past exists physically—empty chairs expect the dead and not in vain. So, turning thus to admit they both remembered, to look again on what they remembered, they might have discovered forgiveness, or at least a moment of companionship. But they had been again too recently in contest, and felt compelled to meet each other's eyes with all the steady honesty of guilt and ask the most hypocritical questions.

Marcia Mae reflected, escaping on the excuse that she had to take a Coca-cola to Cissy, that practically everybody in Lacey felt constrained around her for one reason or another; she wouldn't accept invitations, tell her life story, or remember to speak to people. She scuffed the heels of her loafers at the pleasure of release from this latest encounter. She retained a satisfying impression of Tinker too carefully matched in navy and white, even to navy and white pumps. You would wonder perhaps if in her navy bag there was not a white handkerchief with a navy figure. She regained the leather seat of the convertible and surprised Cissy with the Coca-cola.

"It's not cold enough," said Cissy, feeling.

"I can't help that," said Marcia Mae.

Cissy drank. "I saw you talking to Mrs. Duncan Harper." She smiled her little fat smile.

"Don't be such a brat," said Marcia Mae.

"I want to see Kerney," Cissy complained.

"No doubt you will."

He was near them now, detaching himself from a group of men in straw hats and white shirts. Marcia Mae felt suddenly that she wanted to see him, too. She slid from the convertible seat and went to him. His eyes at least presented her with no discomfort—a born politician on speaking day, trim without elegance in his seersucker suit, what could he be saying to her except, "You and I are the smart ones; we know how things really are." He looked at her so much that way that she actually believed it.

"Cissy awaits," she told him. "She forgot to give you the summons for dinner tonight."

"I haven't got time to talk to her now," said Kerney. "Besides, I already know about it. Miss Nan told me." He waved at Cissy, who had contrived to look impassive behind her blinders and gave no sign.

The platform was empty except for a man tinkering with the microphone. He kept saying, "Testing. Is that all right, Mac?" The words were small in the three big mouths on top of the soundtruck.

"I've never seen such a crowd," said Marcia Mae. "There must be two thousand people here. I always forget how many country people there are."

"It's a common failing," said Kerney.

Still in black for her husband's death, Miss Ada Brevard appeared between them, fanning mightily. Thin and nervous, conscious of a better world where political speakings were not allowed, Miss Ada had but one matter to take up with Kerney and she saw no reason to make a secret of it.

"I have just this minute been told, Kerney, that Duncan is opposed to segregation in the schools! I'm more distressed than I can tell you. Can this possibly be true?"

"Why, Miss Ada," said Kerney, "not that I know of."

"Edna Colquit just heard it with her own ears. She told me. Mr. Colquit asked him right out what he would favor if the Supreme Court ruled out segregation in the schools, and he said in that case we should have to work out some way to comply with the ruling."

"Why, Miss Ada—"

"If you nice young people in politics begin this kind of talk, to whom, oh, to whom shall we turn?"

"Miss Ada, I—"

"You realize what this means to me, Kerney. I, *I* appointed Duncan to office. I was sheriff myself when Mr. Brevard died. Why, I said to Edna, 'It's the basis of our Southern way of life that the black should not mingle with the white.' Our forefathers fought and died, Kerney—" Her voice quite broke. The thought of the culture that had bred her seemed to blow against her like a wind too strong; she was shaken in it, like a high frail bough.

"There, there." Kerney grasped her little arm.

She raised her head high. "If Mr. Brevard had known that any such thing could be in Duncan Harper's mind, he could never, could never, never—"

"He didn't know," Kerney said hastily. "I think you can rest assured of that."

"I said to Edna, 'If he's going to have ideas like that, I shall just have to take the rostrum myself and say I never knew it when I appointed him. I see no recourse.' Is it true that he is hiding that Dozer Negro?"

"Why, goodness, Miss Ada, I'm sure that Duncan—"

"He has always seemed such a sweet boy, such a handsome boy, such a gentleman!" She was as dewy and fresh with tears as a girl, as grieved as an old piano tune.

"Here he comes now," said Kerney. "Why don't you just talk to him?"

"Why, I shall! I will!" She furled her fan for the encounter. Duncan, who was obviously headed for Kerney, tangled immediately in her nets. He floundered amongst them, shifting from one hip to the other, standing here, circling there, but could he be rude to Miss Ada? He could not.

Marcia Mae said to Kerney, "You came a long way from

convincing her of anything good about Duncan."

"You don't convince people like Miss Ada of anything," said Kerney.

"Somebody convinced her of a few things somewhere along the line. She's the most convinced person I've seen in a long time."

"That's just the trouble," Kerney said, "with this whole part of the country. Do you know," he chose suddenly to confide, "a college friend of mine, practicing in New York now, passed through yesterday and called me. I said I didn't have time to see him. What could I say to him? What can we ever say?"

"Look at Duncan," said Marcia Mae dreamily. "In college he was all lean meat and bone. Leanness is a good thing, a good fast thing: people with their foot in the road are lean and fast, like you, Kerney, with your mind churning and burning away. If you stay in Lacey you'll get fat. First the thickening waistline, then the bald spot in the back. You won't be able to get away either, when old ladies stop you on the street. Only you won't be too nice to leave, like Duncan. You'll be too bored to try."

Kerney hardly heard her. Waiting for a word with Duncan, he was more sharply aware of what Duncan was saying. He heard things like: "I don't think we can possibly secede again, Miss Ada. We tried that once, you remember . . . No, I don't say I believe in integration right away, but I do think that whatever the Supreme Court decides to rule, the country sooner or later has to go along with . . . you see, the Constitution. . . ."

My God, thought Kerney Woolbright, he's going to explain the Constitution to Miss Ada. "Tell Duncan I couldn't wait," he said to Marcia Mae. He turned on his heel; and his anger seemed to him at the outset like the loss of temper occasioned by hitting an elbow or at the end of a long day typing a document with the carbon reversed; but it did not fade as it should have: it continued to seethe and fume on his way to the rostrum, to threaten to possess him if he did not find a way to halt it. The Constitution, he thought, the *Constitution*. He felt that he would strangle in a sense of impotence that warred against every instinct of his soul. . . .

From the car under the sycamore shade, Tinker saw Duncan and Marcia Mae come close to collision, exchange a taut greeting, and part.

"Who's that yellow-headed lady with Daddy?" Cotton asked.

"Her name is Mrs. O'Donnell," said Tinker.

Cotton threw a gun to his shoulder. "Pow, Mrs. O'Donnell. Pow, pow!" He was apt to start firing on anybody.

"Hush," said Tinker. "She'll hear you. That isn't nice."

"Pow, Mith O'Donnell," said Patsy without firing anything.

"Testing," said the three big horns from the soundtruck. "I think it's all right now, Mac."

Kerney Woolbright and the electrician passed each other on the rostrum steps.

Duncan came to the car window. "I'm going to sit in the audience, down near the front. Kerney is bound to mention things that concern us both, and I want to be in evidence to back him up."

"Who was that yellow-headed lady, Daddy?" Cotton asked.

"A lady named Miss Hunt," said Duncan.

"I'm named Mith O'Donnell," said Patsy and grinned at him blissfully.

"They asked who she was," Tinker explained, "and I said Mrs. O'Donnell."

"You were right, of course," said Duncan. He pressed his hand into his brow as though his head hurt. "Miss Ada should have brought a Confederate flag to wave. I'll be glad when all this is over." Then he was gone.

the
messenger

47. Skirting the town cagily on his way to Duncan Harper's house, W.B. passed in back of a Negro cabin where a little boy was playing keeps by himself in the back yard. He was crawling around the ring on his hands and knees and shooting hard with a big glass taw. W.B. himself had an agate, and Unker Beck kept a big ball-bearing out of a tractor to shoot with.

The little Negro playing marbles was talking to himself: "Oh, you shoots it and you spins it and you breaks it down the middle, oh you takes it sump'n like this and you goes sump'n like this and— You kin play wif me, black boy, if you got a taw."

"I ain't so black," said W.B. "I half white. I just learned it."

"I half white too," said the boy. "My daddy's a white man, only he died in Mist' Duncan Harper's grocery sto'."

"I seen him do it," said W.B.

"My name is Robert," said the boy, "but they calls me James."

"They calls me W.B."

"Is that your name?"

"Uh-huh."

"You can have some breakfast, want to."

"Thank you, but I can't. I got to find Mister Duncan."

"Mist' Duncan Harper the shurf now in place of my daddy."

"I know hit."

"Who want the shurf?"

The woman who asked this stood at the back door. She was large and blowsy. She wore a soft cotton robe with flowers on it, and she was the pleasing rich color of coffee with a lot of real cream stirred in it.

"I does, Miss Ida Belle," said W.B. "My daddy's sont me to find him."

"Yo daddy? Who yo daddy?"

"My Unker Beck Dozer. He really my daddy. I half from England."

"Sho' nuff?"

"Yes'm. Is."

"Looks like Beck done better than me. How come he ain't ever tole it?"

"He never wanted to hurt Aunt Lucy's feelings."

"Is her feelings hoit now?"

"She don't act like it."

"Well, then?"

"I'o'no'm."

"I does. Beck giving hisself airs. 'Hoit Lucy's feelings.' I got no time for Beck. He give me the pain."

"Where he give you the pain, Mama?" asked the little boy playing marbles.

"Hush up, James. Come here, W.B."

Beyond the back gallery the door stood open on a big room. There was a tall mirror in it on a stand with a heavy gold frame running all the way around. When he used to deliver groceries, he got good at looking in back doors. There was also a record playing softly. The windows had drawn curtains. The glass in the mirror looked like water. The room looked cool.

"You going to Mister Duncan Harper's house?" asked Ida Belle.

"Yes'm."

"Then you go to Mister Duncan's house, but don't you go a step farther. Mister Duncan ain't there, you tell Miss Tinker, or you set there till he come home. Don't you go in town. Don't you go down to that speaking. You know Mister Willard Follansbee?"

"Yes'm, I knows him."

"He come to see me yestiddy trying to get me to say where Beck was at. If he catches you, he'll chop you up and fry you like a chicken, boy. You go to Mister Duncan's and don't you stir a step."

"I ain't right sure," said W.B., "that I wants to go to Mister Duncan's."

"No, now you best do that," said Ida Belle, kindly, like a schoolteacher. "Beck counting on you to do that. Just don't take no chances."

"Yes'm."

When he came into town he walked down the white-folks streets with his head ducked. A white lady inside a house put up a window and said, "Hey, boy!" He stopped and looked at her. "Do you deliver groceries?" she asked.

"No'm," he said. "My name Willie."

"Willie what?"

"Willie Beckwith."

"Well, I reckon you aren't the one." She put down the window.

When he reached Mister Duncan Harper's house there wasn't anybody at home. He went to the back steps and sat down, two steps from the top. He wanted to go home to

Granny and Aunt Lucy. He felt that he had to wait and say what Unker Beck told him to, seeing that it was the day he learned Unker Beck was his daddy. He believed that when Mister Duncan Harper came everything would be all right.

Kerney Woolbright
makes
a speech

48. The town master of ceremonies, the mayor, was announcing that Kerney Woolbright, candidate for the state senate from the Third Senatorial District, would be the first of the legislative candidates to speak. The benches were filling, and knots of talking people loosed to rearrange themselves, turn toward the rostrum and fold their arms, for careful listening.

Kerney Woolbright, no matter what they thought of him personally, was known to be an orator, and people will turn out to hear an orator, and give him attention. Voting is another thing. Voting has nothing to do with speaking, or the size and silence of the crowd. What it does have to do with has yet to be finally discovered.

Duncan Harper gained the front row. There was a country shyness about the way it was vacant, except for a few old men, one deaf, one crippled, one obese, and one habitually drunk. He nodded to them all, and they smiled with what looked like derision, as was their habit. One shook his hand, and he felt the craggy forefinger knuckle that all the fingers had bent and fled from.

Here and there, as he had passed through the crowd that was retracting itself inward toward the rostrum and pulling its scattered elements together, certain phrases were repeated:

"Went to school up North somewhere . . . this nigger business . . . talker, but I . . . him and Harper . . . in the legislature did he . . . school up North but him and Harper. . . ."

Kerney rose, came easily to the microphone, and began to speak without preliminaries. He thanked the proper people, firmly reviewed his career as a Winfield County boy who had gone to school first at the state university, later to Yale in the North from whence he had returned—the instant he got his diploma, it would seem—to the joys of Winfield County. Here he had hoped to settle down to a quiet life as a lawyer, but service to the people of the state of Mississippi seemed to attract him more every day in an age when young men seemed regrettably inclined to place private ambition first, and public duty last in their thoughts, if indeed they thought of it at all. People sometimes told him he ought to enjoy life, make lots of money, and wait for advanced years to serve the public, but he personally thought that when men got to the age of President Truman they owed it to the country to retire. This pulled a laugh, for Kerney's opponent was considerably older than he, and everybody was against Truman.

"A fine wife you're going to make," said Marcia Mae, glancing at Cissy. "You've got to learn to laugh at his jokes."

"He makes me sick," said Cissy. "I wish I hadn't come."

A young man appeared at the flank of the convertible near Cissy's elbow. He was a reporter from a town in another county.

"You're Cissy Hunt, aren't you? I met you over at Moon Lake last summer. I don't guess you'd remember me."

"Oh, sure, I remember. Sure I do."

"I hear this is the fair-haired boy over here that's speaking now. I hear you're engaged to him, Cissy."

"Oh, goodnight. It gets to where you can't be friends with a boy people don't say you're engaged. We're good friends. But, goodnight—"

"It was his speech my boss sent me over here to cover. Seems there might be some angle on the race question in it."

"I don't know," said Cissy. "Politics just confuses me. I just don't know a thing about it."

"Neither one of you is ever going to know," said Marcia Mae, "if you don't listen to what he's saying."

"Oh, he's just on what he thinks about taxes now; that's not much of an issue. Then he'll review his voting record in the legislature and pledge support to the free textbook program. That gets him over to schools, and through the door to the nasty mean hateful old federal government in Washington that wants to exploit our fair Southland and thinks they can tell us what to do and what not to do. Then he gets to segregation and white supremacy, which is what I'm waiting for."

"This is my sister, Mrs. O'Donnell, Bob—"

"Preston. How do you do, ma'am. Cissy, your boy friend's got a good voice."

"I haven't even got a boy friend, I keep telling you. Goodnight."

"A girl like you is bound to have ten boy friends. What's the matter with these hillbillies? Why don't you come over to the Delta?"

"I'd love to. When can I?"

"I want to hear the speech," said Marcia Mae.

"See you later," said the reporter. He unslung his camera and moved across the grass, picking his way around the crowd toward the rows of seats and the red-white-and-blue-draped platform. Up there before a plain wooden rostrum with a pitcher of water, a water glass, and a microphone, a man was speaking. His hands held lightly to either side; his easy forward-leaning stance had been calculated long ago, and the sway of his shoulders, the lift of his chin, the gestures now of his hands, now of the whole arm were like the riding of an expert horseman, who no longer thinks of the rein or the spur, but only of calling the horse to its zenith, and Kerney's horse was the crowd, which had grown as silent as the sky.

". . . And now, my friends," said the three big horns, "I come with reluctance to an issue which lies closer to all our hearts than everything else I have said put together. I say that I speak with reluctance, for there are friends among you to whom my words may give pain. I would ask them to remember that a public servant cannot speak, cannot act, cannot even wish in a private way. Where the public good is at stake, he cannot wish for personal joys. Where he must fulfill a public duty, he cannot hope always to please his friends.

"Good men and women of Winfield County, I know your feeling about the institution of racial segregation in our Southern way of life. I have walked among you these past few weeks and talked with you, and I know your spirit. What you have believed once, you still believe; what you have fought for once, you will fight again to defend, for you are strong, proud people and you do not change. I state to you solemnly, friends, my belief that no man has a right to ask for your vote who cannot serve you from his heart. I pledge you here, from this platform, that no matter what stand the federal government of the United States—the President, the U.S. Senate, or the Supreme Court—may take on this issue, I, Kerney Woolbright, will defend our Southern viewpoint, our Southern traditions, and the will of our Southern people, as long as God gives me breath.

"I come now to a more immediate issue. Exactly two weeks ago this very day, a Winfield County citizen whom you all know was shot and seriously wounded. A Negro man, widely suspected of this shooting and known to have been at the scene of the crime, disappeared immediately afterwards and has not been seen since. I am not the sheriff of this county and it is not my business to say to you what should or should not be done. But it is being said that nothing has been done to bring this Negro to justice, and it is further being said that I, Kerney Woolbright, am party to protecting this Negro as a fugitive from arrest and from whatever due process of the law may follow therefrom. I wish to state to you that nothing could be further from the truth.

"Duncan Harper stands on Tuesday for election to sheriff of Winfield County. Far be it from me to tell you how you should vote. The vote is your sacred instrument of power: let no man dictate to you in whose service you shall enlist it.

"Duncan Harper is said by many to be a friend of mine, and they are right. He is my friend and a friend to all of you. He has brought me cheering to my feet with thousands in the days when he was a national football hero, and all the sports honors this nation can offer were heaped upon his head. But friendship, my fellow citizens, as I have said, cannot and indeed should not make a demand higher than the demands of the public good. I do not attempt to defend or condemn Duncan Harper or any of his actions. I prefer to say simply that he will speak for himself.

"But I, Kerney Woolbright, hereby publicly disassociate my candidacy from the candidacy of Duncan Harper. Inasmuch as we are friends, I love him still. Inasmuch as misunderstanding may malign him, I deplore it. Inasmuch as his will conflicts with yours, I condemn him.

"As a simple citizen of Winfield County, like yourselves, I have a vote to cast for sheriff.

"Duncan Harper will not receive my vote.

"Men and women of Winfield County, I thank you."

Duncan
retreats

49. As Kerney finished his speech, there was at first a stunned murmur from the crowd, a shout or two of "Pour it on, boy," and "You tell 'em, Woolbright," and from somewhere a shrill whistle.

Duncan rose and walked up the trampled grass between the rows of seats. People craned to see his face, but it showed nothing. He walked easily and steadily, for he had once learned well how to pass through a cheering gauntlet as though nothing had happened.

He gained the car and slid under the wheel, reaching for the ignition.

"I'd better take you and the children home," he said. "There's liable to be some ugly doings down here."

"Duncan, no. I'll take them home. You stay here. They may give you a chance to speak."

"Tinker, you know I'm no speaker. That's the last thing I'm good at. I'll wait my turn, give them a chance to cool down. Right now I don't want to see anybody."

"All right." She slid over, releasing the wheel to him. "But I don't think it matters, Duncan, who shot Jimmy or what you ever hear from New Orleans. I don't think anybody cares. I think all they care about is to make sure that everybody they vote for favors segregation."

"Well, maybe so. At one time I thought things might have been different. I know this much: I just have to go along with it the way it's always looked to me. I have to follow it through the way I started it. I can't care too much any more what they want."

"Kerney cares. He cared too much."

"Kerney said he wasn't going to vote for you, Daddy," Cotton said.

"Don't talk to me about Kerney, either one of you."

The family rode silently with him, past the empty courthouse square, the drugstore corner, the stores, with the sign of HARPER & BRO. GRO.

"I always hated football," said Duncan. "I never wanted to play. The coach in high school was nothing but a math teacher who hadn't thought about football in ten years until he saw me and Essie Sanders playing kick and catch after school one day. He watched for five minutes, and the next day talked the principal into organizing a team—the first we ever had in Lacey. But I wasn't trying, I wasn't trying anything at all. I never got to finish the work for my Scout badge because of him and his football team. I used to think I'd do it the next summer, but it was always the next summer."

They had pulled up into their own front yard.

"Go play in the sand pile," said Tinker to her children. "Run on!" she had to order, for Cotton stood needing her. "Look after Patsy for me," she told him. She followed Duncan into the house. Here she fished out a bottle of whisky she had stashed away, and gave him a stiff drink. Twice she sent Cotton back into the yard.

"I only wanted to be a groceryman like Daddy," Duncan told her. "I wanted to walk in the woods on Sunday with my family. I never imagined my name in all the papers, I never dreamed Travis Brevard would walk in my store and die. Tinker, don't you leave me! Promise me."

"Leave you, Duncan? *Leave* you?" She thought he might as well have been imploring her not to start speaking Chinese. In all her life the thought of leaving him had never crossed her mind once.

He turned away from her, and stood facing the cold fire-place, resting his foot on the brass andiron.

"We sat in here, do you remember, the evening after Travis died. We were full of something about to happen. You said we mustn't start running for things." He gave a short laugh, then turned back to her, saying calmly, "They're all too intense for me, you see. Kerney, Marcia Mae, even Willard Follansbee. They are taken and swept by things inside them—here." He laid his hand across his breast. "It must be that I hardly know at all how they feel. Things seem pretty obvious to me, by and large. This Negro thing. Segregation, civil rights— What else is there to say any more but that they should have an equal chance? How can there be anything else to say? But Kerney had to win. If I had felt strongly enough that I had to win, you see, I might have— Tinker, do you understand?"

"No," she said at once. "I think he did an awful thing."

"Yes, so do I. But if I could see how he must have felt!"

"There's never been a time when I didn't adore you," she said.

"They say there's something funny about my family," he went on. "I know people say the Harpers are peculiar. I never knew why, except maybe Uncle Phillip voting for Hoover."

They both laughed.

"If they say it about your family, what on earth do you think they say about mine?"

"Daddy? Daddy."

"Cotton," said Tinker, "if I have to tell you one more time—"

"But I keep trying to tell Daddy. W.B. is out in the back. He says he knows where Beck Dozer is."

"Oh." Duncan left quickly for the back of the house, and Tinker was alone with the boy.

"Come here, darling. Come talk to Mother."

"Mother, Daddy said he never did want to play *football*."

"Well, now. Well, now. I guess Daddy said something he didn't mean, don't you?"

"But Daddy wouldn't do that, would he?"

"Everybody does that, sometimes."

"Even Daddy?"

"Daddy less than anybody. But sometimes even Daddy."

Duncan returned hastily. "Beck is waiting for me down back of Mars Overstreet's store. If I hurry and get him I can put him in custody over in Humphreys County and still be back in time to speak at two o'clock."

"Are you going now?"

"Right now. Yes."

She dusted off her stocking feet and slipped into her shoes. Like the children, she always took them off the minute she got in the door. "I'm going with you."

"You stay with the children."

"The children are all right. Wherever you go today, I'm going too."

When they passed the town square, she was the first to see what had happened. The window of Harper's grocery was broken. There was a jagged hole like a star in the lower half; one point reached several feet upward into the painted letters. If she had known any way to shield him from the sight she would have taken it. Instead she laid a hand on his arm, hoping he would not see.

But he always looked at the store. She felt the shock go through him to the bone.

50. When Kerney Woolbright came down the steps of the rostrum, the forethrust of the crowd was already upon him. People greeted him with relief—in the tangle of everything that had been talked about Duncan and Kerney and Jimmy Tallant and Beck, they were glad to get back to something they could understand without question, the way they understood a sermon on God so loved the world.

Some felt that Kerney should not have said right out that he wouldn't vote for Duncan, but others, arguing the point back into line, said, "Why not?—it's the way I feel myself. I like Harper, but he's said too many doubtful things."

If we had stood together, Kerney thought. If we had stood together.

His thinking went on lonely, like going down an empty valley in a strange country, while Kerney, with his hat in hand and his Lincoln-like stoop for catching every word, remained talking, nodding, listening gravely, shaking hand after hand. When he turned to move away from the crowd, three countrymen with aging boy-faces made him the center of a walking huddle.

"We decided we done fooled around too long," said one.

"We going nigger-hunting tonight," said another. "We hear he's over in Humphreys County."

The third said, "Want to come?"

"I'm due to make a banquet speech in Wayne tonight," said Kerney. "You boys take it easy. Go talk to Tallant."

A leading gubernatorial candidate drew him aside, laid an arm around his shoulder, and talked for a moment, creating a favorable impression. Willard Follansbee stood in his path, wearing his white linen campaigning suit and red tie that stirred memories of Bilbo. The hairs on his hands and those barely subdued to the skin surface of his throat and face appeared richly purple in so white a territory, established with the tropical weight of fuel oil in a bucket. When he removed his straw hat, it was as if one of a species had thrust its head out at the appointed hour. Another effect the white had was to make his teeth look yellow. He put out his hand and Kerney took it, not without nausea.

"Hell of a fine speech," he said. "Just a hell of a fine speech."

Kerney gained the Hunt convertible.

"Can I bum a ride?"

"You certainly cannot," said Marcia Mae. Determined not to so much as look at him, she kept craning her head nervously back, waiting for a rift in the crowd.

"Can I, Cissy?"

"Sure. Hop in."

Marcia Mae turned on her at once. "Don't you know what he's done? Didn't you hear what he said up there?"

"You mean you're not going to let him ride home because of something he said in a speech? That's the silliest thing I ever heard of."

"You mean to say you are? Don't you know he just stabbed his best friend in the back? Publicly?"

"I don't understand anything about it and neither do you. You always want to make a big fuss."

"If you let him in this car, I'm getting out of it."

"Well, get out then," said Cissy.

"Wait," said Kerney. "I'll walk—"

But she had flashed past him, flinging the door shut almost on his finger. He could no more have stopped her than a buzz saw.

"Let her go," said Cissy. "She just gets like that."

He took over the wheel and backed gingerly to make the

turn. People waved to him, and some came up to shake his hand. When he maneuvered the car free on the road to the square, he reached into his back pocket for a handkerchief and felt that something which had been secure there two hours before was now not there at all. He searched again, frantically, prodding into his pockets, halting the car. Then he saw that Cissy was reading from a yellow paper.

"This is the longest telegram I ever saw," she said.

"Give me that." He snatched it. "Where did you get it?"

"It was out on the seat there. It's to Duncan Harper. It's not even yours."

"They brought it to me. I thought it was mine."

"I bet you didn't," she said. "You kept it because it says they've found the man mixed up in that shooting."

"Don't be silly. Why would I do that?"

"Well," she said, "because you didn't want anybody to know it wasn't the Negro after all. How could you talk against the Negro if everybody knew for sure he hadn't done anything?"

Kerney stared at her. "Who told you that?"

"Told me?"

"Will you take off those damn glasses and look at me?"

He reached to unmask her eyes, but a car honked behind him. He drove on, but at the square he took an abrupt swing to the right and picked up speed. He drove away from the direction of the highway, past Duncan Harper's house, past outlying houses, far out, going faster.

"Where on earth are you going?" Cissy asked.

"Who was that you were talking to while I was speaking? Some man with a camera on his back?"

"Oh that was Bob Preston. He works for the Rosedale *Eagle*."

"What did he want?"

"He said I ought to come over in the Delta more and go to parties. It sounded like fun. I bet they have a good time over there."

He swung off into a hard-packed country road, deeply shaded—the cemetery road.

"You must be crazy," said Cissy, "driving way out here."

He swung the wheel again, sharply, entering a lane even more secluded, quiet, abandoned. Through the low oak limbs and sassafras growth, the iron palings of the cemetery fence were visible. The ground lay thick with the droppings of the oaks. When he cut the ignition, something went right on chirping in the brush. There was no feel of houses near.

He reached over himself and stripped the dark glasses from her face.

"Cissy, if anyone ever asks you about that telegram, you are going to say you don't know anything about it. You will do that for me, won't you, Cissy?"

She inspected a chip in her nail polish. She was somewhat out of humor with him, and was getting hungry. She would not look at him. "Okay. I won't say anything."

He was silent for a time—dissatisfaction in his long young face, his thick young springy hair, his lowered lashes, his full, resting mouth. He turned to her, one arm staying upon the wheel just where it had deflected the car into the lane, while the other extended along the back of the seat. He reached out his hand gently.

"Cissy—?"

She drew back from his touching her at all. "I don't know if I want to help you about that telegram or not. I'll have to ask Papa."

"You'll not do any such thing!"

She thought at first that someone else had seized her from behind, actually by the hair, but seeing it was nobody but

Kerney she had some notion he must be going really crazy and tried her little contemptuous manner of flinging free, putting her chin in the air, and saying what she expected to be done for her. But the one who got flung was she, straight down—could Kerney be this strong?—her head struck the doorframe painfully. She struggled up, about to be really scared. "Oh," she said, for her elbow honestly slipped on the leather seat and she fell back, again hitting by accident on a posture, an angle, and a sensation it had been for some time now so pleasing to dream about in bed. "Oh," she kept saying in various ways until his mouth stopped her. She discovered she had been absolutely right in thinking how boring most things were.

When she began to listen again, there was still that bit of chirping in the brush. Her dress was all unbuttoned and her pretty cotton eyelet underthings dragged awry. She did not mind; this was why they were so pretty. She saw the chrome door handle, the sleek gadgets on the dashboard, and above her the rich oak limbs.

"Will you tell?" His head had fallen to rest above her heart.

"Tell? Oh, they'd never let us back together if I told."

"I mean about the telegram."

The telegram was like a stray piece of paper washing up and down in the ocean.

"I don't care about it," she said.

He raised his head. "But I do."

His hand moved through her hair again, caressing and firm.

"Then I won't. I won't tell. Never, never."

51. The big Hunt house stood wide open to gather breezes out of the hot day. Though the people in it were all over it and at considerable distances from one another, their consciousnesses were nonetheless linked and conversant, like music.

Nan stood alone in the dining room, putting out silver for her dinner in the evening. She heard her daughter run in the front door and scamper to her room.

"Cissy? Where on earth have you been? Nellie saved you some dinner in the oven. Is Kerney there? There's enough for him, too, isn't there, Nellie?"

"Yas'm." Nellie answered from way out at the servant's table, shoveling turnip greens, cornbread, potlikker, and side-meat all together on her fork.

"You gwy set there and eat all day, Miss Nellie?" the yard boy asked her from the steps."

"Ef'n I wants to," said Nellie. Conversation did not distract her.

"I want to talk to Kerney for a minute," Jason called, from far off in his office wing, lying on a coarse dark quilt brier-stitched from large pieces of men's suit scraps. He was about to nap, had removed his shoes and coat. The morning paper lay by the narrow bed.

"Have you got anything over your feet, Jason?" Nan asked.

"On a day like this? Lord, Nan."

"All right, you know how you are."

"I know it's hot."

"Don't turn the fan on without putting something on your feet."

From her own room, open on the hall, old Mrs. Standsbury said, "Is Kerney there? Tell him I certainly am glad he broke with Duncan Harper."

Jason laughed. "You're supposed to be deaf, Miss Tennie."

"She hears everything she wants to," said Nan.

"I just think somebody ought to say what they think about Duncan never chasing that Negro. It's going to get so Negroes can come right in the same house with you. It's high time somebody spoke up for law and order. The Negroes will take us all over, don't watch out."

"You hear dat?" said the yard boy from the steps.

"Hears 'em," said Nellie, and drew near her plate an enormous leftover slice of mince pie.

"Kerney!" It was Marcia Mae from the far end of the porch, beyond the corner, knocking a ping-pong ball. She would shove the table against the wall, and play that way alone by the hour. "Kerney, come here!"

He appeared, having threaded through the porch furniture to join her. She kept up the spaced knocking of the little ball: wall, table, table, strike; table, wall, table, table, strike. Her backhand wrist with the little paddle was her silky tennis drive in miniature. She had shed her skirt in favor of a pair of tailored shorts.

"I don't take back anything I said," she told him, sniping the ball. "You betrayed Duncan Harper. You stabbed him in the back."

"I don't recall ever hearing that you stuck by him," Kerney said.

"If I had stuck by Duncan," she said, leaning far forward to catch a small bounce at the net, "I would be a Lacey housewife, putting muffins in a hot stove this minute. And you, after Tuesday, if you had stuck with Duncan, would be a has-been politician, a small-town drinking lawyer. I know how it is. You were afraid of being bored. Nevertheless, I am going to do everything in my power to keep Cissy from marrying you, Kerney."

"It won't do any good," said Cissy, from behind. "I'm going to marry him anyway."

Marcia Mae lifted her palm and let the celluloid ball sail into it. She laid down the paddle and turned. They were standing together, dew-fresh and far too bright. Marcia Mae was not reminded by their moist, parted lips and shining eyes of a small house somewhere, scorched food, and the journey home with news from the doctor's office; instead she could peer through their happiness as through a keyhole into a world where all these sweet young matters were never to be overly valued, like attractive knick-knacks on the gleaming top of a strong desk.

"You understand him?" Marcia Mae asked, levelly.

"What's it to you?" Cissy countered, and lifted her little chin.

Marcia Mae walked through to the dining room where her mother ranked out the silver.

"There's a big one on the way," she warned. "Brace yourself."

"What?" Nan had lifted the coffeepot, and her fingers tightened on its handle. It was as though someone had set off a buzzer system in her nerves, but the pot remained perfectly level.

"She's decided to marry him."

In her mother's face, swift as the tripping of a Kodak shutter or the glint of a narrow blade held into the vision so that for an instant it disappears altogether, Marcia Mae saw unmistakable horror and sickness of heart, and she thought of small, fine bones put to strain beneath the flesh. "I thought she would." She healed instantly—they were in the doorway. "Children!"

"Marcia Mae told you! Oh, she shouldn't!"

"So that's where you were! We couldn't imagine."

Jason came pounding in in his sock feet. "Well, baby girl!" He was kissing her over and over, and wringing Kerney's hand. "As if you didn't have enough handshaking to do."

"I'm going to tell Grand," said Cissy, and vanished.

"You hear that?" Nellie said and stopped eating pie.

"Hear what?" asked the yard boy.

"Miss Cissy, Mister Kerney getting ma'd." She went into the kitchen and came back with a dish of cut lemons. "They needn't think they going have no wedding in this house till cotton picking done. I can't he'p it who they is. All them things is done in the kitchen."

"Who getting ma'd?"

"Miss Cissy. Mister Kerney Woolbright."

The Negro boy was lounging his length against the steps. "I thought they's ma'd already."

"You a crazy nigger," said Nellie. "You know who yo' daddy was? That cross-eyed nigger used to drive Miss Hope Mullens's cows to paster, that's who."

"I ain't never heard that," said the boy.

"Then it's time you did."

"About the speech this morning, sir," Kerney was saying to Jason.

"You couldn't do anything else, Kerney. I wanted to talk to you about it. You probably feel pretty bad over it. But everybody I talked to felt the same way I did, that Duncan's a fine boy and they hate to go against him, but he's lost his head on this Dozer thing. He undertook to say to somebody he thought the niggers would be voting in a few more years. Maybe they will be, but nobody who talks that way can expect to win an office. You couldn't let him ruin your chances. I think, in fact, boy, that you behaved with good sense and courage, and I said to myself at the time, If I ever had a son, I'd want him to be like that. Able to take a thing in hand, and drive it—"

He stopped, and as his voice faded in the shadowy room and his active brown hand unclasped, he remembered a bit behind the two women that he had indeed had a son who had hated him and who had died.

Nan stepped in and put her cool lips to Kerney's cheek. "So welcome to the family, dear."

Marcia Mae went out to the glider on the front porch and hugged her knees. Inside, Cissy had wakened old Mrs. Standsbury out of her nap. She had been dreaming about her girlhood and kept saying, "Marry who? Kerney? Kerney who?"

Jason followed Kerney into the hallway. "I never try to interfere or make suggestions in anything you young people have in mind. Just let me know whenever I can help. It's the main pleasure I get out of life nowadays, helping my children, and you mustn't begrudge it to me. You'll excuse me if I don't come out in my sock feet. I guess you ought to know by now where the door is."

When Kerney passed Marcia Mae he gave no sign of noticing her, and she could not tell if he had pretended this or not. His face revealed nothing of him except his identity: it was as if he had carried his own portrait by.

She rose and reentered the house. Cissy and Nan were still in the dining room, though Cissy had already fetched magazines and they were leaning together near the corner of the sideboard where light came in strongest through the bay window. The approach of a wedding brings out a nineteen-year-old side in every woman, and you would have thought them two girls together, each satisfied at the snail-slow turning of the thick, slick, beautifully photographed pages. "I saved all the June magazines this year," Nan said in her amused voice. "I can't imagine why."

Marcia Mae remembered the spring before she was to have married Duncan, how it had warmed so wickedly, so fulgently toward June, the quarrel over white satin, the heavy paper in the announcements, the search for white camellias in quantity so late in the year, the proud high-arching storms.

"Duncan speaks at two o'clock," she said. "Are you going?"

They both turned quickly—she might have snapped a whip on their backs.

"I'm not," said Cissy. "The only reason I went this morning was to hear Kerney."

"I never try to go out to these things any more," said Nan. "I explained that to Kerney this morning."

Fine, between her eyes, one could see across the room the little wire that would presently begin to throb and tauten, would drag her at last, helpless, stumbling, in agony, into a blackened room, and on a canopied bed, behind a fast shut door, take all its pleasure of her.

Marcia Mae left them together and looked in on her grandmother. The old lady lay propped on two pillows, in her summer dressing gown, an afghan throw drawn up to her waist. She stayed quieter, with folded hands, than the pretty familiar objects that winked on her dresser.

"I hope I don't die before they have the wedding."

"Die!" Marcia Mae laughed. "You're never even sick."

"I'm still going to die," said the old lady. "You don't think I'm silly enough to think I'll live forever, do you?"

"I didn't know it ever worried you," said Marcia Mae. "You read the Bible all the time."

"I didn't say it worried me. Worry's a sin."

"Grand, you remember when all those Negroes were shot in the courthouse back right after the First World War?"

"Remember it? Yes, I remember it well."

"What did Grandfather Standsbury think of it?"

"Think of it? He thought it was terrible, like everybody else."

"I mean didn't he always feel guilty about it, as if he might have stopped it from happening if he had got up there in time?"

"I was mighty glad he didn't get up there till it was over. Those men were murderers, that Acey Tallant especially. Your grandfather couldn't have done a thing with them. He always thought he could, but he couldn't."

"Yet he always felt guilty, didn't he? It haunted him till the day he died, didn't it?"

"I don't know if it did or not. If he thought about it all the time, he never told me. He would never have been one to unburden his worries on his dear ones. He was a mighty fine family man, always loving and considerate. From the day we married till the day he died, there was never anything of what you'd call real trouble between us. My wish was what he wanted—he loved a happy home. I took it all for granted in those days, but God's let me live to see what a precious thing it was. Nowadays, with people flaunting marriage around like a new dress, that is, if they bother to get married at all—why, they carry on worse than Negroes. They don't want to call anything right or wrong. Your grandfather was a far cry—" She stopped speaking, noticing that her granddaughter was gone, but kept on thinking without interruption, smiling faintly, out of great pleasure of spirit, though she felt no undue excitement and had scarcely ever been moved to tears.

Retreating to her high room, Marcia Mae changed her shorts for the corded cotton skirt, ran the silver-mounted comb through her hair, and holding the silver hand mirror to catch the best light, painted her mouth. Blotting Kleenex between her lips, she glanced far down to where three sparrows preened themselves around the leak the garden hose made at the hydrant. Movable sprays ran all day now on the lawn; the yard boy trundled them about to different spots, and still the earth hardened and grass faded from the top half-downward. There where the little birds shook drops from their wings, the ground would not at first absorb the moisture, as perfectly dry cloth takes its time about wetting. Out far, by the edge of the lawn, the leaves on a low maple branch hung dusty, dry, distinct and still. The heat would linger till November yet, but summer was over now, had left the first thing it leaves, the heart, and Marcia Mae knew she would soon be going away. She would take off the house and the town and the people there, like taking off her clothes, one thing at a time, before dressing new from the skin out—new place to live, new job, and somewhere, a new man.

But this I do, she thought, and turned resolutely, dropping the tissue with its red print into the wastebasket, resealing the lipstick, laying down the mirror. This one thing I do.

She caught up her bag, the worn soft leather that pleased her. She ran downstairs.

"Marcia Mae!"

It was her father.

She kept on out the front door, but in the yard she veered, circled the wing of the house and halted under his office windows. "Daddy?"

He appeared back of the screen. "Where are you off to, Marcia Mae?"

"To hear Duncan speak. Do you want to come?"

"I told you from the first, Marcia Mae, that I don't approve of Duncan's ideas in this race. I don't want to be put in a position of having to show publicly what I think of him."

"But I do want to show what I think of him. I want the chance to say I'm for him."

"You cannot play with this nigger business, Marcia Mae. That Dozer Negro has been bound for trouble exactly the same way his father was. If Duncan had handled things right—"

"You mean if Duncan had come to you for orders. If he had taken lessons in how to be a hypocrite."

"You're being very hard. I foresaw trouble for Dozer years ago. I tried to get him to go North. None of this counts with you. I've made money out of this county for forty years, given jobs to everybody worth a plugged nickel, kept this house up and you children fed, clothed, and flying around in automobiles. I reckon this makes me a crook. I wouldn't go down there to that speaking, Marcia Mae. Duncan is talking for something that's going to come, but I tell you it cannot be spoken out for. I reckon that makes me a hypocrite. But I don't want you around where there's any trouble."

"I have to go," she told him. "I have to stand with Duncan's friends. Don't you understand why I have to?"

"I guess so." His face disappeared from the window, then showed again. "You're grown." He vanished, this time for good.

an
army
gathers

52. She drove out, swinging the convertible expertly out of the thick-layered shade into the heat and dust, and skirting the hot square, moved rapidly away toward the schoolhouse and the speaking grounds.

The cars had already gathered, filling the grounds. The benches were tight-packed and people were standing close in and sitting on the fenders of the nearest cars. The loudspeaker gaped open its three monstrous throats. But the spot they all faced, the rostrum, was empty.

Marcia Mae was forced to park on the right side of the

campus and walk a good distance through the car-crowded space.

A game, she thought. You would have thought it was a game. On football weekends at the university, the campus was one big parking lot, and people from every part of the state, from all over the South, too, sat eating their lunches with the car doors open in the dry fall heat. Along the sidewalks from the town, the children sold programs and chrysanthemums with satin ribbons, and shouted their wares from the cold-drink stands. The steady beat of walking filled the air: the flattering, feminine high heels that Southern girls wore to the big games along with their new fall suits, their little hats; the paced, lazy, well-shod, decisive walking of Southern men. Everywhere you heard them say Harper. Close your eyes and it fell out of the air at you, here loud, there soft, here with a Rebel yell before it, there with a furtive handshake on a bet.

In one way or another they were all there to see him, and she, Marcia Mae, for two straight years (the only time in the history of the university) marched as Homecoming Queen between the chancellor of the university and the captain of the team, and received from the Governor of the state an enormous bouquet of white chrysanthemums with satin ribbons eight inches wide, and stood smiling while the three-hundred-piece band arranged on the field to spell "UM" played "Let Me Call You Sweetheart," and a crowd of 30,000 stood solemnly and the men removed their hats, just as if it had been "The Star-Spangled Banner" or news of the President's death or the outbreak of a war. . . . "Jason Hunt's daughter." "Yeah." "From up in Lacey, too." "Yeah." "High-school sweethearts." "So they say." "Never went with anybody else." "Well, he's got plenty, Jason has." "Yeah." "Shows where football will take you, man." "Over the fifty-yard line." "What you talking about? Goal to go."

They're all here again, she thought, on account of him.

People looked at her silently. She saw a tall, angular country fellow she had known as a child but whose name she could not remember. He had a neck like a turkey gobbler's, grizzled, scaly, and fumed, from the sun or some complaint; his eyes were amused and kind. He did not mind being ugly. To him she would never be anything but a funny little girl.

"Why is everybody so quiet?" she asked, half-whispering lest her voice rise over the crowd.

"They don't aim to agree with him," he told her. "On anything." He smiled at her, ever so gently.

"None of them? None?"

"I don't undertake to say none, Miss Marcia. Let's leave it at ninety-nine and some odd per cent."

She thought, I don't believe that, and moved on toward the benches. Just at the end of one toward the back, a man of the town, a friend of her father's, got up and gestured with his hat that she take his seat. She shook her head.

"I'm going further down. Where is he?"

"It's ahead of time yet. I guess he'll come."

"He'll come. It's not like him to back out."

"I don't think it is either."

"He'll come unless something has happened."

"I think so too."

With the touch of his hat, he detained her from entering the heart of the crowd.

"I wouldn't go any further in, Marcia Mae."

"Why? What—"

"Well, I wouldn't, that's all. Listen."

She heard then the hum of the crowd. No sound rose distinctly above any other, but the quality was resolute and passionate. It was like men marching somewhere, nearer all the time. It was like the rustle of hymnbooks in the big tent meeting just after the first number is called. It was as certain as storm and morning, and unreasonable as blood.

The crowd was one.

The instant she realized it, it went through her like lightning. She was terrified.

Jason Hunt, who had followed his daughter secretly, watched her from the shadow of a countryman's pick-up. He saw the halt and start and straightening of her fine carriage, as when in the dark seeded pasture all its own, the thoroughbred smells the wild thing that everybody said left these parts long ago, and the narrow head flings high and the tender ears leap forward. The hoof, trimmed and blackened, has never lifted except to be admired. Through the whitewashed palings the sheathed claw thrusts and touches earth and bears weight. They had said to her all her life: "Don't go too far from town . . . It's Saturday; don't go down on the tennis court by yourself, not in the afternoon . . . Be careful . . . Be sure there's a man along." So this was why.

A young man touched her arm. "Your daddy says he changed his mind about coming. He says for you to come on back there with him."

"No." Even on the one word, her voice shook. She said again, firmly, "No."

She whirled and hurried off the other way, going back to her own car. Somebody obviously had to get to Duncan. Somebody had to warn him what he was about to come strolling into. I can do this for him, she thought. This. At least this. There was some kind of forever in it—the way she thought about it.

The young man went back to Jason Hunt. "She wouldn't come," he said.

Jason watched her drive away, and scratched behind his ear. It wasn't like her to run off. "Okay," he said. "Thanks anyhow."

three
children
play

53. Patsy, Cotton, and W.B., left alone, first ate Puffed Wheat with cream and sugar, then some ice cream and little cakes. They then went to the back door and looked out into the yard toward the sand pile, but the yard looked too big and bright today to play out in. On the way back through the kitchen, Patsy remembered a tin of candy everybody else had forgotten about, and climbed on a chair to drag it down. The candy had grown old and Cotton did not want anything else sweet, but W.B. put one in each jaw and so did Patsy.

In the living room they sat on the floor and started teaching W.B. how to play I Doubt It, but Patsy got the cards sticky and Cotton said they were his cards and put them back into the box. When he felt the sticky surfaces of the cards, Cotton felt he would cry, though not about the cards. There was a feeling he had often now, as if he had swallowed a little light bulb whole. He would try to draw his breath, or yawn it away, but it stayed, cold and hollow, down in his stomach. If he got near his mother when he cried about something, only then would it grow warm and go away.

Patsy said she didn't want to play cards any more anyway. "W.B. is my horse," she said. "I can ride him."

She climbed on his back and put her arms around his neck. W.B. began to trample around the couch on his hands and knees, riding Patsy on his back.

"Giddyap," she said, kicking him with her bare heel.

W.B. made a galloping motion. Patsy squealed.

"Y'all stop," said Cotton. "Don't do that."

But they paid no attention to him. He bent, coming close with the blocking technique Duncan had taught him, and spilled them both on the rug. Patsy tumbled on her fat behind; W.B. sprawled out on his back.

"Y'all play something else," said Cotton.

He was still worried because his daddy had said he didn't like football.

"You're the meanest thing," said Patsy. "I like W.B. a whole lot better than you, and he's colored."

"I just half colored," said W.B. promptly, sitting up. "I also half white."

The children studied him silently.

"If you are half white," Patsy asked, "where *are* you half white?"

"I don't know," said W.B., puzzling. "I hadn't thought to look."

"Then ride me like a horse again," said Patsy. "Let's gallop."

"No," said Cotton, coming between them. "Don't play that."

"You're the meanest thing," said Patsy and hit at him. "Help me beat up Cotton, W.B." It was a grand idea. Her eyes got big. "Together we really could."

But W.B. backed off. "Naw now, Patsy, naw. Let go, Patsy. Les us leave Cotton be."

"Play something else," said Cotton.

"I don't want to play anything else. I don't want to!"

She had started to cry when they heard the knocking at the front door.

"It's Mister Willard Follansbee, I bet," said W.B. "He want to fry me like a chicken. He after me."

"You go hide," said Cotton. "I'll say you aren't here."

But it was only a blond lady, the one they had seen down at the schoolhouse that morning. She wanted to know where Duncan was and he told her just what he'd heard them say:

out at Mars Overstreet's store beyond the Pettico-cow Creek bridge. She seemed an outside lady and spoke in a foreign way.

"Where on earth is that?" she asked. "How do you get there?"

"I don't know," he said.

He stood connecting her with stories instead of anything here, so when she stared, bent, and suddenly kissed him, he wasn't surprised. He wished she had not gone away.

the
stampede

54. Another besides Jason Hunt had wondered at Marcia Mae's departure from the speaking grounds. Unused to making his own decisions, Willard Follansbee was worrying that day with the nervous intensity of a cotton gin. Where was Harper? If Harper didn't come, he, Willard, could speak first. Good. But what if Harper showed up with some last-minute stuff from New Orleans? Bad. What if the nigger got in safe to Harper and told what he knew? Where was Marcia Mae going? The sweat gathered in salty pearls about his brow and trickled down the back of his neck into his collar. What with dust, sweat, and hair oil, his head itched like fire. Was Marcia Mae going to find Harper?

Across the street from the school grounds, a boy came out the screen door of a small sandwich and cold-drink shop, and crossed toward the crowd. Follansbee stood far on the outskirts in his white suit and flaming tie; the boy located him after a moment's search.

"Somebody just called in from out in the country," said the boy. "They say Harper's done got the nigger."

He stood in the offhand way that many Southern boys have, telling the most remarkable news without expression or elaboration.

"When did they call?" Willard demanded.

"Just now. Just this minute."

"Where from in the country?"

"You know Mars Overstreet's store? They were just leaving it."

As the boy left, one of a group of men near Willard had moved to stand at his shoulder. Now the others closed in; among them were the three who had stopped Kerney Woolbright earlier and asked him to go with them to hunt Beck Dozer down.

"I wouldn't be surprised," said Willard, "if Harper just might need our help to bring that nigger in."

"What y'all fixing to do?" a man called to them.

Willard drew his little pack away toward his car, obviously in conference. "You boys take it easy," another voice advised.

Several of the men piled into the car with him. One turned back, changing his mind, and watched them drive away. A friend joined him. "Might as well go see what they're up to." They got in a mud-splashed pick-up, two others crowding into the cab with them at the last minute, and drove away after Willard.

Nobody seemed to know quite what had happened. In watching them go, everybody close by had let the boy get away, back to the sandwich shop. Several people, like bees straying from the central swarm, ran across to question him, but learned nothing; his father had forbidden him to do more than deliver the message. They found him obedient and stubborn as a mule.

Questions flew around. Where was Duncan Harper? Marcia Mae Hunt? Willard Follansbee? Here and there a man turned away from where he was standing and found either his own car or that of a friend who might want to drive uptown in case anything was going on. First, one car went; then, two minutes later, another, this one, like Willard's, with several passengers. For five minutes longer the crowd endured the strain. For five minutes every head was turned toward the empty road which told nothing. The murmur grew into a hubbub. Speculation was instantly repeated as fact: they were bringing the nigger into Lacey; Duncan Harper had found who shot Jimmy; a wire had come from New Orleans for Duncan Harper; the nigger was dead all along; Follansbee and Duncan were in a fight on the square. Through every statement the same thread ran: something was happening somewhere. It seems strange that curiosity can multiply into as strong a desire as wanting to get out of a burning building.

A man said quietly to his wife: "They're fixing to cut loose here in a minute. Let's get out while we can." He caught her by the hand and made for his car, and the stampede was on.

Jason Hunt found himself hopelessly trapped in the rush. Several people had jumped into his car to ride with him, without saying by your leave. Baby, baby, he kept thinking. What had she gone rushing off into this time? He did not see how such a dusty riot of machines would ever untangle. But one by one they shook loose; with a roar of the motor, some old Ford with a rattling fender won a path into the schoolhouse drive and gained the town street. After it came a sleek two-toned Oldsmobile.

Soon they were all free and coursing one behind the other with increasing certainty, for the first to reach the town square were not long in learning that Marcia Mae had stopped at the drugstore to ask the way to Mars Overstreet's store in the country.

55. Mars Overstreet's store was a grocery-filling station, sitting high on a crazy bluff to the left of the road five miles out beyond the tie plant and the Pettico-cow Creek bridge. In the winter when the smaller roads washed out or got too muddy for travel, the store was a sort of branch post office for the neighborhood. There was a dusty radio inside where people came to listen to the World's Series or the war news or the football game, though mainly they came to talk to one another and get the local events thrashed over. Anybody who for one reason or another had decided not to go to town on Saturday afternoon was apt to show up and stand around without saying much. Even today, with the county drained into Lacey for the political speaking, there were two young men in the store along with old Mrs. Overstreet, who being deaf and of no political turn of mind—she did not think women should have had the vote—had been left in charge of the store. She was back of the counter reading the paper, her glasses low on her nose and a yellow pencil stuck in her knot of hair.

The two men were alike—not in appearance, for one was short and dark, the other tall and brown; nor in the events of their lives, for one had just returned home after two years' fighting in Korea and the other was said to be taking refuge in the hills from the husband of a woman over near the River —and were spending all their time together because each felt himself enhanced for other people by an adventurous atmosphere which failed to do him any personal good at all, and each felt that perhaps if he were the other, life might have yielded up the secret. They were, in short, bored to death.

They were never observed talking to one another, only

standing together, each in an attitude. The tall one, the one who had just come from Korea, liked to lean against something without exactly sitting on it, and fold his arms low across his chest the way John Wayne did in the movies. The short one, who was slightly bowlegged, kept his head ducked low with one hand on his hip and the other holding a cigarette the way one picks a berry, so that the smoke had stained between all his fingers and part of the palm. The question Mrs. Overstreet had asked five minutes before—or was it ten?—was still to be heard from time to time in the store. It had been:

"Whyn't y'all at the speaking?"

In order to get rid of it, like swatting a fly, the short one dropped his cigarette on the concrete floor, ground it out with his shoe, and answered through a mouthful of smoke.

"Just didn't go, I reckon."

Mrs. Overstreet finished the funny paper and turned to the editorial page. Her head rose and fell, drawing her eye up and down the columns; she was winnowing out what she meant to read. She released another question into the room:

"Wonder why there wasn't never a write-up in the Memphis paper when Travis Brevard died?"

Then she began to read in earnest.

Her words came and went, came and went. The tall brown one gave a yawn that staggered him.

"Was. Was a nice little squib, about that long." He opened two fingers, but did not trouble to unfold his arms. "Mama sent it to me."

"Funny I never saw it," said Mrs. Overstreet. "I thought I saw everything in the paper. Hardly ever miss a thing."

"Maybe she got it out of another paper."

Mrs. Overstreet took off her glasses and lowered the newspaper. "The *Tribune!*" She could not accept this. "You don't mean Wessie Stevens reads the *Tribune!*"

"No'm," said the tall man. "She takes the *Commercial*, same as everybody."

"Well then." Restored to orthodoxy, Mrs. Overstreet replaced her glasses and put the paper up again before her face. "I hardly ever miss anything. Funny I never saw it." Clearly, she did not believe it had ever been printed.

The shorter man turned a cigarette out of a torn pack, struck a cheap, large-flame lighter to it, and walked to the window. He said something in a voice which never carried beyond the person nearest him, though whether this was its quality or his intention could not be known, and Mrs. Overstreet, behind her newspaper, took a notion that when people spoke they ought to make themselves heard. She absolutely demanded to know what he had said.

Surprised, he turned about, regarding her with beautiful, bucolic, unintelligent eyes, which the woman whose husband was supposed to be chasing him had probably found irresistibly romantic.

"I just said I wisht it would rain."

"Everybody does," said Mrs. Overstreet, impatiently.

"That's all I said."

"What?"

"I said that's all I said."

"Maybe if we'd all quit talking about rain, it would go on and do something."

The two looked at each other, shrugged, and went to the window. They stood there so long, Mrs. Overstreet noticed them. "What is it?" she asked.

"It's somebody driving up in the side yard."

"Getting out?"

"No'm, just stopping. Why, it's Duncan Harper, him and his wife."

"Duncan Harper coming in here?" Mrs. Overstreet laid down the paper on the counter, and put her glasses, which were a great trial to her, on top of it, and came to the window. "He's walking out down the bluff," she said. They all observed that this was true.

The tall man stepped through the side door and stood watching.

"He's coming back towards the bluff with a nigger. I bet you anything it's that Dozer nigger."

"What nigger?" the dark one asked.

"You know that nigger. Took a shot at Jimmy Tallant here last month."

"Sure I know. I used to know him personally. You reckon he's been back there all this time?"

"I reckon he was."

"He's got a nerve," said Mrs. Overstreet. "He's had everybody dancing to his own sweet tune. Using the back of my land to hide in. Look at him, talking along with Duncan Harper. He thinks he's good as I am, now, don't he?"

But she was only marveling. She would have sounded the same if she had been watching an acrobatic troupe.

The dark young man went out of the store to join the other, and the two sauntered across the yard toward Duncan and Beck.

the
challenge

56. When Duncan called from the path down to the cotton house, Beck's woolly head poked out immediately from the door.

"I wants to go into Lacey," Beck told him.

"I can't risk that," said Duncan. "You'll go into the next county for custody."

"How come you think I waited for speaking day if not for

all the white folks to be gathered in town? I wants to go into Lacey like my daddy did."

"I guess you must want to go out of Lacey like your daddy did. Do you long to get dumped in your own front yard like a sack of meal?"

"Times have changed," said Beck.

"I thought times had changed too," said Duncan, "but this morning I found out they haven't. You're looking at the man who's going to get the smallest vote for sheriff in the history of Winfield County."

"On account of me?" said Beck and stopped walking.

"Partly you. Partly Mister Kerney Woolbright turning against me. And mainly people not wanting to vote for anybody with one single liberal thought toward the black race."

"If I had a vote it would be yours, Mister Harper."

"If I could get you one, I would."

"And still," said Beck, "I would like to ride into Lacey."

"I don't give a damn what you'd like," said Duncan.

He was conscious of the biases and willfulness that Beck put himself together with, until his character was as whorled as the grain of a tree that had grown up through the middle of a harrow. There was no way not to think of Uncle Phillip, who was also always pulling against the tide, and just then he recalled for the first time in his life something his mother had told him once when Uncle Phillip had provoked him to the point of murder. "His wife ran off with his best friend," she said. "You have to take that into account. Now don't you ever mention it, especially not to him." I guess it was enough to make a Hoover man of him, Duncan thought, and as quickly as that the gap of sympathy that had stood all these years between his uncle and himself was closed. For he knew now that he too would be seen in Lacey as an eccentric; possibly it would be the only way he could be tolerated. "He went off on the race question," they would say, as though he had taken up some Oriental religion; "It was the strangest thing." Strange enough to take the place of his football record as the story people told about him. Curiously, these reflections did not oppress him. The people around Lacey who were said to be peculiar took up the major part of the town; but perhaps their peculiarity, whether acquired deliberately or incidentally, gave them what they wanted— it freed them from what people expected of them. He felt freer already. I can read more now, he thought, and have a drink in the evenings after work, and just then Kerney Woolbright leaned across the grocery counter, looked up at him with trustful boyish eyes and said, "Do you guess Cissy Hunt would give me a date?" and Marcia Mae, poised to serve beside the fresh chalk line, shook a damp strand from her forehead and flashed him a smile. He heard glass splinter—*who* could have done it? He never wanted to know—and he was back with Uncle Phillip, closer than ever. Cresting the path he saw the two young men approaching them from the store. The day was not over yet.

"Do you mean to say that nigger was back there all the time?"

"We'll help you take him in."

"No need for that. Beck and I are old friends. He came to give himself up."

"You can't ever tell what a nigger will do," said the dark man.

"Sure can't," said the tall one, and hooked a thumb in his belt. "He tried to kill Jimmy Tallant, didn't he?"

"He wasn't the one," said Duncan. "It was a white man did it. Ask Tallant."

"That Jimmy Tallant," said Mrs. Overstreet from the side door behind them and died laughing.

"How do you do, Mrs. Overstreet," said Duncan and tipped his hat.

"Pretty well, thank you, Duncan, considering the heat."

"You can't go by what Tallant says," said the tall man. "He'd just as soon lie to you as look at you. Ask him what time it is, he'll look at his watch and tell you thirty minutes off, just to see what you'll do. Ain't that right, Ed?"

"That's right," said the other.

"That nigger there," said the first, jerking his chin at Beck, "what he needs is for somebody to scare the hell out of him a couple of times. He thinks he's good as I am. You going to have trouble like this till somebody does it to him. I know what I'm talking about."

"I reckon we'll just get on along," said Duncan. "If I thought there was any harm in him, I don't guess I'd have brought my wife along when I came for him."

The two men did not want to give ground.

"I hear you're against segregation, want to let the niggers vote," said the tall one. "Is that right?"

Duncan flushed. "Why don't you go to the speaking and hear what I've got to say?"

"Why should I if you can tell me yes or no right now? Do you or don't you?"

"I haven't got time to waste on you," Duncan said.

"*Waste* on us? You don't talk much like a politician to me. You ask for our vote and you're talking like that?"

"You can vote for whoever you want to," said Duncan. "The way you're talking, I wouldn't want to claim you on my side."

He walked between them, clearing a sort of wake that Beck could follow in. Beck was so carefully expressing neither one thing nor the other that he fell neatly when the tall man tripped him.

"His side," said the dark one and sniffed a couple of times

as though his nose bothered him. "Must think he's still playing football."

Mrs. Overstreet, who had retreated into the store, stuck her head out the door, and called to the two as if they had been her own little children.

"Edward! Perrin! You-all come straight inside right this minute!"

"Duncan!" Tinker cautioned from the car window.

"Don't, Mister Harper," Beck said, from the ground.

They were right. Duncan halted, unclenching his fist, turning away. He helped Beck get up.

"They're just trying to pick a fight," said Tinker. She was leaning across the wheel, speaking from the driver's window. That placed her in the center of the front seat with a space on either side.

"They're never out of one thing they don't get into another!" Mrs. Overstreet called to Duncan.

Duncan slid in under the wheel. Beck had crossed before the radiator and now opened the opposite door of the car. He was about to break the front seat forward and let himself in the back, when Duncan glanced toward him, and his hand paused. In that particular slant of light, Beck's glasses failed for once to shield his eyes.

So it comes down to this, Duncan thought. *To the tiniest decision you can make. To the slightest action. In front of people daring you to do what you believe in and they don't.*

"There's plenty of room in the front," he said.

Beck looked down at Tinker, in recollection of the lady who had bandaged up his hands. For an instant she wavered, then shifted aside toward Duncan. "Of course there's room," she said.

"Well I'll be goddamned," said the tall man to the other. "Do you see that?"

Before Duncan could start the motor, they stood beside

335

him, their faces thrusting in the window. "Somebody's got to stop a thing like this," the tall one said flatly.

"We're in a hurry," Tinker said, feeling just the way Mrs. Overstreet had felt, the way badly brought-up children always make a woman feel. "You-all get out of the way."

The hand of the tall one snaked deftly in toward the ignition key, but before Duncan could strike it aside, Tinker had set her live cigarette on it. The man recoiled with a shriek, carrying away with him on the flesh a good quarter of an inch of burning ash, and fell backward, sprawling over his companion, who had bent downward from the window. Duncan took the chance to back away. As he swirled into the drive, coasting down to the road, "They've thrown us later than ever," he said. "I'll be an hour late to the speaking grounds."

"I wants to ride into Lacey," said Beck Dozer.

"I'm taking no chances with you," said Duncan. "I'll just have to be late."

"I think you'd better stop and see about that front tire," said Tinker.

"The tire?"

"Yes. That boy, that awful little black-headed one. He was up to something with it when he bent down."

"To the tire? What would he do?"

"I don't know. I wouldn't put anything past them."

"It seems to ride all right," said Duncan. "I don't have time to stop," he added.

She relighted what was left of her cigarette. Her brown eyes watched him from the mirror.

"I thought I'd be dead before this time of day," said Beck, riding philosophically, his hand holding to the bar that braced the ventilation window, his legs crossed in his best trousers, his shoes shining under the coat of dust.

The car swayed with the curves. Tinker thrust her heel harder to the floorboard. "Do you have to go so fast, Duncan?"

"I should have told them," he said. "When they asked if I wanted Negroes to vote, I should have said right out, Yes I do. There's no middle ground on this. Kerney's seen to that. I have to come right out with what I mean."

"You were afraid for Beck," she said.

"That's it."

They passed the Negro settlement where the women took in washing, and were gone before the dogs, lazy in the heat and drought, had time to more than lift their tongues out of the dust. They ripped over the Pettico-cow Creek bridge and the dry boards jumped up and clattered. They passed the tie plant. Nearing the highway and the juncture where the road ran out at the Idle Hour, the gravel thickened, the road widened, the curves spun them in wider arcs.

"There's something coming," Tinker said. "Look at all that dust."

Duncan pressed the horn for a couple of blasts and leaned closer to the wheel. He saw no need to slacken speed; he was a quick, accurate driver and he knew the road. But he was not prepared for Marcia Mae.

She came flashing out of a curve ahead, her yellow hair wild in the wind; when she saw him coming, she half-turned back to point behind her. She was calling something. She had always been a terrible driver.

There behind her, bursting from the curve, came another car, jammed with men, and Follansbee at the wheel. She was trying to warn him.

Duncan decided at once to take advantage of the curve to get past both cars, though he was well enough acquainted with Marcia Mae to know she might have some wonderful idea. And she did. With Follansbee coming close upon her, she slammed on her brakes, squinting her eyes and bracing herself for the shock.

Duncan felt a moment of extraordinary pride in her. It wasn't such a bad idea. It had taken nerve. It was even working. There went Willard, skidding on a wild bias through the gravel to his right, unable to swing toward Duncan's half of the road and sure to blam the convertible. Marcia Mae herself had very nearly blocked the road; her radiator had deflected toward him in the sudden stop.

Duncan swerved to skim past her, making it by a thread. Weeds rattled against his fenders. He would have to bring the wheel down sharply left to regain his track, then reverse into the road's tilt—it could be done.

He saw the nose of a pick-up appear in the curve. He cut the wheel down, braking momentarily, and before he could switch back for the quick reversal, he felt and heard it at once—the feeling as though his left knee had given suddenly beneath him at full stride in a tricky run, the sound like gunshot in his ear: a blowout. The wheel leaped violently in his grasp.

a rush
to the
scene

57. Jimmy Tallant had spent the day in his empty roadhouse; he had decided for reasons of health to stay away from the speaking. He heard the first car leave the highway, making for the country, but was too late to see who was in it. When the second passed he was at the window. Marcia Mae's shank of hair signed the sky for him, and zip from over the highway rise came Follansbee, hell for leather, car loaded to the gills, and a country pick-up riding close to his taillight.

It took Jimmy about one revolution of the tires to realize that the only person Marcia Mae Hunt and Willard Follansbee had in common was Duncan Harper. Had the first car been his? And if so, was Tinker with him?

Jimmy's car stood near the entrance; he had fudged a day or two on his doctor's orders not to drive, and had gone into town earlier for a pack of cigarettes. He was bending to the ignition switch when he heard, from a little distance within the rolling country where the road ran, the bang of a blowout followed by a shriek of brakes and crashing of metal. Tinker! His thought came louder than the sounds had. At once he was speeding through the gravel, through shoals of yellow dust that in the still hot day showed no volition either to settle again or ebb into the air currents. Now it thickened to the absolute density of mud; now it cleared on a space of road so innocent that Jimmy wondered if he had already passed whatever had occurred.

He had not. Here at the crest of a curve, with puffs of dust still rising from it, the pick-up lay in a ditch to the right of the road, half-overturned. Two wheels stuck up in the air; he saw the fore one stop turning. Men were crawling out of the cab and sitting along the edge of the ditch. One saw Jimmy pass and ran after him, waving an arm. There ahead was Marcia Mae's convertible stopped in the middle of the road. Not a scratch was on it and it was empty.

Jimmy pulled up behind and stopped.

Marcia Mae shouted to him from the drop at the right of the road.

"Oh God, Jimmy! It's awful! Duncan's tire blew out and he turned over twice, right into Follansbee. Follansbee and all those men are crawling out of a gully, but I can't find Duncan's car at all! Come help me find him, Jimmy—"

"Was Tinker with him? Was she?" He was already over the edge of the slight embankment that sloped, then more sharply dropped, to a ravine split into two rambling wooded sections. "*Was she?*" He shook her.

"Somebody was. There were three, I think."

He pulled away from her. He was listing from his long stay in the hospital, as uncertain of his direction as a feather in the air. "Come on," he said, and plunged down at a run.

"It must be that way," she said, pointing right.

"Here!" He stopped his descent, slipping on the loose Mississippi earth. A large gash in the weeds at his feet showed where a car's weight had struck and glanced off. He thought he heard a cry. He took the short steep way down, half-sliding. Behind him, Marcia Mae stumbled and fell, so that he came to the wrecked car ahead of her, saw who was inside and what had happened and hurried on, searching.

Down a cowpath something alive crawled up out of a shallow ditch and caught him by the knees. It took him a minute to recognize Beck Dozer. The glasses were gone, for one thing, so that his face looked like any colored boy's who had gone and got into trouble on Saturday, but young, very young. Blood was streaming back around his temples as if somebody had beat him over the head.

"Get up, for God's sake," said Jimmy, "and tell me if his wife was in the car too."

"She was," said Beck, shaking like a puppy. "Oh, Jesus, yes. Don't leave me, Mister Jimmy, please."

But he ran again. Where? He circled, thrusting back bushes, weeds, and vines. He called. At last he found her.

She was a little way down the hill from where he had seen the gash in the earth. She had not sailed far, but she had certainly gone high, had succeeded in clearing a clump of small locust trees and landing in a little shady space. By an old stump that had turned white and was sprouting vines and mushrooms he found her lying on her side. She had an arm under her head and looked relaxed and assured there, as if she had chosen the place to take a nap in.

At the sight of her he was suddenly no longer terrified, even though he believed at first that she was dead.

By that time the country road above them was filling with cars; in minutes more the highway itself was blocked and all the traffic on U.S. 82 was baking in the sun. Through traffic could curse all it pleased: a town had turned out to see its own history. Slick with sweat, caked with dust, burned at the touch of metal, fanning, roasting in their own cars, the people of Lacey drove every inch as near as they could to the scene, and some got out to walk nearer while others sat waiting for the news.

Slowly it came back to them, an item at a time, some of it wrong. The highway patrol arrived, clearing a way for the ambulance that had got no farther than the hilltop beyond the Idle Hour where it stood blinking yellow and red, red and yellow, the colors blurring in the sun as fire will do. At last it maneuvered into the country road with its siren purring, and here it crept more slowly than ever, the parked cars shifting and backing to make room, and fresh dust spewing. After a time a doctor, impatient, alighted; he thought he could do better on foot.

Those who had first reached the scene of the wreck were rewarded. Already they had heard all the firsthand stories—stories that would be good for generations. Now they were privileged to see authority arrive and stretchers carried up the hill. Last of all, they witnessed Jimmy Tallant emerge, and walking with him with a cloth to the blood on his head, the Negro man, Beck Dozer.

Seeing the clumps of people gathered on the road and roadsides and in the fields beyond, Jimmy stopped and said, raising his voice so everybody could hear him: "Beck Dozer has got to go into town to the doctor to get his head sewed up. If anybody tries to stop him they've got to stop me first. I'd like to get it straight right now that whoever shot me it certainly wasn't Beck, and it's time everybody stopped making out that it was. I answer for Beck, and if he ever tried to shoot me, I'd take damn careful aim the next time I saw him and shoot him back. But nobody else is going to do it. All this mess—all this—happened on account of Duncan Harper being determined to keep Beck Dozer safe. Well, here he is and he's still alive and he's going to stay alive. I answer for him. I hope that's clear."

A path opened to let him through to his car. The white man and the Negro drove away through silence; not a hand was lifted and not a word was said.

The ambulance had gone ahead of them already, and Tinker had been taken to her mother's house. She had just been knocked out, the doctor said, so he had given her a shot to keep her that way.

When Jimmy turned from the highway into the town road, Beck spoke. "I rides into Lacey," he said. "I rides into town like my daddy did." He held the cloth to his head, sitting by the white man, and watched every street go past.

At the doctor's office they sewed him up, giving him a needle to deaden the pain and afterward a paper box of pills to take in the night in case he waked up hurting. He was wrapped in bandages again, as snow-white as Mister Duncan Harper's wife had got out for him. He paid in cash, and Jimmy Tallant took him home.

Lucy came out to meet him after the car had gone. W.B. stood behind her on the steps, and inside through the window, he could make out the shadow of Granny in the chair by the fireplace.

"Jesus!" said Lucy. "Is you bad hurt?"

"Not too bad."

"What they done to you, Beck?"

"Nothing. Nothing except take care of me. I feel like it's been a year since this morning. My glasses got broken." He reached his son and put a hand on his shoulder, looking down into his eyes.

"I got bad news for you, son. Mister Duncan Harper is dead."

Jimmy gets busy

58. Late Sunday afternoon, a couple of Lacey citizens actually rode out to the Idle Hour and asked Jimmy Tallant if he would allow his name on the ballot for sheriff.

"We hear that Bud Grantham has taken up religion," said one, with an uneasy laugh. "We thought maybe you'd like to take up politics."

Jimmy was sitting on the counter inside the main room of the bare roadhouse, hugging his knee. He wore a clean white shirt with the cuffs turned back, a tie loose at the throat, and a gold tie pin on a chain. His hair was slicked down with water, and he was chewing gum. He looked, in fact, like a country fellow about to go out on a summer date. It was reported later that he didn't even get up.

"You better go easy," he said. "You don't know how I feel about the race question."

They both laughed outright. "We know there's no need to ask you."

"Then you won't be interested to know I favor equal rights."

"We're serious about this, Jimmy. We've checked the law: in case of a candidate's death before election, a write-in vote is legal. We're willing to get out the quiet word all over the county starting this minute, if you'll give us the green light."

"Seriously, then, what have you got against Willard Follansbee? He's still on the ticket."

"Nothing, except nobody wants him. They just don't want to vote for him. If Harper was still in it, Follansbee would win because Harper favored nigger rights."

"I just got through telling you: I also favor nigger rights."

The two stood silent. "We considered you might at least think of it as a compliment."

"I think you haven't counted your blessings," said Jimmy. "If you ask me, you've got the perfect candidate and don't know it. He's not going to get religion like Bud Grantham and feel like the likker business is not godly. He's not going to wonder if a nigger has a right to an equal hearing or a fair deal. On every issue that arises, you gentlemen will not have to ask, 'Where does our sheriff stand?' You will know. I cannot really imagine why you've taken a notion you don't care for Willard Follansbee. Maybe he's not as good-looking as I am. He hasn't got very much chin. But you have to recall that Duncan Harper was even better-looking than I am, and you certainly didn't want him. You think it over and try to be tolerant and remember that not everybody is born with the best looks in the world. As for Follansbee's character, I can personally vouch for him. He is the true mirror of your deepest convictions. Hand-picked by Travis Brevard. Trained in office. Knows his job. Why, if he had been the sheriff appointee instead of Duncan Harper, Duncan Harper would still be alive this minute."

"I said that myself," said one, nodding.

"Of course, the nigger might be dead," said Jimmy.

"Well, I don't think dead necessarily. There's some still think that nigger ought to be run away from here."

"Well, then, there you are. Follansbee would probably see

eye to eye with you. Of course, the way *I* feel, anybody tries anything with Dozer has to answer to me. Personally."

The two looked uncomfortable. "Well," said the spokesman, "if you took up a notion like that about Dozer, everybody would understand. You'd have a right to it."

"I am not to be trusted," said Jimmy. "I am basically unsound." As they left, he said, "Take it easy."

Along about second dark, with the revival singing flooding up from down the highway, another car stopped and presently there came a scratching at the back door. Jimmy went through the dark to open it.

"Evening," he said to Pilston, who came near to fainting in his arms. "I had to say it was Bella wanted to see you," he explained, switching on the light. "Otherwise you wouldn't have come, would you?"

"I reckon not," said Pilston, shrinking down in a straight chair by the lamp as though bracing himself for the third degree or worse.

"You can relax," said Jimmy. "I'll get us a drink. We might as well be sociable. The truth is, I wouldn't harm a hair of your head, Pilston. I would defend you to the grave."

Bella stopped by the roadhouse on her way home from church. "It was just the best sermon yet," she said, just before she saw Pilston. "Mercy!" She thought they might be going to fight over her.

Her innocence came out so truly then that Jimmy lowered his eyes and for once words failed him. She gathered the nature of things all by herself.

"You want me to go on and go with him, don't you?"

"I married you because of what you said about the baby," Jimmy told her. "You knew that at the time."

"I thought I was telling the truth," she said. "It was you I remembered best."

"That's not the way they run these things."

"It might be true still. It looked like you to the life when it was tiny. Maybe it'll look two or three ways more before it's grown. It might get to look like you again."

Pilston shook his head. "You can always tell Indian blood. My mother was a pure-breed Sioux."

Jimmy cleared his throat. "Pilston here has been telling me he's resigned from the gambling business."

"There's not too much future in it," said Pilston, "not in this part of the country anyway. Time you get going good they elect somebody wants to clean you out. There ought to be laws to protect you. Have it one way or the other, but have it permanent. Instead you can't tell. There's no stability." He shot a sly look at Bella. "I told her all this. I had a little talk with Bella night before last. It was while you were still in the hospital."

"That so?" said Jimmy.

"I've put aside a little pile. She knows about it."

"Well now," said Jimmy, "I just as well take my hat and go for a little stroll. Give you two a chance to talk some more."

Bella sat with her feet side by side on the concrete floor. "But it's you I love, Jimmy." That stopped him.

"The thing is," Pilston told her, right out, "he don't care nothing at all about you. He never has, I bet you, and he ain't going to. If a woman loves a man and he don't love her, she can love him more and more, but it don't change him. At least, that's been my experience. Ain't that right?"

"I know it," said Bella. "It's how come I been going to the meeting all the time. I was counting on the Lord to help me."

"Well," said Pilston, "maybe the Lord has. They tell me He moves in mysterious ways."

"He's a sensible-talking man, Bella," Jimmy said, in advisory tones, and left them.

Outside, he found Beck Dozer waiting, and paid him. "He got here before you could get back," said Jimmy.

"Oh, I rode with him," Beck said. "He was over in that Delta bingo place, just like you guessed."

"Do you know if there's anything in the Bible about the father of your children being your legal husband?"

"I don't recall any such," said Beck. "Wouldn't it give some people a number of different wives?"

"They say you can find anything in the Bible," said Jimmy. "When you go home, see can you locate me a text."

"If I finds such a scripture, I might have to abide by it."

"Um," said Jimmy. He was apt to trail off into thinking now, and his thinking always went this way: Why me?

It did not seem possible. If life was blind, how could it suddenly wish him well? Why had not he died in a field in the wood, shot by accident, with Tinker bending over him to help him, instead of Duncan, smashed out of life in a car wrecked by accident, with Marcia Mae covering the sight of him until they pulled her away, and bright blood clung in her hair? And Duncan, the poor bastard, at least was trying to do good; while he, Jimmy Tallant, had never been known to try to do anything good.

He and Beck walked to the front of the roadhouse and, picking up gravel, took turns throwing at a telephone post across the highway. Jimmy struck it first—it rang to the heartwood—and Beck paid him a nickel. They played twice more, and retired in a sweat to a bench by the roadhouse steps.

"I go around in every waking hour thinking on that wreck," Beck confessed. "I think and think, and what I always ask is, 'Why him?' If somebody had to die, why wasn't it me?"

"It wasn't that somebody had to die," Jimmy said restlessly. "He did get killed. It just happened that way. There's nothing to wonder about. You just take it the way it is."

"Mister Harper was a gentleman," said Beck, from the end of the bench. "One is obliged to say it, for it's true."

"You're right," said Jimmy, sitting back with his knee hugged, adding at last with finality—it was perhaps the first time in his life he had ever thought or spoken of Duncan without a lurking scorn—"He was a gentleman."

On the highway coming from Lacey, a car was approaching. Slowing as it neared, it seemed to drift silent on the black strip, the lights widening. The gravel by the roadhouse rustled. The car stopped just beyond the two gas pumps. In the dark it was impossible to make out who the two inside were. Neither Jimmy nor Beck stirred. The figure nearer the wheel spoke without turning his head. His voice identified him as the one who had questioned Jimmy earlier about running for sheriff.

"Did you mean that, Jimmy, what you said about favoring equal rights?"

"I meant it," Jimmy said. He did not move.

In the long pause the insects choired, louder, it would seem, than the revival singing had been.

"You haven't thought it over? Don't want to change your mind?"

"No."

The pause this time was longer yet. Then the one at the wheel started the motor. The car pulled to the edge of the highway, waited while a heavy truck boomed past, then moved away in the direction of Lacey.

"They wanted you to run for sheriff?" Beck inquired.

"Yeah."

"Just for a minute in there, when they got right still, I thought maybe they were going to say, 'Well, equal rights or not, run anyway.' Did you think that?"

"It crossed my mind," said Jimmy.

"They say these matters are very delicate," Beck remarked. "If they had said, 'Run anyway,' I might have shouted 'Hallelujah!' and spoiled everything for another fifty years. You can't tell."

"No, you can't tell."

epilogue

when
the bough
breaks

"I didn't see so much of it," said Mrs. Overstreet. "I never did like nigger trouble, though I understand—ought to by now, goodness knows—that it's necessary sometimes. I just didn't want to watch it, you know. There was Duncan Harper to get him, and them two boys in the store, Perrin Stevens and Edward Price, they run out there. So I started to go in the back room of the store and shut the door. I thought to myself, I reckon I ought to watch, there'll be so many people asking me about it, but I just hope he gets him away from here without nothing happening to him.

"Then I recollected all of a sudden I had seen Duncan's *wife* in the car! I said to myself, It couldn't be right: nobody would go to arrest a nigger with his wife in the car, so the next thing I was fixing to do besides telling Perrin and Edward to behave (always into something, them two) was call her into the store with me if it looked like anything. But by then, bless Pat! Perrin Stevens was sprawled out on the ground hugging his hand where Tinker Harper had burnt him with her cigarette, and Edward Price was sprawled out by him where Perrin had tripped over him. *And* the nigger was up in the front seat.

"I said to myself, I never yet saw a fugitive from justice treated in such style, though they claim there're prisons out in California where they don't want to hurt the crooks' feelings, so everybody acts like nobody never done nothing at all, and they're all just there for fun. A nigger at that! I know he never done it, but didn't anybody know it for sure at that time, least of all Duncan Harper. Well, the boys was upset and I was upset, though I'm sorry as anybody, you understand, that Duncan had that wreck. I don't say, Served him right. Nobody ought to say that. It ain't Christian.

"Perrin Stevens wore his hand wrapped up for a week, but him and Edward never talked so much about it, except to say that if any nigger had to be riding in the front seat along with a white man and a white man's wife when there was a whole back seat empty, and it August, they didn't want to hear nothing about it that time either. But if Edward did anything to the tire I never saw it. I think he more than aptly got knocked over when Perrin drawed his hand back where she burnt him and then Duncan stepped on the gas. You can ask him though.

"Looks cloudy today, though the paper just said: Fair. Continued Warm. I'm so tired of reading Continued Warm. I'm almost tempted to write a letter. Listen, you can call it warm if you want to, but to me it's *hot*. H-O-T, hot. It ain't a hard word. Look it up."

Having listened with his usual good care throughout this declaration, Kerney Woolbright paid his respects and drove back to town. There was a little whipping wind abroad, though it was not yet noon. Dust ran across the road in furrow widths. The iron bridge over Pettico-cow Creek sounded dangerously like thunder.

He parked the car on the square, and began to walk around without seeming to, talking to this one and that one: though apparently in casual progress toward some minor business, he was really not going anywhere at all. People congratulated him on winning the race, and joshed him about the announcement of his engagement to Cissy Hunt, which had appeared in the Sunday paper.

"She had to wait till after the election before she'd say the word," they said. "Cissy's not so dumb."

"No," said the postmistress, who had just locked up for

dinner, "they mailed all the stuff in to the paper on the Monday before the voting. I'll have to take up for Cissy on that. Looks like we're going to get that rain."

Kerney ran into Perrin Stevens, the Korean War veteran, as he was coming out of the pool hall. Perrin stuck his thumbs in his belt and slouched back against the wall with one foot to prop himself.

"Naw, I never said much to him that day, Kerney. Me and Edward come running out of the store to help him, the way anybody would. Then he said the nigger was his friend, that was the first thing that threw us off. It sort of riled me. He never knew at the time, it turned out, but what that very nigger had fired on Jimmy Tallant in cold blood. In cold blood, man. Then he never thanked us neither. And on top of that—put the nigger in the front seat! I'm like you, Kerney. I never heard your speech that day, but I know how you felt. You liked Duncan, he was your friend, but who in the South can go along on stuff like that? I tell you, I been in the war over yonder fighting them damn little varmints, and it's the same story in the Army. I don't care what the nigger-loving reporters write back to the nigger-loving newspapers. I'm telling you because I seen it. It's the same story.

"You can't give them responsibility because they don't know what it is. If you get too many of them in one regiment you might as well call off the war and shoot craps. If you don't segregate them there's always trouble. When one gets out of line, they all get out of line. We had a lot of them in our outfit— smokes, the Yankee boys call them. We had it understood. The PRO—public relations officer, you know—kept writing back how brave they were, and every time one came up for a medal, the CO signed it. He said he didn't want Mrs. Roosevelt flying over to Korea to talk to him. I don't care how much fruit salad they wear. When the situation comes, the whites know how to handle it. Duncan Harper was due a piece of my mind that day—I didn't know at the time he had just heard a piece of yours. His wife burnt my hand, I guess Ma Overstreet told you if you saw her. Look-a there. You can still see the scar. All right. I don't hold nothing against her. Women don't have to figure out too much what their men are up to. She better not ever *talk* to me about it—I'll tell her that right now. And that nigger better watch his step, that's all I got to say.

"Somebody said the other day that Ed Price and me must have had something to do with that tire blowing out, but I'm glad to say I never touched it. It seemed more like a act of God to me, though I'm the last person to say I'd want to see Duncan Harper even with a sprained ankle, let alone dead. I used to be proud to say I was from Winfield County just because Duncan Harper lived here. It don't seem right to think he's dead.

"But, hell, you touch this race thing, Kerney, and it kicks like a mule. A mule. Hell! A elephant."

Kerney had to run for his car, not so much to escape rain which had begun to fall in disks, as to make sure of getting home (three blocks away) in livid lightning and dark at noon like judgment day. The storm was so intense that when he ran into the house from the porte-cochere, the current was already off and his mother, whose occupation was gone the minute she could not cook for him, was sitting in front of the fireplace in the living room, as though ready to receive guests.

"I think it's a tornado," she said to him conversationally when he appeared in the door. "I was in one in the Delta once, and if I'm right the eye should arrive within the next few minutes."

He looked past her. Small branches, broken, went skidding

past on a flood of air, and wet green leaves plastered to the panes. She was usually very nervous about things, so he concluded she must be coping with what she considered real danger instead of the imaginary kind. He broke into a cold sweat and trembled on the stair.

"I wouldn't go upstairs if I were you," she called out. "You're safer on the ground floor."

But he had, obviously, to get to his room; the same as she had to sit with her back straight and legs crossed, as though chatting with people at tea.

The wind was like a large hand laid deliberately to the side of the house. He expected to see the door of his room crush to flinders before he could open it. But he let himself in and, closing the door, lay down in the middle of the bed and lighted a cigarette.

The familiar top of the pecan tree had disappeared from the window; now it came flailing back, fighting like a cat somebody was trying to drown. Lightning exploded in his ear. He sweated at every pore and shivered from cold. His mother had sent him to Sunday school for a few years as a child, but the main thing he knew about religion was looking at some Gustave Doré illustrations either for the Bible or for *Paradise Lost*—he could not remember which. He always thought of those pictures during thunderstorms and how the glory seemed all mixed in with horror: angels like a bee swarm going on forever, and heaven like having opened the door to the jumping-off place. He was always afraid of lightning.

Yet when the phone rang he knew he would answer it, because Beck Dozer was supposed to call him, so with tongue dry in his mouth he hurried through to the extension in the hall abovestairs.

"Hello," said Beck, "I reckon it's dangerous to be using

the phone, but I promised to call you soon as I knew." He sounded cheerful.

"Do you know?"

"Yes, I know."

"Then tell me."

"He's staying over in Stark and eats at a little highway café called the Feed Bag. You know where it is?"

"Yes, I know."

"He's staying there because there's a man in the Delta after him for running around with his wife. But he gets there to eat every evening around six."

"Okay, but I'd better hang up. It's storming. . . . What?"

The phone crackled.

"I said when do you pay me?" Beck asked.

"Any time. I don't care. I got to hang up. . . . Tonight at seven by the old Idle Hour. Okay. Sure."

He dropped the phone in its cradle as if it were red-hot.

After another hour his mother called from the top of the stair.

"We still can't cook; the current's still off."

"I'm not hungry," he replied.

She came to the door. "I thought we were gone that time. I really did."

He lay in his sock feet, his knees drawn up, smoking.

"Come on," she said, "we'll fix some sandwiches and tea. There's ham anyway."

"I'm not hungry, Mother. I'll be down when I get hungry. Now I'm not hungry at all."

"All right. But you haven't been eating enough. You have to keep your strength up. Senator." She smiled fondly, almost tearfully. "Senator Woolbright."

He did not answer and she went away. The thunder kept breaking and mending, breaking and mending, farther and farther away, while the rain made a low loving sound on the roof. When the room grew like a hotbox he opened the window. In late afternoon the sun came through a streak, like dawn at four o'clock. What was green was burning green, and light on the drought-dulled ground seemed about to make rainbows. You could smell all the sweet small limbs and leaves where the storm had broken them open.

Around five-thirty he drove to pick up Marcia Mae and they went to Stark to find Edward Price. Beck had worked well. Kerney entered the little highway place called the Feed Bag at ten past six, and Edward Price was there, eating hamburger steak and french fried potatoes in the far corner, in a booth, alone.

Kerney sat down.

"He better not fool with me," said Edward Price, by way of conclusion to the story of the last time he had seen Duncan Harper. Substantially, his account was the same as Perrin Stevens' and Mrs. Overstreet's.

"But he's dead," said Kerney, rubbing his brow with his handkerchief. There, across the indentation his hatband made, sweat liked to collect. It was cool outside, but inside there, a big electric fan on a pole, hatrack tall, did nothing but make the air closer than ever.

"I know he's dead," said Edward Price, and drank some iced tea. When he put the glass down, crumbs of ground beef and cornbread floated to the bottom along with the stirred sugar. His mouth left an arc of grease at the rim. "He's dead, and that goes to show you. We know what's what about things. We know how we like them."

His nails were broken off, and grease was black under them as evenly as though a woman had done it on purpose as a manicure. His hair had grown too long. But doubtless during the romantic episode in the Delta he had slicked up and looked better, maybe with a white shirt on, the tie knotted low and the top button open, the cuffs turned back once on his wrists, smelling of a good hair tonic, with his large dark heavily lashed eyes and his air of knowing what he meant about things. He might have seemed then what the woman thought she might as well have.

"I voted for you," he said, irrelevantly. "After I heard what you said, and had seen what I saw, I checked to see if my poll tax was paid up and sure enough it was. So I voted for you."

"A good thing to do," said Kerney, falling into his automatic politician's street banter. He found himself staring at the thick-cut, white, fried potatoes on which Edward Price was now engaged in pouring tomato catsup. Kerney's stomach gave a lurch. He did not know if he was hungry or sick, and could not at the moment remember having eaten anything for weeks, though if this were true his mother would certainly be having a fit. He stretched out his arm full length and gripped the side of the table, bringing himself near across toward Edward Price, who stopped with a loaded fork and his mouth wide open.

"Did you do it?" Kerney demanded, in agony.

"Do what?" He put down his fork with the food on it.

"That tire that blew out for Duncan Harper was cut, slit. You could see it. I saw it when I went and looked at the wreck. If it was cut, somebody cut it. Nobody will do anything to you, least of all me. I don't want any trouble. I don't want to tell anybody. I just want to *know*. I've *got* to know."

He had played it all wrong, he realized. In fact, he had not played it at all. He of all people, Kerney Woolbright, who was cagey and smart, a shrewd poker-hand, a born politician. He had not even waited to be called. He had thrown his cards face up on the table, and himself on the mercy of a stranger. He was like the young girl in her first crush, unable to wait to say I love you; he was like the pretty new schoolteacher turning from the blackboard to ask: Who threw that? Who threw it? Who? Tell me! Who?

"Go talk to Perrin Stevens," said Edward Price. "I never had nothing to do with it." He returned to his food; his thick lashes lowered like little curtains over his dark sullen unreliable eyes.

". . . So," said Kerney to Marcia Mae, when he returned to the car, "I lost my head. I didn't play it right. He wouldn't say."

She lighted a cigarette from the dashboard. "It's just as well."

"What do you mean?"

"Kerney, we're both of us sweating blood over this because we want to find an out. We want to say that if Edward What's-his-name cut the tire, then that caused the wreck, then it was his fault what happened to Duncan. But even if we found that out, we'd still be just as much involved as ever. I've thought this over every way in the world, and more often than not I get right mad at Duncan for dying. It's the only unfair thing he ever did." Then she said suddenly, "I went to see Tinker."

"You *what?*"

"Yes, I did. I took myself down, and went by after supper one night so nobody would see me. The little boy came to the door—he's so like Duncan around the eyes. I told him to tell her who I was, and she came right out. We sat on the front porch alone together and I told her why I came running about Duncan that day, because he never realized how vicious people could be and that the crowd was in a terrible mood waiting for him and that I couldn't see him walk in in such an innocent way. She didn't say anything, so I kept on talking. I told her that I had tried to make Duncan leave her, but he wouldn't, just as long years ago I tried to make him leave Lacey and my family and his family, but he wouldn't. So I just gave it over to her like that, you see, Kerney—my whole long love for Duncan. When you tell something you give it away.

"She followed me down the walk to the gate, and I said it had meant a lot to me to talk to her and I hoped it hadn't worried her too much. She said no and said too there was one more thing that I might not remember. She said that in school I once had laughed at a dress her mother had made her. I said, Well, I didn't remember, but I was sorry about it. That seemed to be all between us, so I left. I feel better now. I feel if I hadn't done it, I'd always be like a raw seam, something left to ravel out into time—some vague sort of death. Do you see?"

He did not answer. Having retraced the highway from the Feed Bag to the Winfield County line, he was now approaching the old Idle Hour, which was more a shell every day, since the gas pumps had been taken away and then the windows boarded up. They said that Bud Grantham had gone back to farming and that Jimmy Tallant was buying land and would put cattle in.

He turned into the drive. The gravel was heavy from the rain. He circled toward the back, braked, and cut the motor. It was nearly night, a relieved night; the earth had learned it could rain again.

Down in the wet pasture you could dimly make out from the hill the shaggy lines of green woods beyond, the elbow of a path. Down there a man had walked, flung rocks at a tree, then flipped a half a dollar in the air for a boy to shoot at.

A step crushed the stones, and Beck Dozer appeared.

"I was taking in the sunset," he explained, "along the high-way west. Did you find him, Mister Woolbright?"

"I found him, yes."

"Did he say he cut the tire?"

"No."

"Did he say he didn't cut the tire?"

"No."

"Well. So you don't know, do you?"

"No."

"And I don't know either," said Beck leaning against the car. "I don't know if a single hand was raised against me or not. They do a lot of talking, they'll still go mark the X on the ballot in favor of the man like yourself who says he wants to keep me from marking X on another ballot, but the curious thing to me is that I, Beckwith Dozer, am still alive. I haven't even been run out of town. You use the Negro question to fetch votes with, Mister Woolbright, but to me it's a matter of whether my hide is on my back or ornamenting the barn door. For this I would like to know whether or not he actually damaged the tire. You owe me ten dollars, by the way."

Kerney opened his wallet and drew out the bill. After he had handed the money to Beck he held the billfold open still. "There is someone who knows."

"Who?"

"You were sitting on the far side of the car and didn't see. Duncan is dead. It was Mrs. Harper who kept asking that somebody stop and look at the tire. What did she see that made her think something might be wrong with it? Have you asked her?"

"No," said Beck, after a time. "This I won't do for you, Mister Woolbright. What she knows she knows. Her knowledge is not for sale."

"Well then," said Kerney, "let's put it this way. You see

Jimmy Tallant all the time and sooner or later, maybe right now, maybe not, Jimmy is going to see Mrs. Harper. Lucy goes down to help her. W.B. is always underfoot. Sometime or other, one of you might hear her say and tell the others. Isn't that possible?"

"It's possible," said Beck. "But if it happened, I don't think I would tell you, Mister Woolbright. The only thing I know to tell you to do is to go ask her yourself."

"Yes. Yes, of course," said Kerney. "I could do that."

Late, they drove into the Hunt driveway under the slow-dripping trees. The family was all out in the yard beyond, strolling; it was too wet to sit in the yard chairs, but who could stay out of the cleansed air? They turned and waved. They walked apart from one another, in various directions; here was a flower, there a broken shrub, here a lost tennis ball, yonder a view of the west. Jason leaned in the car window.

"Well, did you find him?"

"Yes, sir."

"Did he say anything?"

"No, sir. I couldn't get a thing out of him."

"Well then. We've done all we can." He looked westward for a minute, then he said, "By the way, Kerney. I've heard a thing or two in town about a matter I probably ought to take up with you. I'm sure there's nothing to it; just if you hear anything, you won't be surprised. The boy at the telegraph office says he delivered to you the message that the man who shot Tallant had been arrested in New Orleans. He said he brought it to you right before the speaking."

A long lavender cloud reclined in the west. It lay easily in a broad cleared stretch of sky, and seemed, what with the thicker lingering clouds above, like an island in a peaceful sea, and Kerney remembered things from English poetry about sailing to the isles of the blest. Few people ever got the chance that Kerney Woolbright had now.

"I remember," said Cissy, and poked her gleaming chestnut head affectionately under her father's arm from where she smiled and crinkled her eyes just slightly at the corners, in the soft way of Southern girls, saying to Kerney without words, "At last, my darling, you are here." She said to her father, "I was in the car when they brought it."

"I see," said Jason, in some alarm, still speaking to Kerney. "But did you know what was in it? Did you read it?"

So, all unheralded, blessed as rain, salvation had broken over him. He paused, setting the words in their proper rank, the way a good lawyer is trained to do. He took another look at the lavender cloud which seemed to tarry for him. He always believed he would have spoken.

"He gave it to Duncan," said Cissy. "They were right near the car. I saw him do it."

"Did you read it beforehand?" Jason asked.

"No, he gave it to him just like it was," Cissy said. "I was right there in the car."

"Cissy, will you please hush. I'm asking Kerney."

"I didn't open it, sir," said Kerney. "I thought that since I had been forced to go against Duncan's platform I no longer had the right to deal in his business. He left orders with the telegraph office to deliver anything to either one of us, but that was when he thought we were still together on the Beck Dozer question."

"So you just turned it over to him?"

"Yes, sir, I did."

"Strange. You would have expected him to get up and make some kind of public announcement. Everybody was curious. Well, he's dead now and we can't inquire, perhaps we shouldn't speculate. Let him rest."

"I feel the same, sir. It's why I never mentioned it."

"Yes. Well, come on in to supper, Kerney. We'll be eating shortly. I smell chicken and hot biscuits. You don't have so much of an appetite in hot weather, but since the rain has cooled things off—well, we'll keep her in there cooking them as long as we can sit there and eat them. I once ate twenty-five, or so Nan vows."

"I *counted* that many," said Nan, joining them, a bough of wisteria in one hand, held outward so as not to drip on her dress. "Look, isn't this lovely? The storm broke it off. Come on in, Kerney, and mix us a drink before supper. We'd love to have you stay."

Dark upon the sidewalk—for preoccupation, no matter how blond you are. is a darkening force—Marcia Mae went from Kerney's car to the house. He was afraid of her, but more afraid of her away than there with her, so he accepted the invitation. While he mixed drinks in the kitchen, the special Collins he could do so well for hot weather, she came through; again at the table as the silver fork tines sank into the tender meat that parted so easily from the bone while the polished knife blade cut the brown grilled crust, he felt her eyes cross and recross him, her face beautiful and pale, for she had been forgetting her make-up, even lipstick, lately, and had to be reminded of it.

As he took leave after supper he met her head-on on the steps with nobody near, and this time he could not avoid her: her eyes were a warrant and cornered him legally.

"I classed myself with you," she told him. "I take it back. I was mistaken. But don't worry. I won't make a big scene. Why should I tell what everybody already knows except Grand, and she doesn't care? They know, but you are one of them now and they will protect you. They will organize themselves for evasions and excuses, they will indulge in endless beautiful subtleties, they will get the door of heaven open for you if they have to unscrew the golden hinges, for your sake and their own. You're safe. Nothing can touch you. Don't worry about anybody, least of all me."

She ran fleetly up the steps past him and indoors. He had no chance to speak. He went down the walk to the car.

A tumult raged in him. He could still go back and say the words to change it all: to make himself an outcast, an exile, a hero. But who would understand? He at least had *understood* what Duncan did. Who would understand him? God, maybe? God by Himself was not enough. Besides, didn't every big politician, statesman, national figure have something of this nature in his past, something he'd had to endure once, to compromise on? It had hurt him to the quick maybe—he would never think of it without pain, never the whole remainder of his life—but this was after all the burden he must bear with him along the way he had to go. The way was service, his country's service: he had to heed the people's will.

He braked suddenly. Without being conscious of it, he had driven wanderingly, around and around the town, and here he was before Duncan's house, Tinker's house. A light burned inside, rounding outward on the hill, cloud-soft upon the darkness. His own headlights stated something strict before him. Between the road there where he was and the hill and house which folded her in, her and hers, darkness was the gulf, darkness the wall, and darkness the only answer; for he could not go in. This final dishonesty he could not commit.

I loved her, he thought, or whispered. I loved her so much.

And fortunately for whatever people might think of him, nobody passed him while he was stopped there, his head laid forward on his arms which were folded across the steering wheel, crying aloud with great innocent sobs, like a little boy.

Library of Congress Cataloguing in Publication Data

Spencer, Elizabeth.
The Voice at the Back Door.
(Time Reading Program Special Edition)
Reprint. Originally published: New York:
McGraw-Hill, 1956.
I. Title.   II Series.
PS3537.P4454V6   1982   813'.54   81-18421 AACR2
ISBN 0-8094-3666-3
ISBN 0-8094-3667-1 (pbk.)